GOLDEN

GOLDEN

A novel

Joni Hilton

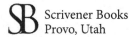

Scrivener Books
Provo, Utah

Cover designed by Jason Robinson
Design and layout by Marny K. Parkin

ISBN 978-0-9895523-8-7

Printed in the U.S.A.

Published by:
Scrivener Books
869 East 2680 North
Provo, UT 84604
publisher@scrivenerbooks.com
ScrivenerBooks.com

TO ORDINARY PEOPLE WHO EXHIBIT GREAT COURAGE—
the courage to speak up, and the courage to listen.

Chapter 1

JANA WATERSON FELT A CHILL IN HER CHEST AS SHE STARED AT the Witch House. She tried to swallow, but her throat was dry. As her tires crunched on the gravel driveway, she realized she had never been this close to it before.

There was the creepy black paint, the crumbling shutters, even thorny vines that clung in jagged veins around the house. And the closer she got, the larger the house loomed. You look up ominous in the dictionary, you see this house, Jana thought. At any moment she expected a cloud of black bats to fly from the chimney.

Slowly she pulled into a parking spot, inching forward until her bumper nestled against a dark thicket of ivy. Didn't rats nest in ivy? She didn't want to open her door. What if she heard creaking doors and moaning ghosts? She glanced over at her passenger, Merry Haines. And Merry was exactly that: Merry. *Should've named that girl Oblivious Haines. Can't she see we're about to walk into the scariest place in town?*

Merry opened her door and Jana closed her eyes. She grabbed her door handle and took a deep breath, as if you could inhale courage and keep it inside you. Then she got out, carefully and quietly closing her door.

And, of course, it didn't latch.

"What are you doing?" Merry asked.

"I don't know. I'm an idiot," Jana whispered. "I'm trying to sneak up on this place and close my door so no one can hear us." But, of course, now she had to slam it so it would fully close.

Woop Woop Woop Woop. Jana's car alarm shattered the silence and she jumped a foot off the ground. She felt blood rush from her head, and she bent over.

"*Now* what are you doing?" Merry asked.

"Trying not to faint," Jana said, simultaneously pressing buttons on her key fob, until the shrieking stopped.

"Come on," Merry chuckled, pulling her along.

They headed up the weed-choked walkway and Jana fought the urge to hum the theme song from The Adams Family: *They're creepy and they're kooky, Mysterious and spooky, They're altogether ooky.*

There were six steps leading to the front door. As Jana began to climb, the wooden steps seemed to sag and creak where they stepped. *Or they're trying to swallow us.*

At the top was a massive door with a brass handle. Jana took a deep breath and reached for it.

THREE WEEKS EARLIER, JANA WAS STARING AT HERSELF IN THE mirror. Was she pushing forty, or was forty pushing her? Either way, she knew she'd seen too much TV, too many skinny models in commercials, too many talk shows about how wrong it is to criticize your own appearance in front of your daughter.

And she agreed with that; she needed to stop whining about losing weight. But she also picked up on the irony that these shows were supposed to make you feel better about yourself, and all she came away with was the certainty that she'd made yet another parenting mistake.

Savannah, her 16-year-old, breezed by to borrow the curling iron, grabbed it and was heading out again, when Jana caught her by the wrist.

"Whoa—you're like a Ninja," Savannah countered. "I just need it for a sec."

"It's fine if you use it," Jana said. "But bring it back. It's the bringing it back that worries me."

"I'll bring it back," Savannah's weary voice trailed out into the hallway.

Jana looked into the mirror again and assessed her battle with gravity and wrinkles, the highlights in her brown hair, the extra fifteen pounds she carried.

What was bugging her wasn't even how she looked. Last night at the Relief Society Meeting a speaker suggested everyone stare into the mirror for five solid minutes without moving. "Look into your eyes, into your soul," the woman had said. "It will take at least a minute to stop looking at your appearance."

True, so far. She stared into her eyes, into her own real self. And the discovery made her jerk her head away.

ETHAN WATERSON WAS AS UNLIKELY A BISHOP AS ANYONE, SO IT stood to reason he became the new bishop of the Larchmont 5th Ward. Shy and uncomfortable in crowds, Ethan chewed his cheeks at ward dinners, planting himself on the perimeter of the seating rather than mingling with the more gregarious folks. Hunched over from years of feeling too tall and standing out in a crowd, at 6'6" he looked more like a reluctant investigator than the leader of a flock.

His cheekbones were high, and pressed his blue eyes into smiling crescents, giving the impression he was jovial. But he was not. He was terrified. A certified public accountant, Ethan was far more comfortable with numbers than with people. It wasn't that he didn't like people; he just had no clue what to do with them.

Amazingly, he had convinced a woman he felt was far above his station, to marry him. To this day he wondered if he had simply caught Jana in a sympathetic moment, or if she felt she had to marry because all her BYU roommates were marrying. She'd laugh that sparkling bell-like laugh of hers when he would confess such worries, and wrap her arms around his waist. And his waist was another thing. It was too skinny. Bony. Like his prominent brow, accentuated by his receding blond hairline. Did he look like a starving Neanderthal Man?

So when the Stake President called Ethan and Jana into his office, Ethan was fairly certain it would involve a calling in the realm of crunching numbers. He literally felt the blood drain from his face when President Morrow called him to be a bishop. His jaw hung slack, and he had to consciously close it to swallow. In all honesty, the one thing he had never wanted to be in his entire life, was a bishop. He had even prayed, years ago, never to become one. Talk about getting no for an answer.

And speaking of no, how many times could that word ricochet through his head until it came tumbling out his mouth? It wasn't a no of unwillingness, it was a no of sheer terror, and the realization that his people skills were virtually nonexistent. He liked the general *concept* of people, it was talking to individuals *per se,* that had him petrified.

"Are you sure?" he finally said, his voice cracking.

President Morrow chuckled. "I'm sure and the Lord is sure." Clifton Morrow was exactly the sort of man you'd picture in a leadership

position. Energetic, engaging, bright, friendly. He even seemed tan
year-round, as if he were an executive constantly summoned to beach-
fronts and yachts. He had a wide, gleaming smile and Ethan could picture him closing deals and making everyone laugh in a board meeting.

Mine would be more like a bored meeting. He looked over at Jana, all
bouncy brown curls and saucy cheeks. How could she be grinning like
that? Beaming—that's the word for what she was doing. Didn't anyone
in this room understand how inadequate he was? Didn't they know the
shock wave that would deaden the congregation when his name was
announced? If "undertaker" had been a calling, that one they would
believe. But Bishop?

Ethan willed himself to accept. He had never turned down a calling,
never intended to. But he also never dreamed he would be thrust into
this much limelight, this much responsibility. And of the two, it was
the limelight he dreaded most. What if the entire ward became inactive
over this?

President Morrow interrupted his near panic-attack as if he could
read Ethan's mind.

"Now, don't worry," he said. "There will be people who stop coming
to church because you're the bishop," he said. Ethan nodded. No surprise there.

President Morrow smiled. "But there will also be people who start
coming to church because you're the bishop. I've seen both happen,
over and over."

Jana was nodding, sharing a smile with President Morrow, over the
shallow reasons some members have, for falling away or coming back.
There was nothing you could do about it, so why worry?

But Ethan was worried. Plenty worried. Had an entire congregation
ever just vanished into thin air? Besides the City of Enoch? And for far
less noble reasons? He was afraid to swallow, afraid any tickle in his
throat might make him throw up.

"Would you like a blessing?" President Morrow asked, again almost
reading Ethan's mind.

He nodded, hoping the Lord would say, "Just kidding." Like Abra-
ham's test in almost sacrificing Isaac. Maybe this would turn out to be

nothing more than a test, to see if Ethan would accept. And, now that he had, the Lord would rush in and rescue him. He could go back into the shadows, back to the comfort of near anonymity.

But it didn't happen. The calling was real. And Ethan became Bishop Waterson.

JANA FELT A RUSH OF WARMTH AND PEACE AT THE MEETING with President Morrow. She knew instantly it was the right calling, that Ethan would make a wonderful bishop. But on the ride home she found herself staring into her lap, almost afraid to look up and catch Ethan's eye. What if he could look into her soul the way she had looked into that mirror? What if he could read her worries, the way he always seemed able to? What if he learned that she was not Bishop's Wife Material?

"Talk to me," he said that night when they were getting ready for bed. "What were you thinking on the ride home?"

Jana turned away, pretending to straighten a towel, but he leaned around into her face, and lifted her chin with one finger. "Tell me what's bothering you."

She took a breath, and then another. Finally she decided she may as well come out with it. "Ethan, there's something I should have told you a long time ago. Something I'm terribly ashamed—" and her voice caught before she could say "of."

Ethan led her to the little bench at the end of their bed, the old padded bench where they always seemed to find themselves for serious discussions.

"Ethan—" She didn't want to tell him. "You know how I've told you that I almost went on a mission?"

He nodded.

"Well, you assumed that I had thought about it and then decided against it. And I let you think that. But—" she took a deep breath and then it tumbled out. "I actually had my call. I went to meet with the Stake President to be set apart, and then I—I backed out."

Ethan put his arm around her. "You were called on a mission?"

Jana felt hot tears spilling down her cheeks.

Ethan held her. "It's okay. You thought you couldn't tell me this?"

"Ethan, I'm so ashamed. I chickened out. It wasn't—" She took a breath. "It wasn't that I felt inspired to wait because I was going to meet my eternal companion, or some justifiable reason like that. I simply—" She shook her head. "I blew it."

Ethan smoothed her hair and whispered. "Why did you back out?"

"I was scared. I was selfish." Jana wiped her cheeks, but more tears streamed down. "I had turned twenty-one and everyone was saying I should put my papers in, and—it all just happened so fast."

"C'mere." He pulled her close and held her, then pressed his lips to her head. "Oh, Jana. If you only knew how much light you radiate." He kissed her hair again. "May I ask where you were called to go?"

"The Missouri Independence Mission," she said. It was the first time in eighteen years that she'd been able to say those words.

Ethan kissed her forehead. "It's okay, Honey."

"No, it's not okay. I should have gone where the Lord told me to."

"So this is why you didn't want to go on that Church History tour." They had been planning a family vacation five years ago, and Jana was adamant about not visiting the Midwest.

Jana nodded. "I can't face the people of Missouri," she said. "I let them down. I let the Lord down."

He held her shoulders and stared into her eyes. "And so you built your own Liberty Jail, and you've been living in it all this time."

Now Jana broke down and sobbed, his words perfectly describing the sorrow she'd been carrying.

"Oh, Jana." He held her again. "Honey, you have to forgive yourself."

"How? How can I ever make it up to the Lord?"

Ethan held her and rubbed her back as she cried. Finally he said, "Jana, you do not need to carry this regret for the rest of your life. You need to move on. You're an incredible woman. You're a wonderful wife and mother. I'm sure the Lord has forgiven you long ago. And you need to do the same."

"How? Even my family was so embarrassed that they've never spoken of it again." She took a deep breath, then released it. "And then I made matters worse by letting you believe a lie."

Ethan studied her face, aching to take away her sorrow. He couldn't even imagine the piercing abandonment she must have felt from her family, people who should have rallied around her. "I wish you had known how much I love you. This doesn't change anything, Jana. If you had told me sooner, I could have helped you. You need to believe in your worth, believe that the Lord loves you—"

"Please forgive me."

"It isn't my place to forgive this."

"But I deceived you."

Ethan held her, smoothing her hair, almost rocking her. "Oh, Jana."

She pulled away. "And now you're the bishop and your wife is—"

"Exactly the wife I want." Ethan drew her hands to his lips and kissed them.

"How can I be a bishop's wife?" Jana asked. "You're going to want everyone to do missionary work and I'm terrified of it."

"Jana, I'm terrified of being a bishop. I'm terrified of missionary work, too. You know I didn't baptize a single soul on my mission."

She nodded. "But at least you tried."

"But I'm not some fireball missionary," he said. "I'm not even good with people in general!"

"Ethan, you are going to be an awesome bishop. I know that."

"And you are going to be a wonderful bishop's wife. I know that, too."

Jana wiped her eyes and stared at her husband, his features as familiar as her own. Oh, why couldn't this pure, unfailing face be the one she saw in the mirror?

"Let me give you a blessing," Ethan said. "And we're both going to take on this new assignment together."

THE 4TH WARD HAD BEEN SWELLING LIKE A BOWL OF DOUGH ON a hot day, ballooning up to nearly 900 members before it was finally split, creating two new bishoprics and one brand new ward, Larchmont 5th. Every auxiliary was affected as members were released and sustained, thrilled and heartsick. There was the usual fallout of members grumbling about losing friends, as if an iron curtain had fallen, and they had no way to contact people outside the new boundaries.

And the boundaries cut a jagged tear through the landscape, scooting around an apartment building here, and sweeping over to enclose a housing development there. Priesthood leadership had to be considered, and finally the new lines were drawn.

Jana's parents were deceased, and Ethan's lived in Florida, unable to make the trip for Stake Conference. Though Jana had enough siblings and in-laws to nearly fill the building, all of them lived in Utah and were busy, or less active and uninterested. But Ethan didn't mind not having an entourage at church—for one thing, it didn't tip anyone off about his new assignment. And it gave him time with his own family that afternoon, to focus on the kids and their feelings about this huge change in their lives.

His counselors' names had come to him during prayer, and both were dynamic leaders. Terrell Moses was a burly veteran with a booming voice and great sense of humor. His dark hair stood on end as if at attention, jolted upward by his sheer energy. The youth adored him and invited him to all their campouts, even if his calling didn't require his attendance. He loved teasing with them, but always held them to high standards. And Tad Lawrence was the silver-haired CEO of a software company that Ethan wasn't even sure he understood. Tad was polished, eloquent, and made you sit up straighter, just listening to him. Both had vibrant testimonies and Ethan was honored to work with them. He also prayed they could fill in for his weaknesses.

"I can't believe you're the bishop," Maddie said on the drive home, her voice a younger version of Jana's, filled with optimism and italics on the words, 'believe' and 'bishop.' She was the sunniest child of all three, and had just arrived at the age Ethan thought was truly perfect for a daughter: Eight. She was still her daddy's darling, with light brown hair like her mother's.

"You and me both," Ethan said.

"Well, I can believe it," Jana said, brimming with confidence. As much as she worried about her own failings, she believed in Ethan's strengths. "Your dad will be a fantastic bishop."

Jana's eyes danced, and Ethan remembered arguing with her, in college, about whether they were turquoise or aqua. In truth, he didn't even know or care what the difference was; he loved watching her fill with passion about minute details, pieces of life he had never even considered. He felt as if he'd been swept up onto a magic carpet, listening to her fervent opinions about everything from breakfast cereal to closet organizing.

"Yeah, congratulations," Josh said. Josh was 13, and already a tangle of arms and legs, just like Ethan had been at his age. Even his unruly, fine blond hair was just like Ethan's. How he hoped Josh would be more confident, more socially adept than he had been. The boy was trying to play sports, trying to make good grades, trying to fit into the Scouting program, but tripping and falling more than clicking into position. Ethan hoped things would even out soon, before the kid simply gave up.

Jana had felt infused with strength and tranquility during Ethan's blessing, and reached back for that again. She wanted to believe every word, that her past was forgiven, and her future filled with promise. It was hard to set aside nearly twenty years of guilt and blame, but she was determined to try. For Ethan. And for the kids.

"And no, it doesn't mean you kids have to be perfect," Jana said, catching Josh's eye. "I don't want you feeling stressed over Dad's calling."

Josh looked visibly relieved.

"Of course the entire ward will be watching you and it will be a tremendous reflection on our family if you make even one tiny mistake," Jana said.

Ethan stopped at a light and glanced into the rear view mirror. "She's being sarcastic, kids."

Maddie released a grand sigh.

"You guys are so easy," Jana laughed. "Seriously, can't you tell when I'm teasing?"

"I knew it," Savannah said. The eldest child, the Laurel.

"Yeah, right." Josh kicked off his shoes.

"You kids don't have to change a thing," Ethan said. And how he hoped they wouldn't. So far they hadn't had any major problems with their kids—not serious ones, anyway. But even he knew the part luck had played. And the fact that they were still young. He also knew plenty of stalwart families whose kids had chosen other paths and plunged their parents into grief and worry, constantly pushing down the tears that would well up at unexpected moments.

"Except we'll all be blessed," Jana said, puncturing his worries. She spoke it as a fact, with the same conviction she had about wearing clean socks.

"Will I get a new bike?" Maddie asked.

Ethan shook his head. "Nope."

"You watch," Jana said, "the blessings will be much better than a new bike."

"Hey, let's drive all the way around the new boundaries," Savannah suggested.

Ethan glanced over at Jana. "Will dinner keep?"

She thought about the stewing beef she had browned this morning, then tossed into the Crockpot with some vegetables and gravy. "It's in a slow cooker—no problem."

Ethan pulled over, then turned to Savannah. "And let me guess. You want to drive." Every time he looked at his 16-year-old daughter lately, she looked more like a movie star and it raised Ethan's blood pressure. He found himself watching for teenage boys at the mall, gawking from side to side like a Rain Bird sprinkler every time he took Savannah there. Why couldn't she pull her hair into a scarf or something? What was that garbage she kept putting on it to make it shine? Is dull hair such a bad thing? And why couldn't she stop wearing lip gloss? Or skinny jeans? Why couldn't burkas come into style? Or pioneer bonnets? He wanted to wrap her in a sleeping bag with holes cut out, for her eyes. And walk beside her like a bodyguard. Even Jana rolled her eyes when he was always suggesting Savannah wear baggy sweatshirts. Finally Jana had to ask him to stop teaching about modesty for every Family Home Evening when his turn rolled around. "Am I that obvious?" he had asked. Yep. He was.

Savannah was an outstanding girl, involved in school government, busy with Young Women—he knew he shouldn't worry so much—but how do you hide a daughter who's becoming a raving beauty without even trying? It was giving him ulcers, he just knew it. Women, as far as he could tell, had no concept of the hormones raging in teenage boys. He felt as if he were living in a constant state of emergency, while his wife and daughter just winked at each other.

Savannah's eyes lit up and she quickly traded seats with Ethan, his bony knees now drawn up under his chin in the back seat.

"I'm the navigator," Josh announced. "Okay, where are we?"

Jana laughed. "Obviously in good hands." There she was, being sarcastic again. *I wonder if that's why I was born in Sacramento. Somebody upstairs thought the sign said Sarcasmento. Somebody with a funny bone. Or a broken humerus.*

"Okay, we're on Marble Street," she said. "Take us from there."

Ethan's temple pulsed as he clenched his jaws. Savannah had only had her license for eight months, and still lacked enough experience to handle a crisis, in his opinion. And with Josh navigating and shouting out turns at the last minute, Ethan could feel his shoulders tightening.

"Hey, they took the junior high out of our ward," Josh said, sounding neither happy nor disappointed. It was an odd combination of red and tan brick, classrooms having been added on haphazardly over the years.

"Yes, looks like it's in the second ward now," Jana said, studying her own map. "The Dayleys and the Hargroves will be in that ward, too." Those couples were their closest friends.

"Aww, my Primary teacher," Maddie pouted.

"You'll get a new one," Savannah said. "Just as good."

"But you'll still be there, right, Mom?" Maddie said.

Jana glanced at Ethan. "Well . . ."

"Mom!" Maddie wailed. "You have to stay in there!"

Jana turned to her youngest child. "They really don't like the bishop's wife to have a demanding, busy calling, Punkin'. And Primary President is pretty busy. So I'm expecting to get released. But maybe I'll still be in there as a teacher—who knows?"

Maddie stuck her lip out.

"Go left on Stripling Warriors," Josh said. This was the nickname the kids had given Stipley Way, named for an early settler. It was dotted with Chinese Elm trees, and houses with double concrete paths for the driveways.

Savannah followed the curving street for a quarter of a mile.

"Whoa—the castle park is in our ward? Cool." Josh had always loved the city park with a castle-themed play structure and slide in it. Jana loved the shady trees where she had spent many an afternoon watching the kids play. She used to meet there with other moms, each one carrying a diaper bag stuffed with apple juice, Goldfish crackers, cheese cubes, and tiny carrots, as if two hours in the park required a 72-hour kit of emergency supplies.

"Now right on El Dorado."

Savannah swung onto El Dorado, and drove around a thick stucco wall, lined with poplars. Suddenly the wall ended and the kids gasped.

"It's the Witch House!" Maddie shrieked.

Savannah almost slammed on the brakes, then caught herself, and pulled over instead.

"No way," Josh whispered. "The Witch House is in our ward?"

"Eww," Savannah said, grimacing as she stared at the massive old Victorian. Like many old homes in Sacramento, it was built more than a hundred years ago, wreathed in scrollwork and gingerbread that was now crumbling and tattered. It didn't help that it was painted deep charcoal, giving it the eerie appearance of a "dark and stormy night" movie mansion.

"That is not a witch house," Jana laughed. "It's just an old folks' home."

"Old witches," Josh said. "They look out the window and cast spells on you."

Ethan shook his head. He remembered hearing similar stories as a youth; it seemed every community had scary folklore designed to keep kids on their toes. And this facility could certainly use a facelift. It even had gnarly vines growing over the windows, as if trying to choke the evil spirits inside. It was hard not to shudder as he stared at it.

"Come on, let's go," he said to Savannah, forcing his voice to sound cheery. "It's nothing to be scared of." Where had he heard that line? And then he remembered: It was the parting counsel from President Morrow, when he'd been called as the new bishop.

JANA PULLED A LOAD OF WARM LAUNDRY FROM THE DRYER AND held it to her chest. She'd done this as a child, enjoying the warmth on cool mornings. It amazed her how many things she still did, left over from her childhood. Blowing into a Popsicle wrapper to loosen it, singing the middle verse of a hymn in alto to copy her mother, wishing on stars, tying her shoes and still thinking of bunny ears. And here she was, the mother of teenagers, yet still feeling like a little girl.

And why wasn't there anything good to eat in the fridge? What matronly woman was going to march into her kitchen and fill her refrigerator with homey snacks? Even after sixteen years as a mother, Jana wanted a mother herself. How did she suddenly become the grownup in this picture?

Talking to Ethan about her almost-mission had been the most cleansing, healing thing she had ever done. Knowing he could forgive her somehow made the Lord's forgiveness seem within reach, as well. She wished her family had rushed in with assurance of her worth, way back then. But ruminating about what might have been only sent her down the path of despair again, so she shook the thought away. She focused on the positive parts of her life, and the genuine desires of her heart. Deep down she knew she was a good person who had simply made a mistake. And, as Ethan reminded her, it was not a mistake that needed to poison the rest of her life.

Jana thought about her eldest daughter as she folded clothes. Savannah was much more mature than she had been at that age. That girl could organize a school dance, star in a play, and head up a community clothing drive all in the same afternoon. Confident and poised, Savannah was a natural leader. When Jana was sixteen, she was still too shy to accept a date, much happier in a library than at a school dance. It wasn't until college that she had finally let her hair down and attended social events.

She put the laundry basket on the dryer and started matching Ethan's socks, rolling them up and stuffing them into one another. Ethan had saved her, really. She was so unsure of herself back then, but Ethan had thought she was dazzling. "You know how to do that?" he used to gasp, watching her crimp the edge of a pie crust in the kitchen of her college apartment.

"You like everyone," he said one time, incredulous.

"Well, we're supposed to," she laughed. Had he missed all those teachings of Christ?

"Yes, but no one actually does it," he said. "I mean, I want to, but . . ." And they had laughed at his honesty. Ethan had made her see virtues she hadn't actually noticed before, especially after the humiliating experience of backing out of her mission. Through Ethan's eyes she realized she really was a kind person, and someone with talents and abilities. She'd grown up in a large, hardworking family without much time for individual applause. Looking back, she couldn't remember any compliments from her parents, just a nod of approval now and again. But Ethan made her feel like a shining jewel. He made her want to be her best self—a good wife, a good mother.

And Ethan was wrong about himself: He thought he didn't like people, but really he was just afraid of saying the wrong thing. Over and over she had watched him give service, never too busy to drive a roommate to a job interview, help another one with his homework, lend a suit to a boy who had none for a wedding. Soft spoken and studious, Ethan thought he was a social disaster, but he was loved by everyone who knew him. So when he hinted that she was exactly the kind of girl he'd like to marry, she didn't hesitate. Ethan embodied the very gospel teachings she wanted her children to learn.

"Hellooo?" Savannah was suddenly standing in the laundry room. "I've been calling you. And you're just smiling at the walls."

Jana laughed. "Oh, I was thinking about your dad."

Savannah frowned as if she had caught them kissing. "Okay, that's just gross. All dreamy over *Dad*."

Jana tossed her some socks to fold. "I hope you find someone half as wonderful," she said.

"Whatever." Savannah began folding. Her brown hair was swept up into a messy bun, and still she looked sophisticated, like an executive in charge of Laundry Administration. Ethan was right—she was captivating.

And now she glanced down at Jana's capri pants and bare shins. "You have Oompa Loompa legs, Mom."

Jana looked down at the orange legs that had resulted from her attempts with tanning cream. "I know! And I can't scrub it off!" She held up a towel. "Of course it's happy to come off on towels, pants, and socks."

Savannah was laughing, now. "Did you exfoliate?"

"Of course I did. I look like I lost a paintball war." She held up her hands. "Plus it left speckles all over my hands like I'm getting age spots on my palms."

Savannah just stared in disbelief. "I'd stick with long pants until it wears off."

Sure, in the heat of a Sacramento August. "Well, I actually had another idea," Jana said. "You know how chevron print skirts are so popular? I'm going to pretend I'm a trend setter and I'm wearing chevron print leggings."

Now her daughter just did her famous eye-roll, and went back to the business that brought her to see Jana in the first place. "So we're trying to find a good service project," she said.

"We who—school or the Laurels?"

"The Laurels."

"How about babysitting for our next activity night?" Jana began piling the folded brown socks and the navy socks in the basket, trying to keep the two groups separated.

"We do that all the time—it has to be something bigger than that. We want to team up with the Young Men, too. And don't say temple baptisms—we just did that."

Jana thought. "How about chalk drawings on the sidewalk somewhere busy, like the missionaries do? A missionary activity?" It was easy to suggest it for someone else.

Savannah cocked her head to one side. "Hmm. Maybe. We'd have to get permission."

What 16-year-old knows about getting permission from the city? This girl amazed her. Did she already know the office to call? Jana wouldn't have known where to start at that age.

"I'll see what I can find out," Savannah said, tossing her socks into the basket and disappearing back into the hallway.

Jana's cell phone rang as she was heading upstairs, so she put the basket on the landing and picked up. It was Mimi Kim, the new Relief Society President, a darling convert from Korea whose excitement over the gospel was infectious. Her first name was actually Mi-kyung, but when Americans struggled with the second syllable, she happily changed it to Mimi.

"I'm giving you a new person to visit teach," she said, as if presenting a new car.

"I figured," Jana smiled. One of her previous sisters was now in the old ward.

"Vera Underwood," Mimi said.

Must be an inactive, Jana thought. "Where does she live?"

"She lives in the El Dorado House. Do you know where that is?"

Was she kidding? The Witch House?

Chapter 2

JANA CAUGHT HER BREATH. *THE WITCH HOUSE.* "I DO. WE DROVE by it just yesterday." Why couldn't she summon the cheery tone she had used with her kids? Then she realized—seeing it from the street is one thing, but walking into that creepy place definitely gave her pause.

An hour ago she'd had to cancel a Primary Presidency meeting for the following day, with one counselor out of town and another expecting houseguests. It freed up the entire morning. "I'll swing by tomorrow," she said.

As Jana turned to head up the rest of the stairway, she noticed the family pictures that lined the wall. Her parents were captured in the plaid jackets and puffy hairdos of the Seventies, smiling as if white belts would forever stay in style. In another, her mom was posed in a country-style, yellow prom dress with a ruffled hem, her dad in a ruffled shirt. They looked like those ruffled chickens at the State Fair. What would her own kids think of her pictures with Ethan someday? Undoubtedly just as dated and out of style.

And then she saw the picture of her grandparents, standing at the vast rim of the Grand Canyon on their honeymoon. Jana had the same wavy brown hair as her grandmother, the same blue-green eyes. Had she lived, her grandmother might be the same age as Vera Underwood. Maybe they'd have traded recipes for the bread-and-butter pickles, the warm chicken salad, the Dolly Madison bars that were so popular back then. Even food went in and out of style. She found herself humming "When I'm Sixty-Four" and could hear Paul McCartney singing the lyrics about grandchildren on his knee, "Vera, Chuck, and Dave," as she placed Ethan's socks in his drawer.

The next morning she sliced bananas over the kids' cereal, then sat down to join them before the bus came. Savannah was already at early morning Seminary.

"Hey, read this," Josh said, turning his Raisin Bran box towards her.

"Kellogg's cereal with one half cup milk plus an 8 ounce glass of milk is a good source of protein and gives you the calcium, Vitamin D and potassium your body needs," Jana read. Then she looked up. "Wait a sec'. You need half a cup of milk with the cereal, and then another whole glass of milk to get the right nutrients? Does the cereal count for nothing?"

Josh was laughing. "I knew you'd appreciate that." He was developing his father's wry sense of humor. "And who drinks a glass of milk when they're having cereal with milk?"

"Does that mean I can have a cookie for breakfast if I eat it with a glass of milk?" Maddie asked.

Jana smiled. "Well, evidently, Miss Maddie. I guess that would turn your cookie into a fitness fiesta."

Maddie laughed and slurped a spoonful of cereal. "I might do it."

"No, you might not," Jana said.

"If they can't offer you all the nutrients you need," Ethan said, "Why are they even mentioning it on the label? Seems they shouldn't even bring it up."

"Like that paint remover," Josh said.

"What paint remover?" Ethan asked.

"The one Mom bought last year, that said 'semi-odorless.' And she said, if you can't say it's odorless, why bring it up at all?'" Josh and Maddie both laughed.

"I still stand by that question," Jana said.

"You think you're buying a healthy cereal," Ethan mumbled as he studied the nutrients label on the box. "I'm telling you, nothing is like it's advertised." *Parenting comes to mind.*

"Like that meerkat show," Maddie said, wiping her mouth.

Jana shook her head, smiling. This happened a few years ago, but remained one of Maddie's favorite stories.

"Remember that?" Maddie said, egging Jana on to tell it.

"I certainly do," Jana said. "I used to *love* meerkats." She noticed Maddie's eyes twinkling. "I thought they were the one pet the entire world had overlooked. Cuddly, cute as a button, right? So when *Meerkat*

Manor was announced as an upcoming TV show, you can bet I wrote the date on my calendar and counted the days until it aired. These darlings would finally make their debut to all the world, and before you know it, would be available as pets."

"And tell what their houses would look like," Maddie said, prompting her mother.

"Well, I just knew they'd have darling underground houses," Jana said, "tidy and swept clean by meerkat moms wearing aprons and using teeny little brooms. Meerkat children would come home from school, hop off the armadillo school bus, and give their moms a big hug. Meerkat dads would take the whole family out for ice cream and I would sit in my family room, watch this, and smile."

Ethan knew his cue and offered his signature giant explosion noise. Even Josh laughed here.

"That is exactly how my image of meerkats crashed and burned within minutes of seeing the first episode," Jana said. "It turns out every meerkat is a crazed gang member out to kill every other meerkat family. Even the babies. You know how they have a guard who stands at attention, apparently watching for hawks or coyotes? Ha—they're watching for other meerkats headed their way in a raid of murdering and plundering."

Maddie was giggling with delight. Jana continued. "Apparently every meerkat ever born is in a full blown panic that their food supply will run out, and unless they eliminate all other meerkat families, they will die. So every waking minute is spent in all-out warfare, either attacking or being attacked. It was a hideous glimpse into a dastardly world that shattered my happy little dreams forever. You want to know what's the opposite of *Downton Abbey*? It's *Meerkat Manor*."

"And remember what we gave you the next day?"

"I do," Jana said, pretending to be miffed all over again. "Little figurines of meerkats in a saucer of ketchup. Very funny."

Maddie laughed and nodded, approving of Jana's anguish as a joyful start to the day.

Soon Ethan left for work and the kids began loading up their backpacks.

"Oh, by the way," Jana said, "I'm going over to Visit Teach a sister who just moved into the El Dorado House."

"You're going *in there*?" Josh asked. Even Maddie whipped around, stunned.

"Of course I am," Jana said, her resolve back. This was the same lilt she remembered in her mother's voice when her older brother had been in the hospital. "Everything's going to be *fine*," her mother had said. And Jana had believed it. For all she knew, the early saints used this same tone to convince their children that crossing a nation on foot would be a snap. What was that called—spunk? No—spunk plus courage. What was the word?

Josh and Maddie went to put their coats on as Jana thought about the retirement home. And it wasn't as if she believed the witch stories, anyway. Her reluctance was because it was a care facility for the elderly. It was going to be depressing. It was going to smell. It was going to be a glimpse into death and decay. She was young, or relatively so. She was Primary President and dealt best with children. Couldn't they have assigned one of the senior sisters to Vera? And there it was: Another uncomfortable truth, that Jana wasn't really crazy about old folks' homes. She felt a wave of shame as she admitted this. After all, she knew logically these people were deserving of respect and compassion. And she had no problem visiting with the elderly members of her ward. It was the "facility." The diapers. The trays of pureed food. She knew these buildings were filled with lonely people, and she stood there feeling shallow and petty, knowing she had always waited for someone else to visit them.

A memory came flooding back. As a child, her mother had taken her along on a visit to Great Aunt Ethel after church one day. Great Aunt Ethel lived in a "rest home." Jill and Annette, two of Jana's sisters, were in tow as well. But Jana was the youngest, only five or six at the time. It was dimly lit, and smelled of liniment and decay. Worn mauve wingback chairs seemed to be crumbling into powder before her eyes, and mustard-and-black oriental rugs released musty odors with every step upon them. Down one hall she could hear a man moaning, then heaving, then moaning again. Another woman, crouched over in a wheelchair, looked up when they arrived, her dark eyes burning holes into Jana's. Then suddenly the woman was seized by a coughing fit, and Jana felt surely the woman would die before her very eyes. The crippled lady gagged, and Jana stared as the old woman threw up, the stench of vomit seeming to fill her entire head.

Jana froze like a statue, unable to walk, the gray damask wallpaper seeming to close in on her. Suddenly she trembled, and her leg felt warm as she stood there trying not to wet herself. But it was too late, and her tiny patent leather shoe filled with urine, her white ankle sock soaked.

"Come *along!*" Jana's mother had scolded, yanking her by the hand.

And then her sisters saw what had happened. Jana remembered it as if through an echo chamber, her sisters' voices cackling through the years, louder every time she thought about it.

"You wet your pants?!" Annette gasped. "Look at her leg, Mom!"

"Oh, way to go, Jana," Jill chimed in. "All over the carpet!"

And Jana knew she would be in trouble. Mom would make her buy a new rug, new shoes, new socks. Who would clean her up? How could she ever live this down? Her sisters would tease her forever. Probably tell the whole family and all her friends.

It was the most humiliating moment of her young life, and Jana had burst into tears. She remembered a nurse coming up with a wet towel, her mother apologizing, her sisters laughing, the sick woman coughing even louder. Her mother had pulled her to their car, an old blue Plymouth with a dent in the back right fender. She rode home sitting on newspapers to protect the seats, her sisters arguing about who had to sit next to her, their mother telling them to be quiet. And she had vowed never to set foot in such a scary place again.

THE BRAKES OF A SCHOOL BUS WHEEZED IN FRONT OF THEIR corner house, and Maddie grabbed her lunch and sweater, a sticky jam kiss on Jana's cheek as she flew out the door. Right behind was Josh's carpool ride to the junior high, so he followed suit. Savannah would now be at the high school, where she walked after Seminary.

The house was empty. Jana cleaned up the kitchen, praying for a change in attitude as she wiped down the counters, and glanced at the clock. There was just enough time to snip some roses for this new sister she was visit-teaching. She figured some flowers might be a welcome treat at a dismal care facility, so she grabbed her clippers and headed to the back yard.

They had lived here since Savannah was five, and had planted an entire bed of rose bushes in a sunny spot near the patio. It provided dozens of blooms for bouquets from April to November, and Jana quickly snipped some buds and blossoms in pink, white, and burgundy. Then, just as she was reaching for one last bloom, she came face to face with a two-inch spider. And that was a two-inch body, not counting the legs. Even worse, it was garish yellow and black, with menacing eyes and blood-curdling fangs.

Jana leaped backward, and dropped both the clippers and the roses. Only now she realized that this terrifying creature was suspended on a round web four feet wide. Heart pounding, she bolted into the house and instinctively locked the door, as if the spider could chase after her.

She dashed to the computer, typed in a description of the creepy thing, and then saw its photo, enlarged enough to ensure that she'd have nightmares for a week. "The orb spider," she muttered, reading aloud. "Be careful not to walk into their circular four-foot webs at night—the fright of this spider crawling over one's face can be terrifying and may cause a heart attack, particularly to the susceptible over 40-year-olds." *No kidding.*

She called Ethan at once. "You cannot believe the spider I just saw in our garden," she gasped.

"Oh, yeah, I saw that a couple of days ago. I meant to tell you about it."

"How could you not warn me? Or get rid of it?"

"I thought it was cool." Ethan was definitely not grasping the gravity of the situation.

"Are you crazy? It's like coming around a corner and bumping head-long into Gene Simmons. It says online that it can cause an actual heart attack."

Now Ethan was laughing. "I'll move it elsewhere tonight."

"Elsewhere as in miles away, I hope," Jana said. She didn't even dare go back for the roses—what if another one jumped out of the flowers? Besides, now it was time to pick up Merry Haines.

Jana had called her visiting teaching companion the night before, to see if she could visit Vera this morning. Merry had an appointment with her obstetrician later, so this was perfect timing. If there could be a perfect time to visit the nearly-dead. Jana shook that thought away, and tried to picture them as happy senior citizens. Surely this place wouldn't resemble the one from her childhood, and no one would throw up as she walked in. And, after her fright in the garden, what could be worse?

Besides, Jana thought of herself as someone particularly patient with the elderly. Hadn't she been the only one who would sit in front of Brother Ames when he got Alzheimers and began singing all the hymns in Pig Latin? Her kids were laughing so hard they shook the bench, and Ethan's eyes were darting back and forth as he stole glances at Jana. The funny thing—besides actually singing in Pig Latin—is that the chorister at the time always dragged the music to such a slow beat that his double wording fit right in. "You" now had two syllables: "Oo-yay." But it worked. And, of course, every line rhymed. So as various members began sitting further and further away, Jana simply sat in their usual pew and enjoyed the performance.

Merry was in her early twenties and expecting her first baby. Jana adored Merry—not only was her cheery nature contagious, but she had just moved to California from Texas and had a charming drawl. Of course, Merry probably saw her the same way Jana thought of Vera, as a woman from another generation, in another stage of life. Jana had been noticing lately that she and Ethan were no longer in the "fun, young couples" category. Newlyweds were treating them differently now, as if they were slightly invisible.

Merry looked like a Scandinavian Madame Alexander doll with blonde braids and pink lips. Had she burst into song as if filming a musical, you wouldn't flinch.

Last month Merry had hopped into the car with a pizza, a salad, and a cake for another sister they visit. Merry's wealthy parents gave them a large monthly stipend which Merry generously used to help others. "These are for the Mezners," she announced.

"Are they sick?" Jana had asked. She thought about Diana Mezner, another sister on their route. Diana was always borrowing money, then spending it on frivolous items like designer handbags and spa treatments. Her ex-husband was still trying to pay off the maxed-out credit cards she had accumulated, and her teenage daughter refused to get a job because Diana would take her paychecks. Jana had arranged for a financial planner to work with Diana, but the solutions seemed short-lived.

"Well, she's going to Vermont to see the fall colors," Merry said, "and the tickets were so expensive that she says she can't afford food, now."

"Excuse me?" Jana was dumbfounded. "Why on earth is she going to Vermont if she can't even put food on the table?"

Merry shrugged. "I think it's on her bucket list. Anyway, I feel sorry for the kids."

"I feel sorry for the kids, too," Jana said, "but I'm not going to enable a spendthrift."

"Well," Merry smiled, "who are we to judge?"

"Uh, we're the people doing the math?"

Now Merry busted up laughing. "You're right, Jana. I shouldn't be providing meals. She probably has more money coming in than I do!"

Jana sighed and shook her head.

"This will be the last time," Merry laughed. And, since the boundaries changed anyway, it actually was.

Merry's family had helped her and Sean buy their house, and occasionally sent them on wonderful vacations. In January they went to a combination spa and dude ranch, where they had signed up for massages, wellness clinics, and spiritual enlightenment meetings.

Jana had met her for breakfast after Merry got back, so she could hear all about it and see the pictures on Merry's phone.

"The manicures were ninety dollars," Merry said. "And most of the facials and massages were a hundred and fifty."

Jana couldn't even do the math, wondering what this trip must have cost.

"They had you put this Tibetan metal bowl on your head and tap it with a mallet," Merry explained. "Then the bowl makes a tone that's supposed to heal you."

Jana didn't need a bowl on her head to hear the humming of her Baloney Meter, but she kept listening.

"And then we signed up for the Horse Encounter," Merry said.

"Oh, you went riding?"

"Oh, no, it's just where you meet in the barn and everyone is assigned a horse, and y'all are supposed to build trust with the horse."

"Anyway," Merry continued, "You try to get the horse to lift his foot for you, but he'll only do it if he trusts you. And mine wouldn't trust me, so the leader of the class asked if I had problems opening up to people in my everyday life."

Jana laughed. "You?" Merry was one of the most gregarious women she knew. "So you're being psycho-analyzed by your horse skills."

Merry shrugged. "Yeah, I thought they were reaching a bit on that one. So then she showed us how to squeeze this place called the cannon bone, so they'll lift their foot. And then we had tools and we cleaned out their hooves."

Jana almost choked on her cranberry muffin. "Wait a minute—you cleaned their hooves?"

"Well, that was why they needed to lift their feet."

"How much did they charge for this class?" Jana asked.

"Fifty-five dollars," Merry said.

Jana busted up laughing. "Hold it. You're saying the guests did their job for them, and paid money to do it?"

Now Merry laughed. "I know, right? Plus, pressuring us, like there's something wrong with us if we can't get our horse to trust us."

"Oh, there's something wrong here, alright," Jana laughed. "Please tell me they didn't charge people to muck out the stables."

"That's exactly what Sean said. And walking back to our room the path was lined with river rocks, and Sean said he bet they charged guests to place those rocks just so in a Rock Alignment class, getting people to landscape for them."

Jana just shook her head.

"So then they gave us a sheet of paper to fill out as we left," Merry went on, "to say what our greatest realization was during our stay."

"I hope you wrote, 'I'm in the wrong business,'" Jana said. And they both laughed the rest of the way there.

Today they'd be meeting their new sister to visit. Jana opened the car door for Merry. "Feeling good?" Jana asked.

Merry rested one hand on her belly as she got into Jana's silver mini-van. She was seven months along. "Oh, just the usual stuff," she said. Her round face seemed even rounder today. "And I am swellin' *up* from this August heat. Plus it's hard to breathe with a baby pressing on your lungs."

"Oh, I remember that," Jana said. "I think Josh was trying to kick his way out—maybe that's what your baby is doing." Merry was having a boy, and Jana pictured him all arms and legs, like Josh.

Merry laughed. "My mom said the same thing."

Okay, Merry's mom was a good fifteen years older than Jana, but now she felt lumped into the same peer group. Suddenly she was the *advisor*. The middle-aged woman with experience on every topic. Jana had turned thirty-nine last April, and it was as if she had jumped into an ocean of old women, all melding together in the minds of the young ingénues on the shore.

"What happened to your legs?" Merry asked.

Jana looked down at her telltale orange-streaked legs. "I got tattoos," she said.

Merry gasped. "Honey, you need to ask for your money back."

"I'm kidding," Jana said, and told her about the tanning cream.

"Well, maybe wear long pants for awhile," Merry said.

Yeah, so I've been told.

"So do you know anything about Vera?" Merry asked. She was rubbing her temples.

"I don't—I guess we'll find out," Jana said. "Are you okay?"

"I've just had a ton of headaches, lately. It's to be expected."

"What we go through to bring these little spirits into the world," Jana said.

"Oh, I know," Merry agreed. "And this is nothing. My sister spends all her pregnancies in the hospital on I.V.s."

Jana nodded; there were several women in the ward who had the same condition. She found herself feeling grateful she'd never been hospitalized except to give birth. And now she was pulling into the driveway of a place where every resident was permanently in a hospital of sorts—and would likely die there.

And that's when Jana's resolve evaporated, as her car crept forward under the looming shadow of the El Dorado House. That's when she parked, accidentally set off the car alarm, nearly fainted, then climbed the steps and wondered which was shaking most—her knees or the steps.

At the top was a massive door with a brass handle. Jana took a deep breath and reached for it. *Inhale and exhale.*

"Hey, I'm the one who should be huffing and puffing," Merry smiled. "You nervous about going in here?"

Jana paused before opening the heavy door, and blocked all thoughts of wet shoes and stockings. "If you won't tell, I'll be honest—yes."

"It's not a witch house," Merry whispered.

Jana swallowed. "Oh, I know. That's what I told my kids. But it's . . . a rest home." *Actually, it's both.*

"Ah," Merry said. "Well, that's true. They can be a little scary. My grandma was in one and I used to visit her all the time just before we moved here. I got used to it." She glanced at the cobwebs clinging to the lantern overhead. "Although I'll tell you what. This one is especially dark and eerie."

"We can do this," Jana said. Gathering her resolve she grasped the cold brass handle of the door and decided to bring a measure of cheer into this gloomy place. And then she remembered the word she wanted, the one for spunk mixed with courage. The word was *pluck.*

Chapter 3

THEY STEPPED INTO THE LOBBY AND INSTANTLY THEIR LUNGS filled with strange smells—musty draperies, disinfectant, oatmeal—a cacophony of odors that begged to be aired out. But the windows were shut tight and blanketed in heavy brown velvet with a thick coating of dust. It looked as if their vacuum cleaner had been working in reverse, spewing out gray powder instead of drawing it in. If they even had a vacuum cleaner.

"Holy Moley," Merry gasped. And then apologized for thinking aloud.

Jana swallowed and glanced around. Tiny flame-shaped bulbs flickered in bronze wall sconces, as if afraid to scatter too much light. The walls were a faded maroon color, now brownish and weak. As they stepped across the black carpet, Jana felt as if she were walking into a pool of ink, where she might be swallowed up forever.

Ahead of them was a tall black counter where a prim woman sat, glaring at a computer screen. Its glow was the only light on her pale face, and as they approached, the woman looked up with slate gray eyes. Her entire head was shaped like a V. Her chin formed a sharp point, then widened to a broad forehead and a mound of auburn hair sprayed into a stiff, massive bun.

"Uh, hello," Jana said. "We're here to visit Vera Underwood."

The woman raised her chin and looked down a small, pinched nose, as if wearing reading glasses. Except she wasn't wearing glasses. Her eyes narrowed, nonetheless. "She's in the recreation room."

Jana and Merry stood there.

"It's down the hall." The woman nodded towards a hall behind a dark, winding staircase.

Jana and Merry stepped away from the desk and Jana resisted the urge to glance back and see what was on the woman's computer screen.

Something told her it would be a list of places where you can buy eye of newt.

Merry took Jana's arm. Jana wasn't sure if Merry was frightened, or if she realized that she herself was, and she didn't care. She was glad to cling right back to her. As they passed various rooms, she glanced in and noticed peeling linoleum floors, faded green curtains, and raised bumps at the foot of the beds, where someone's toes were lifting the sheets away from the mattresses.

A steel nurse's cart was parked by one room, with gray laundry bags hanging on either side. "Good morning, Pearl," a voice was saying from inside a darkened room. Must be a nurse, Jana thought.

A slim, steel bannister was attached to the walls, and a frail gentleman was grasping it as he made his way down the hall, like a child at a skating rink. Further ahead a tiny woman in a wheelchair sat with a gray tabby cat on her lap, stroking its back and humming.

At the end of the hall was a nurse's station where two nurses and a doctor were busy looking at paperwork, one of the nurses placing a folder into a file cabinet as Jana and Merry passed by. The doctor was dictating an exam into his phone, a stethoscope hanging around his neck and a tag on his coat, reading, *Bhupinder Rashid, M.D.*

Jana and Merry saw an open doorway at the end of the hall, with a sign overhead that read "Rec Room." As they stepped into another dimly lit room, they saw half a dozen residents inside, all playing Bingo beneath a lone light overhead. It looked like a movie set for a mafia interrogation.

Jana stared at the wobbly tables, the rickety chairs. More like *wreck* room, she thought to herself.

"I can hear y'all swallowing," Merry whispered, and smiled at her.

Jana sighed and they sat in two folding chairs to wait for the game to finish. A spindly woman with spiky silver hair was reading off the numbers as if it were her hundredth time to do so. And maybe it was.

"N-5," she droned.

"You're cheating again, Howard," one woman said. She had pale yellow hair swept up into a French Twist, and wore orange lipstick. Blue reading glasses hung on a chain around her neck.

"Mind your own business," he fired back. He had one of those tan, angular faces that look carved from mahogany. Like a treasure hunter just off a round-the-world cruise. "You always win, so what do you care?"

"I do not always win," the woman argued. "Vera won last time, didn't you, Dear?"

A woman with tiny white curls in a solid puff around her head smiled. "Oh, I don't know," she said, clearly pleased with herself, but lying. So this was Vera. She reminded Jana of a fairy—light as a wisp, wearing a gossamer pink shawl, and looking as if she could float up and away at any moment.

"Well you did," the first woman said.

Vera shrugged. "Must be beginner's luck." Her eyes twinkled.

"B-17," Gray Spikes said. The residents marked their cards.

Vera gasped. "Oh! Bingo! I guess I won again!"

Howard threw his hands in the air.

"Ha!" the first woman said to him. "You can't even win when you cheat!"

Howard stuck his tongue out at her. "I don't mind losing to Vera," he said. "I'm just glad she replaced Old Tire Iron."

Jana and Merry exchanged glances—who was Old Tire Iron?

Jana stood up and Merry followed behind her. "Vera?"

The woman with the white hair and pink shawl looked up and smiled. Her eyes were crinkled in the corners, from years of a sunny disposition.

"We're your Visiting Teachers."

Vera smiled and held out an arthritic hand. "Well, didn't take you long—I just moved in last week."

"Yes, she's the new girl," the first woman said. Jana thought about this school phrase and how it still clung to anyone new.

"Well, we're happy to meet all of you," Jana said. And then, for lack of better entertainment, the residents all gathered around to see what these strange teachers would teach.

"I guess I should explain that we're not really teachers," Jana continued. "Well, not in the formal sense. We're members of the Church of

Jesus Christ of Latter-day Saints, and every month we visit one another to share a spiritual message and to see how we're doing."

"We have teachers who visit us as well," Merry said.

"I'm Rose," the woman with the orange lipstick said. "So what's your message?" She flipped a switch on her wheelchair to zip up close, startling Merry. "These things are quick," Rose said, by way of explanation. Merry laughed and nodded.

Jana breathed a silent prayer for help, then plunged in. "Our message is about Christ," she said. "And how he's our advocate, pleading our case to our Father in Heaven."

"Aren't they one and the same?" another man asked. Jana turned. It was the gentleman who had been working his way down the bannister towards the rec room. His dark hair was slicked back from his face and needed a trim in back, and his eyebrows were wiry, like cricket antennae feeling the air. He wore a thin, maroon cardigan over a pale blue shirt, and looked as if he might have been a fastidious dresser in his day. He was approaching now, with a cane.

"Oh no, they're separate beings," Jana said. "God the Father is separate from his Son, Jesus Christ."

"Well I've never heard that before," the man said, easing into a chair. His skin looked yellowed and waxy, pulled taut over his cheekbones.

"Use your head, Marvin," Rose barked. "If they were one and the same, how could Jesus have prayed to him?" Then she turned to Jana and Merry. "Sit down, girls."

Jana and Merry complied, almost afraid to set her off.

Marvin cocked his head to one side. "I just thought God came down and became Jesus."

Rose snorted. "Well you thought wrong, didn't you?"

Marvin had raised a crooked finger to make a point, and Jana interrupted. She could sense an argument about to erupt, so she suggested they get acquainted first, and deliver the message later. "Tell us about yourself, Vera. And where you moved from."

Vera struggled to turn her wheelchair around, and eventually got it to face them. "I used to be in an independent living place in Auburn," she said. "But when I broke my hip I just couldn't get the walking thing down. I'm ninety-two." Here she paused for the expected surprise of her listeners, and smiled as everyone expressed how young and lovely she looked for her age. "So I came here, where you can have a wheelchair if you want. We all live on the ground floor."

"Do y'all have children nearby?" Merry asked.

"I have two, and six grandchildren, but they live in Pennsylvania and Michigan. They wanted me to come out there, but I can't take those climates. So they found me a place in northern California."

Jana wondered how on earth they chose this dismal facility, and wondered if it might be to convince their mother to leave, after all. She looked into Vera's lonely eyes and felt even greater shame for dismissing these people, every one of whom was a child of God with value and feelings. And here was a sweet woman whose entire world had been reduced to this charcoal building with its black carpet and brown draperies.

"I notice you have an accent," Howard said, nodding at Merry. "Where are you from?"

"Texas," Merry said, always with Texan pride in her voice.

"Oh, I've been there," Howard said. "Did some work on oil rigs."

"Don't listen to him," Rose said. "He'll tell you he's been everywhere."

Merry was rubbing her temples again, and another woman hobbled over on a cane. Her gray hair fell in loose waves at her jawline, and her skin looked floury and soft, as if she had just dusted it with a puff. "I'm Frances Tennegan," she said. "When are you due?"

Merry smiled. "Oh, not for another two months."

"How long have you had those headaches?"

"Oh, sorry," Merry said, and stopped rubbing her head. "I guess for a few weeks, now."

"I notice you're having trouble breathing."

"Well, I am a little short of breath these days—"

"Stop peppering the girl with questions," Rose interjected. "I notice you're a busybody, Frances."

Frances went on, clipped and efficient. "And you're swollen. Any abdominal pain? Nausea?"

"Some."

"Oh come off it, Nurse Frances," Rose said. She whipped her wheelchair around to face them. "Everybody who's pregnant gets that."

Frances ignored Rose and leaned in. "What's your blood pressure, honey?"

Merry shook her head. "I don't know. But I'm seeing my doctor today—"

Frances frowned, and looked back toward the nurse's station. "Looks like Dr. Rashid has left. Would you mind if I called one of the nurses to check it?"

Merry looked over at Jana, who shrugged. "Couldn't hurt," she said.

Frances motioned to Gray Spikes, the Bingo caller, and asked her to get a nurse and a blood pressure cuff. Soon a middle-aged blonde woman marched over, her flesh jiggling with each step. It was the one who had been filing paperwork earlier. Jana noticed her name tag said, *Theresa*. She wrapped the cuff around Merry's arm and began to pump it.

Listening to a stethoscope and staring at the gauge, she glanced at Frances. "How did you know this?" Theresa asked. Then she turned to Mary. "Your blood pressure is 175 over 110. You should get to a hospital."

Merry's eyes widened. "What? What does this mean?"

"Thank you," Frances said to the nurse. Then she turned to Jana. "Can you drive her to the hospital?"

"What is it? What's wrong?" Merry asked.

"You need tests to confirm this," Frances said, "But you may have preeclampsia."

"And what does that mean?" Merry asked.

"If you have it," Frances said, "It means you're having this baby tonight."

Merry's southern accent filled the room. "Ah'm WHAAT?"

Marvin and Howard both cheered until Rose shot them a glance. "Oh, pipe down, you two idiots. Don't you know how serious this is?"

Chapter 4

JANA DASHED TO THE CAR WITH MERRY, WHO KEPT APOLOGIZ-
ing that they didn't get to finish delivering their message.

"Are you kidding?" Jana said, peeling out of the parking lot. "We can always deliver a message, but you need to deliver a baby!" She was shaking as she drove.

"Slow down," Merry said. "It's not like I'm fixin' to have a heart attack."

Jana sighed. "Do you watch *Downton Abbey*?"

"No, but I've been wanting to. Everybody just raves about it."

"Well, this sounds really lame, but that's how I learned about pre-eclampsia," Jana said. And she decided not to tell Merry that it could be fatal to both mother and baby. "It's just really important that you get your blood pressure down."

"But it's too early to have this baby," Merry said. "It will be premature."

"It will be fine," Jana said, praying that she was right. "Preemies today do fine at this far along." Once again, she could hear her mother's confident voice falling from her lips.

"Well, I'm going to see what my doctor says," Merry said.

Good, Jana thought. *Because he'll want to induce you immediately.*

Merry was dialing her doctor on her cell phone, and told the receptionist she was on the way to the hospital. "Just tell him my blood pressure is 175 over 110." Then she called Sean, her husband, and told him to meet them there. "And bring me a suitcase," she said, "just in case."

Jana swung into the emergency entrance and found herself barking orders at the young man behind the desk. She was in full Mother Bear mode, hoping they were aware of the risk of a stroke or a seizure, but not wanting to increase Merry's anxiety by mentioning it. Soon Merry was in a wheelchair herself, being whisked off to a delivery room.

Jana slumped into a brown tweed chair and called Ethan. "I'll be right there," Ethan said. "Sean and I can give her a blessing."

They must have arrived at the same moment because the two men came rushing through the double glass doors together, banging them open, and headed right for the maternity wing. Sean's face was drained of all color and tears streaked his cheeks. Jana closed her eyes and said a silent prayer. Half an hour later Ethan was back, and said Sean was so shaken that he'd given Sean a blessing as well.

"They're inducing her," Ethan said. "And both their families are on their way."

"I should have noticed the problem," Jana said. "She was having trouble breathing and had a headache."

Ethan put his arms around her. "And how could you have known? Aren't those pretty common symptoms when you're pregnant?"

Jana nodded, but still felt responsible.

"Stop blaming yourself," Ethan said. "Just be glad a nurse was there, and that she got her blood pressure taken."

Jana took a deep breath, then released it. "You're right."

"Here's something to make you smile," Ethan said. "When Merry was filling out the form and it said 'Bp' she wrote 'Waterson.' She thought the Bp for blood pressure meant bishop."

Jana smiled. "I love her."

Just then Stacey Sparks and Doris Hedsun came rushing into the waiting room. "We're her visiting teachers," they said, hugging Jana and eager to see what they could do. "We're already planning for their families to stay with us."

Jana burst into tears. Partly it was the release of adrenalin, partly it was relief that Merry was in good care, but mostly it was because these two women barely knew Merry, yet were willing to open their homes to complete strangers in an emergency. *I love Relief Society.*

SIX HOURS LATER AIDEN OLIVER HAINES CAME INTO THE WORLD at five pounds, eleven ounces, and 17 inches long. Sean called to report that mother and baby were doing fine. Jana had come home to pick up her children and await word, and now released a giant sigh of relief.

"When can she have visitors?"

"Tomorrow," Sean said. "They want to keep them both for a few days' observation."

"Of course," Jana said. "Please give her our love."

"By the way," Sean asked, "Who was the woman at the El Dorado House? I wanted to thank her for saving Merry's life. Maybe I can go over there tomorrow."

"It's Frances something," Jana said, unable to recall the last name. Then, after hanging up, she turned to Ethan. "I think I'll go over and thank her as well."

"I'll come with you," Ethan said. "Savannah, you'll need to watch the kids until we get back."

"You guys make some sandwiches for dinner," Jana said.

Immediately the kids began howling.

"Or you can come with us," she added.

Instant silence. Jana smiled. "That's what I thought."

"You can't go back there," Maddie said, as if they had just made it through a mortar attack and were going straight back into a shoot-out. "The witches will cast a spell on you, just like they did on Sister Haines. And *she* ended up in the *hospital!*"

Jana wondered what this girl would be like in her teens if she was this dramatic now. "They are not witches and they did not cast a spell. In fact, one of them saved her life. I think she's a retired nurse, and she's the one who told me to rush Merry to the hospital."

Maddie sighed and went into miniature mother mode. "Be careful."

Josh joined in. "And remember who you are. And don't be out late."

Ethan ruffled Josh's hair, grabbed the car keys, and they left. Jana buckled her seat belt and sighed. "There isn't enough time between our house and the El Dorado House to prepare you for it, so I'll just . . . let you see for yourself."

"And draw my own conclusions?" Ethan asked.

"Yyyep," Jana said, popping the P. Why try to describe that place? It would exceed her description, anyway.

Sure enough, Ethan's jaw dropped when they went inside. His head rolled around like a teenager's eyeballs as he took in the cobwebs and flickering candelabras, looking this way and that at all the creepy appointments. If a skeleton had jumped out of a closet he wouldn't have been a bit surprised. He thought about saying, "What—no harpsichord music?" and then remembered his goal to be less sarcastic now that he was a bishop.

"You could have prepared me a bit," he whispered to Jana. She grinned.

The same woman with the V-shaped head was sitting at the desk and looked up. Looked down. Somehow managed to look up from the screen yet down her nose.

"We'd like to see Frances," Jana said, "and thank her for helping us today."

This time the woman didn't even speak, just nodded her head in the direction of the rec room again.

"Do we—" Ethan started to ask.

"Just follow me," Jana said. Great. Now she was a tour guide at the Witch House.

This time the smell of institutional food wafted down the hallway—grease, tomato sauce, starchy gravy—and she tried not to think about Great Aunt Ethel's place. She glanced at Ethan. He didn't seem eager to penetrate the bowels of this hideous building, either, because he wasn't taking his usual long strides. It was as if he hoped smaller steps could postpone the inevitable.

And she was right. Ethan was appalled at the musty appearance of the place. *When had they last cleaned it—the 1930s? How could they stay in business? Didn't the health department check on places like this?*

They went into the rec room, where the lone light overhead was now flickering. Probably a ghost, Jana couldn't help thinking.

And there was the Bingo group, eating pasta and canned peaches. "Hello, again," Jana called out. "This is my husband, Ethan. And this is Vera, Frances, and Rose, and on this side are Howard and Marvin."

Ethan whipped around as he stared at his wife. How did she already know everybody? What was it with women who could enter a building and get totally acquainted within ten minutes? It would take him six months, he was sure of it.

Jana apologized for interrupting their dinner, but they seemed glad to have a better alternative. Ethan made the rounds, shaking hands, then held Frances's in both of his, and thanked her for her sharp attention to Merry's condition.

"Well, my years of nursing come in handy," she said, gesturing to the residents. "Especially around here."

The men grumbled, the women laughed, then Jana reported on the new baby. Everyone cheered the new baby's name, and all but Vera toasted to Aiden Oliver with their glass of wine. Jana stared. *Well, there's something you don't see every day. At least if you're LDS.*

She stood behind Vera, with her hands on Vera's shoulders and looked back at Ethan. "This is Vera Underwood, the one we visit teach."

"I'm new," Vera said, as if this somehow covered everything.

Ethan pumped her tiny hand. "We'll make sure you get some great home teachers as well," he said.

"What? *More* teachers?" Rose bellowed.

Ethan smiled and pulled up a chair, happy to explain any facet of the church. Jana smiled as she watched him describe home teaching, and compare it to the Savior's ministry.

"That's a good idea," Marvin said. "I'd like to sign up for that."

"You got it," Ethan said. Jana flinched. He could do that? He could assign home teachers to nonmembers?

"Well if he's getting one, I want one," Rose said, sounding exactly like Maddie for a second. Heaven forbid someone get something that girl didn't get, and throw the entire universe out of whack.

Ethan pulled out his cell phone to make notes. "Who wants one?" he said. He looked like a car hop taking an order.

Little Vera was beaming, and raised her hand. Rose raised hers as well, and both Howard and Marvin had their hands up. Frances shrugged and said, "I'll share with the others."

"Hey!" Rose shouted to the four other residents in the room. "Who wants a teacher?"

They all looked up from their meals and frowned at her.

Rose waved them away. "They're just killjoys," she whispered to Ethan.

He laughed and typed in their names.

"It's free, right?" Rose asked.

"Completely free of charge," Ethan smiled. "And now we'd better let you get back to your dinner."

"Oh, yeah," Howard teased. "We'd hate to miss any of this." The others laughed, and Ethan shook their hands again.

"I like his manners," Vera whispered to Jana, nodding her head towards Ethan.

She smiled. "Me, too."

As they headed out, Jana paused beside Rose's wheelchair for a moment. "Who was Old Tire Iron?"

Rose laughed. "Oh, she was dreadful. Mean as a hornet. Finally had to move to an Alzheimer's care facility."

"Oh, I'm so sorry," Jana said.

"You kiddin'?" Rose chuckled. "Best thing that ever happened to any of us was when she couldn't remember who we were, anymore."

Well, I guess there's that.

"And now we have this sweet little Vera," Rose said.

Note to self: Do not be a crotchety old woman someday. Or a crotchety woman of thirty-nine right now.

Ethan and Jana had to push past overgrown bushes along the walkway back to the parking lot. As they got in the car Jana asked Ethan if he really could assign them home teachers.

"Absolutely. Visiting teachers, too."

"So were you scared in there?"

Ethan smiled. "Well, this place definitely needs some positive PR. But first," he said, "it's going to get some TLC."

Chapter 5

"NO WAY." THIS WAS SAVANNAH, REACTING TO HER FATHER'S news that the next ward project was going to be sprucing up The El Dorado House.

Jana was pleased to see all her children in complete and adamant agreement about something, but wished it could have been about keeping their rooms clean, or washing dishes cheerfully. "Come on, it will be fun," she lied. But when she turned her back to them she stretched her eyes as wide as she could and mouthed to Ethan, "Are you crazy?"

Ethan ignored her, his blue eyes twinkling. "I already have some ideas," he said. "I'm calling the place tomorrow to see if they'd like a . . . what is that you girls watch on TV?"

"A design makeover?" Savannah asked, her face still ashen with shock.

"Yep—a design makeover. That's what we'll give them."

"But the kids don't have to help, right?" Josh said. Maddie was already shaking her head no, as if trying to send subliminal signals to her father.

"They certainly do," Ethan said. "It will be a project for the entire ward."

Jana gulped, but then raised her eyebrows as if it could raise her spirits. "Hey, Savannah—you wanted a big service project for the mutual kids—this would be perfect!"

Savannah stared back and forth from Ethan to Jana, as if her parents had visibly lost their marbles that very instant. "No way! You won't get one soul to come within twenty feet of that place!"

"She's right," Josh said. "No way."

"No way," Maddie parroted.

Jana laughed. "Oh, come on—we're not fraidy cats!"

Savannah squinted. "Where do you get these expressions?"

"And," Josh said, "we totally are fraidy cats."

"Totally," Maddie said.

Ethan did what he always does when he wants to calm the atmosphere, and slipped a church music CD into the sound system. "Let's make a list of everything that place needs." He pulled a sheet of paper from the computer printer.

"A gigantic bomb," Josh suggested.

Jana wondered if she was to blame for the sarcasm in this family.

"Seriously," Savannah agreed.

"Come on," Ethan said. "Let's all gather around the table."

Sighing and eye rolling, the kids finally slumped into chairs when Jana brought out a tub of strawberry ice cream and some bowls. Spoons clattered on the table as she dropped them in a heap.

"Of course, you kids haven't seen inside, so you might not realize all that can be done there," Ethan said. "But what can we do outside?"

"Get those fairies to undo all the vines," Maddie put in. She loved the movie, *Sleeping Beauty,* and was obviously thinking about the thicket of thorns Maleficent caused to grow over the castle.

"Cut vines," Ethan said as he wrote. "We definitely need a yard crew."

"Why can't we just do a chalk project?" Savannah whined.

Jana scoffed. "That's small potatoes," she said.

"Another weird expression."

"Still, a chalk project is nothing compared to this," she said. "This will beautify the entire neighborhood and mean the world to those people inside."

"The witches," Maddie whispered, grabbing a spoon and digging into her ice cream.

"Okay, Rule Number One," Ethan said. "No more calling them witches. Besides, some of them are men."

"Warlocks, then," Josh said. Ethan gave him a look.

"One of them looks like that fairy in *Sleeping Beauty*," Jana said. "The one named Fauna."

Maddie's eyes grew round. "Really?"

"Really. I'll introduce you sometime. Her name is Vera."

The kids sat silent.

Jana stopped scooping. "That's what we need to do," she said to Ethan. "We need to give their names to the ward members. So they realize these are real people."

Ethan nodded, thrilled that Jana was getting on board with his idea. He truly felt prompted to do this, and just knew it would bless the entire ward.

Savannah sighed. "It needs paint."

Ethan beamed and wrote it down. "What color?"

She shrugged. "Anything else."

Jana laughed. "How about we submit a color scheme to the owners, for their approval?"

"A scheme?" Josh asked.

"Yes—it's a Victorian, so they usually have three colors for all the woodwork. Like the 'Painted Ladies' in San Francisco." The kids had always enjoyed the colorful side-by-side homes in Easter egg pastels they'd seen on trips to Alamo Square.

"Blue and white," Josh said.

"No way—it should be mint green," Savannah argued.

"Pink! Pink! Pink! Pink!" Maddie chanted, now waving her spoon.

Ethan laughed. "I have a feeling we're going to need to give each auxiliary an assignment, and let them make some of their own decisions."

"Primary gets the painting," Maddie said. "And we'll pick pink."

"We'll see." Ethan had now divided the paper into segments, listing all the projects that came to mind. "Somebody needs to clean the carpet."

"And the draperies," Jana said.

"And paint the walls," they both said together. Within minutes they had added lighting, flooring, walls, and window cleaning to the list.

"Where's the budget going to come for all this?" Savannah asked, making Jana wonder once again which one of them was the adult and which one the Disney cartoon watcher.

"Well, I know we can get all the labor donated," Ethan said. "But we might have to ask the city to help us out. Or the owners."

He went to his computer. "I'm going to make this the topic of Ward Council this Sunday." He began typing a meeting agenda.

"Operation El Dorado House," Josh said.

Maddie had sidled up to her mother and was now whispering in Jana's ear. "But I'm still scared to meet that fairy witch."

Jane scooped her into her arms. "You will adore her," she said. "I promise."

AFTER THE KIDS WERE ALL BUSY WITH THEIR HOMEWORK, JANA reminded Ethan about the spider. He went looking, but now it was dark and the spider was nowhere to be seen. "I think they only come out in the daytime," he said.

"To scare the living daylights out of people," Jana said.

"I think so," Ethan said. "I think that's in their job description." But he had noticed the roses and clippers on the ground, and brought them in. "Sorry you had such a scare."

"Why can't they make their webs out front and scare away the burglars?"

Ethan laughed. "That would be better than a barking dog, I think. And certainly better than National Night Out."

"Oh, don't get me started," Jana said. Two weeks earlier Kristi Hargrove had invited her to the one she was hosting, to raise awareness of crime.

"Oh, you'll raise awareness, alright," Jana had told her friend. 'It will start when everyone returns home and finds their place ransacked. They should call it National Burglar Night."

"No," Kristi said, "The police will be there telling us how to prevent burglaries."

"Yeah, and the Number One way is to stay home," Jana said. "How is this not a giant signal to every thief in the nation to get out his Zorro mask and make the day of it? Okay, night of it?"

Now Kristi was laughing. "It's not like they know about it."

"How can they not?" Jana asked. "You and I know about it. The whole country knows about it, and that would include burglars. I believe they get the same flyers stuck in their door that I do, and they're probably all high-fiving one another this very minute, at Louie's Hideaway Bar or someplace. Maybe they're even divvying up our addresses.

"And then, while our kids are jumping in a bounce house, and we're sampling the potluck offerings of our neighbors, thieves will quietly be loading our jewelry and electronics into their utility vans."

"So that's a 'no' RSVP," Kristi said.

"That's right," Jana said. "I'm doing National Night In."

Kristi laughed. "How are we friends? We have nothing in common."

"That's right," Jana said. "Except we keep forgetting that." Two women, paired up like those 'opposites attract' couples, sharing little besides a sense of humor, and the pledge to lead a Conga line at one another's funerals.

"Well, at least I no longer expect you to come running with me," Kristi said. "I'm doing a 5K tomorrow."

"Let me know when you have a ½K," Jana said. "I think I could run that."

"That's like a few blocks!" Kristi laughed.

"Oh. Well then, better make it a ¼K."

"You really should start something like that. It would be hilarious."

"But then all the burglars would hear about it and rob our houses while we're there," Jana said. "I'll keep an eye on your house for you tomorrow while you're out ruining your knees."

"Deal," Kristi said.

THE NEXT DAY ETHAN DID INDEED FIND THE SPIDER, AND TOLD Jana it was taken care of as he headed out to work.

"Are you sure it's gone?"

"Positive."

"And what about the web—did you get rid of that, too?"

"Yep."

"So everything's really gone?"

Ethan smiled. "You can hire somebody else, but I think my rates are good."

Jana glanced out the back doors.

"Yes, you are totally safe," Ethan called, and disappeared into the garage.

Jana clipped a few more roses, this time for Merry in the hospital. She arrived to visit along with half a dozen of Merry's relatives just in from Texas. Merry had once told her how vehemently they were opposed to Marry's baptism, but today their happy drawls swirled around the new mother and her little bundle. "Idd'n he just precious?" one aunt asked, inhaling the sweet new-baby fragrance of little Aiden's scalp.

Merry's mother nodded. "Ah worship that chawld."

Merry was noticeably less swollen and in great spirits. Though her blood pressure was still a concern, it was coming down. Sean looked utterly lost and exhausted, trying to manage sudden houseguests, his job, and the medical situation. He ran his fingers through his bedraggled hair, and rubbed his bloodshot eyes. Two of the relatives were staying with a visiting teacher, and the ward was rallying with meals, but it was still Crisis Management.

Jana told Merry about taking Ethan to the El Dorado House, and how it had hatched a ward project.

"Take before and after pictures," Merry said, "or no one will ever believe it."

"What I can't believe is that my kids are actually willing to help," Jana said. "Josh was even texting a friend of his about weed whackers and shovels."

Merry smiled. "Well, keeping them outside is probably a good idea." Then she winked. "Magic spells and all."

Jana leaned down to hug her, then whispered in her ear. "Hey, maybe we can turn it into a spa, and get people to pay for the opportunity of cleaning it up."

Merry laughed, then whispered back, "And make them feel guilty if they can't get the weeds to trust them."

Jana prayed as she drove home—why were so many of her prayers said as she was driving, these days?—and asked for help to be strong about this whole thing. Strong, and forgetful. Remembering the childhood incident at Great Aunt Ethel's place wasn't doing her a bit of good, and even elicited negative feelings about her sisters. She thought about a recent Sunday School lesson about grudges and past hurts we all carry like rocks in a backpack, as if they're actually valuable treasures. *I just need to put down these rocks.*

That Sunday Ethan presented the project, handed out a list of the residents' names, and got unanimous support from every auxiliary leader. Assignments were made and a date was chosen, subject to the approval of the owners.

"Were you nervous?" Jana asked him later.

Ethan was sitting at his desk in the home office, and now he leaned back in his chair. "Surprisingly, no. I think I was so sure this was inspired, that I just never doubted."

Jana smiled. "Kind of like being the bishop," she said.

Ethan stared at his wife and tried to decide if she was more beautiful or brilliant and realized she was both, in exactly equal proportions.

"Okay, yuck again," Savannah said, sighing as if she had come upon someone licking the floor.

Jana laughed. "You always catch us in romantic moments."

"No, I always catch you in disgusting moments," Savannah said. "So the youth are doing the windows? And weeding? Aren't those the worst jobs?"

"Nah, not with a squeegee," Ethan said. "Plus the bishopric will be helping you."

"What if there are snakes?" Savannah asked.

"I'm sure they're more scared of you than you are of them," Ethan said, suddenly remembering a farmer's words when he was a boy.

Josh happened by just then. "Did someone say there are snakes over there?"

"See?" Jana said. "This is how rumors get started. I'm sure there are no snakes at the El Dorado House."

Josh slid onto a brown leather love seat in the office. "Did you know we're selectively breeding rattlesnakes that don't rattle?"

"Who is?" Jana asked. *What a stupid endeavor! Who would do such a thing?*

"Society is," Josh said. "Because we kill the ones that rattle."

Suddenly Jana and Savannah locked glances, realized what this meant, and screamed.

Ethan got up from his desk and tried to calm them both down. Josh just sat on the love seat and laughed.

"They could be anywhere!" Savannah cried. "They could be in our house!"

"And we'd never know it!" Jana shouted.

"Oh my gosh, I can never relax again as long as I live," Savannah wailed.

"Okay, everybody just calm down," Ethan said, guiding both of them to the love seat and motioning with his head for Josh to move.

"This is not funny," Jana growled to Josh. "You have scared us both to pieces."

Just then Maddie rushed in to see what the commotion was. "What's going on?"

And every family member knew there would be no peace in Whoville if Maddie found out what Josh had just said. They all just swallowed and stared at her.

"Nothing," Savannah said.

"That's right. Nothing," Jana echoed.

Maddie put her hands on her hips. "Well it had to be something."

"It's nothing that concerns you," Ethan said.

Maddie sighed, twirled around, and left. Ethan turned to Josh. "You will not be sharing any more snake information in this house."

Josh shrugged and headed back to the hallway.

"Or laughing about it," Jana said. Josh looked back and grinned as he walked out.

WITHIN TWO WEEKS ETHAN HAD APPROVAL FOR THE PROJECT from the owners, along with their selection of paint chips—a soft, buttery yellow, a creamy white, and gold trim. The owners were a group of investors who were more than happy to let a local church make "cosmetic improvements," as long as the ward members signed waivers to protect them from lawsuits, should anyone get injured doing the refurbishing. Surprisingly, they even made a small donation for paint and light fixtures. It turned out an inspector had already reported the outdated wiring, so the owners put Ethan in touch with the company doing the electrical work as well.

Since the upstairs was only used by the staff for office space and storage, the improvements would all be focused on the downstairs living space.

Four people in the ward had rug shampooers, and the High Priests would be cleaning the carpets. The Elders' Quorum would be painting the exterior, while the Ward Missionary department and the Sunday School would paint inside—pale taupe with crisp white trim. The Relief

Society would sew new curtains for the residents' bedrooms, and dry clean and re-hang the heavy brown draperies in the lobby.

Professionals were coming in to repair peeling linoleum and one brother, an electrician, was going to supervise the installation of new lighting in the lobby and recreation room, working directly with the firm already hired to upgrade the inside wiring.

A boy working on his Eagle Scout Award asked if he could install a new wheelchair ramp to replace the old one, along with new handrails, and a prettier bannister rail in the main hallway.

Once the building itself was done, the entire ward would meet on a Saturday to tackle the grounds, pull weeds, and trim bushes. A landscape architect in the 2nd ward had already agreed to sketch out a design, and a local nursery was donating the plants, which the ward would help plant under his direction.

The Primary decided to stay out of the work zone, and make a separate project at the ward building: Giant posters to hang in each resident's room, including photos and facts about their lives. Jana realized that the scariest lady in the entire building was the woman at the front desk, but she was planning to ask her for this very sort of information, so the kids could put together the collages. She loved children's art and was excited to see the joy and color it would bring to those drab rooms. She hoped the approval of the buildings' owners would ensure the woman's cooperation.

A week later the interior painting began, and Jana figured she had procrastinated long enough. It was time to officially meet that chilly receptionist.

Plastic tarps crinkled beneath her feet as she stepped across the black carpet in the lobby. The ward missionaries and Sunday School teachers had already removed switch plates, taped off windows, and were rolling a soft shade of taupe onto the walls. Even the smell of wet paint was a welcome change from the previous odors. The heavy curtains had been taken down to be dry cleaned, and even with the windows still obscured by tangled vines, the light level was decidedly up.

Renovating some old building was infinitely easier than doing missionary work, and she was grateful Ethan had chosen this project, instead of something that meant talking to strangers about the gospel—which still made her heart race. Jana had a testimony; there was no doubt in her mind that the church was true. But sharing it with others reminded her of her failure, so she had consciously avoided it all these years. And that terror was not something easily set aside.

The woman with the auburn bun was watching without expression, her mouth a horizontal line of red lipstick. Her green sweater was buttoned up to the neck as if this were January, not early September.

"Hi, I'm Jana Waterson—we met a week ago?" Jana stepped up to the black counter.

"They're in the rec room," the woman said.

For just an instant Jana wondered if this bit of information were the only thing the woman knew how to say.

"Oh, it's you I was hoping to speak with," Jana said.

The woman frowned, her eyebrows coming together. "Me? What about?"

"Well," Jana said, wishing she had a name to slip in here. "First, may I ask your name?"

"It's Helen."

"Nice to meet you, Helen." Jana explained her art project, and noticed too many of her statements were looping up like question marks, her voice hoping for the woman's approval.

Finally the woman shrugged. "Well, go ahead if that's what you want to do. But I don't have any information for you. You'll have to get it from the residents, themselves."

"They didn't fill out any questionnaires about their interests, or their lives?"

"Nope. All we have is private medical forms."

Jana thought how sad this was, that these people had agreed to live out their lives in utter anonymity. Not one soul had taken a personal interest in them, or knew their backgrounds. But she nodded and thanked Helen before going down the hall to say hi to Vera.

How was she going to collect the life story of all twelve residents? And then her cell phone rang with the answer.

Chapter 6

"MOM, I NEED TO CALL GRANDMA WATERSON," SAVANNAH SAID. "Can you give me her number in Florida?"

"Sure," Jana said, glancing in the residents' rooms as she walked by. "What's this about?"

"Mrs. Ames gave us an assignment in History. We have to interview three people who were born before 1940. We have to ask what their childhoods were like, the inventions they've seen, the moon landing, stuff like that."

Jana smiled. "Gee, where could we find a whole bunch of people born before 1940?"

Savannah gasped. "No way. I am not interviewing those people in the Witch House. I mean the El Dorado House."

"Why not?"

"Because! It's creepy in there."

"Hey, it's creepy at Grandma Waterson's house in Florida," Jana said. "She keeps the door open to a screened-in patio and the humidity makes mushrooms grow under the swamp cooler."

"You are making that up."

Jana laughed. "Ask your dad, then. He can't lie because he's the bishop."

"Well, I don't have to see the mushrooms if I call her on the phone," Savannah argued.

"You don't have to see them if you come over here, either," Jana said. "And you'll have a dozen people to help you make it the best report in the entire class." That last line clinched it, and Jana knew it would. "Might be a good project for the whole Mutual," she said. "And we actually need background on these folks for the artwork the Primary is doing."

The giant sigh on the other end of the call told her Savannah was caving in. Turning in the best report of the semester was like nectar to this hummingbird. And heading up a huge project was the perfect thing for a daughter who loved to direct activities. Jana found herself imagining Savannah as the Social Director for a cruise line someday. Maybe she'd bring her mom along to the Greek Islands or the French Riviera.

"Well, you look happy," Vera said, snapping Jana out of her reverie.

"Oh—yes, yes I am," Jana stammered, suddenly aware that she was standing beside Vera's wheelchair. She put her cell phone away.

"Me, too," Vera whispered, as if this should be kept a secret. "I can't wait to see how this place will look."

"It's pretty exciting," Jana agreed. "Merry finally got to bring the baby home, so she told me to tell you hello."

Just then Vera turned her head and called out, "The baby is home, now!" in a louder voice than Jana knew the tiny woman could muster.

Frances and Howard hobbled over as quickly as they could, and flamboyant Rose beat them all by zipping past in her "speed chair." Today she was wearing a sequin-covered baseball cap.

Howard turned and called to a small group at a table in the back, "Hey, Marvin—the baby's home!"

The entire group raised a cheer as if they were all related to little Aiden. "Thanks to Frances," Marvin shouted, and the entire room cheered the retired nurse.

Frances blushed, waving away their attention, but was clearly pleased with their praise. "I'm just glad everyone's okay, now."

"So what's our lesson today?" Rose said. Her thumbs were looped through the chain holding her blue glasses, like a farmer looping his thumbs through the straps of his overalls, relaxed and ready to be entertained.

Jana gulped. She actually hadn't prepared one, having come by just to meet Helen and get background information. And since there wasn't any, interviewing Vera herself had become Plan B. But they were all meandering over now, like cats to a bowl of kibble, so quickly she made one up. Besides, Savannah and her friends would be handling the interviews just fine.

"Today we're going to talk about families, and why they're important," Jana said.

Suddenly she realized she had picked the worst possible topic. Here were a dozen people whose families never even came to visit, if they even had any family left at all, after burying loved ones over the years. What was she thinking? These people were the very picture of disconnected living—no spouses, no nothing. She tried not to cringe.

"Families *are* important," Rose threw in. "Young people today don't seem to realize that."

A chorus of muttered agreement rose up as elderly heads nodded at one another. Jana just knew one of them would soon burst into tears about children who never visit.

"That's true," Marvin said. "They don't even get married and some of them decide not to have children."

"It's a disgrace," the tiny woman with the gray tabby cat said.

"Families are the only way you keep a society going," one bald man in the back said, building his volume like a campaign speaker. "The minute the family breaks down, pphhfft!"

Frances and Vera nodded.

Jana smiled. She had been wrong; these people weren't here to whine about loneliness or uncaring relatives—they believed in families! They wanted to talk about how families impact society.

"God was very clear about it," Jana said, summoning courage. "He told Adam and Eve to have a family, and that's been the directive ever since." Suddenly they were all staring at her. *Well, it's now or never.* She took a deep breath and launched into the Plan of Salvation. She told them about living with God as spirit children before they were born into families, and how families were meant to be together forever. She could see the surprise on their faces as she told them about having Heavenly Parents and a plan to get back home again.

Frances and Howard were frowning—almost scowling—at this strange doctrine, and Howard essentially turned away. Deciding this was a lot to chew on, Jana thanked them all for listening, then hugged each one goodbye. Though she could see they weren't all on board with the doctrine, not one of them refused a hug. And, as she walked back down the hall, she felt a prompting. She needed to bring the Primary kids here and have them sing "Families Can Be Together Forever."

Sure enough, by the time Jana got home Savannah had texted the other Laurels and Priests to enlist their help with the interviews. "I am *not* going in there alone," she said.

As long as you're going in. And she knew Savannah's fears would evaporate as soon as she actually met Vera and the others.

Slowly the text messages came back—only three Laurels and two Priests would agree to go into the El Dorado House, even with Savannah reminding them that they could use this information for their high school history reports.

The Witch House? Are you kidding me? No way.

I have to work that night. (Savannah: But I haven't picked a night). Whatever night you pick, I have to work.

I am not going anywhere near that place.

Too much homework.

Soccer practice—sorry.

And on and on. With only six youth, including herself, agreeing to interview twelve residents, Savannah realized she would have to invite the entire mutual and just hope six more would sign on.

Once Josh realized the deacons were included, he reluctantly caved in. But for a week and half no one else would commit to it. Finally when Ethan offered a pizza party following the interviews, one Teacher and two Beehives signed up. They would still be short-handed, but the leaders offered to fill in, and interview the remaining two seniors. Then they could pass along the information to the Primary kids who, undoubtedly, would have a ball painting the posters.

"HEY, LET'S TAKE A PLATE OF COOKIES TO THAT NEW FAMILY down the street," Jana called out to the kids the next day. They had already been floating through the kitchen like lazy sharks, snitching bits of dough. "Can't—Scout planning meeting," Josh said. "But I'll take some cookies to the scouts." Carefully he lifted the chocolate chip cookies from the cooling rack and stacked them on a paper plate.

Jana's plate was already loaded and covered with foil. "It will only take a minute," she called to the girls who were both in the family room.

"I'm coming," Maddie said. She knew her own future cookies could depend on her cooperation, and Savannah was eager for a break from the computer anyway. They both pulled on hoodies and headed down the block with Jana.

"I love doing this," Jana said. "It's such a slice of Americana, greeting new people with a plate of cookies or brownies." It seemed so few people did this anymore, and she was glad to involve her daughters, and continue the tradition.

"You move in, you get cookies," Maddie said, then held a pointer finger in the air. "It's the law."

"Well, it's not really the law," Jana said.

"It's Mom's law," Savannah added. "And she always takes them a flyer about local stuff to do, and when church is."

"It's good information to have," Jana said. "Oh, hey, there's someone, now."

Just then a man in a navy blue parka came walking down the driveway. The garage door was up, and you could see bunk bed frames and bicycles among the many boxes.

They hurried to meet up with him. "Hi there," Jana called. "We're the Watersons—some of your new neighbors."

"I'm David," the man said, seeming rushed and not terribly interested. He had a dark mustache and wore a gray baseball cap.

"We thought we'd bring you some cookies," Jana continued.

David took the plate without even breaking his stride, got into a white pickup truck parked at the curb, and drove off.

Jana and the girls just stared.

"Okay, something is wrong with that," Savannah said.

"Yeah, and the something is that he drove off with the cookies," Jana agreed. "Why didn't he go inside and ask his wife and kids to come out and meet the new neighbors?"

"Or at least take the cookies into the house, instead of just driving off with them?" Savannah continued.

Maddie stared back and forth from her sister to her mother, waiting for one of them to hit upon the answer.

"Oh, my gosh, he could be a burglar," Jana said. "It's the perfect explanation, right? I mean, technically he wasn't even in the house. Maybe David—if that's even his real name—was probably just casing the joint, and then took off with that family's cookies!"

"Yeah!" Maddie said, eager to jump on the drama wagon.

"I doubt he was a burglar," Savannah said, her voice not very certain at all.

"Seriously," Jana said, liking this theory more and more, "What person—myself excluded—could eat an entire plate of 16 cookies by himself? Surely he would take them inside to share, maybe grab a couple of them for the road, and then leave. Right? And anyone with any manners at all would call his family to come out and get acquainted."

"Unless . . ." Savannah said.

"Unless he's a thief on the run, that's what," Jana said. "So now we're aiding and abetting and feeding a criminal. Possibly even a criminal master mind."

Maddie's eyes danced, and she couldn't wait for her father's car to pull into the garage before dashing out to meet him and shouting, "Guess what? A burglar moved in down the street!"

Ethan came in, sat down at the breakfast bar, and listened to her retelling of the whole Cookie Caper. He turned to Jana. "You just feed the drama machine when you do this."

"We fed a burglar," Maddie corrected him. "A real burglar!"

"And that's why I'm never going to National Night Out," Jana said, winking at Ethan. "In fact, I'm going to drive by there from time to time and see if that same guy even shows up—or the kids who own those bikes and bunk beds."

Savannah was stirring some corn chowder on the stove, and turned to her father. "You've got to admit, that was pretty weird behavior."

"Weirder than some woman driving by and spying to find you again?"

Jana shrugged. "Hey, we live in a crazy world."

She looked up and Ethan was smiling and nodding, pointedly in her direction.

SPEAKING OF A DRAMA MACHINE, ETHAN WAS FLABBERGASTED at the number of fires he had to put out as bishop. He pictured himself cast in a reality show similar to *Candid Camera*—only this one would be called *Guess What, Bishop?*—where people secretly installed a camera in a bishop's office, then hired actors to pop in with wild predicaments, to see what the bishop would do. Already he'd had to explain that you cannot receive food assistance and then turn around and sell it on the corner, that you cannot have Poker Night for a Relief Society Activity, and that the missionaries cannot be lifeguards at your pool party, even if one of them is an award-winning swimmer. This week he'd gotten three calls complaining that the Ward Librarian, Sister Friedman, was charging late fees.

"Just like a real library," she had happily admitted, when he called her on Saturday to verify the claims.

"We can't actually do that," he said.

"Well I'm doing it," she replied. "These people have got to learn to be more responsible. And then, with the money we collect, we can buy all kinds of wonderful church books—"

"No, we'll need to return the money you've collected—" Ethan started to say.

"Well, I won't do this calling if you're going to restrict my entre-preneurial ideas," she said. And Ethan had had to scramble to find a replacement that very night. Good grief; was he going to have years of this craziness?

FORTUNATELY THERE WAS GOOD NEWS THAT SUNDAY. IN WARD Council, the Ward Mission Leader and Sunday School President reported that the interior painting of the El Dorado House was finished, flecks of white in their hair as evidence.

It had six downstairs bedrooms for the residents, each one with two twin beds. Six women were housed on one side of the building—two women in each of the three bedrooms there—and six men lived in three identical rooms on the other side. The Relief Society was busy sewing white linen curtains for all six bedrooms, and also had decided to tie a colorful quilt for each bed. They had borrowed four quilt frames from the stake humanitarian department.

Ethan coughed to conceal the fact that he was choking up, so amazed at how willingly everyone had helped. Even the painters had gone the extra mile and included the bedrooms, not just the common areas. When he walked through on Saturday, the entire place looked lighter and brighter. Two of the nurses kept going on and on about the difference it was already making in the moods of their patients. This week the linoleum would be fixed, lighting would be upgraded, and, with several retired High Priests volunteering to help, the carpet would get a thorough cleaning. Undoubtedly it would be ideal to replace that black carpet, but the budget was maxed out as it was, so new flooring of any kind was out of the question. But new floors or not, the place now seemed to sparkle. Countless hours of loving service had virtually injected it with the spirit of generosity.

"Is it my imagination, or is everyone suddenly smiling more?" Jana whispered to him just before Sacrament meeting started. He was wearing the maroon and yellow tie Maddie had made him for Father's Day three years ago, and Jana decided a man was never more handsome than when he was wearing some monstrosity his child had made.

Ethan beamed. She was right; this project had energized the entire ward. Elderly Sister Hastings was playing the prelude music, her soft hands gently brushing "Because I Have Been Given Much" onto the keys. It seemed the perfect song for the gratitude he was feeling.

"Hey," he whispered, pulling Jana aside. He hated to break the glowing moment, but had no choice. "You know I'm going to have to release you." In addition, she'd been the Primary President for three years, now.

Jana sighed. "I know, but can you wait until the kids go sing to them?"

He smiled, but shook his head. "I need to do it today. We've already called a new President. And next weekend is General Conference."

Jana sighed. "But we're going to be singing this Friday afternoon."

Ethan paused.

"Look, I know hardly anyone will come," Jana said. "It might even be just Maddie."

"You can still do it, even if you're released."

Jana brightened. "That's true." But her heart sank at suddenly realizing this incredible calling was coming to an end. Then she looked up at Ethan as he sat down with his counselors, and realized he was the perfect example of accepting change. What a difficult thing this had been for him, yet he had done it with his whole heart. Suddenly she got an idea. A flirty, fun idea for the man who still made her heart pound. She tore a strip of paper from the Sacrament program, scribbled on it, then hurried up and handed it to him. But two other people wanted to speak with him before the meeting started, so Ethan just held the note in his hand.

Finally, after the song and prayer, she was standing up in Sacrament meeting, being released from Primary. Her first counselor, Eva Henry, became the new president. Ethan still hadn't opened her message.

And then a speaker stepped to the podium and Jana watched as Ethan unfolded her note. He frowned, then looked quizzically back at her. His eyebrows scrunched and he shook his head. She grinned back, nodding. She had written, "You look hot!" on the note.

Ethan nudged Terrell Moses, the counselor beside him, and showed him the note. Jana could read Ethan's lips asking, "Do I look hot?"

NO! Jana was mortified—this was a private, frisky note that Ethan wasn't supposed to share with anyone!

Terrell smiled. Even worse. Terrell got the meaning of the note, while innocent Ethan was thinking he looked sweaty and overheated. And, of course, Terrell glanced down into the congregation, right at Jana, whose face was contorted with agony, and absolutely crimson.

Terrell chuckled, then whispered to Ethan, who then blushed deep red and shoved the note into his pocket. As best he could, without the entire ward noticing, Ethan stared at Jana with "What were you thinking?" pulsing from his eyes.

And she stared "What were *you* thinking?" right back at him.

After the meeting, they gave each other wide-eyed glances, and Eva Henry saw it. "Are you upset about being released?" she asked Jana.

"No, no, it isn't that," Jana said. "It's—it's something else. Eva, you are the perfect choice."

Eva's eyes were filled with the realization that she was now in charge, and she nervously kept pushing blonde bangs away from them. "Will you still help the kids make those posters? And handle the singing thing this Friday?" she asked.

"Absolutely," Jana promised. "You know you can count on me for whatever you need."

Eva smiled, and swallowed hard.

"You will be wonderful at this. The best president ever," Jana whispered.

Eva forced a smile, then hugged her. "I'm going to miss you so much."

"I'll be right here. You know that." But when they pulled apart, they both had wet eyes, as if this were goodbye at a train station in the 1940s. Seeing one another get so emotional, they both laughed. "It's going to work," Jana said.

"I know, I know," Eva agreed.

Jana made her way through the crowd, and darted into Ethan's office and he shut the door.

"What was that?" Ethan asked.

"A private message!" Jana shot back. "I can't believe you showed it to Terrell!"

Ethan stood there, fuming, a tumble of feelings in his head. On the one hand, he felt stupid for sharing it with Terrell, but on the other hand, he was flattered that Jana had given him the note in the first place.

He took her in his arms. "Well, I'm sort of mad *at* you and *for* you."

Jana laughed, then kissed him. "You big dope."

Ethan gave her behind a quick pat as she headed out.

Jana rounded the corner and bumped into Kristi Hargrove, whose ward met earlier in the same building. Kristi told her the High Priests and Young Mens' Presidency had just been shuffled around in her own ward, and her husband, Doug, had been released as the Young Men's President. It had been a huge calling and Doug had recently had to take on a second job, as well. In addition, Doug was now caring for his ailing parents, and truly needed a less demanding assignment.

"I have to tell you," Kristi said, "Doug was so relieved. When they asked him to be the Assistant Executive Secretary, Doug said, 'You had me at assistant.'" She and Jana laughed.

Jana went into the Primary room to tell the kids how much she loved them, and to assure them everything would flow along smoothly. She tried not to glance around the room one last time, at the darling sheep the kids had made from cotton balls, now stapled to a bulletin board with the kids' own shining faces in place of the sheep faces. Or the bright green family tree on another bulletin board, with ancestor photos in each of the apples. It isn't as if you're moving away, she told herself. You can still come in here and see what the kids have been doing. But she found herself fighting back tears.

Then Eva winked at her, and she told them about the singing opportunity that Friday. As if on cue, all the kids blanched with horror, and even several teachers raised their eyebrows. "Honestly," she said, "you will love these elderly people. And they will love you."

"To eat," a boy on the back row muttered, just loud enough to elicit laughter.

"Come on," Jana said. "We're fixing up their house and I think they'd just love to have some darling children who they can—"

"Turn into toads," a girl on the next row said.

Jana sighed. This was going to be a tough sell.

And then Ethan walked in. "Hey, kids," he said. "How many of you have a grandma and a grandpa who live close by?"

A sprinkling of hands went up. Suddenly every kid wanted to say where his lived and what they gave him for Christmas.

"How many of you have grandparents who live far away?" Now most of the hands went up. "Do you think they miss you?"

Heads nodded.

"And do you wish you could see them more often?"

More nodding. Two comments about Skype.

"What if you could have a grandma or a grandpa right in our neighborhood? What if you could adopt one and visit them all the time?"

Slowly he painted the picture of how much love the kids would receive, and how much joy they could bring to someone who was lonely. He spoke about an old woman named Vera, another named Rose, and a man named Howard.

Then he asked if any of them had ever heard something that wasn't true. "Has anyone ever heard a lie about one of your friends? Or about yourself?"

Hands shot up. "Tawny Mitchell said I cheated, but I didn't," one girl reported.

"It's a terrible thing to spread lies about someone, isn't it?" Ethan said. "What if someone said your house was haunted, and no one should ever come and play with you?"

Jana watched their faces as the kids imagined this happening to them.

"That's what has happened at the El Dorado House," Ethan said. "People have spread lies about it. But there are no witches there. In fact, witches don't even exist. And none of you need to be afraid of that house or of the people inside."

The kids were listening and Jana found herself flooded with gratitude. Even if no one showed up this Friday—even if they still thought it was too creepy to consider—she was thankful for a husband who knew how her idea was going to be received, and who came to her rescue.

That afternoon she divided the list of families with the new Primary Presidency and they called all the Primary kids' parents to ask them to bring their children to sing at the El Dorado House. None of them jumped at the chance, but most of them said they'd think it over and talk to their children. Jana figured maybe four children would show up, and at least that would be a cute little a capella quartet.

That night she and her own kids watched family videos, while Ethan and his counselors met with the various people who were being released, and called. Savannah popped popcorn and drizzled it with melted white chocolate, an addictive combination that Jana tried (unsuccessfully) to avoid.

"There I am, riding that horse," Josh said, staring at the TV screen. The video showed him bouncing along, his chubby two-year-old cheeks jiggling under a red cowboy hat as a pony trotted around a circle in a park.

"And there I am," Savannah said.

"Where?" Maddie asked.

"I'm the one behind him—the pink ballerina," Savannah said. But of course. She smiled at the camera as her horse passed by, five years old and already a princess.

"Where am I?" Maddie asked, reaching into the stainless steel mixing bowl that held the popcorn.

"You weren't born, yet," Jana said. "You were still in heaven, waiting to join us."

The pony ride came to an end and Jana noticed a happy, white-haired couple lifting another boy down from his pony.

"There's the kid with the grandparents," Josh said. He'd seen this home movie so many times he knew all the bystanders caught by accident on video.

The kid with the grandparents, Jana thought. Her own kids didn't see themselves as kids blessed with grandparents. What a vital part of childhood they had missed! Suddenly she realized how sad it was that her kids hadn't known elderly people who loved their chubby cheeks, their princess costumes, their sticky hands. Sure, they had parents who adored them, but that grandparent element had never materialized. Her own parents had died of cancer and a heart attack just months apart, before Savannah was even born, and Ethan's parents were too far away to be there for the pony rides and birthday parties, the school plays and piano recitals.

And then she thought about the senior residents, themselves. Very few had children nearby, or children at all. Only Marvin had a son about an hour away who visited every couple of months, and the others either had children who had forgotten about them, or children who only came around during the holidays. They might welcome surrogate grandkids as much as the children would benefit.

She should have done the very thing Ethan was suggesting this morning—she should have adopted some loving seniors as grandparents to her children. It wasn't as if their wards hadn't been brimming with older folks who would have loved that opportunity. But she hadn't done it. And now her kids had missed the chance.

"I'm so sorry you kids didn't have grandparents," she said, thinking aloud, but raspy with regret.

"Oh, Mom," Savannah said. "Like it was your fault."

But it was my fault, Jana thought. *I should have reached out.*

"Dad says you can find some at the Wit—I mean the El Dorado House," Maddie said.

Josh and Savannah whipped around to stare at their mother.

"Well, it's true," Jana said. "We're hoping the Primary kids will do just that. So many of them have no grandparents nearby."

"I am not picking out a grandpa at that place," Josh said.

"Neither am I," Savannah said. "I'm interviewing them, but that's it."

Maddie chewed a mouthful of popcorn and swallowed it. "Well, I might. If it can be that Fauna Fairy one."

Jana smiled. Maybe there was hope that at least one of them could find a grandparent.

That night as they climbed into bed, Jana asked, "Do you think our kids will be permanently damaged by not growing up with grandparents close by?"

"Welcome back," Ethan said in his best pretend radio D.J. voice. "And for those of you just tuning in, welcome to the ten-thirty to eleven o'clock portion of Jana's Worries."

She laughed and punched his arm. "Not funny."

"I can set my clock by you," Ethan said. "You always start worrying just as you get into bed."

Jana paused. "Okay, but in my defense there seems to be an awful lot to worry about."

Ethan smiled and kissed her. "Not grandparents. Not burglars moving into the neighborhood. Not a Primary singing performance at a rest home."

Jana sighed.

"Everything will work out," Ethan said. "Have faith."

Chapter 7

THE NEXT MORNING ETHAN GOT A PANICKY CALL FROM MIMI'S first counselor, Lachelle Marks. "Bishop, I'm at the dry cleaners and they've lost the draperies."

Ethan sighed and told his secretary to hold down the fort for half an hour, then jumped in his car and headed to the dry cleaners'. Ethan was grateful this was his own accounting firm, and he could leave at a moment's notice. The liquid amber trees were already turning colors, somehow knowing in the heat of September that fall was just around the corner. He waited for a man with half a dozen shirts on hangers, to pull his car out before taking his parking spot.

"They're trying to get me to take these other ones," Lachelle was saying as he walked in. Lachelle was a petite woman who owned one of the top temp agencies in town. She was organized, sharp, and a shrewd negotiator. He knew; hers was the company he always called when a staff member was suddenly out sick. Lachelle's husband, Ty, was a lobbyist at the State Capitol, and most people saw them as the power couple of the ward.

And now she seemed to be standing in a face-off with the stout Ukrainian owner of a local dry cleaners'. The smell of steamy linen mingled with the exhaust of a FedEx truck that pulled up to double park and make a delivery next door.

"I am telling you, these are same," the man said, struggling with his English. His face was flushed and his features rosy, as if the very air imparted a pink tint.

"I brought you brown draperies," Lachelle fired back. "And these are hot pink."

"Come in back, I show you," the man said. "You see how much dirt we take out." He turned and waved his arms to show how serious he was about proving it.

"I seriously doubt that these draperies were pink," Lachelle said, then turned to Ethan. "Bishop, what would you like to do here?"

Ethan stared at the draperies. They were velvet. They were gigantic. They were definitely bright pink. But who else could have brought in so many heavy, velvet draperies?

"Tell you what," he said. "Let's take them and hang them up and see if they fit. Then we'll know for sure."

"Yes, yes—you take and you hang," the man said. "You see."

Lachelle rolled her eyes as Ethan paid for the massive pile of fabric. "But if these don't fit," she said to the shopkeeper, "I will expect you to refund every penny."

"Yes, yes," the man said. "You see." He and Ethan helped her load the curtains into her red SUV.

"Do you have someone there to help you hang them?" Ethan asked. "I have to get back to work."

Lachelle held her palms up as if to say, *Are you kidding?* "Of course I do. With ladders. I will let you know within the hour if these fit."

Ethan smiled. "You know, those could actually be the right curtains. I mean, maybe they really were that dirty."

"If so, those were the filthiest draperies in history," Lachelle said. She started up her car and drove off.

Ethan's dashboard jingled with a cell call from Jana as he was driving back to the office, and he told her about his visit to the dry cleaners'.

"Maybe I'll pop over to help," Jana said. "I'll let you know how it goes."

Ethan felt immediate relief. Maybe this was why they were called the Relief Society, because they kept rescuing the men from tough situations. And if anyone could smooth over a furious Lachelle, it would be Jana.

Then, fifteen minutes later, even before he could park his car under a shady oak at the brick building of his accounting firm, his phone rang again.

"I assume you're sitting down," Jana said, "since I've caught you in the car."

"Yep," Ethan said. "What's the word?"

"Well, I drove over there and Lachelle was up on a ladder, hanging the drapes. And they fit. Perfectly."

"Well, that's a relief," Ethan said. "So they're pink, now?"

"Oh, they're pink, alright. But there's another surprise."

Ethan waited.

Jana drew in a breath and then said, "The carpet is purple."

"What!" Ethan turned off his engine.

Jana was outside the El Dorado House, standing on the porch and unsure whether to laugh or cry. "When I got here the High Priests were using those rug shampooers, and had already made about six swipes across the lobby. Ethan, that rug is now purple."

"How can it be purple? Are they putting some kind of dye on it?"

Now she had to laugh. "No—Ethan it was originally purple and it only turned black over the years because no one ever deep-cleaned it. All they did was surface vacuuming."

"But who would install purple carpet and pink draperies?"

"Well, this is the part you need to be sitting down for."

And then it hit him. "No. No, I do not want to hear about this."

"Well, you're going to have to hear it," Jana said, still laughing. "When the electricians went upstairs they had to move some file cabinets and they found an old newspaper article and a couple of pictures. Apparently—"

"No." Ethan squeezed his eyes shut and groaned.

"It was a . . . what can I say? A house of ill repute, back in the 1950s."

"Oh, good grief." Ethan was leaning back on his head rest now, wondering how on earth his quiet little life as an accountant had turned into a scandalous drama that would sweep through the stake. Maybe he could just live in his car, never move from this spot, and have take-out delivered forever.

"Now, don't worry," she said.

Ethan recognized that tone. It was the one she always used to comfort the kids when a disaster was looming.

"Seriously," Jana went on. "It isn't as if it's still going on, Ethan. Lots of old buildings have colorful backgrounds. Speakeasy bars, gambling halls—and they could become a . . . a church or something today. It's like looking into your genealogy." Jana sat down on the top step.

"My genealogy, specifically?"

"Okay, *one's* genealogy. It's the sort of thing you discover, sometimes."

"Yes, but the residents are not going to want to live in a bordello-themed rest home, Jana. And we cannot afford to roll up the carpet and buy new draperies."

"Well, here's the thing," Jana said, running one finger along the chipped bannister as she spoke. "The residents love it. It's bright, it's cheery, and they're all gathered around watching the carpet come back to life. A couple of them are cheering every time another purple stripe is revealed."

"Please don't say revealed."

Now Jana busted up laughing. "You should come and see it. It looks like a completely new place."

"I'll bet."

"They should be done by mid-afternoon, and then tomorrow it's supposed to be dry."

After hanging up Ethan kept his eyes closed, trying to imagine how this could possibly be an acceptable outcome. For him, anything but beige was daring.

He called the Department of Health, got redirected twice more, and finally found someone who could tell him how a care facility could have a carpet and curtains that filthy. Apparently the El Dorado House had passed all the cleanliness requirements for food and medical care, but nothing required frequent rug shampoos, or dry cleaning of draperies. Over time, even if you vacuum, textiles can become soiled and change color.

Jana went back inside where Lachelle was now laughing with three other sisters who had come over to help.

"Can you believe this?" Lachelle was saying. "I mean, I was positive these were not the same curtains. I've got to apologize to that dry cleaner!"

Jana saw the delighted grins on the faces of Vera, Rose, Howard, and Frances. Then she remembered that pink had been the "in" color in the 1950s—you found pink bathroom tiles and pink fridges in older homes all the time. And while this was a much deeper shade of pink, it probably felt nostalgic to them, like a homey touch of a happier time. She went over and hugged them. "You like it?"

"I love it!" Rose shouted. "And those carpet cleaners are hunks!" Rose whirled her chair around and held up her cell phone. "I'm going to take a selfie with those guys in the backround."

Seniors take selfies? Jana glanced at the elderly high priests working the machines, then back at Rose. This could be the best day she'd had in years.

"Let's have a report on that baby," Howard said. Today he was wearing a navy-and-cream V-neck pullover, and looked like the captain of a rowing team.

"Oh—mother and baby are doing fine," Jana said. "I'm sure she'll bring him in for a visit as soon as he's strong enough."

They all cheered, nudging each other as if this were their very own grandchild.

Vera tugged on Jana's arm and Jana leaned down. "I hope you brought a lesson today. We have to go in for lunch in a few minutes."

Jana froze for a second—she had only come over to see if the draperies fit. Then she thought about the *Preach My Gospel* manual her family was studying. Why couldn't she just use that as the basis of a little message each time she visited? "Okay, Vera. We can chat over lunch."

Vera beamed.

As they headed into the rec room, Rose lagged behind. "Hold on," she said. "I'm posting this on Instagram." Rose was on Instagram?

Jana gave her a thumbs up, then sat down at a table with Vera, Rose, Frances, and Harriet, the tiny woman with the gray cat.

"Where is your cat today?" Jana asked her.

"Oh, she's in her crate," Harriet said. "With so many workmen coming and going, I didn't want her to get out." Harriet was wearing a row of jangly bracelets, her tiny wrists looking almost too small to support them. Her black sweater had gold trim, and a tiny gold barrette was in her wispy, white hair.

Trays of turkey, potatoes, and limp zucchini were soon brought to the residents.

"Don't you want some?" Vera asked.

"No, no—I'm meeting a couple of girlfriends for lunch in half an hour," Jana said. Every month or so she tried to get together with

Michelle Dayley and Kristi Hargrove, her best friends. Summer had slipped by with all their family vacations and sports competitions, so this was their first get-together since June. But it was a friendship that always picked up where it left off, no matter how long they'd been apart. And they couldn't wait to hear about the El Dorado House project.

"Hey, Howard, come and hear this," Rose shouted across the hall.

Howard waved her away. "I've already got my own religion," he called.

"He's a party pooper," Rose said. "Go on without him."

Jana smiled and said, "Today's lesson is about the Restoration." Then she went on to describe the Apostasy and the need for God to call a prophet in this dispensation. She found Joseph Smith's account of the First Vision on her cell phone and started reading it to the women. Glancing up halfway through, she noticed Vera mouthing along the words and realized that Vera had it memorized. "You finish it, Vera," she said.

"Oh, you're the teacher," she said, shaking her head.

Jana smiled. "But you have it memorized."

"What?" Rose said. "You have that story memorized, Vera? Well, let's hear it."

Frances leaned in as well, and Vera shyly picked up where Jana had left off. At the end, Vera's eyes were glistening, and Jana found herself tearing up as well. She remembered some words from the last Stake Conference: *When you bear your testimony, other people hear their own.*

It was silent as Rose, Harriet, and Frances sat, thinking about what they had just heard. They had finished their lunches and were now staring at Vera and Jana.

Frances looked skeptical. "Hmm," she said. "I'll have to think about that."

"And I have to go see the carpet," Harriet said.

"Oh, me, too," Rose said, pivoting around and then zipping off in her motorized wheelchair.

Jana stood up as the other women left, then she leaned down to hug Vera. "Thank you for doing that," she said. "I felt the Spirit as you spoke." Vera patted her hand, and Jana walked back through the lobby where everyone was again gathering to cheer on its colorful progress.

The drapery panels were up, now, in all their pink blazing glory, and the residents were overjoyed.

Jana sighed. It was hard to compete with the brassy makeover the ward had inadvertently provided. And she could tell the Restoration lesson hadn't gone over well. Perhaps these women were just listening because they were lonely, or because Jana was someone new to talk to. They seemed respectful, but doubtful about her message. And the men and the other two women wouldn't even listen.

Maybe Kristi and Michelle would cheer her up.

Chapter 8

THE CAFÉ WAS BUSTLING AS JANA WALKED IN A FEW MINUTES late. Waitresses filed by with bowls of steamy tomato soup, crusty bread, and salads piled high with croutons. Kristi and Michelle were already sitting at a table in the center, with water glasses and a lemonade, waiting for Jana. Kristi was a striking blonde with an angular bob, who made everything she wore look like a runway fashion. Slim and stylish, she even looked good at Girls' Camp. To Jana's way of thinking, that was the ultimate test. And Michelle was equally beautiful, but understated with sleek, brunette hair pulled into a chignon, and little makeup, if any. She was blessed with smooth, olive skin and thick lashes.

"Just what I need," Jana said, sliding into her seat and taking a long sip of her lemonade.

"Wait until you hear the awful news," Michelle said.

Worse than a bordello and a bunch of people who aren't interested in the Restoration? Jana thought.

"Merry Haines has gone inactive," Kristi said.

"What? That's crazy!" Jana said. "I know her. She would never do that."

Michelle, the quieter of the three, nodded. "She called me last night. She said she doesn't want to come to church anymore."

"Are you kidding? That's crazy!" Jana couldn't believe what she was hearing.

"Her family from Texas has convinced her that she only joined the church so she could marry Sean," Kristi said.

"That's crazy," Jana said.

"Stop saying that's crazy," Kristi fired back. "It's true. And it's a disaster. You need to tell Ethan and get him over there."

"Well, we all need to go over there," Jana said. "Plus I don't believe it. I've heard Merry bear her testimony to the sisters we visit teach. Maybe she has postpartum depression or something, and she isn't in her right mind."

Michelle shrugged. "She sounded pretty sure about this."

Jana stood up. "Well, we can't just sit here and eat a Cobb Salad. Let's go!"

"Is Mimi your Relief Society President?" Kristi called across the parking lot, dialing the minute Jana nodded. "I'll call her."

As they drove over to Merry's house in tandem, Jana called Ethan. He answered with, "So how are your buddies coping with you being in another ward now?"

"Oh, that is the least of our worries," Jana said. Then she told him what she knew so far about Merry.

"That's crazy," Ethan said.

"Thank you. That's what I said."

"Call me as soon as you leave, and let me know how it goes."

She promised to give him a full report, then pulled up in front of Merry's house. And it was just like Merry—surrounded by bright yellow mums, with a sunflower wreath hanging on a cherry red door.

Merry opened the door. "I thought about just not answering," she said. "But I wasn't reared to be rude."

Still, she didn't invite them in, and didn't flinch when they begged her to reconsider. "Y'all need to respect my choice," she said, as if delivering a memorized line.

After twenty minutes of expressing love and concern, bearing testimonies and pleading with her to come back, the girls were turned away. Merry thanked them for coming by, but said she really wasn't interested. Reluctantly they went back to their cars, and Kristi and Michelle drove off. Jana picked up her phone to call Ethan, then slipped it into her purse again and went back and knocked on the door.

"Can I at least see that darling Aiden?" she asked. "Please?"

Merry sighed, and slowly swung open the door. A wicker bassinette was near the leather sofa, and Jana stepped over to where he was sleeping. Sunlight filtered through the branches of an elm tree outside the window, and curved around his tiny head.

"Oh—he is so gorgeous!" Jana said. And he was. A perfect little bundle, with rosy cheeks just like his mother's. "Can I pick him up?"

"I'm not supposed to let him get around people, yet," Merry said.

Jana thought about the parade of relatives who had undoubtedly just marched through. She turned to Merry. "Can we at least still be friends?"

Merry sighed. "I'm having a really hard time right now, Jana. I mean, you will always be my friend. I know that. But I have to distance myself from the church right now. My family situation—I just have to pull back. Please don't try to change my mind."

Jana decided to grasp that straw. "Okay. Deal." She stared into Merry's face, trying to find a glimmer of hope there. "You know, that baby is all they talk about over at the El Dorado House."

Merry looked away. "That's nice."

"And speaking of which," Jana smiled at her. "Did you know that place used to be a . . . house of ill repute? In the 1950s?"

Now Merry's eyes widened. "Are you serious?"

Jana laughed, hoping Merry would join her. "Can you believe it?"

"That's crazy," Merry said.

Well, at least we use the same expressions.

Merry shook her head. "That's worse than being a witch house. How did you find this out?"

"They found an old photo of the madam and her girls," Jana said. "Then when we cleaned the carpet and draperies, they turned out to be bright purple and pink."

Merry shook her head in disbelief. Jana sensed it was time to leave, so she headed out, hoping Merry would let her keep in touch. And she said a silent prayer for Sean as well. Heaven only knew what he had to be going through.

ETHAN AND MIMI BOTH TRIED TO VISIT MERRY THAT EVENING and the next day, but Merry was resolute. And all Sean could do was tear up and ask them to keep her in their prayers. Several of the young moms reached out to invite her to the park with Aiden, but Merry had closed the drawbridge and wouldn't return their messages. She wouldn't even take calls from Kristi or Michelle.

"I'm going to call her every week," Jana told Mimi. "At least for now she'll talk to me."

Mimi was grateful, and like everyone else, completely perplexed. "I'm going to give her to you to visit teach, if that's okay."

"Of course," Jana said.

"Looks like you have all less-active sisters on your route," she said.

"But Vera's strong," Jana said. "She even told the Joseph Smith story when I was there. And we'll do all we can to get Merry to come back."

"I'm asking the Priests to take the Sacrament to her," Mimi said. "How about Sister Orton?"

Jana thought about her third assignee, Carlita Orton, who would never let her in, and whose teenage son even lied for her, saying she wasn't home when she had just watched her go in. She knew who Carlita was from seeing her at the high school, but they had never actually met.

"I'm still working on her," Jana said. "I take things over and leave them at the door, but she won't let me in."

"Yet," Mimi said, always brimming with optimism.

"Yet," Jana agreed.

MUTUAL WAS WEDNESDAY NIGHT, AND ETHAN DROVE SAVANNAH, Josh, and a vanload of Priests and Laurels to the El Dorado house to do interviews. He cringed when they piled into the van and Savannah had to sit between the two Priests in the back seat. Why did that big Dobson kid have to call shotgun and force the girls to climb over legs and laps to sit down?

Ethan had already spoken to the whole group about not perpetuating ridiculous witch stories, and about having compassion for the people they were about to meet. "Some of these men are veterans who put their lives on the line for your freedoms," Ethan said. "Some of these people built the community, taught school, and made contributions. Let's treat them with dignity and respect."

Terrell Moses was driving another two in his convertible, and the Young Men and Young Women's Presidents were bringing still more. Soon they were all clamoring up the front steps.

As they burst into the lobby, Helen jumped. "I'm sorry," Ethan called to her. "Weren't you expecting us?"

"I was expecting a group of young people," Helen said. "But not a herd of elephants."

"Okay, let's all settle down," Terrell barked to the boys. Ethan envied the way he could shout out commands, yet still seem cool and accepting. The kids quieted down at once.

And then they looked around. Sure enough, the carpet was bright purple. The new lighting left no doubt about it. As they all craned their necks around to stare at the hot pink draperies Ethan realized what it reminded him of: A cartoon show about bunnies, where the kitchen walls were bright orange, and all the rooms looked as if they were carved out of tree trunks. He half expected the Road Runner to go zipping by.

And then one did! Rose came flying into the lobby in her wheelchair, the straps of her blue eyeglasses flapping in the wind. "Who are you?" she hollered, wiggling her glasses in an effort to focus. Ethan caught himself wondering how Helen found the youth group startling, but not an apparently crazed grandmother in a hot rod wheelchair.

"Hi, we're the Young Men and Young Women from the Larchmont 5th Ward," Savannah said, stepping forward and taking charge.

"The fifth ward—where is that, in an insane asylum?" Rose came back.

"It's the Mormon church," Ethan said, already wishing he'd said The Church of Jesus Christ of Latter-day Saints.

"Oh—I remember you—you're Jana's husband! And you kids are part of the big project! Well, come on in." Rose wheeled around 180 degrees and went rocketing down the hallway.

"Man, I want to ride that thing!" one of the boys whispered.

"Well, keep livin'," Terrell said. They all laughed, and followed Rose down the hall. Meatloaf and potato aromas came wafting down the hall from their earlier supper.

Soon Savannah had the clipboards divvied up and kids were tentatively knocking on open doors as they peeked into the bedrooms and rec room at the residents. Then, one by one they sat down with their elderly counterparts and began asking questions.

Ethan followed the Dobson boy into Marvin's room. Marvin was reclining in his bed, wearing a satin smoking jacket. With his black hair slicked back, he looked like Errol Flynn, or some glamorous Latin star from the golden age of movies. He looked every bit the part of what used to be called a dandy.

And Todd Dobson was the exact opposite—a beefy wrestler with sandy hair, freckles, a pug nose, and a greasy sweatshirt. It was as if a bulldog were trying to interview a panther. Todd glanced down at the questions about Martin's age and childhood, looking for a point of reference. "Do you like sports?" he finally asked.

"I can tell you who won every World Series since 1967," Marvin said.

Todd grinned.

"Well, I'll leave you two at it," Ethan said, and stepped next door to Chester's room. Chester was small in stature, almost birdlike in his movements. With piercing eyes, Chester darted about his room, no cane needed. You could tell from the sun spots on his skin that he spent a great deal of his life outside, and sure enough, he was just telling one of the Priests about the horses he had trained. On his wall were pictures of a smiling man in yellow harlequin jockey silks, posing beside chestnut-colored thoroughbreds in flower-filled winners' circles at various race tracks.

"Is that you?" the boy was asking.

"Which one?" Chester teased. "The horse? Nope—I'm the other one."

Ethan saw the light of recognition in the boy's face as he grasped the fact that he was talking to a jockey who had evidently won dozens of races.

The next bedroom was empty, so Ethan moved on to the rec room, where he saw the other four men at tables with their young interviewers, each one animatedly sharing his past, reliving glory days, and even giving advice to the kids. "And you should treat your education like a job," Stanley was telling one of the youths. "Give it your full, best effort, every day . . ."

Stanley was barrel chested and bald, with a rosy complexion that made him look overheated. But he laced his fingers together and spoke in calm, measured tones. "Back when I taught elocution . . ."

"Wait—electrocution?" the boy stammered.

Stanley sighed and shook his head. "That's the trouble with schools today. They don't teach the classics anymore. You kids should be studying Latin, Greek, and memorizing poetry. You should be learning how to enunciate and speak before groups."

"Oh—we give talks at church," the boy piped up. "Most of us have done that since we were little kids in Primary."

"Well, I like that," Stanley said. "That's excellent."

Ethan made his way to the back of the room, where Howard was chatting with Josh. Despite his son's reluctance even to come tonight, they seemed to be getting along great. Howard was describing the coal he had to shovel into a train engine, years ago, and Josh was hanging on every word, typing notes on the laptop Ethan had let him borrow.

Raymond was sitting backwards on a chair, rocking against a table where another boy was listening to his story about how he met his wife. "We courted in those days," Raymond was saying. His skin was crepey, almost scaly, yet still you could tell he'd been a handsome man. He was tall, like Ethan, and folded his feet beneath him the same way. Ethan couldn't help wondering if he'd be like Raymond one day, pouring out his life story to a youth who was taking it all down on an electronic device of the future. And suddenly he missed Jana—what if he should lose her one day and become a widower? No one ever thinks they'll end up alone at a facility like this. Everyone says, "Just pull the plug," yet no one can really do that. These people probably had said exactly the same thing.

It made him wistful. He wanted to check on Savannah, the girl who was growing into a facsimile of her mother, right before his eyes. Since Herb, the sixth man, was in the restroom anyway, he wandered over to the women's side of the building.

Even from a distance he could hear Rose's raucous laugh, and followed it to her room, where Savannah was typing madly on her cell phone, taking notes as Rose said, "And we never even heard of a microwave oven, honey."

Right next to her in the same bedroom, Frances was telling a Laurel, "And when John Glenn came back after orbiting the earth, I knew I wanted to be an astronaut."

The girl was scribbling old-fashioned notes on a yellow legal pad. "And did you do that?" she asked.

Frances stared at her. "You have no idea, do you?"

The girl shook her head.

Frances smiled. "It wasn't possible in those days, Sweetie. They didn't let women become astronauts. But I loved science. So I became a nurse."

The girl stared, shocked that an entire career was closed to Frances and other women her age. "Wait a minute," she said. "So what other careers could women not have then?"

Frances laughed. "Trust me. You do not have enough time or paper."

Ethan thought about the huge changes these people had seen—some for the better, but not all. They certainly noticed a decline in manners, ethics, patriotism, and morals. He went to the next room, shared by Vera and Harriet.

Here a bubbly Laurel was telling Harriet, who was wearing a dark red house coat made from some kind of fuzzy fabric Jana would know, all about her own love of cats. It was an interview in reverse, but the two of them seemed happy to have found a kindred spirit, nonetheless.

Vera was talking about "Gold and Green Balls" to her interviewer. "They were all the rage in the church, before the 1970s," she said. "We were called M-Men and Gleaners. And in those days, we really knew how to dance." Vera asked the girl if she could look up swing dancing like she did in the forties, on her cell phone. Suddenly both Laurels in the room were glued to the video, one of them shouting, "Shut! Up!" and forcing Ethan to wave away Vera's concern, saying, "That's a good thing."

"Oh my gosh, I want to learn how to do that," one of the Laurels said.

"Well, come on over and we'll have a dance here," Vera said. "There's room in the lobby, I think. We can teach you kids how to do it."

Ethan smiled. This was exactly the connection he was hoping the kids would have. He headed to the next room, shared by Pearl and Lorraine, the two women Jana hadn't yet been able to meet. Jana was hoping Ethan could bring her some information about them, but their room was empty. And then he heard laughter coming from the sitting room (or was it the parlor?), adjacent to the lobby.

As he got closer, he felt as if he had wandered into a private women's party, like a bridal shower or the lingerie department.

"I am telling you, that's the last time I wore an inflatable bra!" Pearl giggled in a crackly voice, her audience of Lorraine and two Young Women leaders heaving with laughter and wiping their eyes. They looked as if they'd known each other forever.

Ethan stopped in his tracks, unsure of whether he wanted to listen in on this conversation. And then, as he turned to head back up the men's hallway, he saw Helen at her desk. And for the first time in weeks, she was smiling.

Chapter 9

THE KIDS CHATTERED NONSTOP ON THE WAY TO THE PIZZA PAR-
lor, each one amazed at the life stories they had just unearthed.

"Bishop Waterson, have you ever heard of a flibbertigibbit?" This was
Portia Ferguson, the Laurel who vowed never to date any boy whose
last name was Carr, so she wouldn't accidentally fall in love with him
and end up named Portia Carr.

"No, what's a flibbertigibbet?" Ethan asked.

"It's a flighty, scatterbrained girl who won't stop talking," Portia said,
laughing. "Like me!"

How this girl saw this as a good thing escaped him, but she was
clearly tickled with a new label for herself.

"I think I'm going to start a blog or a website or something and call
it that," Portia went on.

The kids all laughed. "Did someone call you that?" Todd asked.

"Well, not exactly," she said. "Harriet—the one with the cat—she
said that when she was young she was a bit of a flibbertigibbet, and it
sounded exactly like *me*. Right? I mean, I'm super hyper and I'm always
talking, so I figure that's a good word for me."

Ethan could see her in the rear view mirror, waving as she spoke,
animated and enthusiastic as usual. Behind her were the two priests
who came along, both rolling their eyes. Portia would undoubtedly go
off to college and marry a quiet, studious introvert who would find her
exactly the jolt of personality he'd been missing.

But Savannah was sitting in back, wedged between the two priests
who were quickly weary of overly chatty girls. And that made Ethan
nervous. What if they both thought Savannah was exactly their type?
She was gorgeous, for starters. And smart as a whip. He stared at them
in his rear view mirror, to see if he could pick up on any signals.

"Dad—lookout!" Josh, trapped beside Portia, shouted just in time
for Ethan to yank his wheel and avoid hitting a pickup truck.

Ethan flushed, his neck burning. Thankfully, they were just pulling up at the pizza joint where he pulled over onto the gravel, and parked under the red neon sign, relieved to have barely missed a collision.

As the kids piled out and darted into the restaurant, Savannah hung back. "I know why you didn't see that truck," she said. "You were watching Austin and David in the rear view mirror."

Ethan opened his mouth to deny it, but nothing would come out.

"You've got to stop being so overprotective, Dad. Honestly, it's like you think you have to watch me every minute."

Every second, actually, Ethan thought. *You have no idea.*

Savannah stormed off, and Ethan followed behind. How did fathers ever relax? How did they not grab every boy by the collar and threaten to beat him to a pulp? If Jana were here she would be telling him to get a grip and stop ruining Savannah's life. And she'd be right.

"Sorry," he muttered sideways to Savannah as the kids all stared up at the menu board behind the counter. Then, to the group, "You kids go grab some tables—I'll get us some pepperoni and sausage." Austin high-fived him, approving of the choice.

The other groups arrived, and Ethan told them the same thing. Then he ordered the pizzas and some pitchers of root beer from yet another high school kid who he could swear kept staring off in Savannah's direction. Was he imagining this? Was he going crazy?

The kids were all clustered together with their leaders, leaving Ethan and Terrell alone in a booth. "Okay, counselor," Ethan said, lowering his voice. "I need some counsel."

Terrell leaned in, fiddling with the salt and pepper shakers.

Ethan took a deep breath. "How do you back off and stop worrying about your teenage daughter?"

Terrell was clearly stunned. "Savannah? Why would you be worried about her? She's a fantastic girl."

Ethan pushed his lips out, thinking. "It's the boys I'm worried about."

"Ah." The light of recognition went on in Terrell's eyes. "Hey, I have three boys and Shanice is just now 7 months along with our first little girl. So I have no idea what it's like to have a teenager daughter."

Ethan nodded. Of course. How could Terrell understand?

"But," Terrell said, leaning in even further to whisper. "The other night I stared at Shanice's belly and literally said, 'You will not date until you're 45.'"

Ethan laughed. "What did Shanice say?"

"Nothing. She was asleep."

Ethan pictured his big, burly counselor hovering over his sleeping wife, already worrying about an unborn baby girl. So he wasn't alone.

Terrell shook his head and went on. "I don't know how dads cope. Just fake it 'til you make it, I guess."

Ethan nodded. He did need to present a more confident image to Savannah. Like most teens, she saw it as a mistrust of her, rather than a mistrust of the entire male population. "And I need to have faith," Ethan said. "Faith that the Lord is watching over her, and that she won't get duped by some—" he sputtered, trying to find other words than con artist, charmer, and jerk.

"I know," Terrell said. "But she has a good head on her shoulders. She knows what she wants in life. She won't get duped."

"Lotta dupers out there," Ethan mumbled. "In and out of the church."

"Don't we know it," Terrell agreed. "We were two of the dupers!"

Maybe that explained it, Ethan thought. He was so girl crazy in high school, obsessed with one girl after another, and knew exactly what was going through these boys' minds. Lucky for Ethan he was gangly and goofy, and spent the bulk of his teenage years just dreaming of what could be. His mission helped him prioritize, and, fortunately, he met Jana soon afterwards.

Ethan glanced over at Josh, who was twirling a straw and suddenly poked himself in the eye at that very moment. Yep, the apple doesn't fall from the tree. Ethan saw Josh struggling to fit in the same way he had at that age, and wished he had a magic formula for social skills that he could just pipe into Josh's brain. It would make junior high so much easier.

Finally the pizzas were ready and the kids inhaled the gooey wedges, their cheeks and fingers greasy with tomato sauce. Soon oily napkins were piled up on metal trays, sodas were polished off, and they were back in their cars, headed to the church.

Once home, they were greeted by Maddie, who couldn't wait to hear all about the "wi—wi—women, I mean," despite Jana reminding her it was past her bedtime.

"Oh, they were pretty amazing," Savannah said. "And that one—Vera—really does look like Fauna."

Maddie's eyes twinkled. "I get to meet her on Friday, when we sing," she said.

Jana took a breath. *I hope it's a "we," and not a solo of just Maddie.*

Savannah made copies of the interview forms for her report, then she and Josh handed them to Jana, so she could get the Primary kids to make posters about their backgrounds and interests. She was really going to miss this calling.

After family prayer everyone else went upstairs, but Jana sat at the kitchen table and glanced through the questionnaires. A kitchen clock, usually drowned out by the commotion of a busy family, now ticked loudly in the otherwise silent room.

Ask me about Pearl's inflatable bra! it said at the bottom of one. Jen Hudson, one of the Young Women leaders, had evidently had quite the interview.

Vera wants to teach us swing dancing, Portia wrote.

Frances never got to be an astronaut. Chester was a jockey!! Marvin used to live by Yankee Stadium. Jana pictured each of the residents as she read about them, so glad that at least some of the kids had agreed to participate. And she found herself thinking about Merry, and all that she was missing.

Ethan knocked on Savannah's door before going to bed. "Hey, Kiddo." Slowly he swung it open.

Savannah was sitting up in bed wearing a 49ers T-shirt, writing in her journal by the light of her nightstand lamp. She looked at Ethan and sighed.

He could only imagine the description she was writing for his behavior tonight. He hoped he wouldn't feature too prominently in her telling of the day's events. "Hey. Can I come in?"

"Fine."

Oh, boy. *When a woman says "fine" it never is.* Ethan pulled the desk chair around to face Savannah and sat down. He took a big breath. "I want you to know I love you," he said. "I know I can be a really over-protective—" again he couldn't think of the right word. Instead, "duper" came to mind, but he wasn't about to share that.

"It's just so embarrassing, Dad," Savannah said, her words bursting out in the torrent she'd held in. "You're always glaring at every guy around me. Like some, I don't know, creeper or something. They're not all trying to steal away your little girl, you know."

Oh, I'm afraid they are, Ethan thought. *You have no idea.* "I do trust you," he said.

"Apparently not," Savannah snapped. "And, for the millionth time, don't say it's them you don't trust."

But I don't. I've been them.

"I mean, you practically wrecked the car because you weren't even watching the road," Savannah continued.

Ethan sighed. "I need to lighten up."

Now his daughter sighed. "And so are you going to?"

Probably not. "I'm working on it harder than you think."

Savannah shook her head, put down her journal and turned off the light. "That was nice of you to get pizza for everybody."

"Goodnight, Honey."

"Goodnight." She filled the word with the same emphasis she used when she said, "Whatever."

Ethan bumped into Jana in the hallway, then motioned her into the bedroom and relayed the evening's events as they got ready for bed.

"If you're this nuts—okay, I don't mean nuts," Jana said. "If you're this concerned—"

"We can go with nuts," Ethan said.

Jana laughed. "Okay, if you're this crazy when she's sixteen, what are you going to be like in another year or two?"

Ethan pictured himself in a padded cell. Or smiling with a faraway expression, heavily medicated. Would someone please explain to him why there couldn't be LDS convents or nunneries where girls could be locked up for a few years?

"You have to let her be a teenager," Jana said. "Let her have fun and have friends who happen to be male. She isn't interested in Dave or Austin, anyway."

Ethan put toothpaste on his toothbrush. "How do you know?"

"She told me."

As he brushed, Ethan realized he'd made it impossible for Savannah to open up to him, especially about guys. He was one of those dads who freaked out at the mere mention of boys. "I've been an ogre."

"See? You're even foaming at the mouth," Jana teased.

Ethan spit into the sink. "I want her to feel she can talk to me."

"Then you're going to have to stop acting like a parole officer. And I don't want her to become one of those girls who gets married too young, just to get out of the house."

Ethan's head snapped up and he stared into the mirror. That could happen? He could be pushing her right into the arms of some duper? This was the first time he had considered that his actions might backfire.

"Aha," Jana said, suddenly using a German accent and trying to imitate Sigmund Freud. "I think we've made some progress in your treatment, ja?"

Ethan was speechless, his mind whirling with new resolve. There was a fine line between suffocating a child and being too permissive, and he was determined to find it.

AFTER PRAYING THEY CLIMBED INTO BED, A FAINT CLOUD OF perfumed lotion wafting into the air as Jana arranged the covers over her blue nightgown. Jana thought about the folks at the El Dorado House. "I wonder if we'll end up in a home," she whispered.

Ethan turned to her. "Hoping or dreading?"

She looked over at him. "Be serious. None of those people planned that. But there they are."

"I'm counting on dying before that can happen," Ethan said.

"I'll bet they all said the same thing." Jana propped her pillow up.

Ethan sighed. Propping the pillow up meant a long conversation, and he was tired and ready for sleep.

"I've actually prayed that Heavenly Father will give me some warning before I go," Jana continued. "I want to know when it's my time."

"Oh, great," Ethan mumbled, then lowered his voice to sound like a booming angel, "Here it comes, Jana, now's the time—wham!"

"No, not like that," she laughed. "Like a day ahead."

"Why?"

"So I can prepare! So I can let you and the kids know."

Ethan stared at the ceiling over their heads and wondered if all women wanted to talk like this when their husbands were exhausted and wanted to sleep.

"I can just see it," he said. "We'll all be gathered around your death-bed. I'll be saying, 'It's almost three o'clock—that's when she said she'd die. Oh, no—it's 2:58. Now it's 2:59! Oh no, no—there she goes! Three o'clock! Oh, no! Jana? Jana? Are you there?'"

Now he raised his voice to a squeak, to mimic her. "I'm still here. I feel fine." He paused. "Guess I'll get up, now. Anybody want anything from the store?"

Jana was laughing and poking his stomach, now. "That is not how it will be."

Ethan continued his impersonation of her. "Gee, I thought he said the 13th. Maybe he said the 31st."

Now Jana was dissolved, her eyes watering.

Ethan went on, still with a squeaky voice. "Maybe it was three o'clock Eastern Death Time—no, Hawaii Death Time—"

Weak from laughing, Jana tried pounding on his chest. "That is not funny."

"So it isn't enough to manage your life, now you want to manage your death."

Jana put her pillow back down and fell onto it. "I'll probably die laughing, anyway," she said, "with you the cause of it."

"How did I know I would somehow get the blame for this?"

She kissed him. "It's a given when a man marries."

Ethan sighed; there was more truth in that statement than she knew.

Chapter 10

ON THURSDAY MORNING JANA SAT BEFORE A GLOWING COM-
puter monitor, sending emails and texts, reminding parents about the
singing presentation on Friday afternoon, for the El Dorado residents.
She promised ice cream cones to every child who showed up, but knew
the place looked as scary as ever, since the outside cleanup and landscaping hadn't even begun. It would take more than bribery to get them
to overlook the gnarled vines and ominous black exterior.

And then she decided she simply couldn't keep worrying about it.
She'd take Maddie and if Maddie were the only child there, so be it. She
could meet Vera. And it wasn't as if the residents knew about her plan,
anyway. Nobody was expecting even one child to sing, let alone a group.

In the meantime, Jana had signed up to babysit two pre-schoolers
for Yolanda Bonner, a young mother who had recently moved into
the ward. Yolanda had to have outpatient toe surgery, and Jana was
happy to watch these new kids who were easily the best behaved in the
entire ward. Each week they sat through Sacrament meeting with nary
a wiggle, not even a peep.

When she arrived around noon, Yolanda had the kids all set up
to color at the kitchen table, while she and her husband, Jess, went to
the doctor's office. And the kids didn't disappoint. Charlotte, 3, was so
meticulous she even had her crayons lined up in a row. Her black hair
was pulled into a ponytail, and her little fingernails were painted hot
pink. Quietly she filled in the squirrels and bunnies in her coloring
book while Noah, 2, held the crayons in his fist and colored bold zig
zags on blank paper. Noah liked to stick his tongue out of one side of
his mouth as he worked, and still had chubby arms and enough baby
fat to make his T-shirt roll up to reveal a round tummy. The kids were
amazingly well mannered, answering "yes" instead of "yeah," and saying "please" and "thank you" whenever they needed something.

Finally Charlotte asked Jana if she would read to them, then led her to a little corner of the family room with low shelves of childrens' books. "Which one would you like?" Jana asked.

"Which one would *you* like?" Charlotte smiled. Good grief—how does someone raise such polite, unselfish kids? Jana scanned the row of books and saw an old favorite, Dr. Seuss' *Green Eggs and Ham.* She hadn't read it in years, so they all curled up on the sofa and Jana began reading.

Jana remembered using this book to get her kids to branch out and eat more vegetables. If a whimsical goon can discover he likes green eggs and ham, they could certainly learn to like spinach, right? But as she read it today, she saw an entirely different message, and couldn't wait to share it that evening with her family.

"First of all," she said, as she ladled peas onto everyone's plates, "those Bonner kids are geniuses. You ought to hear their vocabularies! And they are so well mannered it's unbelievable."

Josh was smiling and shaking his head. "You always say this about little kids."

"Well, not all little kids," Maddie reminded him. "There were those ones at the airport."

This was true. Jana had shared a distinctly different impression of some lawless renegades at the airport a few months ago, practically mowing down travelers as they roared through the terminal. "However, the Bonner kids were exceptional," she said. "But that isn't even what I wanted to tell you. It's about Green Eggs and Ham."

"We're not having that I hope," Savannah said.

"No—but you kids all liked that book, right?"

They shrugged. Finally Ethan said, "I always liked it. If I remember right, it was written on a bet. Bennett Cerf bet Dr. Seuss 50 bucks that he couldn't write a book using 50 words or less. And not only did Seuss do it, but it went on to become a best seller."

"Did Bennett Cerf pay him?" Josh asked.

Ethan laughed. "No—as I recall the story, he never did."

Jana stared at her husband. How did he have so much trivia stored in that head of his?

"So what did you discover about Green Eggs and Ham?" Ethan asked.

Jana beamed. "Well, everyone thinks this is a book about trying new foods, right?"

They all nodded.

"Wrong! This entire book is a tribute to nagging! Little Sam wants the big creature to try a new dish and will not relent until he wears the guy down. Will he eat them on a boat? Will he eat them with a goat? On a train, in the rain—"

"Yeah, we get it," Savannah said.

Jana sipped her water. "Finally the big character caves in and what do we learn? That little Sam was right! Not only were the green eggs and ham delicious, but persistence is the root of all success. Nagging wins the day!"

"Oh, great," Josh whined. "Now she thinks this justifies bugging us to clean our rooms."

"It totally does," Jana said. "Seriously, if one person will not clean up his room, and the other person reminds them, who's the protagonist and who's the antagonist here?"

All the kids were sighing and shaking their heads now, and Ethan was laughing.

Jana was on a roll. "Think of how it applies to life," she said. "If you don't pay a bill, do you accuse your bank of being a pesky busybody? No; you realize that they will stop pestering you when you comply with the rules."

Ethan was grinning. "I like it. Hey, let's make it a rhyme. Let's see. 'Do what is right'—"

"Oh, good night!" Maddie said. And the entire family busted up laughing.

FRIDAY MORNING HER ALARM RANG IN THE MIDDLE OF A DEEP sleep and Jana fumbled for the off switch. She glanced over at Ethan's side of the bed, but he was already up. Groggily, she stumbled into the bathroom.

Ethan was shaving, and glanced over at her. "Have you looked outside?"

"No—why?" She glanced through the bathroom blinds just as a crack of thunder rolled overhead. It was pouring rain. "Oh, great. The perfect weather to go with that scary house."

It was early in October, now, and Jana was afraid this would happen. The fact that Halloween decorations were everywhere in town didn't help, either.

"Hey, it can be a Waterson Family Concert," Ethan said. "No one will be the wiser."

Oh, they'll be wiser, alright—wise enough to ask us not to do this again. Singing wasn't anyone's top talent in this family.

The kids all bundled up and left for school, then raining or not, Jana needed to run to the drugstore for some skin creams Savannah *had* to have because she would *rather die* than appear in public with a pimple on her chin. Just a simple errand, Jana figured.

Then, as she was checking out, the clerk said, "You know, you can get a ten-dollar coupon if you buy one of these." She pointed to a stack of white boxes on a display at the counter. The boxes were about six inches square. "All you pay is the sales tax, and then you get a ten-dollar coupon."

Okay, I hate story problems. In fact, I hate all math problems. How can this possibly work? Jana hesitated, trying to figure out how you could buy something and actually end up with more money, when the clerk said, "Here, I'll show you."

First the woman voided everything Jana had just bought—the skin cream along with some pantyhose, toothpaste, and deodorant, and started all over. "While you're at it, you may as well get a couple more," she said. "But each one has to be a separate transaction."

Wow, I'll get thirty dollars off my bill, Jana thought. And only now she glanced over to see what the boxes were. In gigantic lettering on one side, it read, "TESTOSTERONE" and on the other side, "WEEKEND WARRIOR." Jana cringed. Did it really have to be testosterone? She glanced around. But thirty dollars was thirty dollars, so quickly she stacked three of them on the counter, and waited for the magic to happen.

Except it was dark magic. The clerk's computer jammed and she then had to call her manager, who apparently had to finish the entire

Lord of the Rings motion picture trilogy before he could come to the front, but who finally arrived. By now two more people were in line behind Jana. While the manager and the clerk pulled receipts from the machine and tried to untangle the three refunds, Jana noticed three more people getting in line. Now all of them were craning their necks around to see what was holding things up.

The boxes, meanwhile, had seemingly grown to the size of shoeboxes, and from fifty feet away you could read "TESTOSTERONE." She considered turning them, but "WEEKEND WARRIOR" would then show. Jan could feel heat creeping up her neck and blooming crimson on her face.

She forced a chuckle. "Boy, my husband is really going to laugh when he sees these," she said. No one believed her. To the rest of the world, she was a fortyish woman in obvious desperation, loading up on the one item that could save her marriage. In public. At Walgreen's. With a growing line behind her.

There were now twelve cash register receipts on the counter, and the clerk—no longer Jana's bargain buddy, but her mortal enemy—was trying to match up which receipts went with which purchases, and which enormous white box, each one now the size of a television set, could rest atop each of the three piles. The lettering of "Testosterone" was practically blinking in red neon and Jana could feel sweat dripping down her back.

People were shifting from one foot to the other now, sighing and wishing they hadn't gotten in line behind a crazed woman in the throes of unrequited passion. Jana thought about turning and saying to the lady behind her, "This is such a good deal," but then realized she had no idea how to explain the mathematics, and the woman would just think she was making it up anyway. As a matter of fact, Jana began wondering if the clerk were just making it up, as well.

Finally they got all her purchases into bags, including the oven-sized testosterone boxes, and she dashed out into the rain like a robber. She was already dreading Ethan's reaction when she showed him the clever way she saved thirty bucks, and she could only imagine what the kids would ask. But, hey. At least they now had a year's supply of something else.

Ethan took off from work early, and came in from the garage holding one of the white Testosterone boxes. "Were you saving these for a Christmas present?" he asked.

Jana had been unloading the dishwasher and now turned, flushing beet red, and laughing. "What were you doing in the food storage room?"

Ethan smiled. "Uh, wasn't aware that room was off limits. Is there something I should know?"

Now Jana told him the whole story and Ethan just shook his head. "Well, at least we have some white elephant gifts if we get invited to one of those parties this Christmas. I'm already imagining the looks on their faces as they open these."

Jana leaned her head on his arm. "Not exactly something you expect to get from a bishop."

Ethan drew in a sudden breath. "Oh, you're right. We'd better throw them away." He headed to the garage again, then glanced back at her, blushing. "That is okay, isn't it? I mean, you weren't saying—you didn't want me to—"

"Throw them away!" Jana called. "Of all the things we don't need."

Now Ethan smiled, and Jana laughed. This was easily more than thirty dollars' worth of embarrassment.

It rained steadily throughout the day, the kids all stomping muddy feet on the floor as they came home from school, Savannah first, then Josh, and finally Maddie.

Maddie had planned to wear a favorite pink sweater so she'd be ready for the singing, and carefully ate some red grapes as an after-school snack, watching that none of them dripped on her sweater.

"I'm ready to go," she said, her mouth full of fruit.

Josh, downing a peanut-butter-and-jelly sandwich, laughed. "You'll get soaked," he said.

"I have an umbrella," Maddie sang back, emphasizing the "ella."

"How about we all go?" Ethan said, giving Josh a look that said this wasn't really a question.

Josh scowled. "Oh, come on! In the rain?"

"I thought you liked the man you interviewed," Jana said, loading ice cream cartons into a cooler of ice.

"Howard? I do like him. But that doesn't mean I have to visit him twice a week."

"It's not like this is our new schedule," Ethan said. "But, given the weather, we might not get much of a turnout, and we can use a few extra voices."

Josh laughed. "I am so not singing."

"Me neither," Savannah said, sweeping into the room in a terry cloth robe, with her hair in a towel. "Plus I just washed my hair."

"Well, then you won't care if it gets wet," Jana said. "Come on, pin it up in a quick bun and throw on a skirt. I think we're going to have to fill in for the Primary kids today."

Savannah stared at her mother. "You're kidding, right?" Then she looked at Ethan and knew staying home was not an option. "You people are ridiculous," she muttered. "Plus I have homework." Reluctantly, she stomped upstairs to change.

"I'll put this in the car." Ethan said, lifting the cooler and carrying it to the garage.

Jana grabbed a shopping bag. "And I'll bring the cones." She yanked the kids' raincoats from the closet as she went by.

"I get to drive," Savannah announced, as if this were the price of her participation. She came down the stairs wearing a long sundress over a white T-shirt top, and threw on a yellow windbreaker as she headed out.

Ethan opened his mouth to object, not sure if Savannah could handle wet roads yet, then closed it again. *And if we all die, I will at least get credit for not being an ogre today.*

Savannah started up the car and backed out, the windshield wipers beating a steady rhythm.

"I guess the workmen won't be able to attack the landscaping tomorrow," Jana said, thinking aloud as she stared out at the rain.

"Nope; they'll have to wait another week, looks like," Ethan said. Water was already streaming through the gutters and more rain was predicted for Saturday.

"I'm meeting Fauna, I'm meeting Fauna," Maddie sang in a nanner-nanner tune, bouncing on the seat.

"But remember her name is Vera," Jana said.

Lightning lit up the sky and there was another crack of thunder. Maddie jumped. "Are you sure it's safe in there?"

"You'll be fine," Josh said.

Savannah pulled into the parking lot, which wrapped around the back of the building. "What's going on?" she asked.

Jana covered her mouth with both hands and gasped. The parking lot was full of members' cars. Primary kids and their parents were everywhere, hurrying along under umbrellas and splashing through puddles as they made their way up the weed-snarled walkway.

"They came!" Jana gasped, her eyes pooling with tears.

"And I am off the hook," Josh announced.

Quickly Savannah parked and the Watersons piled out. Ethan grabbed the cooler and they rushed up the steps. People were shaking water off their umbrellas and jackets, and stepping into the lobby.

Jana couldn't hold back her tears of joy as she hugged the children who had come through for her. And knowing she wasn't their Primary President anymore made her all the more emotional.

Parents were dumbfounded, staring at the garish carpet and draperies, then catching themselves and trying to look utterly calm, as if wanting to model composure for their children.

"I *love* this!" Maddie exclaimed, turning in circles as she surveyed the explosion of pink and purple. "I want my room to look like this!"

Jana chuckled. Indeed, if not for the bordello history, this could look like a little girls' fantasy tea party house, swagged in candy colors as bright as frosting.

She had cleared the possible performance with Simone, the social director—the tall woman with the spiky gray hair who had run the Bingo game. And now Simone was standing with Helen at the counter, both of them smiling at the cheery faces of almost thirty children and their parents.

Jana rushed over. "Thank you so much for letting us do this."

"Thank you for setting up such a lovely surprise," Simone said. She looked thrilled to be given a break from reading off Bingo numbers.

Jana looked down at the counter, then back up at Helen. "Did you—did you paint this, Helen?"

Helen's mouth curved up into her blushing cheeks. "Well, Vera did most of it. Black just didn't seem to go with everything else, now."

Jana stared at the counter, now covered with a mural that looked like a French impressionist painting of people dancing in a meadow—*elderly* people dancing in a meadow. Laughing, the wind in their hair, scarves billowing, and brilliant flowers swaying all around them.

She turned back to Ethan. "Have you seen this?"

Ethan came over, hand in hand with Maddie. "Is that the same counter?"

"Oh, this is beautiful," Maddie whispered, as if coming upon a true masterpiece.

"Helen, this really makes the whole room," Jana said.

"Well, Vera sketched it out and did most of the painting," Helen said. "I just helped."

Simone smiled at Helen, then back at the Watersons. "It's amazing, isn't it?"

Maddie tugged on Ethan's hand until he leaned down to her. "I want to live here," she whispered.

"I'll go round everybody up," Simone said, and went off down the hallway, her shoes clicking on the linoleum.

Jana glanced over at Savannah and Josh, who had caught the crowd's enthusiasm now, and were helping usher children into the parlor where the piano was. She had been so sure no one would show up that she hadn't arranged for a chorister or a pianist.

Quickly Jana scanned the crowd of parents for people with musical ability. One of the moms, Bobbie Skidmore, had played piano for Primary last year and was an accomplished pianist. And one of the dads, Luke Sanchez, belonged to a barbershop quartet , and often filled in to lead the music in Sacrament meeting. Both waved away her apology for the last-minute request, and eagerly jumped in.

"What are they singing?" Bobbie asked, sliding onto the piano bench. Her red hair was swept into a ponytail, making her look as young as Savannah.

"'Families Can be Together Forever,'" Jana said.

Bobbie waited, thick black-framed glasses perched on her nose. "That's it? Just one song?"

Jana swallowed. With this many kids it did seem a shame to sing only one tune. "Okay, then "I Am a Child of God," and then—what ones do you know?"

Bobbie smiled. "I know all of them, Jana. How about "A Child's Prayer"? They're all rehearsed for the Primary program, anyway."

Perfect. Jana's heart flooded with gratitude. For the kids, for their parents, for Bobbie, for Luke. For this being October, when they always had their Primary program. This thing was actually going to work. She turned and saw Ethan across the lobby. "Will you pray?" she mouthed to him, folding her arms.

He nodded and she realized she was most thankful for Ethan—he was the one who had convinced the Primary kids to open their hearts and have compassion for the El Dorado House residents. Those kids had gone home and convinced their reluctant parents to get up on a rainy Saturday morning and bring them to sing to old, forgotten people in a scary, black house.

Parents backed up to make room for the seniors who were now wheeling and walking into the lobby. Several men gathered chairs for those who were hobbling with canes, and soon all the residents were seated.

"Welcome to our concert," Jana said, wishing she'd thought of a name for it. "Our opening prayer will be given by Bishop Waterson."

Ethan said a prayer, and then Jana nodded at Luke. He stepped over to the cluster of children and swept his hands up in a giant mustache motion in the air. By the time they were singing "all eternity" Jana was fanning her watery eyes. Savannah, a few feet away, caught her crying, then simultaneously smiled and shook her head.

The residents clapped and cheered at the end, something you never hear when you sing at church, and the startled kids exchanged happy grins. Then Luke and Bobbie went on to the second song. Jana noticed Ethan's eyes glistening as well, and two other moms were dabbing their eyes, too.

They began the last song. Soon it was time for the beautiful counter melody finale about God hearing our prayers. Jana had already noticed the amazing acoustics as the children's lilting voices swirled around them, but now their voices lifted as if to blend with angels', filling the entire room with the spirit.

By the time the children were singing the harmonious conclusion, Jana noticed Marvin shuffling in, late. Tears were streaming down his cheeks, and his chin quivered as he stood off to one side, listening.

As the children finished the final song, the residents and nurses cheered, and those who could gave a standing ovation. Jana stared into the faces of the Primary kids she loved so much, and saw them beaming at their parents, every one of whom looked amazed at the magical moment they had just witnessed.

"I have three new favorite songs," Rose shouted. She'd been holding her cell phone up, taking a video of the kids.

The entire room buzzed with delighted voices as the choir filtered back to their families, many of them stopped by residents who wanted to thank them for such beautiful singing.

"Thank you for planning this," one of the moms whispered to Jana, a catch in her throat. "I wasn't in favor of coming here, but I've learned something today."

Jana hugged her. "It was Ethan who talked to the kids about it," she said. "Thanks so much for bringing Emmie and Ben."

"Encore! Encore! Encore!" Howard, Raymond, and Chester were chanting for another song, Howard and Raymond waving their canes.

Jana glanced over at Bobbie, who motioned her over to the piano. "How about the entire group—all of us—sing 'There is Beauty All Around'?"

Jana spun around. "Hey, everyone—before we have ice cream, how about we all finish with one more song? All the families—let's sing 'There is Beauty All Around.'"

Some of the kids were yanking on their parents' arms, begging their moms and dads to join in. Vera had scooted her wheelchair over to join in as well, and soon the entire assemblage was raising the roof.

After the last round of applause the families slowly made their way to the rec room where the ice cream would be served.

As Jana turned to join them, she noticed Marvin had quietly crept up behind her. He was standing there, his eyes glistening. "I wasn't going to come out," he said, clearing his throat. "I'm not interested in your church.

Plus Herb is sick, so I thought I'd just sit and keep him company . . ." Marvin waved his free arm, still leaning on his cane. "But when I heard those kids . . ." And now Marvin bowed his head and cried. Looking up, he could barely speak. "It was the most beautiful thing I've heard—in years."

"Oh, thank you, Marvin." Jan hugged him. "I'm so glad you liked it."

Marvin tried to say something else, but was too overcome. He just squeezed their hands and then made his way back to Herb's room.

"Hey, Marvin, wait up!" It was Rose, shouting from across the room. "I'll show Herb the video."

Marvin turned and looked visibly relieved, as if this would be the highlight of Herb's life.

Ethan and Jana headed to the rec room where Simone had set up a table for the ice cream serving. Jana was amazed at the difference in the mood of the room, with four bright lights overhead, replacing that lonely single light that had been there, before.

Josh and Ethan began helping Jana scoop ice cream into the cones, and Savannah tried to fan out the paper napkins. But her attempt at aesthetics was destroyed by the eagerness of the kids grabbing any napkin they could reach.

"Whatever," she muttered.

"Whoa—you're filling up the cone?" one boy asked Josh.

"Of course," Josh said. "That's how my mom taught us to do it."

Jana noticed him carefully scooping up thin ribbons of ice cream to pack down into the pointy sugar cone, before piling a round scoop on top.

"Awesome!" the boy said, and Jana saw him dash over to his parents to tell them about it.

"I bet his mom always served hollow cones," Josh whispered to her, as if this indicated seriously flawed parenting.

Okay, one point for me, Jana thought.

"Offer a cone to the residents," Ethan said as one child after another swarmed the table.

"Some of our patients have diabetes," one of the nurses said, "but they should let you know. I'll keep an eye out." Her name tag said "Shanika," and she seemed the ideal blend of stern rule-following and genuine compassion. Ethan found himself wishing he could ask her how she found that perfect balance.

All around, the kids and their parents were bustling among the residents, getting acquainted. Jana hoped some of them would choose to "adopt" these older folks, but just seeing them chatting and laughing was wonderful. She couldn't wait to see the posters these kids would draw for them.

Maddie was tugging on Jana's sweater, now. "When do I get to meet Vera?"

"Go on," Ethan said. "We've got this." He handed her a vanilla cone to take along.

Jana wiped her hands and took Maddie over to Vera, who was sitting in her wheelchair wearing a pale blue shawl this time, at the same table where they had first met.

Maddie handed her the cone and Vera's whole face lit up. "Why, thank you!" Vera said.

"This is Maddie," Jana said. "My youngest."

"Oh, you did a beautiful job today," Vera said.

"Thank you," Maddie said. Jana could tell she was studying her to see if she truly resembled the fairy, Fauna. "Which do you like better—pink, green, or blue?" Maddie asked.

Oh, good grief—she was quizzing the woman to see if she really was Fauna—the green-clad fairy in the *Sleeping Beauty* movie.

Vera paused, giving this due consideration. "I think I like green best, because that's the color of nature."

Maddie beamed as if she had been praying Vera would get this right.

"How about you?" Vera asked.

"Pink," Maddie said. "But I like green, too."

Vera smiled, looking more like a twinkly Fauna every minute.

"Did you really paint that box desk thingy in the lobby?" Maddie asked.

"Yes. I've always liked art," Vera said. "Do you like art, Maddie?"

Maddie inhaled a gallon of air so she could give full emphasis. "I love it!" She threw her head back as if she might faint.

Right up there next to Drama.

"Could you teach me art?" Maddie asked.

Vera looked as if she'd been waiting all her life for this question. "I would love to!" Soon the two of them had arranged a date, and Maddie fairly floated out of the room when it was time to leave.

As the families filed out, Jana overheard a little voice saying, "I'm going to make that one guy my grandpa." She beamed. It was Will, a little five year old. She had no idea which guy he had chosen, but was tickled that a connection had been made.

"I'm just saying it's the most popular flavor in America." Howard was licking a vanilla cone and arguing with Rose again, near the doorway. His hair fell over one eye in playful, rogueish fashion.

Rose waved her chocolate cone. "How can you prefer it to chocolate? Vanilla's even a word people use to describe boring!"

Jana chuckled; these two could literally argue about anything.

"Well, I am anything but boring," Howard countered. "I've been to more countries, and had more daring adventures than anyone you'll ever meet!"

"Blah, blah, blah," Rose sneered. "You never went to Norway."

"Oh, here we go with Norway again," Howard said.

Their voices faded as the Watersons made their way down the hall.

Jana chuckled. "I think Howard is sweet on Rose."

Savannah released an exasperated sigh. "Mom, where do you get these expressions?"

"Well, you have to remember I was the baby in my family and my parents were in their forties when I was born. So I was kind of raised with the vocabulary of a previous generation."

"Which I love," Ethan interjected. "And I think she's right about those two."

"How can you think that?" Josh asked. "All they do is argue. Even when I was here the other night, he was looking for ways to pick a quarrel with her."

"Exactly," Jana said. "Howard tries to get a rise out of her, just so they can talk."

"Hmm," Savannah said. "So when guys keep bugging you and saying stupid things it's because they like you?"

Ethan swung his arm around her. "Welcome to the mysterious world of the male mind."

Josh shook his head. "Well, I'm never doing that."

Ethan laughed. "Wait until you like some girl and have no idea how to talk to her. You won't believe the stupid things that will come out of your mouth."

"Okay, but Howard should be over that stage," Savannah said.

"Oh, some men never get over that stage," Jana said. Then quickly, "Present company excluded, of course." She squeezed Ethan's arm and he laughed.

As the various families gathered their coats and umbrellas from the sitting room and went back out into the rain, Jana gratefully shook their hands.

Then, with only the Watersons remaining, Jana threw her arms around Ethan. "You are totally responsible for this," she said. "I love you, Ethan. Thank you so much."

Ethan was knocked back on his heels. "What are you talking about? You're the one who arranged everything."

"But it was you who got them to do it," she said. "That speech you gave in Primary. That's what did it."

Ethan held her and kissed the top of her head.

"Do you think we should meet Herb?" Jana asked, turning to Ethan and the kids.

"I can offer to give him a blessing," Ethan said.

The Watersons headed back down the hall, this time to Herb's room.

Shanika was pouring some water for him when they stepped into his room. Herb coughed and sipped, coughed and sipped. His skin was ashen, his scalp speckled with age spots. He spilled a few drops of water with a shaky hand as he held the glass to his lips. Marvin was sitting in a chair not too far away, looking worried.

"We're the Watersons," Ethan said. "My wife—"

"Oh, I've heard about you," Herb said with a hoarse voice. "You're the one who comes to teach Vera and Rose." He glanced at the kids. "And was that you kids I heard singing?"

"It was me," Maddie said. But of course.

"Well, it was just wonderful." He wheezed and coughed again, handing his glass to the Shanika.

"This is Savannah, Josh, and Maddie," Jana said. They nodded their greetings as Herb struggled to breathe.

"We're sorry you're not feeling well," Ethan said. "I'm a bishop in the Church of Jesus Christ of Latter-day Saints, and I can give you a blessing if you'd like."

"Sure, why not?" Herb said.

"Would you mind if I called another brother to help me?"

Herb shrugged. Since he didn't know what the blessing entailed in the first place, he just lay back on the pillow and rested after the exhaustion of coughing.

Luke had been last to leave, so Ethan thought he'd catch him before he got too far away. Sure enough, Luke had stopped for gas only a block away, and was easily able to swing back onto El Dorado to help out.

Marvin watched as Jana and the kids stood with their heads bowed. Then Ethan and Luke administered to Herb.

Out in the hallway Ethan thanked Luke for helping out. "I didn't feel impressed to tell him he would recover," Ethan said, lowering his voice.

Luke nodded. "I don't think so, either. But a blessing of comfort is a good thing, too."

As Luke walked away, Maddie whispered, "So is that man going to die?"

"Well, not right away," Ethan said. "But at some point. Whatever is Heavenly Father's will."

Josh and Savannah were somber, but Maddie had no problem switching gears. As the other main nurse, Theresa, rolled a cart down the hall, she asked, "Did you hear us sing?"

Theresa smiled. "I certainly did. That was as good as it gets, Honey."

Maddie took a huge bow, and Savannah whispered, "She is such a ham. Honestly, Mom, you've got to rein her in."

Jana sighed. Why not let Maddie drink in the praise? Life offered up enough discouragement. She decided to let her youngest child enjoy her moment in the sun. Besides, those ice cream-packed cones were *also* as good as it gets.

Chapter 11

ON THE WAY OUT, JANA ASKED HELEN IF SHE'D GOTTEN AN ICE cream cone.

Sheepishly, Helen raised two fingers, and Jana laughed. Then she leaned in to Helen. "Painting this desk was the best idea," she said.

"Well, I couldn't help overhearing the interviews the other night," Helen said. "And I could just picture Vera dancing at those balls. Then when she said how much she liked to paint, I put two and two together."

"And got five," Jana winked. "What a gorgeous piece of furniture it is now." She slipped her hooded raincoat on. "I guess we'll have to wait until next Saturday for the landscaping. So I'll see you then."

Helen looked crestfallen, so Jana quickly added, "Or I might drop by before that."

Helen smiled softly and the Watersons left.

ON SATURDAY THEY GATHERED IN THE FAMILY ROOM TO WATCH General Conference. And, as always, Jana felt the talks were exactly what she needed to hear, and squeezed her husband's hand whenever a speaker spoke about forgiving oneself. Nothing filled her with such strength and determination to go forward and do better.

That afternoon Ethan and Josh took off to join with the men for Priesthood Meeting at the Stake Center. Jana pulled out three aprons, getting ready to make their traditional Conference Cinnamon Rolls with her daughters, but Savannah headed up the stairs, instead.

"You don't want to make cinnamon rolls?" Jana called up after her.

"I have homework," she called back down.

Jana turned to Maddie who shrugged, "We can just do it our own selfs."

It didn't seem the same, and Jana wondered how much homework a girl has to do on a Saturday night. But she dug into the baking project and enjoyed seeing Maddie getting some individual attention for a change.

Maddie was particularly excited to punch down the dough after letting it rise in a greased bowl. She wanted to use the "grownup rolling pin," and Jana smiled as she watched her youngest daughter trying to roll it into a huge rectangle. Finally they smeared it with melted butter, cinnamon, and brown sugar, then rolled it up tightly and cut it into fat sections.

"Now we let it rise again," Jana said.

"Again?" Maddie's patience was being tested. "It keeps having to rise!"

Jana laughed, and covered the rolls with a dish towel. Suddenly she heard Savannah laughing, up in her bedroom. *Must be talking with friends. So much for the big homework night.*

The rolls went into the oven just before Ethan and Josh got home, filling the house with a heavenly aroma.

"Oh, man," Josh said, puffing his chest out as he inhaled. "Cinnamon rolls!" He and Ethan shared glowing reports of the talks they'd heard, as Jana ladled up some chili and cheese she'd made the day before.

"Who else eats like this?" Ethan asked, eagerly downing the chili. "First the world's best chili, and then cinnamon rolls!"

Maddie took it all in stride. "That's Conference time," she shrugged.

Soon the rolls came out of the oven and Jana drizzled them with shiny, white frosting.

Ethan swept her into a tight embrace. "I love you more than finding stray pieces of popcorn in my shirt after going to the movies with you."

Jana laughed.

Ethan looked around for his eldest daughter, who would normally have made a comment about what cheesy parents she has. "Where's Savannah?" Ethan asked.

"I'm right here." Savannah came fluttering into the kitchen, inhaling deeply and reaching for a roll. Her face was flushed and she was grinning.

"Well, you certainly look happy," Jana said.

"Of course I'm happy," Savannah said. "It's cinnamon rolls!"

But Jana had a hunch it was something far more than cinnamon rolls that was making her daughter float on air. *Savannah has a crush on somebody.*

THAT NIGHT ETHAN ASKED JANA TO MEET HIM IN THEIR BED-
room. Something in his tone sounded very official.

"You're issuing me a calling, aren't you?" Jana smiled. Her mind
whirled with the possibilities.

As they sat on their padded bench, Ethan took her hands in his. "I
want you to know I have been praying about this," he said. "And I feel
absolutely certain this is a calling from the Lord."

Jana gasped. Her chest felt it might burst and suddenly she knew the
calling. "You can't be asking me this," she whispered. "You want me to
be a ward missionary, don't you?"

"No," Ethan said. "I don't want it. The Lord wants it."

Jana's eyes welled with tears as she stared at her husband. "But you
know how hard it is for me to—"

Ethan was nodding. "I do know. And that's what I told the Lord.
Several times. Believe me, I have been pleading your case, Jana."

She sighed. "Oh, Ethan."

"I promise he would not let me call you to anything else. And people
have asked for you—believe me, there are several callings I wanted you
to have."

"How can I do this?"

"Just pray about it," Ethan said.

"I don't need to pray about it," Jana said. "I got that feeling in my
chest and knew it even before you said it. Either that, or it's a hot flash."

Ethan laughed. "Well, then have faith. He's going to help you over
this hump once and for all."

"The one calling I never wanted . . ." Jana stared into space, shaking
her head.

Ethan held her, then pulled back. "Don't you think he knows your
heart? This is your chance to finally put away this blame you've been
carrying. He wants you to believe in yourself, Jana."

Again, the warmth in her chest. The Holy Ghost wanted her to
believe those words.

"I've never thought I could do missionary work," she said. "It's like
I had my chance and that was it. And now I've felt, I don't know, not
worthy to do it."

Ethan listened. "Those sound like messages from the adversary. Like, *Now you've done it,* the way he wants us to believe we're hopeless when we stumble. Like we can never come back."

Jana froze. Those very words, *Now you've done it,* had seared themselves into her mind years ago, like a slap in the face. "All this time," she said, thinking aloud.

"You'll be set apart and you'll have a blessing," Ethan said. "You cannot fail with the Lord's help." He hugged her. "I promise."

Jana smiled. "I love you, Bishop Waterson."

"I love you," Ethan said. "And you're going to be great at this. I know it."

AFTER THE LAST SUNDAY SESSION OF CONFERENCE, JANA MADE Sky's-the-Limit Pizzas, another Conference tradition. Each person got their own wad of pizza dough, rolled it out, and then could put any and everything they wanted on it, as long as they ate it. She watched as the kids—who thought they were highly adventurous, but who picked virtually the same toppings each time—piled on the pineapple, artichoke hearts, barbecue sauce, and cheese.

Except Savannah seemed distracted.

"Aren't you doing olives?" Maddie asked. Olives were Savannah's favorite.

"Oh, yeah," she said, and sprinkled them on.

Then, as Savannah started to put hers in the oven, Ethan said, "What—no cheese?"

"Oh, yeah," she said, turning back and grabbing a handful of shredded mozzarella.

Jana knew something was up, and that something was a boy. That night she could hear her daughter's voice through her bedroom door, filled with lilting laughter again. Jana knocked.

Savannah opened the door, quickly muttering, "I'll call you back," into her cell phone, and tossing it onto her bed.

"Can I come in?" Jana asked.

Savannah swung the door wide, smiling. "Sure."

Jana sat on the bed with her, their usual spot for intimate chats. "So? Anything new going on?" Savannah had always been open with her, sharing her frustrations, her opinions, her hopes and dreams.

"Nope. Not really."

Jana glanced at the cell phone. "You sure?"

Now Savannah frowned. "Positive. Geez, Mom."

There was a palpable chill in the air and Jana realized, for the first time, that Savannah wasn't going to tell her about the boy she'd been talking to. And that could only mean one of two things: Either Savannah no longer saw her as a confidant, or the even worse alternative—Savannah was hiding something.

Chapter 12

JANA WANTED TO TELL ETHAN ABOUT SAVANNAH, BUT THE phone rang and soon he was putting on a shirt and tie.

"I need to go and give Sean a blessing," he said. "Merry and the baby are at a friend's house."

"Oh, I'm so glad. He must be worried sick about her."

Ethan nodded. "I'm glad you're reaching out to her. She's gotta be so confused right now."

"Trying to keep the peace with her family, and adjusting to a new baby," Jana said. "I was going to call her tomorrow."

While Ethan was gone, Jana decided not to share her suspicions about Savannah just yet. Maybe in a few days, if the situation warranted it. For one thing, she wasn't certain that Savannah was being sneaky. But she was absolutely certain Ethan would not handle it well if he found out she was being deceptive, particularly if a boy was involved. And she could just picture the fireworks if she and Ethan shared their suspicions with her.

Jana knew it wasn't likely to be a boy from their own ward, probably someone from another ward in the stake, from Seminary. But why be so secretive about it? She mulled over the possibilities, picturing various kids from other wards, and wondering why Savannah felt she had to hide this. On the other hand, this was her daughter's first crush, and she couldn't blame her for wanting some privacy. Maybe she was scared it wouldn't work out. She decided to give the girl some space, and let her come forward when she was ready.

MONDAY MORNING JANA'S PLAN WAS TO PICK UP SOME DIAPERS for Aiden, then some barbecued ribs for Merry, from a little Texan diner she knew Merry loved. About an hour before school was out, she headed to the market.

All at once a white Hyundai came barreling out of a parking spot and smacked right into the passenger side of Jana's mini-van.

Jana slammed on the brakes and threw it into park, stunned at what had just happened. Then she got out of the van to check the damage. So did the other driver.

It was Carlita Orton, the inactive sister who would never come to the door! She was wearing khakis and a tan tunic, her black hair slicked back with a gold zig-zag headband.

"What is wrong with you?" Carlita was shouting at Jana. "You could see I was backing up!"

"Wait just a minute," Jana said. "I was already behind you when you came flying out of there." She looked around for witnesses.

Two teenage boys came over. "You backed into her," one of them said to Carlita. Then, turning to Jana, "I saw it and she was at fault."

"Oh, what would a young kid know?" Carlita yelled, then turned her fury on Jana. "You can't just scoot behind someone who's backing out. Look what you've done to my car!"

Carlita's bumper and trunk were crunched, and both of Jana's side doors were bashed in. Jana could only assume that Carlita had pressed the gas pedal all the way to the floor as she came screeching out.

"You'd better call the cops," the other teenager said.

Jana began dialing.

"Good," Carlita sneered. "You're going to have to pay for this! You should watch where you're going!" She tagged on some choice words and a label or two for Jana.

"Hey, *you* hit *her*," the first boy said. Jana felt a surge of gratitude for this kid who was sticking up for her. Without him, her take-the-blame reflex would be kicking in and she'd be questioning whether she was, indeed, at fault here.

Carlita marched right up to him and leaned into his face. "Yeah, because she drove right behind me! I was backing up first!"

"No way," the kid went on. "You can tell by where you hit her that she was already behind you."

Several other shoppers were craning their necks and staring at the scene as they pushed their carts by. Carlita turned on them as well. "Did you see this? This woman has totaled my car!" Then she whirled around to Jana, again. "You'd better have insurance!"

Jana quickly snapped pictures on her cell phone, before Carlita could move her car.

Just then a police car pulled in and Jana felt an immediate wave of relief. Two officers got out and Carlita began shouting her side of the story to them as well. Then they turned to Jana, who explained her version of the wreck. A couple of other cars started to turn down the aisle, then noticed the commotion and moved on.

"And are these your sons?" one cop asked.

"Nope, just bystanders," the first boy said. "But we saw the whole thing and this lady is right. That one just backed out without even looking."

Jana wanted to hug them.

Insurance cards were brought out, the boys signed a statement, and a report was written.

"You can't listen to them," Carlita screeched, motioning at the teenagers. "What are they—17 years old?"

"We can see what happened from where the cars are situated, Ma'am," one of the officers said.

"I have to be someplace," Carlita snapped, getting into her car. Rolling down her window she sneered at Jana, "You'll be hearing from my lawyer—I am gonna sue you for everything you've got!"

And then Jana said something she regretted. She leaned down and said, "Well I just happen to be your Visiting Teacher and I'm counting this as a visit!"

Carlita scowled and peeled out of the parking lot, leaving Jana and the cops behind.

"What was that you said to her?" the second officer asked.

Jana sighed. *The only comeback I could think of.* And what a pathetic one it was. As if she had finally won some kind of battle, when it was as if she had thrown a handful of feathers at Carlita. *Think you can dodge me, eh? Well, I'll show you!* As if Carlita gave a hoot about whether she was visited or not. Jana imagined Savannah at her side, saying, "A hoot? Seriously? Where do you get these expressions?"

She turned to the policeman. "It was just . . . nothing. We go to the same church." She shrugged, then thanked the policemen for their help and they drove away. The teenage boys were still there, so she shook their hands, then they disappeared into the market as she slowly inched into a parking spot.

She dialed Ethan. "Carlita Orton just hit me."

"What! She assaulted you?" Ethan pictured his wife standing at the door with another plate of cookies, being punched in the face by a less-active sister.

Jana sighed. "No, no, I mean she hit me with her car."

"What? She drove into you? Are you in the hospital?"

Jana struggled not to laugh at their miscommunication. "We had a car accident," she said. "She didn't know it was me."

"Are you okay?"

"I'm fine," Jana said. "She backed into the side of the van. It was her fault and two young guys witnessed it and talked to the police for me."

"Police came?"

"Well, Carlita was rather, uh, hostile, so I thought I'd better get everything documented. And I took photos."

"Where are you? I'll be right there."

"No, it's fine, honestly," Jana said. Then, knowing her husband wouldn't take no for an answer, added, "I'm at Safeway." She felt too jangled to drive, anyway, and was glad to sit still and calm down for a moment.

In a few minutes Ethan pulled into a nearby spot, and bounded out of his car. Jana got out and hugged him.

"Are you sure you're okay?"

"Well, I'm embarrassed, for whatever that's worth," Jana said.

"For getting in a car wreck? I thought you said it wasn't your fault."

"No, I'm embarrassed for telling her I was her visiting teacher and I'm counting this as a visit."

Ethan stared at his wife, the woman with the beautiful brown curls and the brilliant mind. "You what?"

"Look, I've been trying to see her for, like, a year, Ethan."

"And so you visit taught her at the scene of an accident?"

Jana was getting flustered. "Well, it's not like I delivered an actual message," she said. "I'm not stupid."

Ethan was rubbing his chin now, struggling not to laugh.

Jana slumped back down into the driver's seat. "Okay, it was a ridiculous thing to say. Plus now she knows who I am, which is not going to make her want to come to church anytime soon."

"Do ya think?"

Now Jana couldn't help laughing. "I think maybe she needs a new visiting teacher."

Ethan shook his head and smiled. "Oh, I don't know. You two have some shared history, now."

"That's not funny." Jana sighed. "So the car is all smashed in."

"I can see that. But it's drivable, right?"

Jana nodded. "And now we have to get estimates and go through that whole ordeal."

"And she had insurance, I hope."

"Yeah. The cops said her insurance will have to pay for it. But she said she's going to sue me."

Ethan smoothed her hair and leaned down to kiss her. "We'll deal with that. She won't get far if she's to blame. You want to go home and rest? I can pick up take-out for dinner."

"No, I have dinner already planned. But I was going to take some stuff to Merry Haines."

"Do it tomorrow," Ethan said, glancing at the damage. "Trade me cars so you can pick up the kids. They're obviously not going to be able to use those doors."

"Oh, yeah," Jana said. She was due at Maddie's grade school in 15 minutes.

Just then the two teenage boys came out of the supermarket. "Hey— there are the kids who saw it and talked to the cops," Jana said, getting back out of the van. She waved.

Ethan looked around and the boys came right over.

"These are the boys who signed the witness statements," Jana said. "Dylan and Chase, right?"

Ethan shook their hands and thanked them profusely, then introduced himself.

"Oh, I know who you are," Dylan said. "You're Savannah Waterson's folks."

"You know Savannah?" Jana asked.

"Yeah, she goes to our school. We're seniors, so we get out earlier. She's a really great girl."

So this boy was helping Jana in order to make points and date his daughter? Ethan's jaws were clenched and pulsing.

Jana was already sorry she had told Ethan where to find her.

"But you were totally in the right," Dylan rushed in to say. "We weren't just defending you because we're friends with Savannah."

She's friends with seniors? Senior boys? Ethan took a deep breath and swallowed, trying to summon patience.

Jana could see Ethan building up a head of steam and quickly stepped between him and the boys. "Well, it was wonderful that you came to my rescue," she said, almost walking the boys away from Ethan. "I'll have to tell Savannah."

"No prob," Chase said.

"Yeah, tell her hi," Dylan added.

"Will do. Have a good day." Jana waved, to further encourage them to leave. Then she turned back to Ethan. His eyes were narrow slits, now, watching as the boys walked off.

"I can see your brain smoking," Jana said. "Calm down, Honey."

"Were they even telling the truth to the police?" Ethan asked. "Or was that just to impress you, because you're Savannah's mom?"

"Absolutely the truth. I can show you the pictures," Jana said, getting her cell phone out and checking for the shots.

His voice was a hiss, now. "What is she doing hanging around senior boys?"

Gently Jana pushed Ethan down into the van's driver seat. "I have to pick up Maddie and you have to get back to work. Take a deep breath. She is not running away with a couple of senior boys."

Ethan closed his eyes and rested his forehead on the steering wheel.

"Love how you came to comfort me," Jana teased.

Ethan sat up. Once again the tables were turned and it was Jana who was the strong one. "You have three hours to compose yourself," she said.

"That's not enough."

"Hey, Savannah, we met some of your classmates today. Really nice guys and they were nice enough to help your mom. Chase and Dylan."

Ethan glanced at her.

"Repeat after me."

Ethan sighed. "Okay, I will say something to that effect." He thought for a second. "But—but—"

"No buts, Ethan. You have to get a grip and relax."

Ethan stared at the clock on the dash board. Three hours were definitely not enough.

Chapter 13

"STOP TAKING PICTURES OF THE CAR AND COME IN TO DINNER," Jana shouted, hoping her voice would carry through the laundry room and out into the garage. Now that Ethan had driven the van home, the kids were all out there snapping photos and posting them throughout cyberspace.

Maddie was the most dramatic, of course, saying it looked like a charging rhinoceros had hit the car.

"But your mother was the picture of calmness," Ethan said. "She even managed to do a little visiting teaching at the same time."

Jana stared daggers at him. Her "visit" was more of a threat, and they both knew it. Luckily the kids ignored that and wanted to hear all the details of the collision.

"First, it's Josh's turn to say the blessing," Ethan said.

Soon they were passing honey-glazed chicken thighs around the table, with Asian rice and plum sauce.

"There's not much to tell," Jana said. "The other driver backed out, hit our car, and then the police wrote up a report." She wiggled her eyebrows at Ethan, trying to cue him to speak up about Savannah's friends.

"And guess who happened to be in the parking lot and saw the whole thing?" Ethan said, picking right up on her hint. "Two boys from Savannah's school."

Savannah jerked her head around to stare at her father, and see if this story would end with his punching their lights out.

"Very nice boys," Jana said, realizing she was prompting Ethan, but determined to get that out there.

"Yes, very nice boys," Ethan parroted. "Chase and—" Then he went blank. His brain was already trying to erase all memory of these creatures and the names were first to go.

"Dylan?" Savannah guessed.

"That's it. Dylan," Ethan said. Subject closed. He hoped he had managed to maintain his sanity long enough to change the subject, now, and check off the "amiable dad" box.

"He and Chase are always hanging out together," Savannah said. "So what did they do?"

"They gave a witness report to the police," Jana said. "And I'm glad they were there to vouch for me—the other driver was completely at fault."

"That's cool. So they came over to help you?"

Ethan bristled. Why did this story have to continue? Boys saw, boys signed, boys left.

"Yes," Jana said. "They were a huge help."

Savannah smiled. Ethan frowned. Savannah buttered a roll, and passed them to Maddie. "Dylan's really sweet that way."

Ethan could feel his eyes bugging out, and wished he could manually push them back into his head. He stared down at his rice to hide his panic.

"He's actually interested in the church," Savannah went on.

I'll just bet, Ethan thought. He knew a dozen guys like this in high school, who pretended an interest in the church just so they could date the cute LDS girls.

"Oh, no kidding," Jana said. "That's wonderful." And then a queasy feeling came over her. *This is the kid she likes. This is why she wouldn't admit she was on the phone with him, because she knows he's a nonmember and we wouldn't approve of her dating him.* Her appetite was completely gone. Jana stirred the food on her plate, and tried to act natural. Her immediate goal was to run interference between Ethan and her daughter, to keep things from escalating.

Ethan stole a glance at Savannah. Her face was flushed, her eyes twinkling. She was interested in this kid! To occupy his mouth he gulped down half a glass of milk.

"Well, they both seemed like nice boys," Jana said. "Maybe they could come to church sometime."

"Yeah," Savannah said. "Dylan's friends with Eli Skaner from the 2nd Ward, by the way. I told them about the El Dorado House, and Dylan wants to help out with the landscaping this Saturday."

No, no, no, no, no, Ethan thought. He thought about leaving the table. What would he say? *Excuse me, I need to step out and have a heart attack?*

Just then the phone rang and Ethan sprang from his chair like a cheetah. "I'll get it," he said.

Jana stared at him. Poor Ethan; he had maintained such composure so far. But this was pushing his limits. Come to think of it, maybe it was a good thing the phone rang to rescue him from talking about these boys with Savannah.

And then she heard Ethan's voice crack. "Dylan? Uh, she's having dinner right now . . ."

Savannah lit up like a candle and dashed to the phone. "I can take it," she said, reaching for the land line.

Ethan covered the mouthpiece and whispered, "Taking a call during dinner?" to remind her of their family rule not to interrupt dinnertime with phone calls. "And it's Family Home Evening night."

Savannah gestured to her father, standing there with a phone in his hand, who had just done that very thing. Ethan sighed.

"Hi, Dylan," she said. "No, it's okay. Yeah, I'll call you back. Okay. Bye!" She came back to the table, beaming. Ethan slumped into his chair.

"So this Saturday could be a missionary moment," Jana said, kicking Ethan under the table.

"Cool," Josh said.

Ethan took a bite of chicken and chewed it, not tasting a thing. Savannah was smiling that megawatt smile of hers, and glancing at her cell phone, resting on the counter. The family always left their cell phones there, on vibrate, during mealtime. The idea was to put them away so they could focus on one another. But Savannah's focus was clearly on Dylan now, phone or no phone.

And why had he called the land line? As if reading Ethan's mind, Savannah said, "Dylan must have called the house because my cell phone didn't ring through."

"Well, I hope he can help out on Saturday," Jana said. "That's a gigantic job and we need every person who can pitch in." She looked over at Ethan, hoping he'd muster up a nod, at least. Nothing. "The missionaries will be there," Jana continued, trying to catch Ethan's eye. "Maybe they can see about teaching him."

"Yeah, maybe so," Savannah said.

Ethan was forcing a smile, now, but it was more of a grimace. Jana was just glad that Savannah was too preoccupied to notice.

"HOW DID I DO?" HE ASKED JANA THAT NIGHT AS THEY GOT ready for bed.

"You get a B," Jana said.

"Only a B? That was an A-plus performance!"

"No it wasn't." Jana dried her face. "If she had been paying any attention whatsoever she would have seen you writhing in pain, like I did."

Ethan scowled. "But I said the right things."

"Okay, a B-plus. Certainly A for effort." Jana hugged him. This was definitely not the time to tell him his daughter had been on the phone with Dylan earlier. And maybe the boy would join the church, after all. "Isn't it cool that our daughter is sharing the gospel with her classmates?"

"You two are so naïve." Ethan shook his head. "If that boy is sincerely interested, I'll—I'll—buy you a chocolate shake."

Jana smiled. "Deal." Then she turned away and sighed. If this were an acting class, her own performance tonight would have earned an A-plus.

ON TUESDAY SAVANNAH HAD BOOKS AND PAPERS SPREAD ALL over the dining table as she studied for a big test, and Jana sensed this wasn't the best moment for a heart-to-heart with her daughter.

She spent the next morning getting estimates and dealing with insurance companies, finally getting the van into a body shop, and a rental car to drive. Then Jana decided to try, once again, to deliver some diapers and a meal to Merry Haines.

When she knocked on the door she could hear Aiden crying, so she knew Merry had to be home. But then Sean opened the door. Aiden was in his arms, red-faced and miserable.

"Oh, Sister Waterson," Sean said. "I'm so glad you're here. Come in."

Jana came in, setting the take-out bags on the counter, and the diapers on a chair. "What's going on?"

"Merry's in the hospital," Sean said. "I can't be with her because they won't allow babies in—"

"Wait—what happened?" Jana asked.

"She broke her foot," Sean said, his words coming out like a rain of bullets. "Just this morning. She tripped over the rug in the nursery. I drove her to the E.R., but I couldn't bring Aiden in. Then I called work and said I couldn't come in—"

"Oh for heaven's sake," Jana said. "Do you want me to watch Aiden so you can go over and be with Merry?"

"Well, he's crying and I don't know what he wants," Sean said.

"Show me where his food is and I'll make sure he's fed and dry." Jana reached for the baby and took him in her arms. "Don't worry about a thing."

"But she's going to be mad that I let you in," Sean said.

Jana sighed. "Sean, this is an emergency. Blame it on me, say I insisted."

Sean looked from Jana to the wailing baby, then back again. "I'll come back as soon as I can."

"Don't hurry. I can be here for hours if you need me."

Sean looked as grateful as anyone Jana had ever seen, then quickly showed her where the baby bottles were, grabbed his keys, and left.

Jana changed Aiden's diaper, then warmed up some milk and rocked him as she tried to get him to drink. She looked around the pale periwinkle nursery and imagined Merry sitting in this very spot, looking at these same walls, holding this same little boy. His name was spelled out in a cheery graphic on the wall. Did she sing him Primary songs? Did she wonder if their family would be together forever?

Slowly Aiden settled down and finished off half a bottle. Jana burped him, then rocked him until she felt his little body go limp, sleep taking over. Carefully she lay him in his crib, and then quietly prayed for all of them.

She put the barbecue dinner in the fridge, and in about an hour her cell phone rang. It was Merry.

"Merry, hi—I'm so sorry about your foot," Jana began.

"Thanks, Jana," she said. "Sean just left, so I wanted to call and speak with you privately."

"Sure—whatever you need—"

"I appreciate y'all coming over, but we really don't need anything. Sean should be there in a few minutes. And I'll probably be able to come home tonight. So thanks, but we're going to be just fine on our own."

"Well, I'm happy to help in any—"

"The best thing you can do," Merry said, "is just respect my wishes."

Jana wanted to say, *Oh, come off it, Merry—I know you're still in there!* "Of course," Jana said. "I left some dinner for you in the fridge, and a bag of diapers in the nursery."

She could hear Merry take a breath and release it. "Well, thank you."

And I'm counting this as a visit, Jana thought. This was becoming her new motto.

A few minutes later Sean came in, full of apologies. "I just pray her heart will soften," he said as Jana headed out.

"Don't worry about it," she told him. "We're on the same team, here, just loving her and praying she'll come back." She headed down the walkway, then turned back. "And really do call me if she has a hard time getting around and needs some help."

Sean nodded and closed the door.

JANA HAD ALMOST AN HOUR BEFORE SHE NEEDED TO PICK MADdie up, so she swung by the El Dorado House to say hi to Vera and the others.

Helen smiled from the splashy reception desk. "How's everything?" she asked.

Well, except for a daughter who's giving my husband and me gray hair, a car smashed by a less active member, and another less active one who wishes I'd fall off the face of the earth, excellent.

"Well, let's see," Jana said, not wanting to lie, and trying to buy some time. "I'm getting a new calling." She figured it wouldn't hurt to tell Helen in advance.

Helen frowned, her eyebrows sloping down below her auburn bun. "What's that?"

"A new job to do at church. Instead of being in charge of the children, I'm going to do some missionary work."

"Like those boys on bicycles?"

"No, just helping them," Jana said. "I'll still be living at home."

"Why can't you work with the children?" Helen was clearly dismayed.

"Oh, I can—and I will. I mean, I'm helping them make those posters we talked about, this Saturday morning. But in our church we're all volunteers and we do various jobs. We switch around all the time. So someone could be teaching Sunday School for a couple of years, and then maybe lead the music, or work in the church library, or help out with the Scouting program—just wherever the Lord needs you."

"And how do you know where the Lord needs you?"

"Our bishop gets revelation," Jana said. "He feels inspired about where you should serve."

"And they don't pay you."

"Right. Not even the bishop draws a salary," Jana said. "They have regular jobs. For example, my husband is an accountant. Bishops can be anything for their regular job."

Jana noticed Chester and Stanley in the parlor, lowering their newspapers as they eavesdropped.

Helen shook her head, amazed. "But those missionary boys get paid, right?"

"Oh, no, they actually pay to be missionaries," Jana said. "Many of them save up from the time they're little children, and then totally support themselves. Girls are allowed to be missionaries, too. And they set aside their schooling and everything else to serve all over the world." She swallowed, remembered the words of her blessing, and allowed peace to settle into her heart.

"Do you get to pick where you go?" Chester, the ex-jockey, was making his way over, spry and quick for a man his age.

"Oh, no," Jana said. "You just apply and then wait for your call. It could be anywhere from Okinawa to Oklahoma, as my dad used to say."

Chester shook his head and whistled. "Why would a young kid do that?"

Jana opened her mouth to tell him, then got a sudden burst of inspiration, herself. "How about I bring a couple of them over sometime, and they can tell you, themselves?"

Helen was still frowning. "So everyone's an amateur, running this thing."

Jana laughed. "Pretty much. But we get lots of training and help. And it's the Lord's church, Helen. So he's not going to let it fail."

Now Stanley, the elocution teacher, was wheeling over, his lower lip jutting out and reminding Jana of Winston Churchill. "I like the training," he said, as if he'd been asked to give this whole idea his stamp of approval. "I understand your children give speeches."

"Yes, they do," Jana said.

"And they did a fine job singing," he went on. "That's good, getting them out in public, teaching them how to perform and conduct themselves."

"Thank you, Stanley. They had a wonderful time."

"One of them took a bit of a shine to me," Stanley said. "Little boy named Will."

Jana grinned. Will Duarte was the little five-year-old who had said he was adopting a grandpa here—so it was Stanley! "Oh, he's a wonderful boy," she said.

"Yes, I told him there are many fine men named William, and he has a lot to live up to." Stanley was already taking his grandpa duties seriously.

"I'm so glad you told him that," Jana said.

Stanley went right on. "There's William Shakespeare, William Wordsworth, William Yeats, William Blake, William Faulkner—"

"I had an Uncle William," Chester said, "and he was a rascal. And let's not forget Billy the Kid—"

Stanley hefted his torso around to face Chester. "I trust you to keep that information to yourself," he said, more of an order than a request.

Jana laughed, imagining tiny Will hearing about famous writers, and realizing he'd probably find Billy the Kid a lot more exciting. "Well, I'm sure he'll be in good hands with you for his adopted grandpa, Stanley."

He nodded, quite certain she was right.

Chester just shrugged. "Willy Shoemaker, now there was a fine jockey."

Stanley raised his voice slightly. "That boy is not going to become a jockey."

"Why not?" Chester argued. "Maybe he'd like to be a jockey."

Stanley snorted. "Preposterous."

"It's a noble profession," Chester said. "He'd be a lucky man if—"

"He will study the arts, science, medicine—"

"I think he should choose for himself—"

Jana looked over at Helen, who was shaking her head, then left Chester and Stanley arguing about Will's future as she headed down the hall to say hi to Vera.

The hairdresser, Carrie, who came twice a week to cut and style the residents' hair, was just taking a break, and nodded at Jana as she passed by, pulling a pack of cigarettes from her sweater pocket. Carrie's short hair was auburn with magenta streaks, and Jana once told her how wonderful she made all the women look. "You listen to them and do their hair the way they want it," Jana said.

Carrie had been looking weary, but now she brightened. "Thanks for saying that. I was just wishing I could do more exciting stuff, but you've reminded me I'm here for them, not for me."

Today Vera was in her bedroom, watching TV with Harriet, her roommate. Harriet was stroking Misty, her gray cat, who actually seemed to be watching the action on the screen.

"Oh—I won't interrupt," Jana whispered, starting to back out again.

But Vera pressed the pause button on her remote. "It's okay," she said. "We taped this, so we can watch it later." They were watching an old Clark Gable movie, and happened to freeze the frame just as he was striking a debonair pose.

Harriet looked up and smiled as well, always happy to have a visitor.

"Well, I only came to say hi," Jana said. "I have to pick up Maddie from school in a few minutes."

"How's that baby Aiden?" Vera asked. "And why hasn't his mother brought him by?" Vera looked more relaxed in her wheelchair now, turning it easily to face Jana.

"Oh, he's still so new," Jana said. "But I'm working on it." She decided not to tell Vera about Merry just yet, and changed the subject. "Maddie sure is excited to have an art lesson with you."

Vera beamed. "She has the soul of an artist, I can already tell."

Harriet smiled. "And she likes cats."

"Yes, she does," Jana said. "Hey, maybe she can draw Misty." Harriet had told her the cat's name, and Harriet seemed pleased that Jana remembered it.

"What's this about being married in heaven?" Harriet said. "I thought your marriage was over when one of you dies."

Oh, wow. A whole discussion about eternal marriage and sealings.

"I told her I'm planning to be with my Theodore when I die," Vera said, to explain Harriet's sudden interest in the topic.

"It's true," Jana said. "If a couple is sealed in one of our temples, then they're married for eternity. Isn't that a wonderful thought, Harriet?"

"Well, not to me it isn't," Harriet said. "I want nothing to do with the man I married."

Vera laughed and Jana sat down in a chair beside Harriet's bed. "Oh, it's not like you're stuck with someone you don't love, Harriet. Both people have to be worthy of that blessing, for one thing. Even if you're sealed in the temple, not everyone's marriage will be an eternal one."

"Then what happens to a woman like me?" Harriet asked. "I have to be alone forever?"

"No, no—let's say you joined our church, Harriet." She paused, to see if Harriet found this idea plausible. She couldn't tell, so she continued. "And let's say you went to our temple and you lived a good life and did everything you could to get home to Heavenly Father. You will receive every single blessing, Harriet. You'll have a wonderful husband in the next life."

"Who?"

Jana chuckled. "Well, I don't know who, but Heavenly Father will find you the perfect man."

Harriet cocked her head to one side, thinking. "So . . . maybe Clark Gable?"

Now they all laughed. "Who's to say?" Jana said. "Maybe it will be Clark Gable."

Harriet smiled in approval, content with that notion for now, at least.

Jana hugged them both goodbye, stroked Misty's head, then headed out to pick up Maddie, leaving the residents to their dreams: Harriet to her newfound romance, and Stanley to his newfound grandson's future.

Chapter 14

SAVANNAH SPUN AROUND FROM THE COMPUTER SCREEN AND smiled at Jana. "Check it out," she said.

Jana looked up from the cooling racks where she was placing two loaves of pumpkin bread. Maddie was working on a math assignment, Josh was at a basketball practice, and Ethan was at the church, conducting interviews.

She had been wanting to have a moment alone with Savannah, to speak to her about being untruthful and about not dating a non-member, a policy their family had agreed upon. But on Wednesday Savannah had been busy at school and then at Mutual, and now it was Thursday and she'd been completely occupied again, typing nonstop for the last two hours. "It's my report on the people at the El Dorado House," she said.

Jana wiped her hands and came over. Savannah had used information from the Mutual kids' interviews to write about the residents' memories of life almost a century ago.

Jana sat down and began reading. On page after page, Savannah described their lives. "Vera Underwood grew up before the invention of credit cards, seat belts, or television. There was no Scotch tape and no McDonald's. She used to go sledding in the winter, wearing hand-knitted gloves. In the summer she would roller skate, and loved the feeling of the wind in her hair. Her favorite thing was to make dolls out of hollyhock flowers and twigs, and pretend they were forest fairies."

Jana gasped. Maddie would love this. She kept reading. "Today Vera's tiny frame is almost lost in her wheelchair, yet in her youth she spun across the dance floor in sparkling gowns, and won big band dance competitions. She loved attending her church's 'Gold and Green Balls,' where she met Theodore, the man of her dreams and the best dancer on the floor. Vera worked as a telephone operator, and soon became Theodore's 'steady girl.' They married after Theodore came home from fighting in World War II, and Theodore went on to become a successful banker. Vera had every luxury she could want, and studied art at the local college. She even sold many of her paintings. But Vera was heartbroken not to have any children. After ten years they were finally blessed with a boy and a girl, and Vera felt her life was at last complete. But again, her joy was short-lived, as Theodore died suddenly in his sleep when the children were still in elementary school. Today Vera keeps his photo in a locket around her neck, and looks forward to seeing him again in the next life, where her Mormon faith teaches that she will be eternally married to him. Her son and daughter live back East, but come to visit twice a year with her six grandchildren. All their pictures hang in her small room at the El Dorado House.

"Vera has known both heartache and joy, triumph and loss. Despite her loneliness, she does not give in to self-pity. She has taken the talents she has been given—strong faith, artistic ability, and dancing—and has offered to share those with others."

Jana looked over at Savannah and smiled. "You captured Vera perfectly."

Then she went back to the report. Chester described the glory days of riding on the backs of gleaming thoroughbreds, right to the winner's circle. "Horses are smarter than you think," he had said. "And you've got to get to know each one's personality."

Chester remembered the invention of the jet engine, radar, and the atomic bomb. And then, in a section that brought tears to Jana's eyes, she read, "Chester enlisted to fight in World War II. The shrapnel from a bomb lodged in one knee, and ended his career as a jockey. But Chester has never once regretted his sacrifice, and felt it was an honor to serve his country."

"The greatest generation," Jana whispered.

Savannah leaned in. "What?"

"That's what they call them," Jana said. "They had the greatest patriotism, the best work ethic, the most integrity. It's never been matched since. These are heroes, Honey."

Savannah swallowed. "Wow."

"I can't wait for Dad to read this," Jana said. "He'll love it."

"I wanted to write about Marvin and how he loved watching Mickey Mantle play baseball," Savannah said, "But I had to share the list with two other kids who had the same history assignment."

"I like Marvin," Jana said. "He really seemed to enjoy the Primary kids' singing."

"Yeah," Savannah agreed. "And he seems like such a good friend to Herb." She paused. "And what a dresser, right? What do you call that— Dapper Dan?"

They laughed. "See? You're learning my lingo," Jana said.

Savannah rolled her eyes. "Lingo . . ."

Jana went back to the document, eager to see what Savannah had written about Rose, the most outspoken, gregarious one of the bunch.

"Rose Haugen grew up on a farm in Minnesota, wearing gingham skirts and skinny dipping in the lake," it said.

That sounds like Rose.

"Rose used to get in fights, just like a boy, defending her little brother. Then one day she found out it was her little brother who had arranged all the fights! Needless to say, Rose taught him a lesson, as well.

"Rose jumped into life with both feet, always the first to take a dare, first to ride a horse bareback, first to bleach her hair blond—something very brazen in those days. She also found she was first to get into trouble at school for playing hooky, and first to get stitches for jumping off the roof.

"After high school Rose decided the farming life was not exciting enough for her, and went off to Europe, staying with relatives in Norway. But after a year she came back, and was the first in her family to attend college, and the first in her hometown to march for Civil Rights. Rose was born in 1928, the year Amelia Earhart became the first woman to fly across the Atlantic, and Rose always believed this meant she was destined to be first in everything she did."

Jana smiled. "So she never married?"

Savannah shook her head. "Nope. She said men were intimidated by her."

Jana laughed. "I can see that. She's a fireball, and it would take a particular man in that era to appreciate that."

"Someone like Howard." Savannah smiled.

"Yes. Someone like Howard, with a spirit of adventure."

"Too bad they couldn't have met back in their twenties," Savannah said. "And Pearl was quite an adventurous woman, too. She's the one whose inflatable bra exploded from the high altitude when she wore it on an airplane."

Jana laughed. "Is she in this report, too?"

"No—I had to let Portia write about her. But you're almost to the end."

Jana kept reading. The next part was about Frances, who remembered being alive before penicillin, television, and ball point pens. Frances was the one who had wanted to be an astronaut, a career closed to women in those days. But she had persevered and become a nurse, and to this day was using her skills to help everyone around her. Savannah had written about these people's heartaches and losses, yet their determination to be useful, their dedication to service. Every one of them saw war take loved ones. They lived through The Great Depression. The Dust Bowl. Hard work and hard times. Babies lost to diseases now eradicated. Racism. Communism. Nazis. It was hard to imagine these people had been alive to hear the voices of FDR, Hitler, Winston Churchill, and Orson Welles on radio. And yet they had.

And then Savannah spoke of their humor, their spirit, their dreams. These people were not finished, simply because they had tallied up 80 and 90 years of experience. They had been shuttled off to a "rest home," ignored by the community and even seen as witches and monsters, yet they were still vibrant, still wanting to contribute. "They have so much to offer," Savannah wrote, "and it is we who stand convicted. We are the monsters. Our crime is neglect, and the price is the wisdom of the ages."

Jana caught her breath and realized her daughter's words had brought her to tears. "Oh, Savannah," she said.

"Do you like it?"

"It's exactly what everyone needs to know." Jana turned and looked up at her daughter. "You nailed it."

"So I guess I like old people, now."

Jana laughed and swept Savannah into a hug. "That's not just a great report," she said, "it's written by a great woman." Again, this just didn't seem like the time to bring up Dylan.

Ethan had picked Josh up from his basketball game, and came in with him now, both of them raving about the delicious smell of the pumpkin bread.

Jana called them over as they came through the door. "You, too, Maddie—come and hear this." Then she asked Savannah to read it to the family.

Soon they were in the kitchen with warm bread and cold milk, all chattering about the residents who had now become their friends.

"I can't believe they didn't have computers or cell phones," Maddie said.

"Hey, *I* didn't have computers or cell phones," Jana said. Maddie stared at her in disbelief, and Jana chose not to share the list she had just read on Facebook, of all the other things this new generation had, which she hadn't even heard of in her childhood.

"You didn't write about Howard?" Josh asked.

"No—I had to share the list with other kids who had the same assignment," Savannah said. "I had to skip Stanley, Lorraine, Marvin . . ."

"Tell us about Howard," Jana said, pouring more milk for her son. "You interviewed him, right?"

"Yeah, he's pretty cool," Josh said. "He had a hard life, taking odd jobs wherever he could get them. He'd hire himself out to oil fields, or on boats, sometimes shoveling coal on a train. He even put up circus tents, whatever he could do."

"He was a roustabout!" Jana exclaimed.

"Honestly, where do you get these words?" Savannah stared at her mother.

"That's what those men were called," Jana said.

"I guess he went all over the place," Josh explained. "All different countries. He never got married, but I think he would have made a good dad."

Ethan smiled, and wondered what traits Josh was picturing.

"So he doesn't have a family?" Maddie asked.

"Nope."

"That's sad." Maddie bit into a second cookie.

"But one time he hunted treasure for some guy," Josh said, "and the guy left him a bunch of money in his will. I think that's how Howard pays to live at the El Dorado House."

"My goodness, the stories he must have," Jana said.

"The stories they all must have," Ethan added.

"I know, right?" Josh said. "It's like Howard has all this experience and stuff, and no one to pass it along to."

Ethan glanced over at Jana, then back to Josh. "Shall we make Howard an unofficial grandpa?"

Josh laughed. "I doubt Howard would want that. He's pretty independent."

"Well," Jana said, her wheels turning. "We can ask and see what he says."

Josh shrugged, but Jana could see him stifling a smile.

"Well, I definitely want Vera for a grandma," Maddie announced.

Savannah rolled her eyes. "What a surprise."

"We can't do this and then pull away, though," Jana said. "If we do it, we need to commit to it and be there for them."

The kids all looked back at her as each one nodded.

"That's what they would have done," Savannah said. "The greatest generation."

THE NEXT MORNING JANA TOOK THE SECOND LOAF OF PUMPKIN bread to her hairdresser, Ernie, who had been cutting her hair for years. Ernie was short for Ernestine—a stout, jovial woman with short silver hair and hoop earrings.

"Wow, thanks," Ernie said, placing it on the counter. Two other stylists zoomed over and cut themselves a slice. Josie, the talkative brunette who worked in the corner, took one bite and said, "Needs nuts."

Jana sat there, speechless.

But Ernie whipped right around. "Oh, let me give you your money ba—Oh, wait."

Josie slunk back to her corner and Ernie shook her head. "Sorry about that. Some people are so rude."

Jana waved it away. To be honest, she wished she had Ernie's ability to think quickly on the spot. "I wish you could follow me around and be my spokesperson," Jana laughed. "You have no idea how often I could use your skills." It usually took her a day before she could think of good come back. Instead she muttered ridiculous things like, "I'm counting this as a visit."

JANA PRAYED ABOUT SAVANNAH, AND HAD THREE THOUGHTS. First, she wanted to give Savannah time to think about Dylan and come forward on her own. In addition, this sudden crush could blow over. And third, Dylan might be genuinely interested in the church, could maybe even serve a mission one day. She decided not to jump to conclusions, but just to observe things between Savannah and Dylan on Saturday afternoon, when she brought over the Primary kids' posters to the El Dorado House.

Since she wouldn't be there that morning, she wanted to hold off telling Ethan everything that had transpired. The last thing she wanted was for Dylan to show up and have a confrontation with Savannah's dad. It would be unforgettable, and probably from Savannah's point of view, unforgivable as well.

So she gave her daughter plenty of chances to open up and confess, but Savannah was staying busy and unusually reclusive.

Saturday morning brought a cacophony of sounds to the El Dorado house, in the form of tree trimmers, saws, and weed whackers. Dust and dirt filled the air as overgrown shrubs were unearthed and hauled to a giant dumpster.

Ward members swarmed over the grounds, while Ethan and two other men analyzed a diagram of the sprinkler system. Mutual kids were filling wheel barrows with weeds while men on extension ladders were pulling debris from gutters and trimming back branches. Termites could not have been more thorough.

"Whoa, these vines are like iron," Austin said, trying to cut them away from the windows with a lopper.

"Years of neglect," Chad Henry said, making *thwack! thwack!* sounds as he attacked the base of the vines with a hoe.

Ethan just hoped they could get it all cleared out in one day. The Elders' Quorum was scheduled to paint the exterior the following Saturday—if weather permitted—so they needed to get the property cleared by nightfall. Mimi had sent around a sign-up sheet for Relief Society sisters, to drop by with lunch and dinner—a stroke of genius.

Ethan glanced up at the windows the kids were slowly unveiling as they snipped the vines, and saw Marvin and Chester waving back. Already the grounds were looking more spacious and open. Occasionally one of the seniors would step out onto the porch to watch, squinting in the sunlight for a few minutes.

As huge bushes were pulled away, the giant black structure actually looked more foreboding than ever, looming over them as they worked. But he knew it would have to look worse before it looked better.

A couple of youths screamed out as they found spiders in their hair, and one boy needed the first aid kit for a small cut. Josh tripped over a stone and landed in some thorns, but waved away any bandages. Otherwise, they were like army ants, methodically attacking dead brush and unruly limbs, scooping it all up into piles, then lifting the piles into the dumpster.

If he hadn't seen the sketches made by the landscape architect from the 2nd ward, Ethan would have been worried they were leaving it too barren, but he knew that in a couple of weeks it would be filled with new greenery, flower beds, and clean walkways. Mature trees towered over them, and Ethan was grateful there were so many they could keep. Once cleaned up they lost their menacing look, and actually seemed inviting. The tips of the maple and oak leaves were just beginning to turn crimson and orange for autumn, and the transformation was already astounding.

A row of poplars lined the wall behind the building, forming a tall screen that obstructed the apartment complex next door. And some of the hedges were staying, too, nicely blocking the trash areas and the air conditioning unit.

He watched Josh clumsily battle some limbs that kept swatting him in the face as he tried to break them into manageable pieces. His heart broke for him. Had Ethan been that uncoordinated as a kid? Probably. Would Josh ever enjoy sports, or be unathletic like his dad? And why hadn't Josh joked around with the other kids when everyone first arrived? Had Ethan passed on a social misfit gene? Was Ethan too busy, as a bishop now, to help his own son deal with peer pressure and popularity? He sighed. Even if he had time, what would he tell his son? He certainly had no answers when it came to social acceptance.

On the other hand, Ethan was relieved that Dylan hadn't shown up. Hopefully the boy was all talk and Savannah would lose interest in him. Last night he had talked to the kids about being the hardest workers on any project, and was pleased to see Savannah pushing a full wheel barrow over the uneven ground, wobbling it towards the dumpster.

"Whoa, lookout," someone called, and Ethan turned to see Josh nearly falling on a weed whacker as he backed up without looking. Instinctively he took a step toward his son, wanting to rescue him, but then saw that Josh had recovered on his own. He was relieved to hear Josh say, "Maybe I'll just work here for a while," as he dropped to a stationery position along a walkway and began pulling up handfuls of weeds with other deacons and teachers.

"Mr. Waterson?" A teenage voice was right behind him. Ethan turned. "Hi—I'm Dylan."

Ethan forced a smile and lied. "Good to see you, Dylan."

"I brought gloves and a shovel," Dylan said.

Ethan noticed the shovel wasn't new, but worn from years of use. He did not want to like this boy, or discover that he was a hard worker. And that would have been a lot easier if the shovel had looked brand new. *Probably his dad's shovel.*

"Oh, Dylan, hi!" Savannah was coming across the property now, obviously having kept an eye out for her friend. She was tucking a strand of hair behind her ear, smiling like a girl in a slow motion commercial for Gatorade.

Ethan needed Jana. Jana would know what to say to keep him from saying, "Well, thanks for coming. Bye!" or "Dylan, you work on the perimeter, Savannah, you go home." But Jana was at the church helping the Primary kids make posters. She wouldn't even be one of the women arriving with donuts or tacos in another hour.

"Come on, I'll show you where we're working," Savannah said. And the two of them walked off. Dylan had blond hair, blue eyes, and looked like a surfer. Or, with those broad shoulders, maybe a swimmer. Tan, strong features. *Leave Sacramento. Run away to L.A. and become a movie star, Dylan.* Ethan closed his eyes and tried to repent of his thoughts.

"Need a rest?" It was Terrell Moses, his counselor, who had just arrived with an ice chest full of bottled water and sodas.

Ethan turned to Terrell and shook his head. "You have no idea."

"So is this a boyfriend?" Terrell nodded at Savannah and Dylan, who were over by the dumpster now, laughing together.

"Don't even," Ethan said.

"Whoa, whoa, got it," Terrell laughed. Then he leaned in and whispered, "So this is the kid you're worried about?"

Ethan nodded. "She says he's interested in the church, but—."

"But you think he's just interested in her. I'll keep an eye out," Terrell said, and headed in their direction.

Ethan knew he couldn't keep standing there, blinking like a lighthouse, so he looked around for Josh. The other deacons were still weeding, but there was no sign of Josh. He hoped he hadn't gotten injured.

"Bishop, where should I put this?" Portia Ferguson was holding a black bag filled with the morning's orange juice cups and muffin wrappers. "They don't want it with the green waste in the dumpster."

"Oh, I'll take it," Ethan said. "I'll put it in the trash around back." Ethan knew right where the garbage cans were and headed off with the bag. Just as he rounded one of the hedges he stopped. There was Josh, sitting by the wheelchair ramp, on the steps outside the kitchen. He was holding a bag of ice on his knee.

"What happened?"

"Oh, nothing. I just tripped and hit my knee on a sprinkler."

"Are you cut?" Ethan looked under the ice at the red, swollen knee.

"No, just banged it a little."

Ethan put a hand on Josh's shoulder. "You need to go home?"

"No way. Plus I want to ask Howard about that grandpa thing."

"You really like him."

"Yeah, he's cool."

"But is he ready for a totally cool grandson?"

Josh laughed. "Guess I'll find out."

Ethan sat with him for a few minutes. "That was nice of the cooks to give you some ice."

"Yeah." Josh took the bag from his knee and examined it. "I think it'll be okay, now."

"Do you want Savannah to come along?" Ethan was hoping he could use this excuse to pry her away from Dylan. He lifted the lid of a trash can and dropped the bag in.

Josh shrugged and stood up, testing his knee.

Ethan realized Josh wanted this to be his own thing with Howard, not a family affair. "How about you go in and see him, and just let us know how it goes?"

"Yeah, okay." Josh walked off, trying not to limp.

Then Ethan circled around the house, and came up the side just in time to see Dylan teaching Savannah how to dig with a shovel. *Didn't she already know how to do that? I'm her father—I'll teach her how to dig.*

"Like this?" he could hear her saying. One of her feet was on the blade, trying to press down. Suddenly she saw her father and jumped. "Oh, my gosh, you scared me, Dad!" Her eyes filled with disappointment that he was apparently spying on her.

"Sorry—I was in back with Josh—he banged his knee." Ethan forced himself to keep walking, as if he had a purpose, though he did not.

Terrell was about 20 yards away, pretending to be raking, and caught his eye. They winked at each other and Ethan felt ridiculous. He was not only spying on his daughter, but he had his counselor spying on her as well. Ever so slightly he tilted his head, to tell Terrell where to meet up with him, then went to the front steps and waited.

Soon Terrell came strolling by. "Do I look nonchalant?" he asked.

Ethan hung his head. "I am a pathetic, overprotective father."

Terrell chuckled and sat beside him. "Who isn't?"

"So?" Pathetic or not, Ethan still wanted to know what was going on between his daughter and this interloper.

"So nothing seems to be happening. I mean, you can tell they like each other, but they're not exactly alone, so . . . not much can happen, Bishop. He is pitching in and working."

"Well, at least there's that." And, for just an instant, Ethan felt a wave of hope that the kid really would look into the church. Maybe he was completely sincere.

Just then Mimi and two other women showed up, and all work stopped as the entire assemblage swarmed their cars for lunch. Ethan grabbed a taco, downed it in half a minute, then picked up a hedge trimmer and got to work on the bushes below the front porch. He never had much to say in a giant crowd, anyway. And hovering over Savannah was not going to earn him any points.

Soon he could see Josh's legs hurrying down the steps and he turned off the trimmer. "Hey, ready for some lunch?"

"Oh, there you are," Josh said. "He said yes! I mean, he's not interested in the church—he made that really clear. But he likes the grandpa idea."

"Fantastic," Ethan said, high fiving his son. "I thought you were dashing out here for some tacos." But tacos, he was happy to see, were not nearly as exciting to Josh as having Howard as a brand new grandpa.

Chapter 15

"THAT LOOKS LIKE A CAMEL, NOT A HORSE," JACKSON BAKER said. He was watching Brighton Stills make a giant hump on the back of the tan animal she was drawing.

"Of course it's a camel," she retorted. "They didn't come on horses!"

"What are you talking about? Of course he rode horses." Then he turned to Jana. "Sister Waterson, she's ruining the poster."

Jana sighed and went over to the six-year-olds who were painting the poster about Chester. Each resident had been assigned to a group of children, then their Primary teachers had read them all the information about Rose, or Marvin, or whomever. The kids were wearing oversized men's shirts backwards, for smocks.

"What's the problem?" she asked.

"She's making a camel." Jackson had his hands on his hips now.

"I get to tell it," Brighton said, standing up. "It's for the wise man."

"What wise man?" Jackson and Jana both asked in unison.

"The wise man Sister Adams told us about."

"Uh oh." This was Sister Adams, now, coming over after stepping away to deal with her one-year-old. "Let me look at his description again." She unfolded the paper and began reading.

But she didn't need to. Jana remembered. It said, "Chester is a wise man" and Brighton had taken it literally to mean one of the magi who visited Christ. This was like the time she had said, "Well, that's one for the books" to Savannah at this age, and Savannah had asked, "What books?"

"You're both right," Jana said, putting a hand on each of the kids' shoulders. "He did ride horses and he is very wise." Then she explained to Brighton that someone can be a wise man and yet not be one of the Three Wise Men. "But the way it's written," she said, "that would be very easy to assume. I should have been clearer."

"Let me help you," Sister Adams said, and soon they had smoothed over the hump and sketched a man riding him. "Brighton, how about you paint his clothes? They had yellow diamonds on them."

Now Brighton had forgotten all about the camel mistake and was eagerly dabbing yellow paint into diamond shapes on his jockey silks. The other kids, having heard about the lavish flowers presented to the winners, were making a splashy border of brilliant blooms all around the edges.

Harriet's poster almost looked like the cover of a book. It showed a woman with a silvery beehive hairdo, dressed in a bright red gown, smiling. And on her lap was a gray cat the size of a goat. It was comical, yet whimsical and welcoming.

Marvin's poster showed a huge stadium at a baseball game, and a little boy with dark hair cheering from the stands. Marvin as a child—brilliant!

Vera's poster, micro-managed by "I'm her granddaughter" Maddie, showed a joyful fairy flying through the air, clad in green, of course.

"She looks like the fairy from Sleeping Beauty," one boy complained.

"Thank you," Maddie said, completely unaware that this was a complaint.

Jana stared at the happy painting, and noticed Maddie had Vera dabbing paint on the leaves of the trees around her. "Maddie, you made her wand into a paint brush!"

Maddie smiled. "Yep."

Jana stared at the pink and yellow splotches on the leaves. "It's like she's bringing autumn to the world."

"Yep."

Maybe Maddie really *did* have art talent. Jana wanted to stay and watch as her daughter kept painting, but it was not to be.

"Sister Waterson," Charlie Marks was calling. "Do you think Stanley looks like Humpty Dumpty?"

She came over to where the 11-year-olds were working. Yikes. They had captured Stanley's bald head and full face in a perfect egg shape. Even worse, they had placed him atop a wall.

"You drew Humpty Dumpty!" Sasha Gorman was shaking her head in dismay.

"I was putting him on top of that wall by the El Dorado House," Charlie said.

"I wanted to have him dressed in graduation clothes," another girl put in, "because he was a teacher."

Jana seized on this idea. "Oh, I think that would solve it," she said. "A cap and gown?"

"Okay, but it has to be blue," Charlie said.

Soon the "egg" was topped with a jaunty blue mortarboard cap with a gold tassel, and from the neck down was draped in a floor-length blue gown. Now he seemed to be standing in front of the wall, instead of sitting on it.

"I think he should have a whiteboard," another kid said. "Let's look up some Greek letters and put them on there." Soon his Primary teacher was Googling "Greek letters" on her iPhone, and the entire scene became an indoor classroom instead of an outdoor wall. Another kid drew a stack of books nearby. Definitely no egg references. *Whew.*

The 7-year-olds were working on Rose's poster, a wild collage of all her exploits—jumping off a roof, waving from an open-air bi-plane to depict her flight to Norway, swimming, marching in a parade. Hilariously, she had the blond French twist, orange lipstick, and the blue reading glasses, even as a child. And her clothes were garish florals and plaids, as bold as Rose. This was one reason Jana loved children's art—it was fearless. Like Rose.

And then she saw the poster for Frances, the retired nurse. She had expected to see Frances in a nurse's uniform, taking care of patients. But instead, Frances was zooming into outer space in a rocket, waving from a big window and grinning from ear to ear. Huge flames shot out from under the rocket, and stars twinkled in the dark sky all around her. "You made her an astronaut," Jana whispered, a catch in her throat. "She will love this!"

Raymond's poster showed him hiking in the woods, Pearl was holding a giant cake she had baked, and Herb, the one who had been sick, was shown lifting weights—the picture of health. Lorraine was wearing a pink ballerina's tutu and a crown, and Howard was dressed as a pirate, holding aloft a treasure chest dripping with sparkling jewels. Jana laughed—this one captured his swash-buckling stories perfectly.

By noon parents were coming to pick up their kids, and thankfully the artwork was finished. All twelve residents had dazzling posters that captured their earlier lives in vivid color and detail. The parents were astounded at the excited telling of each resident's story, and several kids begged to go by later in the day, to see their work on display.

"Ethan—I mean Bishop—will help me hang it this afternoon," Jana said. "And I'm sure you can drop in anytime to see it."

Lachelle Marks was helping Jana scoot the tables and chairs back in place. "Hey, how are you coping with having your husband gone so much, now that he's the bishop?"

Jana looked up. "Honestly?"

"Honestly."

"Well, I'd be lying if I said there weren't times I could use his help with the kids. And times I just want to vent, you know how we do with our husbands."

Lachelle nodded, chuckling. "Oh, I do."

"And sometimes my house is a wreck—I mean, you have to choose your battles. But then I realize how blessed the whole family is. I seriously can feel it. And I'm just honestly grateful."

Lachelle hugged her. "Thanks."

"For what?"

"For whatever you're sacrificing so the rest of us can have a great bishop."

"Oh." Tears suddenly spilled down Jana's cheeks and she waved at her eyes with her hands. "Why do we fan our eyes when we cry?" Both of them laughed.

By the time Jana and the other Primary staff cleaned up the art supplies and gathered the newspaper that had lined the work surfaces, the paint had dried. Carefully they loaded the posters into Jana's van. They were curling a bit from the wet paint, but Jana already had permission to nail them in all four corners, on the walls. And she had all the tools in her van. Maddie hopped into the front seat and they took off, Maddie eager to see Vera's reaction to her artwork.

WITH SO MANY PARENTS LEAVING THE EL DORADO HOUSE grounds to pick up their Primary kids from the church, the number of workers on the property had dropped by half. And the taco-and-donut break had taken almost an hour. Ethan began to panic. What if they couldn't clean up this huge property in time for next week's painting? The Elders' Quorum would be trying to set up their ladders in bushes and rubble.

A squirrel was darting down one of the tree trunks for bits of taco shell left behind, then scurrying back up again with it. Ethan glanced over at a grassy area where the teenagers were sitting to eat. Savannah was sitting with Dylan, of course. *How many tacos does a person need? Why can't they stop laughing and get back to work?*

Thankfully, Jana's van pulled into the drive just then. Ethan turned off the trimmer and jogged to the back parking lot to meet her. "Dylan's here," he said, as soon as she opened her door and got out, leaving Maddie inside, out of ear shot.

"Wow. Thanks for the warning."

"You're being sarcastic."

Jana gave him a look, still trying to downplay the whole thing. "I think it's good that he's here. Maybe he'll take the discussions." She opened the back hatch.

Maddie climbed out, now, and ran around to hug her father. "Come and see the posters." She pulled him to the back of the van.

"How about we hang these?" Jana said.

"But there's so much work to do on the yard—"

Jana leaned in and whispered. "You mean so much spying to do?"

"That, too."

"You have dozens of people here," she said. "What do you think is going to happen?"

Ethan's mind whirred with the possibilities. *Dylan's going to ask her out, she's going to accept, then we'll say no, then she'll sneak out anyway, then she'll run away with the circus, marry a clown, and we'll never see her again.*

"Come on," Jana said, grabbing two hammers and the box of nails. "We can get this done in half an hour."

Ethan sighed and looked down at the artwork for the first time. "Oh, wow. This must be Harriet." He lifted them individually, to see the one beneath. "Oh, look at Chester. With a smiling horse! Who's this—Lorraine as a ballerina? And Rose—that's her, all right. And look at Frances!"

Jana grinned. "Aren't they incredible?" She watched as Ethan reacted to each one. "This is going to cheer up their rooms and lift their spirits like gangbusters," she said.

"I heard that," Savannah said. "Another weird expression."

Jana spun around and laughed as she saw Savannah and Dylan coming up the drive. "Well, it will," she said. "Look at this amazing art."

Savannah and Dylan helped them take the posters from the van. "These are so cool," Savannah said. "Want us to help you hang them?"

"Oh, it's okay," Jana started to say. "Dad and I—"

"We'd love your help," Ethan interrupted. *This way I can keep an eye on that kid.*

Savannah and Dylan walked ahead with the posters, Jana giving Ethan a sideways glance. "I know why you're doing this," she whispered.

Ethan covered his forehead with his hands. "You stay out of there and stop reading my mind," he said. "That's private property." Then he called to Josh who hurried over to join them.

"Looks like your knee's doing better," Ethan said.

"Yep," Josh said.

"What happened to his knee?" Jana asked.

"Oh, nothing," Josh said. "Just hit it on a sprinkler. But it's fine, now."

Jana watched as he walked, to make sure. They climbed the steps and went into the foyer, where nearly all the residents were glued to the windows, watching the undergrowth get chopped up and hauled away. Next to seeing their carpet go from black to purple, this was probably the most action this place had seen in years.

"Wow," Dylan said, taking in the hot pink draperies and purple carpet for the first time.

Savannah laughed. "I know—pretty wild, huh?"

"I thought this was a Halloween spook house," Dylan whispered to her.

"Not anymore."

And now the residents came swarming over to see their posters, a crush of canes and wheelchairs.

Jana held her hands up. "Let us surprise you," she said. "Everyone wait here until we're through."

Helen helped herd everyone back into the parlors, simultaneously craning her neck to peek at the posters, herself. Simone brought in some crackers and cheese, as if hosting a reception before the unveiling of a masterpiece.

"Smart thinking," Ethan whispered as they headed down the hallway to the bedrooms. "Otherwise we'd be in here an hour."

One by one, they hung the art, two posters per room. And it was nothing short of spectacular. "It's like a museum," Savannah gasped as the posters went up. "Look how much happier this room feels."

"I like the horse one and the pirate one," Josh said. "Totally cool." Then, turning to Maddie, "Of course, the one of Vera is the best."

Maddie beamed.

"Children's art always captures such joy," Jana said. She watched her daughter and Dylan, clearly enamored with one another, but trying to look casual. She was going to have to force a conversation with Savannah that night, whether the timing seemed right or not.

As they hung the last poster Jana glanced at the time. Thirty minutes on the button. "I guess we can let them in, now." She caught Helen's eye and nodded to her.

"Time to get back outside to work," Ethan said.

"But can't we wait and see their reactions?" Savannah pleaded.

Ethan glanced over his shoulder as Marvin came clacking along the bannister, as quickly as he could hobble. The surge of excitement was almost tangible. "Yes. Of course."

Marvin's room was closest to the lobby, so he was first to see his poster. "Hoo-eee! That's me, right there!" He poked his cane at the boy in the stadium. Jana had never seen him so elated. "And I'm in even better seats!"

Howard roomed with Marvin, and arrived just seconds later. He threw his head back and roared with delight. "Yessir, a pirate's life for me!" Then he waved his cane like a sword. "And that's one good-looking pirate, I'll tell you."

Nurses were popping into the rooms to see the new artwork as well. "Oh, aren't these jazzy?" Shanika said.

Theresa nodded. "I love it!"

Chester's and Stanley's room came next, and Chester clasped his hands together and shook them over his head like the champion he was.

"All right! That looks like one of my favorite colts, matter of fact."

Stanley stood before his poster, almost in reverence. "Those wonderful kids," he said softly. "Just marvelous."

Herb was in the third room, sitting up in bed, having been there when the posters went up. "Hey, Raymond," he called to his roommate. "Isn't this something?"

"Raymond looked at Herb's poster showing Herb as a weight lifter and smiled. Then he looked at his own, and shook his head in disbelief. "Did those kids know that I like to hike?"

"We told them all about you guys," Josh said.

"Well, I'd like to go hiking there," Raymond said. "With all those trees and flowers—even a deer. Who thought of that?"

"The kids did it," Jana said. Sunbeams had paired with the 11-year-olds on this one, which explained the scribbly blue sky *and* the delicate deer.

They crossed over to the women's rooms, and could hear Rose even before they arrived. "That is me all the way," she was shouting. "Look at me! Look at that!"

She was almost hollering, but her roommate, Frances, wasn't listening. Frances was sitting on her bed with happy tears streaming down her face as she saw her own poster, of herself in the rocket. "I love it," she managed to say as the Watersons arrived. "It's absolutely perfect." Then she got up and thanked them, hugging Jana. "It's the most lovely thing I've ever gotten."

Vera seemed to be waiting for Maddie as they got to the next room. As soon as Vera saw her, she waved her over and held her in a hug. "It's magical," Vera said. "And you are a great artist." Maddie looked over her shoulder at Jana, and grinned.

Harriet was already talking to her cat, Misty. "See that? That's you up there." Then she looked up at the Watersons. "This was a wonderful idea."

Jana caught a glimpse of Dylan, who seemed genuinely touched by the gratitude of these seniors. He kept glancing at Savannah and smiling. She could see why Savannah was drawn to him, but that didn't excuse breaking the family rules and then hiding it.

Various residents were now wandering into each other's rooms to check out the rest of the posters, and their raves echoed down the hallways.

In the last room, Lorraine and Pearl were already arguing over whose was the best poster. "But my pink cake actually glitters," Pearl was saying.

"Not as much as my crown or my tutu," Lorraine was firing back.

"Oh, they're both gorgeous," Jana said. "And they capture your tremendous talents, don't you think?"

Pearl nodded. "Well, yes, but mine is still better."

"Nonsense," Lorraine said.

The Watersons backed out quietly, leaving Pearl and Lorraine to their debate. The kids chuckled as they stepped into the foyer. Helen was just coming back from the men's bedrooms. "You have really done a grand thing," she said. "I've never seen them so happy."

"Well, you ought to visit Pearl and Lorraine," Savannah said.

"Oh—they don't like their posters?" Helen was stunned.

"Oh, they like them," Jana said. "They just can't agree on whose is best."

Helen pursed her lips to hold in her laughter and shook her head. "Those two."

"Well, back to work," Ethan said. The kids started filing out.

"You may have some Primary kids coming by to see their art on display," Jana said. "They're all so excited."

"The El Dorado Museum is open," Helen smiled.

"Starting with this reception desk," Jana winked.

Just then Charlie Marks burst through the front door, pulling his parents, Ty and Lachelle along. "He couldn't wait," Lachelle laughed. "And I think the Wickhams are just parking, as well."

Ethan turned to Helen. "It's going to be a busy afternoon."

THAT NIGHT ETHAN WHISPERED TO JANA, AFTER THE TWO younger kids had gone to bed. "Something bothering you?"

Jana was folding laundry in the bedroom and looked up. "No. Why do you ask?" Now *she* was lying!

"You just seem . . . a little distant. Like something's bugging you."

More than you know. Jana wanted to tell him everything, but had decided to talk with Savannah first, in case the girl was genuinely sorry. Maybe give her a chance to apologize and set things right, before Ethan overreacted.

"No, everything's fine," she said, cringing with every word.

Ethan came over and helped her fold. "Well, I've been wanting to tell you something."

"Is it about Dylan?"

"No, but I was glad he had to leave after cleanup." Dylan's father had tickets to a football game, pulling the boy reluctantly away from Savannah just as the final load of brush went into the dumpster that evening.

"It's about the kids and this adopt-a-grandparent thing." Ethan told her about how happy Josh was that Howard agreed to be his grandpa. "It made me realize how much our kids have been missing, not having our folks in their lives. I really think this is going to be wonderful for them."

Jana nodded. "I agree. I know Maddie's thrilled to have found Vera. I wonder if Savannah will click with one of them."

"Right now I think she's busy clicking with Dylan."

The laundry was done and Ethan sat down on their bench, and began untying his shoes. He turned to Jana. "Can't you see the situation? Savannah is at least ten times prettier than any other girl in the entire high school. She's smart—probably a genius, she has the best personality in the world, and there isn't a guy on this planet who wouldn't like to be her boyfriend."

Jana nodded, placing the folded laundry in the dresser. "She also has a good head on her shoulders. Just relax and enjoy that blessing." *And I hope she searches her heart and comes forward.*

Outside their room, Savannah had stopped short, listening. She had intended to knock on the open door, then go in and ask if she could borrow a scarf from her mother for church tomorrow. But now she pressed her back against the wall, and leaned there instead, just smiling.

Chapter 16

JANA STOOD BEFORE THE DRESSER AND LOOKED AT HERSELF IN the mirror. Enough tip-toeing. "I think I'll go and have a chat with her," Jana said. She closed the last dresser drawer.

Outside, Savannah hurried back to her room.

Ethan stood up, holding his shoes. "Why—is something up?"

Jana tipped her head back and forth. "Ahh . . . I just want to see." Jana took a deep breath, said a silent prayer, and headed down the hall to Savannah's room. *I really hope she isn't on the phone with him again.*

But she was busy at her desk, and pretended to be surprised when her mother knocked.

"Hey, can we talk for a minute?" Jana asked.

Savannah turned around.

"Come and sit on the bed," Jana said.

Savannah plopped down, the bed bouncing as she sat.

Jana paused, praying for inspiration. She'd gone to a parenting class years ago, where the teacher said not to ask questions that allow a child to fib, but to tell them what you already know. Don't set them up to be caught red-handed; just put all the cards on the table. "Look," she said. "The other night when you said you had homework—"

"What night?"

"A week ago. When we were making cinnamon rolls. I know you were talking with Dylan, and you didn't want me to know—"

"Are you accusing me of lying?" Savannah's eyes shot open, her face suddenly red.

Jana sighed. "And then today—you two act like you're a couple."

Now Savannah squinted. "I can't believe this! You don't trust me!"

"Savannah, I've never had reason to doubt you before. But for the last few days, you've been secretive, you've been—"

"You're worse than Dad! You guys think every guy is the enemy. What if he's interested in the church? Do you expect me to completely ignore every guy who's not a member?"

"I expect you to be forthcoming with me. Not hide what's going on." Jana reached out to caress her, but Savannah pulled away and stood up.

She was trembling and raised her voice. Her body language, alone, told Jana she had nailed it. "Well nothing is going on!"

Jana just looked at her daughter, wishing she would tell the truth. "Nothing?"

"That's right—nothing! Except we're friends. And he does want to know more about the church. So I'm being a missionary. That's all!"

Jana looked down at Savannah's feet and remembered them in tiny crocheted booties when Savannah was a baby. Then little Velcro tennies, then patent leather Mary Janes. Somehow she saw her daughter's entire life in shoes—*shoes!* And she could feel her eyes stinging.

She had no idea how to handle this. And the parenting class idea was an epic fail. She just knew she couldn't stay and watch Savannah dig the hole any deeper. She stood up. "I'm always here if you want to talk," she said. Then she walked out of the room, Savannah staring daggers as she left.

"And you owe me an apology!" Savannah shouted after her.

Jana saw Ethan coming out of their bedroom and motioned him back inside.

"What's going on? Did I hear shouting?" Ethan backed up, sitting on the bench with his wife.

Jana wiped her cheeks and composed herself. If Ethan saw how heartbroken she was he'd march down to Savannah's room and "get to the bottom of this." And that would backfire right now. Jana took Ethan's hand. "I need to speak calmly with you."

"I can be calm," Ethan said.

"No, I mean *I* need to be calm," Jana said. "First of all, I know you have the gift of discernment as a bishop. And you certainly have it as a husband, and you were right. Something has been bothering me for more than a week."

"What? Savannah?"

Jana fought to maintain composure. "I wanted to talk to you about it earlier, but I kept hoping she'd come to me and open up first. I was afraid you'd—"

Ethan took a deep breath. "Explode."

Jana nodded.

Ethan released his breath and closed his eyes. "Okay. That's fair. I can get crazy when it comes to boys. And this is about Dylan, isn't it?"

"Ethan, she's seeing him. Or whatever that means these days. They're talking on the phone, I can tell she's, well, smitten."

"I knew it! I knew it!" Ethan brow was glistening.

"She says she's just doing missionary work, but this is the first time she hasn't shared a crush with me, and the first time she ditched the cinnamon roll baking so she could talk to him on the phone. She said she had homework, but—" Jana shrugged.

"So you think she's being sneaky."

"I hate that word."

Ethan sighed. "So do I. But why would she hide it if there's nothing going on?"

"Exactly."

Ethan stood up. "We need to nip this in the bud."

"But is a big confrontation the way to go?"

Ethan was already heading out the door. "She needs to understand the family rules."

Jana was right on his heels as he knocked on Savannah's door.

"I'm going to sleep," came an angry voice.

"You don't sound very sleepy," Ethan called.

Silence. Then the door swung open. "So you told Dad," Savannah smirked.

"You will not speak to your mother that way," Ethan said, striding into her room. "And of course she told me—why wouldn't she? Our daughter has a secret relationship with some kid from school, and I'm not supposed to know about it?"

Jana put a hand on his back and Ethan paused, glancing back at her.

"Savannah, you know the rules," Jana said.

"Oh, so I can't be friends with nonmembers, now?" Savannah was not backing down.

"Come and sit down," Ethan said.

"I don't want to sit down," Savannah argued. "I am being accused unfairly."

"I am not going to ask you something that gives you the chance to lie," Ethan said, as gently as he could. Jana noticed he'd been thinking of the same parenting class. "I'm just going to remind you that our family rule is we do not date nonmembers. Friends, yes. Boyfriends, no."

"And we're just friends!" Savannah repeated. Loudly. "Now I'm going to bed!"

Ethan looked at Jana, both of their faces filled with worry. Jana nodded toward the hallway, and Ethan followed her lead. Once more in their bedroom, Jana whispered, "You've reminded her. She knows the rules." They knelt for prayer. "Maybe this will be enough," Jana said. "Maybe she'll break it off."

"I hope so," Ethan said.

THE NEXT MORNING SAVANNAH STRODE CONFIDENTLY INTO THE kitchen as Jana was making breakfast.

Never one to skirt an issue, Savannah brought it right up. "I know what you and Dad are thinking," she said. "And you'll just have to see that you're wrong."

Jana smiled. "Good. I'm glad to hear it. Then I apologize for jumping to conclusions."

"Wrong about what?" Maddie asked, her mouth full of Cheerios.

"None of your beeswax," Savannah said.

Jana smiled. Savannah was using her expressions without even realizing it.

Ethan was already at Bishopric Meeting, and Josh came bounding down the stairs as the phone rang.

"Would you like to get that?" Jana asked. *Let's see if it's Dylan this time.*

Savannah confidently snapped up the phone. But it was Eva Henry, the new Primary President. She was violently ill with the flu, and wanted Jana to attend Ward Council for her.

"Sure," Jana said. "But don't you want one of your counselors to do it?"

"Already asked—one's on her way to her brother's mission homecoming and the other has sick kids herself."

"I'll be glad to," Jana said. Then she turned to Savannah. "Can you drive me to church, and then come back and get Josh and Maddie?"

Savannah shrugged and nodded.

They drove in stiff, formal silence as if they were strangers, Jana thanking her for the ride, and Savannah muttering, "No problem," as she let Jana off at the curb.

Maybe this was enough of a shakeup to get Savannah back on track. Maybe she's already ended things with him.

Jana headed in for the meeting. Ethan brought up the Action List of members they were trying to reactivate, and asked Mimi why Sister Garfield wouldn't come to church. "Well, she's divorced and says it's hard for her to look around and see all these happy married couples," Mimi explained.

"Did you tell her we're not all that happy?" Sherman Avery, the ward clerk, asked. Everyone laughed and it was just what Jana needed, to lighten her mood.

And there was Mimi, who had never married, yet was brimming with joy and optimism, her commitment unfazed by those around her. She didn't dodge Sacrament meeting on Mother's Day, or get mired in self-pity when the Primary kids sang and she had no children. She just jumped in and served. And if couples were going to the temple, Mimi would ask for a ride. She was actually the epitome of a mother in Zion, Jana decided.

"Maybe I'll do that," Mimi laughed. "Really, you can't imagine how many women don't come because they think we're so perfect. And they won't fit in."

How on earth have we built that image? Jana thought. This is the PR triumph of the century, the very definition of irony. I'm sitting here dreading missionary work and even hate stepping inside a rest home. My daughter is rebelling against the family rules, and we're just hoping and praying we don't drive her away. Even among Jana's siblings there were enough failed marriages, addictions, and apostasy to supply an entire ward Action List. They were far from a perfect family.

Years earlier, as Relief Society Secretary, Jana had been asked to compile a list of single sisters and it outnumbered the married ones. Divorced women, single moms, widows—there were actually very few families who fit the picture-perfect image. Yet the less-active sisters somehow overlooked the dozens of people turning to Christ with their challenges, and focused only upon the Von Trapp Family Singers who appeared to have it all.

"I think the walls would fall down if I came," one sister told her, years ago. Jana had been her visiting teacher and knew of her struggles with the Word of Wisdom. Yet, despite assuring her that church was exactly where she needed to go to find help and comfort, this sister was convinced that she had to be perfect first.

Jana had wanted to say, "That is ludicrous," but she sensed the woman was looking for excuses, not logic. And even with plenty of each to choose from, that sister chose reasons not to come, instead of reasons why she should.

Jana wished she could climb into the head of each of these hesitant members and convince them of Christ's love for every single person. They needed to stop comparing themselves unfavorably with others, and just embrace His gift and renew their covenants. This wasn't a country club with an exclusive membership.

"This isn't a country club with an exclusive membership," Ethan said.

Jana's eyes popped at his uttering the same line she was thinking.

"Everyone's a sinner, and this is our clubhouse," Ethan went on.

Again, the group chuckled.

"Not that we come here to revel in our sins," Ethan said, "but, well, you know what I mean. This is where we can repent and recommit ourselves to follow Christ. We need to love these people back into activity."

Jana thought about Merry Haines. Her reason wasn't a feeling of not fitting in—it was that she was buckling under family pressure. But the remedy still seemed to be love. Jana marveled at how many problems all had the same solution.

Ethan gave duties to each auxiliary, clear assignments about how to reach out to each person on the Action List. And when Merry's name came up, Jana volunteered to be the point person.

And then, in the hallway, she bumped into Stacey Sparks. "Jana, I have to talk to you." Stacey was one of Merry's visiting teachers who had opened her home to Merry's relatives when Aiden was born. Stacey was a pale, heavy-set woman. Her big brown eyes filled with fear.

"What is it?" Jana and Stacey went into an empty classroom and sat down.

"I'm worried that I must have done something to offend Merry. Or maybe my kids—they're such a handful—maybe they made Merry's family wonder what kind of crazy church she had joined—"

Jana shook her head. "Trust me, Stacey, you did not cause Merry to go inactive."

"But I must have done something—she won't return my calls."

"What is it with us women?" Jana asked. "We blame ourselves for everything!"

Stacey sighed. "We do."

"We need a blame-a-holics group or an intervention or something," Jana said, getting Stacey to laugh for a second. "Seriously. Who is nicer than you, Stacey?"

Stacey tried to wave away the compliment.

"I'll answer it for you," Jana said. "No one. You are it. How many people would open their home to complete strangers? Complete anti-Mormon strangers? If anything, you set the perfect example of Christian kindness."

Stacey began to smile. "I just worry. My kids are so high energy."

"Everybody's kids are high energy," Jana said. "Yours are hardly the worst. In fact, they're adorable and anyone visiting your home would be impressed by them."

"Then why won't she return my calls?"

"She's trying to honor her family's request and I'm sure she feels torn. Maybe she even feels guilty that she's pulled away," Jana said. "Believe me, you are not the cause of this."

Stacey released a giant sigh. "Okay. Thank you for making me feel better."

"Just keep reaching out," Jana said. "That's what I'm going to do. I'm still going to be her friend."

Stacey nodded. "That's all we can do. And pray for her."

"For her and for Sean," Jana said. She couldn't keep from wondering how devastated he must be feeling.

As they rose to leave, Jana suddenly wondered, just for an instant, if she might also have contributed to Merry's doubts. Then she mentally shook herself. Why was it always easier to give advice than to embrace it yourself? And why, when so many women were so fearful of offending someone, were there still so many people who were nevertheless offended? No matter how carefully you tiptoe, you cannot avoid certain toes. Just one more of life's many ironies.

It reminded her of a phone call she'd made to ask Jennifer Pope if she could help Sister Smith pack up to move, when she'd been the Compassionate Service Leader. Ethan had watched as Jana had said, "Hi Jennifer, it's Jana Watson. Did I catch you at a busy time? Oh, good. Hey, you know the Smiths are moving? Yes, I know—it's such a great opportunity for them . . . Yes, they are. We're going to miss them . . . I know! All the way to Montana . . . And that youngest one is adorable . . . Oh, absolutely—they'll have to enroll in new schools and find a new pediatrician . . . Exactly . . . Did you? Oh, that's a good idea. Well, anyway, some of us are meeting at her house tomorrow at ten to help her pack. It's so hard for her with the little ones around . . . Tell me about it . . . So can you come over and help? Oh, that would be so fantastic. Thank you so much . . . Yes, see you then. Okay, have a great day. Bye-bye!"

Ethan watched her hang up and then said, "Let me tell you how that conversation would have gone between men. 'Hi Bill, can you come over to the Smiths tomorrow at ten to help them move? Great. See you then.'"

Jana laughed. "I just can't be that cut and dry. It seems so, I don't know, curt."

"Maybe that's why Curt is a guy's name."

"It just seems so businesslike."

"Exactly," Ethan said. "Professional. Efficient. You women are so afraid of hurting each other's feelings or being bossy. You're always apologizing, always tip-toeing."

And he was right. "If I spoke that way to other women they'd think I was unfriendly," Jana said. "I'd feel I was too abrupt." Although she did recall some women making quick requests like that, and it hadn't bothered her in the least. Why couldn't all women simply stop *worrying?*

During Sacrament meeting Jana was sustained as a ward missionary, and found herself hoping the full-time missionaries hadn't been paying attention, and wouldn't be calling her to help for awhile. Then she closed her eyes and pushed that thought away. She needed to be not only willing and able, but enthusiastic. Yikes.

Ethan smiled at her from the stand, and she smiled back and gave him a thumbs up. Ethan's shoulders visibly relaxed. He couldn't help worrying about Jana, and how stressed she must feel, being thrown into missionary work. But he'd felt genuinely inspired, and knew she could do it.

As he glanced toward the back of the chapel, he suddenly noticed Sister Friedman, the woman who had been charging late fees at the library. Only now she was sitting at the end of a bench, with a big cinnamon-colored dog in the aisle. He squinted. The dog appeared to be wearing a service dog vest, but was pulling at the leash and sniffing everyone who walked by.

He asked his counselors if they knew anything about Sister Friedman's dog, but this was news to them as well.

Throughout the meeting the dog kept pulling at the leash, getting up and then sitting down again. Sister Friedman's hair was pulled into a gray bun, and she was wearing tortoise-rimmed sunglasses. What kind of dog was that, anyway? It sure was fluffier than most service dogs—was that a labradoodle? After the meeting Ethan headed down the aisle.

"Sister Friedman," he said, "Are you training dogs, now?"

"Oh no," she said. "This one is already trained. It's a guide dog for the blind."

And that's when Ethan realized why she was wearing sunglasses. He looked down at the vest, clearly homemade, with "Service Dog" written in black Sharpie.

"My eyes aren't so good anymore," she said. "So I need a guide dog for the blind."

Okay, you cannot bring your dog to church by dressing him up and pretending to be blind. This dog was not even close to an actual, well-behaved service dog, and now that everyone was milling about and moving on to Sunday School, the dog was yanking this way and that, trying to make a dozen new friends.

Naturally the Primary kids were completely distracted—although not as distracted as the dog himself—and were fawning over him and getting licked in the face.

Ethan sighed. "How about we talk for a minute in my office?"

"Oh, I don't know if Bucky can find it," Sister Friedman said. "Maybe another time."

She started to head out, but Ethan stayed with her, following her to the foyer and then out the door where they could talk privately. *You're sure getting around well for a woman who needs a guide dog.*

"Sister Friedman, I know Bucky isn't a real guide dog," he said.

"He has a vest."

And I could dress up like a surgeon, but you wouldn't want me taking out your tonsils. "I can see that," Ethan said. "And it's a really sharp-looking vest. How long have you had Bucky?"

"Oh, a little while."

"I'll bet you miss him when you're away."

Sister Friedman shrugged.

"You know what? I'd miss him, too. He's a cool dog." Ethan stroked Bucky's head. "But you can't bring him to church. We love you, Sister Friedman. And we want you here. Can you come without Bucky?"

"Oh, fine," she snapped, pulling off her sunglasses. "These things make the room too dark, anyway."

"I'm so glad you understand," Ethan said. "Do you need someone to help you take him home, and then drive you back?"

"Nah, I drove here myself," she said.

Ah. Like all blind people do.

Sister Friedman turned as she loaded Bucky back into her Chevy, and called out to Ethan. "But I'm still taking him to the movies!"

Ethan smiled. It didn't surprise him a bit.

AFTER CHURCH, SAVANNAH SEEMED TO BE HER OLD SELF, TEAS-ing with Josh in the car and acting as if her fury of the previous night was completely forgotten. Jana decided to let it go; maybe this was Savannah's way to put the ugly mess behind her and start fresh. That day's Sacrament talks, the Sunday School, and the Relief Society lessons were all about repentance and forgiveness. And maybe Savannah had had an epiphany.

As usual, Jana had felt the prickly recognition that the talks were exactly what she was supposed to hear as well, and couldn't wait to talk with her closest Sister, Rebecca, that afternoon.

Rebecca was six years older, but the two of them seemed to have the most in common. And Rebecca's maturity, like Savannah's, reached far beyond her actual age. She was dark-haired like their mother, with strands of silver already taking over. Plump and vivacious, Rebecca was the family reunion organizer, the fun aunt all the cousins wanted to visit, and the best cook, hands down. It was Rebecca to whom Jana often turned for advice, especially now that Ethan was often tied up with interviews. She didn't want to share her concerns about Savannah, though. If it was all resolved, why bring it up?

"So I'm thinking I need to apologize to Carlita Orton," Jana said, aware that she'd have to explain the whole ridiculous, sneering comment she'd made at the scene of the accident.

"Who's Carlita?" Rebecca asked.

Jana bit the bullet and explained. Soon Rebecca was laughing, then apologizing for it, then laughing again.

"So it was not my best missionary moment," Jana admitted.

"At least you didn't say, 'And I'm putting your name in the temple—take that!'"

Jana sighed. "Only because I didn't think of it."

"So now you're thinking of apologizing? Not for the collision, right?"

"No, not for hitting her, because she's the one who hit me. But for saying I was counting this as a visit."

"Well, you could go ahead and try," Rebecca laughed. "But didn't you say she threatened to sue you?"

"Yeah."

"And have you heard from her attorney?"

"Not yet."

"Has her insurance company agreed to pay for damages?"

"Yeah."

"Then she's probably not suing you. Hey, what have you got to lose?"

Jana sighed. "More face."

Rebecca laughed. "Let me know how it goes."

Jana called out to the kids that she had to see someone on her Visiting Teaching list, and that she'd be right back. A roast was slowly cooking in the oven with some vegetables, and except for tossing a salad, Sunday dinner was taken care of. She grabbed her keys and headed to Carlita's house.

It was a small, stucco house with curved walls and a couple of round windows, built back in the Art Deco era. Jana remembered the style from an architecture class she had taken in college.

Birds were clamoring in one of the maple trees across the street as she parked and walked up to Carlita's home. She knew Carlita could see her through the door's peep hole when she rang the bell, and figured Carlita would once again pretend not to be home.

But suddenly the door swung open. There was Carlita, glaring at her. "Yes?" Carlita was wearing a white tank top and cut-offs. Her black hair was pulled into a ponytail braid.

"Carlita, I came over to . . ." Jana started over. "I said a really stupid thing and I'd like to apologize for it."

Carlita's chin was still jutted out, but she was listening.

"I shouldn't have said I was counting that as a visit," Jana said. "That was . . . cheap and, and idiotic. That's not how to visit teach someone."

Carlita's nostrils flared as she inhaled. But she was still listening.

"When you said you were going to sue me, it was the only thing I could think of. Plus I really have been trying to visit you and I was mad that you would never let me in."

"So you took advantage of our car wreck."

Jana sighed. "So I took advantage of our car wreck."

"That is pretty desperate."

"I know. I'm sorry."

Carlita folded her arms. "Are you counting this as a visit, too?"

"No, no—I promise. I just wanted to apologize."

"Well, now you have," Carlita said, and closed the door.

Jana closed her eyes, then spun around and marched back to her rental car. The rental car she had because of Carlita. She definitely needed to work on her attitude.

"Hey," she said to Ethan that evening, serving him the warmed up roast dinner he missed with the family, "when you said that thing about church not being exclusive, I had just been thinking of those very same words."

Ethan smiled. "We do that all the time."

"Jinx," they both said, looping their pinkies.

"Oh, barf," Savannah said, coming into the kitchen at exactly that moment. "I can't believe you two just did that."

Jana laughed. "Dad and I say the same thing all the time."

"You're going to be one of those old couples who wear matching Hawaiian shirts, I just know it," Savannah said, putting a bag of popcorn into the microwave.

"What are you kids doing?" Ethan asked.

"Josh is writing the missionaries and I'm letting Maddie wear that prom dress we bought at D.I. that time."

"What?!" Ethan almost shouted. "She's eight years old!"

"I know, but she likes to play dress-ups with it. I told them I'd make popcorn if they'd write to the missionaries, and Maddie's already done."

Ethan was breaking out in a sweat. The last thing he needed was for another daughter to grow up and start acting like a woman. Just as he opened his mouth to demand that Savannah let Maddie be a little girl and stop dressing her like a teenager, Maddie came waltzing into the kitchen.

"Do I look like Fauna?" Maddie asked. She had wrapped a cone of cardboard with a green scarf and tied it under her chin. Now she was waving a pencil like a wand, and waving it over everything in the kitchen, as if spreading magic fairy dust. "And you," she said to the toaster, "can become a cat. And you," addressing the bread box, "can become a pet dog!"

Ethan released a sigh of relief. The microwave beeped and Savannah disappeared into the family room with the popcorn and Maddie in her green fairy gown.

"You thought she was going to be all glammed up with makeup and high heels, didn't you?" Jana said.

Ethan nodded. "I almost lost it."

"I know." Jana rubbed his shoulders. "One day she really will grow up, Ethan. And you're going to have to accept it."

"But not yet."

Jana smiled. "No, not yet." She wondered if all fathers had this hard of a time watching their little girls grow up and decided her own dad had probably felt the same way.

Ethan swallowed some potatoes. "This is really good." He took another bite, then a gulp of milk. "So," he whispered, "did you two talk any more about Dylan?"

Jana shook her head. "Seems to have blown over completely. Let's hope."

Ethan nodded. "Maybe she prayed about it. Or heard something in Young Women's."

Jana had wondered the same thing. But the turnaround was awfully sudden. Something about this seemed far too easy.

Chapter 17

On Monday Jana clicked her cell phone's vibrate button on and off. On meant the elders could reach her. Off meant she could hide. *Oh, grow up and do this.* She clicked it one last time, to "on."

And it rang.

"Hi, Sister Waterson," came the cheery voice of Elder Jamison. "We were wondering if you could join us tomorrow at one o'clock, to teach a lady on Drake Avenue."

Jana sighed. "I'll be there," she said.

And she pulled up at one o'clock on the dot. Her fingers left damp little prints on her steering wheel as she parked in front of the house, but she focused on the words of her blessings, especially the one setting her apart and promising her miracles.

"Wow," she had whispered to Ethan at the time. "Miracles."

He had smiled. "You know what I thought of? I thought of the miracle of forgiveness, and how *you* will be one of those miracles."

Jana nodded. "Believing in myself. Forgiving myself." She could use that miracle.

Drake Avenue was a shady, tree-lined street, reminding her why she loved Sacramento. It was the trees. When she had taken Savannah to the capitol on a field trip, the guide had explained that Sacramento had more trees per capita than any other city in the world, except Paris. And Paris only edged out because they had annexed an entire forest.

And it was a brilliant mid-October day with one of those blue skies that look so saturated with color you think you're wearing tinted sunglasses. She turned to the house. Jana also loved how Sacramento was filled with such a variety of architectural styles, and this one was Arts and Crafts style—a charming bungalow with wide white eaves and gray stone walls. With three rivers running through Sacramento, there was no shortage of rounded river rock.

The elders were just taking off their bike helmets as she turned off the car. Elder Jamison was tall and red-haired, one of those outgoing elders whose enthusiasm was never dampened. He was from a small farming town in Utah, and made Jana think of a crowing rooster, thrilled every day when the sun came up.

Elder Torrisi was the shorter, quieter one, but bore a penetrating testimony, filled with the spirit. His parents had emigrated from Italy and ran a small grocery store in New York. He was their third son to serve a mission and loved to bear his testimony on Fast Sundays.

Jana joined the elders on the porch as Elder Torrisi rang the bell. A woman about her own age answered the door and invited them in. Her name was Stephanie Wilcox, and she had a head of shiny copper-colored curls, a sweet smile, and wore black horn-rimmed glasses.

Jana felt immediate peace, and thought of Boyd K. Packer's imagery of having the faith and courage to walk to the edge of the light, and then a few steps into the darkness, before discovering that the way ahead is lighted for a footstep or two.

Stephanie invited them in, where they sat on comfy sofas amidst stacks of books. "I'm a librarian," she said. "It's also an addiction."

"What a wonderful addiction to have," Jana said, and could hardly wait to pick her brain about the books she liked to read.

Stephanie listened as the elders spoke with her about Christ's ministry and love for all people. Stephanie had been raised without a specific church, but with a general idea of Christianity, and seemed eager to soak in this new information.

"But tell me about the Book of Mormon," she said. "How does that tie in?"

Elder Torrisi's eyes glistened as he bore testimony of the restoration, and of Christ's visit to the Americas.

Stephanie was nodding, but she seemed impatient at the same time. "So it's a history, basically."

No, it's another witness of Christ. Jana looked to the elders to explain it.

"Yes," Elder Jamison said, "but it's so much more than that. If you only read it for the history information, you will miss the incredible gospel truths, and the power in it."

"It's another witness of Christ, and his visit to the Americas," Elder Torrisi added.

Stephanie leaned back, pressing against the sofa cushions. "But the story—the history—is the part that interests me," she said. She pushed her glasses up on her nose. "I just want to see what all the fuss is about, and what the book says."

What all the fuss is about is the restoration of Christ's actual church. It's the second-most exciting news since the resurrection. Jana could hardly contain herself, but didn't want to interrupt the elders, or worse, be argumentative.

"We invite you to read it," Elder Jamison said, handing her a copy.

"It was written for us, for our time," Elder Torrisi said. "The prophets who kept this record saw our time in a vision. They wrote for future generations."

Stephanie shrugged, then stood up, a clear signal that the meeting was over. "Okay, I'll read it. Thanks."

"Great—we'll check back with you," Elder Jamison said.

"Oh, I'll let you know if I have any questions," Stephanie said. "Don't call me; I'll call you."

Jana swallowed. *She actually said that?*

Jana rose, feeling a bit rushed out of the house. Stepping back into the sunlight she turned to the elders. "So did she just want a free copy of the book? Is she even interested in religion?"

"Well, maybe not yet," Elder Jamison said.

"But wait 'til she reads it," Elder Torrisi smiled. "It might surprise her that she's going to feel the spirit."

"I hope so," Jana said. Then she realized she hadn't contributed a single comment to the lesson. "Sorry I didn't have much to say."

"No, it's great that you were there," Elder Jamison said. "And she didn't give us a whole lot of time to talk."

True. But next time Jana hoped she'd be a little bolder. For now she was just grateful that she had felt a burning desire to teach, instead of a knee-jerk reaction to run from the room. One step at a time, she decided.

The next day Jana decided to swing by and say hello to Merry, maybe offer to watch little Aiden so she could get a nap. But Merry was on her crutches, just buckling Aiden into his car seat in the back of a friend's car, to take him to a checkup at the pediatrician's office. Merry didn't introduce her friend.

"Thanks for the meal last week," Merry said, talking quickly so she could hurry away. She put her crutches in, closed the back car door, then hobbled into the front seat. She rolled down the window. "But you don't need to keep checking on me," she said. "We're fine. And I'm really not interested in coming back to church."

Her friend's SUV bounced over the dip in the sidewalk as she backed into the street, then drove off. Jana stood in her driveway and wondered how many women could give her the bum's rush this week. Carlita did it on Sunday, then Stephanie on Monday, and now Merry on Tuesday.

That evening the elders came by to get an update on their dinner calendar, which Jana was now coordinating. She noticed a gap in the schedule, and wrote her own family down for the Sunday after this.

"So, Elders," she said, giving them each a slice of Meyer Lemon pie, "how often do you get rejections?"

They both laughed. "We don't count," Elder Torrisi said.

"I'm not sure we could count that high," Elder Jamison laughed.

"And it doesn't bother you?"

Both of them shrugged. "Not anymore," Elder Jamison said. "You get used to it."

"Besides, you're still doing the Lord's work," Elder Torrisi said. "Even if people say no, you succeed by extending the invitation."

Ah. She felt a wave of embarrassment at having had three rejections so far, when they probably had ten times that every week. She determined to redefine success, and wrote down what Elder Torrisi had said.

Over the next few days she paid visits to less active sisters, but most weren't home. The few she was able to catch seemed cordial, but unmotivated to try attending church again. Over and over she reminded herself that just reaching out was enough.

At home, she felt similarly brushed off by Savannah. All week her eldest daughter had been swamped with homework, and apparently legit homework, judging from the books and papers spread out over the dining table, and Savannah's near monopoly of the family computer. Jana hoped this meant she really had cooled her interest in Dylan.

By Friday night Savannah was ready for a break and planned a movie outing with some girls from the Student Council. It had been raining all day, but it didn't seem to dampen her enthusiasm for a night out. As she was getting ready Jana knocked on her bedroom door.

"I know you're whirling," Jana said, "but I just want to let you know how proud I am of the choices I see you making. You're a dedicated student, you're a wonderful sister to Josh and Maddie—" How could she diplomatically say, *And you've given up on Dylan?* "And I'm glad you're sticking to the family rules."

Savannah's exaggerated eye-rolling could become an Olympic event. "We're still friends," she said, her voice more than a little irritated. "He still says he's interested in the church."

Jana paused. "Well, that's good."

Savannah bugged her eyes out, this time as if to say, "Are you through? Is there more? Or can I get back to my life, now?"

Jana decided to leave it at that, and left the room.

That night she and Ethan watched Savannah hop into the carload of girls who came to pick her up, and Jana found herself muttering a line she would have thought only Ethan would say, "At least they're all girls."

Ethan squeezed her shoulders. "My sentiments exactly."

SATURDAY BROUGHT AN EVEN BIGGER DOWNPOUR, CAUSING THE painters to postpone their work on the El Dorado house for another week. Even worse, it was too stormy for the kids to do anything but get on each other's nerves and quarrel, leaving Jana ready to ground every one of them. Finally she decided to get them busy in the kitchen helping her make cake pops, with the idea of delivering them to various less-actives that night, if the weather broke.

But it didn't, and soon the kids were devouring the entire project, fighting over who got which ones, and making Jana wish she'd never dragged out all the ingredients and made this mess in the first place.

Ethan had been helping a member move all day, and when he finally dragged in, he took one look at Jana and the messy house, and realized that despite working outside in torrential rain, her day was probably worse.

"The kids were just at each other all day," she sighed as they climbed into bed that night. "They tore the house apart and practically tore each other apart as well."

"And so you rewarded them with cake pops?"

"Apparently."

Ethan laughed and pulled her close. "That's what I love about you. You think of clever consequences."

"Shut up," she sighed.

Ethan laughed again and kissed her. "At least this week is over," he said. "And tomorrow is a brand new day."

She turned to him and fluffed her pillow. "That's what I'm afraid of."

The next morning Maddie was wailing about a missing pink sweater, which she *had* to have or she could *not* sing in the Primary Program.

"It's probably in your hamper," Savannah said.

"And if it is, there isn't time to wash it," Jana said, "Wear that cute black-and-white one Aunt Rebecca sent you."

"I left that one at school," Maddie said. "Remember?"

Jana seemed to remember something about that. "Did you check the Lost and Found? That was a really expensive sweater."

"I did and it wasn't there," Maddie said. "Someone must have stolen it."

"Well, just choose something else."

Maddie stomped off to her room and soon reappeared in a red jacket. Josh, who had missed her earlier theatrics said, "Oh, that's a cute jacket, Maddie. Looks like Christmas," at which point Maddie stifled a scream and fled back to her room to change again.

"Let me guess," Jana smiled at Josh. "You're hoping all your future children will be boys."

Josh smiled. "That thought has crossed my mind."

Finally Maddie settled on a multi-color speckled sweater, but groused about it all the way to church.

As usual, the Primary Program was phenomenal, with the usual Sunbeam or two yelling out the songs with fervent gusto, and three or four kids forgetting their lines and having to be prompted, but looking adorable nonetheless.

"Maddie, you did a great job," Ethan said to her afterwards.

"And you looked lovely in your sweater," Jana added.

By now Maddie was quite confident both those statements were true, and skipped off to class with her friends.

"Please tell me I was not that hot and cold," Savannah muttered.

Jana just smiled. *We are not out of the woods on that one.*

AFTER CHURCH JANA DECIDED TO STOP BEMOANING HER WEEK of rejections and the drama in her family, and simply roll up her sleeves and try again to visit Carlita. If she slammed the door in her face again, so be it. At least she will have reached out.

She got dinner started, told the kids she'd be back shortly, and drove over to Carlita's house. Stepping on the porch, she reached for the doorbell, and then stopped. *Am I a glutton for punishment?* Then she figured she truly did have nothing to lose, so she rang the bell.

Carlita looked irritated as she opened the door, giving Jana a huge sigh and a weary glare.

"Hi, Carlita. I just wanted to see how you're doing."

"I'm doing fine." Carlita began to close the door again.

"Did I tell you I've always liked your house?" Jana asked.

Carlita frowned. "My house? My house looks like a ship."

"Exactly," Jana said. "It's Streamline Moderne. Do you know Art Deco?"

"Who?"

"It's the style of your house. It's called Art Deco."

Carlita was chewing her cheek, now. But at least she wasn't glaring any more.

"Back in the 30s, designers changed Art Deco. They got rid of the more ornamental parts, and used lots of horizontal lines and curves—kind of made it aerodynamic. It showed up in cars, clocks, radios, toasters. You've probably seen diners, train cars, and hotels that look like this," Jana went on. "It's kind of exciting to see a Streamline Moderne home—they're not that common."

"So why does it look like a ship?"

"Oh, they loved using nautical elements," Jana said. "Like a big ocean liner. Port holes, railings."

"You're telling me this is a thing."

"A really cool thing," Jana smiled.

Carlita stared at her for a few minutes. "My insurance company says I was at fault."

"Yeah." Jana shrugged. "Sorry."

"So I was really upset that day. My kid was in trouble at school and I was in a hurry to get over there."

Jana nodded. "Understandable."

"And then when we had that accident, it was, like, one more thing I didn't need."

"I've had days like that." *Wait. That was my day.*

Carlita sighed, "Anyway, when the cops came it was like the last straw."

"Yeah. I know."

Carlita turned away, then looked back at Jana. "So I guess I don't totally hate your guts."

Jana beamed. "Thank you."

Suddenly they both laughed, and Jana said, "Can I help in any way—I mean, are things okay with your son?"

Carlita rolled her eyes. "He got suspended. Lit the auditorium drapes on fire."

"Oh. Wow."

"I'm making him pay for it, though," Carlita said. "He goes back to school tomorrow—it's been two weeks—but he's still grounded. And he has to earn the money."

"It's not easy being a single mom," Jana said. "I know you work full time just to support yourself."

"Are you a single mom?"

"No, no I'm not," Jana admitted.

"Then how do you know how hard it is?"

"I don't. But I've heard."

Carlita stared at her. "Okay, you're honest, at least."

"Listen, Carlita, if I had just gotten word that my kid was in trouble at school for doing that, I don't know how I'd drive."

Jana heard a door open and then close inside the house, and Carlita stepped out onto the porch. "He doesn't have any good role models and I'm working six days a week."

"Okay, this sounds crazy," Jana said, "but do you have dinner plans?"

"MOM, THAT KID IS PRACTICALLY A JUVENILE DELINQUENT."
Savannah was helping her set two extra plates at the table.

"Precisely."

"What's a juvenile ink thing?" Maddie asked. She was folding napkins and tucking them under the forks.

Jana turned on some music and placed butter and rolls on the table. "It means he needs some good people in his life and he needs to know God loves him."

"He tried to burn the school down!" Savannah was almost shouting. Josh and Maddie whipped around.

"Is that true?" Josh said.

"Well, not everyone enjoys school—" Jana began.

"Are you kidding me?" Now Savannah was definitely shouting.

Jana stopped and gave her a look.

Savannah lowered her voice. "Oh my gosh, Mom. You guys don't want me around Dylan, but you're inviting Cody Orton over for dinner."

"It isn't that we don't want you *around* him—" Jana began.

"Oh, even I can tell that," Josh called from the kitchen, where he was dumping ice into glasses in the sink.

"If Dylan joins the church—" Jana began.

Now Savannah was sighing, rolling her eyes, and shaking her head as if a miniature tornado were raging inside there.

"So what's the deal with Cody Orton?" Josh asked, bringing glasses to the table.

"I visit teach his mother," Jana explained. "She's the one who accidentally hit me in the parking lot."

"WHAT?" All three kids in unison, all staring at her.

"You're having that lady over for dinner?" Maddie had her hands on her hips, now. "She smashed our van!"

"Wait—she hit our van, then her son tried to burn the school down? Does Dad know about this?" Josh asked.

"No; he's interviewing people at church." Jana glanced at the clock. "He should be home in a few minutes, just as the Ortons arrive. I tried to call his cell, but he didn't pick up."

And then, all at once Savannah was muttering, "Why would you ask these terrible people to come over?" at the same time Josh was saying, "I think you should have talked with Dad" at the same time that Maddie was saying, "What if they bring a bomb?" Then Savannah started saying "Oh my gosh" over and over, and soon Maddie was crying and the oven timer was buzzing.

"Okay, everyone settle down." Jana pulled the roast from the oven and set it on the stove top to rest. "Maddie, stop crying. These people are not going to pose any kind of danger here." Then she cast an accusing eye at the older two, for getting Maddie all upset. "They need our love and our help. They need to come back to church."

"Without any matches," Savannah muttered.

"And after some driving lessons," Josh added.

Jana laughed as she stirred the gravy. "Okay, very funny, you two. That's the last comment about the—the thing Cody did."

"The arson," Savannah corrected. "Just calling it what it is."

"Okay, fine," Jana said. "He's been punished, he's having to pay for it, and it's none of our business."

"Uh, excuse me," Savannah said, "I go to that school."

"Okay, it's a little bit our business, but we're not going to discuss it while they're here," Jana said. "Or the car crash. No comments. Promise me."

Reluctantly, the kids nodded.

"Cody doesn't have a good role model," Jana went on. "He needs to come to church and become part of things. Meet some good men. Good families." She dumped a bag of salad greens into a bowl. "So be nice."

And then the doorbell rang. Maddie, who usually jumped up to get the door actually took a step back, and glanced over at her mother.

Jana wiped her hands on a towel and went to the door. "Carlita, Cody—come in!"

Cody looked as if he'd been dragged to the dentist. His hands were in his pockets and his hair was in his eyes. But he and Carlita stepped in.

"Hey, Savannah," Cody mumbled.

"Hi Cody," Savannah said.

Jana suddenly realized that Cody was no more excited to have dinner with Savannah than she was with him. No doubt he saw her as a popular, social girl in an entirely different crowd. She imagined the conversation he'd had with his mother probably mirrored the one she'd just had with her own kids—and probably Carlita had reminded him that he was grounded, and had to do what she told him to.

Carlita had thrown a pale blue denim shirt over her tank top, and Cody was wearing a black T-shirt with a dirt bike logo on the front.

"Well!" Jana said, untying her apron. "I hope you're hungry. Dinner's ready, so please sit down." She made introductions, then motioned to two chairs for Carlita and Cody. "I'll toss the salad, and we'll have a blessing."

They scooted into place as the kids helped Jana bring food to the table. She hated to start without Ethan, but he told her not to hold meals for him, now that he couldn't predict his schedule. She asked Josh to say the blessing, and soon they were passing around slices of roast, potatoes, and vegetables.

"Kids, the Ortons live in that wonderful house I've pointed out to you," Jana said. "The Art Deco one."

"The one that looks like a boat?" Maddie said.

Cody chuckled. "That's the one."

"I wish our house looked like a boat," she said. "Or a tree house."

"Tell them about the poster you just made," Jana said. "You had trees on it, remember? For Vera?"

"Oh," Maddie said, winding up for a great tale, "I have a new grandma who looks exactly like the green fairy in Sleeping Beauty."

Jana glanced at Carlita and saw her smiling. Maddie said, "You know the Witch House? Well, guess what? It isn't witches at all—it's old people!"

Everyone laughed, and then Maddie, with Josh and Savannah filling in the blanks, told of the ward project to fix up the El Dorado House. Josh showed a scrape on his elbow from the yard cleanup day, and Cody actually looked interested.

And then Jana heard the garage door go up. Soon Ethan was walking in, startled to see two visitors at the table.

"Oh—these are the Ortons," Jana said, smiling broadly. "I tried to call you, but I think your phone was off."

Ethan just stared, trying not to look stunned. "Oh, right," he said, finally, pulling his cell phone from his pocket and turning it back on again. "Nice to meet you both." He shook their hands, then pulled out a chair and sat down. *The Ortons? The woman who crashed into our van? The kid who set that school fire I heard about? What is Jana doing?*

Jana could see her kids checking out Ethan's reaction, then glancing at one another.

"I hope everything's still hot," Jana said.

Ethan waved away her concern and filled his plate. *I hope someone explains what's going on.*

"I was visiting Carlita this afternoon," Jana said, "And I thought, why not have them over for dinner?"

Yes, why not? A woman who wants to sue us, a kid who wants to burn down his school. Yes, that's what I would do as well: Invite them over for dinner! Had his wife taken complete leave of her senses?

"Sorry about the damage to your car," Carlita said.

"Oh, well, the insurance companies have that all worked out," Ethan found himself saying. He wanted to ask Jana what on earth she was thinking. It felt as if fireworks were popping in his veins.

"Carlita works at The Bread Shoppe on Fremont," Jana said.

That's it? That's all we're going to say about the crash and the estimates and the body work and the rental and the expense? And to think, a few minutes ago, he'd been starving.

"And Cody's a junior at Easton," Savannah said. "We had American History together last year."

Ding ding ding ding ding. If this boy is interested in Savannah we will share a jail cell: Him for arson, me for assault. He looked over at Jana, but she was buttering a roll. *Was this a ploy—invite over a completely inactive LDS boy so Dylan will look like an acceptable alternative?* His head was darting back and forth from Savannah, who had positioned herself at one end of the table, and Cody, who was gulping down ice water at the other. He was trying to detect any interest, but no one would look him in the eye.

"So, Cody, what classes do you like most?" Jana asked.

This is an outrage—my wife is talking to him like he's a date Savannah has brought home, and we're getting to know him. And we already know plenty about that kid, believe you me.

Cody cleared his throat. "I guess mechanics," he said.

"Wait," Maddie said, one finger in the air. "You guess or you know?"

Now Cody laughed. "Mechanics."

"What kind?" Josh asked.

"Cars, mostly."

Ethan's eyes were drilling holes into the boy's cranium, but Cody just ate his dinner, oblivious to the scrutiny. The family was acting as if this were some kind of normal experience, and yammered on with Cody about car mechanics. He looked over at the woman who had totaled his own car. Okay, not totaled—Ethan took a deep breath and composed himself. *Give them a chance. Be forgiving. Look at Jana. This can't be easy for her. What an amazing woman. What on earth does she see in me? Why did she even marry me?*

Ethan caught himself again, and stabbed some of the lettuce in his salad. *But does Savannah actually like this kid? Is she one of those girls who likes the rebel, the kid on the edge?* He pictured her standing in a circus holding a balloon between her teeth as Cody snapped a whip to pop it, both of them wearing leopard-print leotards.

He looked over at Jana, who now had not only caught his eye, but was crossing hers, in an effort to send exclamation marks through the air and into his brain. Suddenly he realized he'd been cramming lettuce into his mouth until his cheeks were bulging like a hamster's. Quickly he swallowed what he could and wiped his mouth. Jana was shaking her head. He definitely needed to get a grip.

Furthermore, as their bishop, he needed to try to help them, not judge them. Carlita looked haggard, as if she were really struggling with life. She'd been on the list of people he'd been wanting to visit as a bishopric, but after the threatened lawsuit, he thought he'd wait a bit. Looking at her now, though, he realized this might be a chance to mend fences. Maybe that's what Jana had been trying to do. And here he was, stuffing his face like a lunatic.

He turned to her son. "So, Cody, we're thinking about a car mechanics night in Young Men's." Okay, in truth only he was thinking about it, and only just now. But it was a great idea and he was going to push for it. "Would that interest you?"

Cody glanced at Carlita, then shrugged. "Sure. I guess."

Maddie gasped and raised one finger again, as if catching him. "You guess—"

Cody smiled at her. "I would."

Maddie exhaled and smiled back.

"She's tough," he said.

"Oh, you have no idea," Savannah laughed. "She keeps us all in line."

Maddie beamed.

Soon carrot cake was served, milk was poured, and Josh was telling Cody about a Mustang his friend's dad owned.

"Cody, some men are painting the El Dorado House this Saturday," Jana said. "But the Saturday after that we're putting in the landscaping. We sure could use some help if you're available."

Cody saw his mother nod, and said, "Sure. I mean, I guess. I mean, I know." Then he smiled at Maddie.

Carlita laughed, now. "He's pretty good with yard work."

Jana had thought she saw a little twinkle in his eye, when she had mentioned the cleanup they'd done. The nursery was supplying plants, but the labor force would still have to come from the ward. And, whether he wanted to join in or was being forced to do it by his mom, she was glad he'd be mixing in with other men.

Ethan watched as Jana guided the conversation around Carlita's work, Cody's interest in cars, and their unusual home. As the dishes were cleared, he felt ashamed for being so sure she'd lost her mind. Ironically he had just been advising an elderly couple to serve a senior mission, and here he had been, the worst missionary in the entire ward.

"I'm sorry," he whispered in her ear as he helped load the dishwasher, once the Ortons had left.

She chuckled. "Honestly, Ethan. I wish I could crawl inside your brain, sometimes."

"No you don't."

"You're right. No, I don't." She hugged him and gave him a kiss.

"Dis-gus-ting," Savannah sang as she swept by, putting the leftover rolls away.

Maddie and Josh brought in dishes and glasses, plunking them down on the counter, then took off for the family room, where Josh started showing Maddie how to navigate Family Tree on the computer.

"I do wish I'd gotten your call about having company," Ethan said to Jana. "It was a bit of a shock, you have to admit."

Jana laughed as she rinsed off the roasting pan. "I'm sure it was."

Now Savannah came over to them again. "And let me guess. You thought I had invited Cody over."

Ethan stammered, his face flushing.

"I knew it," she said. "You looked like a minion with those big round eyeballs. I can only imagine what it will be like at my wedding. You'll be there on a stretcher, with an IV in your arm."

"Oh, he'll have had a stroke and died long before that," Jana said.

Savannah was drying the salad bowl. "I haven't even gone on a date yet!"

"Exactly," Jana said. "That's when he'll have the stroke and die."

"Ha ha ha," Ethan said. "You two are a laugh a minute."

Savannah whirled around, smiling. "But as long as we just had Cody over, could we have Dylan over sometime?"

"Whoa, wait a second," Ethan said. "Just because we had Cody over doesn't mean—"

"Why not?" Savannah shouted. "You two are completely unreasonable! Here you have Cody over—"

"Because I'm fellowshipping his mother," Jana said.

"You weren't honest with us about that relationship—" Ethan began.

Now Savannah spun around and threw her dish towel onto the counter. "You want honesty? I honestly think you guys are the strictest, meanest parents in the world!" She bolted from the room and they could hear her stomping up the stairs.

Jana turned to Ethan. "Well, I was going to say that the dinner went pretty well."

He sighed. "Yeah, right up until this very last minute."

Chapter 18

glaring, finally softening when she needed Jana's help with a history report. Jana decided to leave the topic of Dylan alone for now, and just try to re-establish some sense of normalcy in the house. By bedtime Savannah seemed at least cordial.

On Tuesday morning Jana planned to meet the missionaries at the El Dorado House. She hadn't forgotten her promise to Chester and Stanley, to bring some elders by to tell them why they were serving a mission. Besides, now that she was a ward missionary, why not include the El Dorado residents? Granted, it was the longest shot imaginable, but with all the time she was investing there, she wasn't making many other contacts.

"How does this outfit look?" she asked Ethan as he came into the kitchen, tying his tie. She stood in his path.

He stopped to consider her question. "Fine," he said. Fine was always the right answer.

"No it doesn't," she said. "Something's wrong with it." Jana looked down at her legs and feet. She was wearing a navy striped top, white jeans, a short navy jacket and ballet slipper-style shoes.

"It reminds me of something, but I can't think what," Jana said.

Savannah came waltzing into the room on her way to school. Seminary had been cancelled that morning. "You look like a mime," she said.

Jana gasped. "I do! That's it! Oh my gosh. I look like Marcel Marceau."

"Who no one has ever heard of," Savannah said, grabbing a piece of toast and heading out.

Jana turned to Ethan. "Do I look like a mime?"

Ethan clapped his hands to his cheeks and mimed, "No."

Jana's eyes narrowed into slits and she was about to ask him why he never told her the truth about her appearance, when Maddie came flying into the kitchen on the Drama Express. "I can't find my tan sweater—do you know where it is?"

Jana shook her head.

"This means I'm going to have to wear the black one!"

Jana just looked at her.

"And the black one doesn't go!" Maddie wheeled around and left again.

"And this is why men learn not to get involved in fashion matters," Ethan said, scooping up some papers and heading off to work.

Just as Jana heard the garage door close, Josh called to her from upstairs. "Mom, have you seen my science report? The one on Mars?"

Maybe it ran away with Maddie's sweater. "Look under your laundry basket," she called back.

"How come you know where Josh's report is, but not my sweater?" Maddie asked, coming around the corner, clearly bedraggled from crawling under her bed, searching.

"Like it's showing favoritism," Jana laughed. "Did you look in the car?"

"The car! I left it in the car!" She relaxed immediately. "Why are you dressed like that?"

"Well, I was about to change—"

"You can't change," Josh said, zipping his jacket as he whizzed by and grabbed a granola bar. "I have to set up for the science fair early, remember?"

Jana sighed and grabbed her keys. "Let's go."

"Why didn't you kids think of all these things earlier?" she asked as they pulled out onto the street.

"I was half asleep!" Maddie said, perfectly describing herself during scripture study that morning.

"I did tell you," Josh said, and Jana realized she, herself, must also have been half asleep. That might even explain the outfit she was now stuck wearing to the El Dorado House.

After dropping off Josh and Maddie, she headed over to meet the missionaries. Climbing the steps she noticed someone had hung a fall wreath on the door, and stacked some cheery orange pumpkins on the porch. With its black paint, now it looked even more like a

Halloween-themed mansion, the sort of place that would host a spook alley in a couple of weeks. Jana couldn't wait for the painters to brighten it up.

Helen looked up from her desk and smiled. "We had quite the parade last night."

"Parade?"

"Well, three families from your church came by for that Monday night thing."

Jana smiled. "They did?"

"It seems they want to adopt some of our residents as grandparents. It turned into quite a party."

"Oh, I hope it's okay."

"I think everyone got quite a kick out of it," Helen said. "They also brought those decorations on the porch, and some delicious pumpkin bars."

Jana wondered which members had stopped by. Will's family, for sure. "You keep such long hours, Helen. It seems you're always here."

"Well, I live upstairs," Helen said. "Simone does, as well. I handle the books and the nursing staff. Simone's the social director and oversees the kitchen."

Just then Dr. Rashid came breezing through the lobby. "Looking good," he said, one arm sweeping to indicate his approval of the refurbished interior. "Outside, too. Good to see this place getting fixed up."

Jana smiled as Dr. Rashid disappeared down the hallway. Then she turned back to Helen. "Do you have children, Helen?"

"Two boys, both married. No grandkids, though. Both live in Arizona. One of them is coming to visit today, in fact."

"Oh—you must be so excited."

Helen smiled. "Actually, I'm a bit nervous."

"Oh—why is that?"

Helen tried to keep from smiling as she reached into a drawer. "I've been reading this."

Jana gasped as Helen held up a Book of Mormon.

"I got it from Vera," she said. "I just thought I should see what you people were about, since you kind of took over the place."

"Oh—we didn't mean to—"

"No, I mean that in a good way," Helen said. "I just wanted to know why you folks were all so happy and really seemed to care, and, well, once I started reading, I—" Helen stopped short, her eyes brimming with tears. "Well, I love this book."

Now Jana felt her eyes stinging as well, and she rushed over to hug Helen. "Oh, that's the best news I could have heard."

Helen wiped away her tears. "Well, it won't be good news to my son. He's a minister."

Jana held her breath. "Oh, my."

"So we'll see what happens," she said. "He's in town for a pastors' convention."

Just then the elders breezed into the entryway, their bikes stashed under the stairs.

"Elders," Jana called, "Guess what?"

The young men stepped over to the desk, both breaking into broad smiles when they saw the book Helen was holding. Jana waited for Helen to tell them.

"I've been reading your Book of Mormon," she said. "And I think it's true."

"Wow!" Elder Jamison said. "Golden!"

"What does that mean?" Helen asked.

"It means you're golden," Elder Torrisi said. "It means you've been searching for the truth, and you recognize the restored gospel quickly. You're open to the whisperings of the Holy Ghost."

Helen's mouth curved slowly as she listened, finally smiling broadly as she recognized herself in this description.

"Helen, can we teach you about the Church of Jesus Christ of Latter-day Saints?" Elder Jamison asked.

"Well," she said. "I have to call the laundry service and take care of some other things here on the computer, but how about in half an hour?"

Jana's heart was pounding. "You're going to love it!" she said, realizing she sounded like someone recommending a good movie.

She and the elders headed down the hallway to the room shared by Chester and Stanley. They weren't there, but Elder Jamison poked his head in and saw the Primary kids' posters. "So which one's which?"

"Chester is the jockey on the horse," Jana said. "And Stanley used to teach speech and diction."

Elder Jamison said, "I like horses," at the exact moment that Elder Torrisi said, "I like speech."

They laughed, and Jana guided them into the rec room. She waved to Pearl, Frances, and Lorraine, who were watching an exercise video—yet not moving a muscle—and they happily waved back.

Then they saw Marvin, Stanley, Chester, and Howard playing poker at a card table. Jana made introductions, and said, "Well, I promised to answer your question, Chester."

"What question was that?" he asked. "I'll raise you three beans."

The men were playing with dried pinto beans, and Chester slid his beans into the center.

"You wanted to know why these boys would save up and pay to serve a mission, and leave their families and their schooling for two years."

"Oh, that's right." Chester smiled up at them.

"Well, in my case," Elder Jamison said, "I've wanted to serve a mission since I was a kid. So I did all kinds of work around the farm to earn money." He looked at all the men, then back at Chester. "I took care of the horses—"

Chester lit up. "You ever break any?"

"More than I can count," Elder Jamison said. "Quarter horses, though. Not thoroughbreds."

"Still counts," Chester nodded. "Still counts."

Elder Jamison smiled and continued. "I put half of all I earned into a missionary savings fund. And then I got a basketball scholarship, so that covered my first year of college, but then I gave that up to come out here and meet you."

Stanley nodded in approval. "A well-spoken young man."

Chester frowned. "But why? Why would you do that?" He turned to Elder Torrisi.

"Because it's true," Elder Torrisi said, softly. "Once you pray about this, once you know that Christ's original church is restored upon the earth, you just want to share that news with everyone you can."

The men stared at him. All holding their poker hands, all gathered around a small pile of beans.

"And it wasn't just so you could see the world?" Howard asked.

"Oh, no," Elder Torrisi said. "It's because we're serving the Lord—we go wherever we're sent."

"And you don't get paid?" Howard said.

"Not a penny." This was Elder Jamison.

Howard whistled and shook his head. "Hogwash, I say."

"Don't be rude, Howard." Rose was wheeling towards them, Harriet coming up behind her, with Misty on her lap.

"Well, he can believe what he wants," Howard said. "I'm just saying I wouldn't put my life on hold like that for two years unless I was gettin' paid. Big time."

"Oh, ignore him," Rose said, pulling the elders away. "Come and talk to us; we're much nicer." Today Rose was wearing a brilliant chartreuse caftan, the same orange lipstick and the same blue glasses.

"Thanks for stopping by," Chester said, as if trying to soften Howard's brashness.

"Afraid none of us are takers," Stanley said. "But we respect your choice."

"No problem," Elder Jamison said, as ebullient as if they had just signed up for the discussions. "It was great meeting all of you."

Jana had to admit she was disappointed; she had felt certain Chester might show more interest. But the elders weren't the least bit disheartened, and happily began chatting with Rose and Harriet, on the way to join up with Pearl, Frances, and Lorraine. Harriet was telling Elder Torrisi about Misty's latest hiding spot, under the sink.

Jana kept glancing around for Vera, wanting to thank her for sharing the Book of Mormon with Helen, but figured she was in her room.

Rose glanced over at Jana as she wheeled across the room. "So is this your Halloween costume? You're going as a mime?"

Jana sighed. Halloween was still a week and a half away—why would she be wearing her costume now? "Oh, maybe."

Just then Vera came wheeling in, beaming.

"Vera!" Jana called.

"You look wonderful," Vera called. "Marcel Marceau, right?"

I am driving straight home after this and throwing these clothes away.

Soon Vera had joined the other women gathered around the blaring TV, still watching the exercise show purely for entertainment. "I guess you spoke with Helen," Vera said.

Jana leaned down and raised her voice over the volume of the exercise show. "Yes—and she's reading the Book of Mormon, thanks to you."

"Oh, it was thanks to all of you," Vera insisted. "I just gave her the book when she asked me for more information."

Rose was leaning in to hear the conversation, but the TV was too loud. Suddenly she shouted, "Turn that off, Ladies. Just for a minute."

Frances held up the remote control and pressed a button. "What's the matter?"

"I want to hear this," Rose said. "What's this about Helen?"

"She's reading the Book of Mormon," Jana explained. "Vera gave her a copy."

"Well I want one!" Rose said. "I didn't know you were giving them out."

The Elders exchanged excited grins and dug through their backpacks for another copy.

"Oh, she just has to be first," Frances muttered, and snapped the TV back on again.

"Anyone else want one?" Elder Jamison shouted above the din.

The other women shook their heads as Rose looked up at Jana. "How far is she in the book?"

"I—I don't know," Jana said.

And with that, Rose zipped out of the rec room to ask Helen herself.

Oh, I hope she isn't just reading it to finish before Helen does. But at least she wants to read it.

Jana and the elders followed her out, and sure enough, Rose was quizzing Helen about how far she had read.

"I'm only in the Alma part," Helen said. "But I'm so anxious to get to 3rd Nephi. Vera says that's her favorite."

"What's 3rd Nephi?" Rose demanded.

"It's the chapter when Christ visits the people."

Rose was thumbing through her book to find it. "What's a Nephi?"

Elder Torrisi smiled at Elder Jamison. "Rose, Helen, could we teach both of you?"

The women looked at one another, then nodded, and they all stepped into the parlor. Helen sat primly in her brown blouse and tweed slacks, on a straight-backed chair. Jana couldn't help noticing the contrast between circumspect Helen and flambouyant Rose, and how marvelous it was that the gospel was a perfect fit for everyone.

And she felt ashamed for judging Helen so harshly when she first met her. The severe hairstyle, the sharp, unsmiling features. She should have been listening to the spirit, not fault- finding.

After a heartfelt prayer by Elder Torrisi, Elder Jamison launched into an excited explanation of the great apostasy, the reformation, and the restoration. As he spoke, Jana could see the light of understanding in Helen's eyes. "It all makes sense," she said. "Of course it would have to be restored."

But Rose was the one who surprised Jana most. Rose, never before at a loss for words, was completely quiet, her eyes riveted on the elders. Finally Elder Jamison noticed her silence and said, "What do you think about this, Rose?"

She took a deep breath, then whispered, "I have been searching for this my entire life." Huge tears rolled down her cheeks. "I knew it was gone. I looked for a religion that fit the Bible, and every time—" she paused and wiped her eyes. "Every time I found mistakes. They weren't doing things like Jesus said to. Or it was invented by some person, instead of by Jesus. I know they meant well. And they did a lot of good work. I know they tried to follow the Bible, but—"

"It was changed," Helen said. "Is that what you mean?"

Rose nodded, crying.

"I know exactly what you're saying. It's like everyone wants to follow the Lord, but—they're guessing. They're teaching good things, but they don't really have—" Helen searched for an explanation.

"They don't have Christ's authority," Elder Jamison said. "They don't have the Priesthood like we do."

Both women nodded. Jana's eyes filled with tears as she felt the Spirit, and she knew Helen and Rose were feeling the same witness.

And then, as if right on cue, Helen's son arrived.

Chapter 19

LIKE HELEN, HE WAS TALL, WITH A HEART-SHAPED FACE AND thick auburn hair, but he stood in the doorway as if a fierce wind had blown him in. And he was glaring at the missionaries. "What have we here?" he demanded to know.

Elder Jamison popped right up and held out his hand. "How do you do? I'm Elder Jamison, and this is Elder Torrisi."

Helen's son wouldn't shake his hand, just stood there.

"Oh, Derrick, you made it," Helen said, jumping up and trying to give him a hug. "How was your flight?"

"Nevermind my flight," Derrick said. "What's going on here?"

Jana bit her lip and prayed for Derrick to calm down and for Helen to stay strong.

"These are missionaries from the Mormon church," Helen began, her voice quavering. "And this is Jana, and this is Rose."

Derrick folded his arms. "I'm Pastor Sturvis," he said. "I'd like to know what you think you're doing."

"We represent the Church of Jesus Christ of Lat—" Elder Jamison started.

"Oh, I know exactly who you are," Derrick said. "And my mother is not interested in your religion. Mom, you don't have to sit here and listen to this."

Jana could see Helen swallowing, and trying to find the right words. "Well, actually, I—I've been reading the Book of Mormon."

"What on earth for? That's nothing but a phony document written by a phony prophet. We believe in the Bible. Don't get sucked into this, Mom."

"Well, they believe in the Bible, too," Helen said.

"Not the same way we do. They're not even Christians."

"Actually we are Christians," Elder Torrisi said. "We'd be happy to explain—"

Derrick held up his hand and laughed. "No thanks. Mom, you need to tell these boys to get on their way."

All this time Rose had been facing away from the doorway, but craning around to watch Helen's son. Suddenly she did a 180 in her zippy wheelchair and startled him. "Excuse me?" Now she slowly rolled her chair over to Derrick and waved her hand, gesturing to Jana and the elders. "These are our guests. And you have no business marching in here telling them to leave." She turned to Helen. "I'm sorry, but your son is out of line."

Derrick set his jaw. "Well, I'm not saying the rest of you can't listen, but my mother doesn't need to hear this nonsense."

Jana stood up. "I believe you owe me an apology. That's my faith you're disparaging and calling nonsense. I would never do the same to yours."

Derrick literally took a step back and raised his palms. "No disrespect intended. But my mother already has a faith, and I don't appreciate seeing her brought into a—a cult."

Both elders quickly jumped in to assure him it wasn't a cult, but he brushed them off. "Mom, this needs to stop right now."

Helen glanced back at Rose, who looked ready to leap from her chair, if she could have. Then she glanced at Jana who was also standing firm. "Derrick, I've been reading and I honestly want to know more about it. They have some answers that—"

"No they don't," Derrick said. "I can show you websites, Mom, and tons of books that disprove everything they're saying."

The elders were glancing at one another, unsure whether to get into a point-by-point debate with him.

"Well, I'm sorry, but I'm staying," Helen said.

Jana smiled. Good for Helen, standing up to her son.

And now he sneered. "This is ridiculous! You'd listen to these teenagers—and a mime—over your own son who's a minister?"

Jana's face burned red, but she held her tongue.

"I just know how I feel when I read the Book of Mormon," Helen said. "And I want you to respect that."

Now he rolled his eyes more dramatically than Maddie could ever duplicate. "Are you insane? This is total bunk!"

"That's the third time you've been rude about their religion," Rose said, gesturing to Jana and the elders. "I pay to live here. You don't. That makes this my home and I'll thank you to leave."

Derrick turned to his mother, sputtering at Rose's defiance. "Are you serious? You want to hear this?"

Helen was shaking, but took a deep breath and said, "I want to join this church."

Everyone's eyes popped at that, and Helen suddenly smiled, seeming to have surprised even herself. But, now that she had said it, she was bubbling over with confidence. Jana's eyes suddenly filled with tears and she clapped her hands.

"You can't!" Derrick shouted.

Helen planted herself firmly before him. "I can and I will. I've prayed about this and I know it's the truth, Derrick."

"I'm checking into a hotel and we'll talk about this later," he snapped, sweeping back out as quickly as he had blown in. ". . . lost her mind," he muttered as he slammed the front door.

Helen turned to Jana and the elders, beaming. "Well, I guess that's that."

Jana could feel the Spirit rushing in again, once Derrick left.

Rose seemed to feel it, too, and smiled. "Sorry I was so abrupt with your son, Helen."

"No, he was in the wrong," Helen said. "I raised him to be more polite than that, so I apologize for his behavior." Then she turned to the missionaries. "So when can I get baptized?"

The elders were elated and set a date with her. "But we still have more to teach you," Elder Torrisi said.

"I have to get back to work," Helen said, "but maybe this evening?"

The elders arranged to come back at seven, then closed with a prayer and headed out.

"And I want to be there, too," Rose said. "Helen what are you going to do about your son?"

Helen shrugged. "He's going to have to accept this."

"But he's going to put up a fight," Rose said.

Helen pursed her lips together, thinking. "I know what I feel. And I'm a grown woman, for goodness' sake! I can decide this for myself."

Jana caught her sleeve as she headed back to her desk and gave her a hug. "I'm so proud of you. And happy for you."

"Me, too," Helen said. "I can't wait to tell Vera."

"I'll go get her," Jana offered. And she and Rose headed down the hallway.

Simone had arranged a trivia game in the rec room, and Vera was just heading out of her bedroom to attend, when they caught up with her.

"Helen wants to see you," Rose said. Jana was proud of Rose for not stealing Helen's thunder with the big news.

Vera turned her wheelchair to the lobby, and motored the other way, with Jana and Rose following. As she arrived, Helen got up from her chair and came over to hug her. "Vera, I've been reading the Book of Mormon and I want to join your church."

Vera gasped, then covered her face with her tiny hands. "Oh, my. Oh, my." When she lowered her hands, her eyes were glistening. "This is the best news you could ever give me, Helen."

The two of them wiped tears away, then Helen told her about her son's visit and the scheduled meeting that evening.

"May I join you?" Vera asked.

"Of course," Helen said.

"That would actually be perfect," Jana said, "since I have to fix dinner and take my kids to Scouts and piano—" *And change out of this silly outfit.*

"We've got it, we've got it," Rose said, as if in charge of the resistance effort.

Jana could hardly pull herself away, but was eager to tell Ethan the news, and enlist his prayers for Helen's son to accept her choice. She didn't even stop to change clothes, and drove straight to his office, rather than call.

"Well, look at you," Ethan said, noticing her wide grin as she rounded the corner into his office. "You look like you just . . . let's see, like you just heard Dylan is moving to China."

"No, that's news that would make *you* smile," she laughed.

Ethan leaned back in his leather chair. "So what's up?"

"Helen wants to be baptized!"

Now he sprang forward, his hands flat on his desk. "Are you serious?"

Jana nodded, suddenly crying too hard to speak. Ethan rose from his chair and held her. "This is phenomenal."

Jana took in a deep breath, then exhaled. "Vera gave her a Book of Mormon and she felt the Spirit, reading it."

"So awesome."

"I know." Jana wiped her eyes. "But her son is a minister and flew in from Arizona today. He thinks we're a cult and is totally furious."

"Does she need my help? Should I go over there?"

Jana thought. "Might not hurt to offer. Especially if he should come back this afternoon." She sat in a chair opposite Ethan, as he pulled his phone from his pocket and dialed.

"Helen, hi. This is Bishop Waterson. Congratulations, I hear you're going to get baptized . . . yes, that's what Jana was just telling me . . . I see . . . I see. Do you want me to be there if he shows up again?"

Ethan looked over at Jana and shook his head as he listened to Helen. "Okay, well, you have my number and if you need me there, just call . . . . Oh, she is? Okay. Very good. . . . Yes. . . . Bye." Ethan shrugged and put his cell back into his pocket.

"What did she say?"

Ethan shrugged. "She says she can handle it and needs to do this herself. Good for her. And she says Rose is going to be right at her side, too. Is Rose looking into the church, or just looking for a fight?"

Jana laughed. "Maybe both. She's going to read the Book of Mormon. I think she wants to finish it before Helen does. And she's the one who asked Helen's son to leave."

Ethan whistled. "Well, it's going to be an exciting afternoon at the El Dorado House."

"And then the missionaries are coming back tonight to teach the next discussion," Jana said. "That tiny little Vera is some missionary."

Ethan smiled. "So are you."

"Me? I haven't done anything."

Ethan twirled back and forth in his chair. "I think the Primary kids have made a big difference. And seeing how our families are. You set all that up."

"After you decided to take on the entire place and give it a makeover."

"Come on," Ethan said, "Let me take you to lunch."

THEY PULLED UP TO THEIR FAVORITE MEXICAN RESTAURANT, with yellow ceramic pigs and giant red chilies in the foyer. Taped Mariachi music was blaring from the speakers and a waiter swept by with a huge bowl of guacamole and a basket of tortilla chips. Velvet sombreros lined one wall, and orange-striped serapes were draped over the railing. Jana decided she was wearing the least outlandish décor there.

"Two?" A perky hostess led them to a booth in the dining room and placed two maroon menus on the table. "Pedro will be right with you," she said. Jana glanced around the familiar, garish room and almost gasped. Merry and Sean were sitting in the corner booth a few yards away, with Aiden on the seat in a carrier.

"Merry, hi!" Jana said, rushing over. "Wow, so good to see you guys. How's your foot?"

Merry stuck it into the aisle. "Well, I got a walking cast this morning."

"I thought we'd celebrate," Sean said.

Ethan shook his hand, then leaned in to see Aiden, in the carrier. "That's one handsome boy."

"Oh, look at him," Jana said.

Merry stiffened, and glanced at Sean.

Jana could see their chance meeting wasn't a welcome one. "We'll let you two be alone—you three," she smiled, turning back with Ethan.

"Listen, I hope you'll tell Frances how grateful I am for her help," Merry said, calling her back.

Jana started to say, *oh, of course*, but then stopped. *Frances saved her life. This shouldn't be a message relayed second-hand.* "You know, I'm heading over there tomorrow morning. Maybe you could come and tell her in person—and bring Aiden, of course. They're dying to see him."

Merry glanced at Sean, who shrugged. "Up to you."

She thought for a moment, then said, "Well, I really do owe her a personal thank you."

"Great. Can I pick you up at, say, ten-thirty?"

Merry nodded. "Now that I'm in a walking cast I can get around better."

"Okay—see you then." Jana wanted to scoot away before she changed her mind, then high-fived Ethan the second they slid into the privacy of their own booth.

"Now, don't get your hopes up," Ethan said. "She's just doing the proper thing."

"I know, but it's a step in the right direction."

"I can't believe Helen is joining," Savannah said that night, as the kids all wolfed down smoothies and sandwiches before heading in different directions. "And that her son is a minister!"

"I would have thought she'd be the last one to—" Josh shook his head, at a loss for words.

"It just goes to show you can't always tell from first impressions," Jana said. And she felt her own guilt pulsing like a neon light as she said it.

"Do you think Rose will get baptized, too?" Maddie asked.

"You never know," Jana said. "But that was my impression today. She's going to start reading the Book of Mormon."

"I wonder if Helen's son came back." Savannah tapped her fingernails on the table.

Jana finished off her smoothie. "I'm sure I'll find out in the morning. You kids keep them all in your prayers, okay?"

The next day the sky was overcast and showers were predicted. Ethan decided to work from his home office, and Jana got ready to head over to the El Dorado House. She worried Merry would cancel and prayed the rain would hold off until the afternoon. At ten-thirty she knocked on the door and Merry opened it, Aiden's carrier in one arm.

"Where's your mini-van?" Merry asked, as she buckled Aiden into the rental car.

"Oh—had a fender bender," Jana said. *Should I tell her it was Carlita who hit me? That was the sister we kept trying to visit.* "It's in the shop. Should be back next Monday." Then she went for it. "Guess who it was that hit me?"

Merry looked over.

"Carlita Orton."

"What?" Merry was stunned. "Did you tell her who you were?"

Oh, yeah. Maybe I don't need to share every detail of that. "I did," Jana said. "Long story, but I ended up having her and her son over for dinner."

"You are kidding." Merry shook her head. "We tried for a year to see her."

Jana laughed. "Will miracles never cease, right?"

"That is truly amazing," Merry said.

Jana tried to fill the silence as they drove, by jabbering about her kids, so Merry wouldn't be able to reiterate her stance on never coming back to church. Soon she was pulling into the back parking area.

"Wow—this place looks totally different," Merry said.

"Oh, yeah," Jana said. "They took out all the underbrush and dug up the weeds. Painters are coming this Saturday, and then next week the new landscaping will go in. It's been quite a project."

"It has more windows than I thought," Merry said.

"I know—once they cut all the vines off, it was pretty amazing."

"Sean's planning to help with the paint," she sighed, sounding almost disappointed that he was still involved.

Jana was determined to keep it upbeat. "The Primary kids made posters of each resident," she said. "They're gorgeous and really brighten up the bedrooms."

Aiden was sucking on a pale green pacifier as Merry lifted him out of the car. "Well, I don't want to be long, if that's all right with you. I just want to thank Frances."

"No problem," Jana said.

As they climbed the steps, Merry said, "I wonder whose bikes those are."

Suddenly Jana glanced beneath the porch and realized the missionaries must be there. "Oh—those must be the elders' bikes."

Merry held the banister and stopped. "Jana, are you setting me up?"

"What? No—heavens, no, Merry. I had no idea they'd be here."

Merry looked at her skeptically. "Really?"

"I promise!" Jana felt irritated that Merry would accuse her of lying. "Two of the people are taking the discussions tonight, but I had no idea the elders would be here this morning."

"They're taking the discussions?" Merry looked almost as stunned as Derrick Sturvis had been. "Are y'all kidding me?"

"It's Helen and Rose," Jana said. "You remember—the receptionist? And that gregarious blonde lady?"

"The last two I would ever have imagined," Merry said. Then, shaking her head, went inside, with Jana following.

"Are you kidding me?" Merry gasped, when she saw the purple carpet and pink draperies. Then, seeing Helen look up, whispered, "I mean, you warned me, but . . ."

"Oh, I was just going to call and invite you over," Helen said to Jana. "The elders happened by and I thought you might like to join us."

Jana wanted to cast a "told you so" glance at Merry, but then thought better of it. She noticed the elders were sitting in the parlor, looking just about as incongruous as possible, surrounded by the gaudy furnishings. "Hey, Elders," she called.

They stood up and came over to shake hands with Jana and Merry. "Vera and Rose should be joining us, soon," Elder Jamison said. "We invited a few of the others to sit in as well, but—"

"Let's just say they weren't ready," Elder Torrisi smiled.

"That's putting it mildly," Rose hollered as she wheeled into the room. "But they can't dictate what Helen and I do. And if we invited these boys over, then they get to be here." Rose was wearing a sparkly silver pantsuit she must have had since the '80s.

"Howard and Lorraine were quite vocal about not wanting to join in," Vera whispered as she wheeled close to Jana. "But that's their choice. Besides, Carrie's doing their hair this morning."

Jana deliberately avoided looking at Merry, who was nodding her agreement when Vera said "their choice."

"Now let's see this little man!" Rose bellowed, her arms outstretched. "Can I hold him?"

Reluctantly, Merry took him from his carrier and handed him to Rose.

"Oh, he is his mama's boy through and through!" Rose shouted, almost startling Aiden. "I don't know what your husband looks like, but this boy is your spit and image!"

Merry smiled.

"What did you do to your leg?" Rose asked, and Merry began explaining how she broke her foot.

As Merry told Rose the story, Jana stepped aside to ask Helen how her afternoon meeting with Derrick went.

"Well," Helen said, "he's not happy with me. When I told him I had to choose for myself he stormed out again. But I called and told him I love him and would always want to see him. That's all I can do."

Jana hugged her. "But that had to be hard, seeing him so angry with you."

"It was," Helen said. "But I honestly feel the Lord comforting me, and giving me strength. If my son pulls away because I'm following the Lord, then he'll have to answer for that."

Jana squeezed her hand, and the two of them rejoined Rose and the elders.

Vera was holding Aiden, now. "What a beautiful baby," she was saying. "Oh, I'm so glad you brought him by."

"And you look like you haven't even had a baby!" Rose said to Merry. "I'm fatter than you are! Good grief, I look like a Hershey Kiss with legs." Jana stared at her broad hips in the silver outfit, and smiled. Rose had described herself perfectly.

"Is Frances available?" Merry asked, back to the business at hand. "I just came by to thank her."

"Oh, forget about Frances," Rose said, baby-talking Aiden. "It's your Auntie Rose you want to see, isn't it?"

Merry actually chuckled at Rose's antics.

"I'll get Frances," Jana said. But when she got to the rec room and told Frances that Merry was there with the baby, Marvin overheard it and shouted to the group, "Hey—Baby Aiden is here!" and suddenly the seniors were cheering and parading en masse down the hallway to the entryway.

"I'm so sorry," Jana mouthed to Merry as she got closer. "They all wanted to come." She turned to the crowd. "Maybe you can go in the sitting room to see the baby." It was a mirror duplicate of the parlor, just on the other side of the lobby, and Jana figured they could see Aiden there, without feeling roped into a missionary lesson.

Merry took Aiden back from Vera, and stepped across the hall. Rose, Vera, and Helen sat down with the elders in the parlor, and Jana sat beside Helen.

It was pure pandemonium in the sitting room, as voices whirled around Merry and Aiden. Pearl and Harriet were cooing over him as the men clamored to get closer.

"Now there's the little guy we've known since before he was born," Raymond was saying, as excited about this as if it were his very own grandson.

"He's our first actual baby," Stanley said, as if announcing an artifact discovery.

"And he's got a strong grip—lookit that," Howard was saying.

"I just wanted to say how grateful I am that you sent me to the hospital when you did," she could hear Merry saying to Frances, trying to get a word in edgewise. "I'm sure it's why we're both alive today."

"It was all in a day's work," Frances said. "As a nurse I'd seen that many times before."

"Well, thank you," Merry said. "My husband and I both thank you."

"I met him," Frances said. "He came by. Nice man. You have a lovely family."

Jana turned her attention back to the elders. "And that's part of Heavenly Father's plan," Elder Torrisi was saying to Rose and Helen, "for families to be together forever." Jana glanced across at Merry, and noticed her staring into the parlor, then quickly looking away.

"Look how wise he looks," Chester said. "Like he remembers us."

Elder Torrisi continued, across the hall. "And we were all together in the pre-mortal world before we were born. Then our Heavenly Father sent us to earth where we prepare to return to his presence . . ."

"Think of all that lies ahead for him," Frances was saying. "All the experiences he'll have."

"And because no one can live a perfect life without sin," Elder Jamison said, "Christ offered to be our Redeemer, to atone, and pay the full price for our sins."

In all the commotion, Misty had jumped down from Harriet's lap and was hiding under an end table. It gave Harriet the chance to hold

Aiden up in the air, and Jana could hear her saying to him, "What a precious thing! Don't you wonder what life is all about? Now you get to find out!"

". . . and God's purpose is to bring to pass the immortality and eternal life of man," Elder Torrisi was saying, as Vera, Rose, and Helen soaked it all in.

Jana stared back and forth from room to room, and realized one room was asking the questions, and the other room was providing the answers. Here was a new little soul, fresh from heaven, embarking upon the journey back home to his Father in Heaven. If only she could combine the rooms.

Soon Merry had had enough of Aiden being passed around like a kaleidoscope, and swept into the parlor. "We should go now," she said.

Jana excused herself just as the elders were asking Helen and Rose if they'd like to attend church the next Sunday. Both of them were nodding as she grabbed her jacket and headed out. The residents all waved from windows as she and Merry drove out onto the street.

The wind was whipping up, but the rain held off, and she was able to get Merry and Aiden home before the first crack of lightning lit up the sky. "Boy, they sure are crazy about Aiden," Jana said, trying to fill the silence. "I guess they feel part of his life."

"I guess so," Merry said. "Well, thanks for driving."

"My pleasure," Jana said. "That was sweet of you to thank Frances. I'm sure it meant the world to her."

Merry forced a stiff smile, then hurried into her house with Aiden just as fat droplets began hitting the windshield.

Chapter 20

JANA HAD TO SWING BY THE SUPERMARKET FOR MILK AND EGGS, then realized she needed at least a dozen other items, as often happened. By the time she got out to the parking lot the rain had grown into a major downpour. Heavy sheets came down in torrents, as if buckets of water were literally being poured from the sky.

She ran to her car under an umbrella, the grocery clerk helping her load the trunk as quickly as possible, then she took off.

Jana fiddled with the buttons on her loaner car, and finally found the windshield wipers. Immediately they began smacking back and forth, flinging the rain with the fury of a machete-weilding warrior. Jana pulled out onto the street.

Three houses from home, she reached up to touch the button where the garage door opener was put temporarily, so she could pull into a dry garage. Except the door did not go up. Instead, a sunroof Jana hadn't even noticed hummed open, allowing raindrops the size of almonds to pelt her head like a cartoon of a chipmunk firing nuts from his cheeks, machine gun-style. Bam-bam-bam-bam-bam. And the entire interior of the car was getting drenched along with her, like a surprise ice bucket challenge.

Of course she screamed. But it was raining like a monsoon so there was no one around to hear her. Wildly she pressed every button on the roof, but none of them would close the sunroof or open the garage door. Jana's hair and face were being pummeled and her clothes were wringing wet. Now she was in the driveway, screaming and soaked, with her sunroof wide open and the garage door clamped shut.

Her purse and some papers on the seat were drenched, and Jana had no idea how she'd ever dry the carpet or upholstery. She keep pressing buttons and finally the garage door opened. Incredibly SLOWLY. The second she knew the roof would clear, she zoomed in, the antennae flipping like a rubber band.

Ethan, having heard the door go up, came out into the garage to greet her and saw a dripping wet version of his wife, furiously stabbing at the roof to try to close the sunroof. It would not. Jana threw open the door and leaped from her unheated hot tub, red-faced, humiliated, and totally sopping. Her hair was plastered to her face in rivulets and she was panting.

Ethan's lips curled into a smile. Calmly he reached into the car, pressed a button, and the sun roof hummed closed.

"That was NOT working a minute ago," Jana growled as she stomped into the house. And like all good husbands, he knew better than to argue.

Ethan made her some hot chocolate while she toweled off and changed into dry clothes, then wrapped her in a blanket on the sofa.

"It had to rain one day before I get my own car back!" Jana said, still mad. She took a sip of the hot chocolate. "I can tell how much you want me to calm down by how many marshmallows you put in the cocoa." There were fourteen little marshmallows floating on the surface.

Ethan smiled and sat beside her.

"I hate rental cars where you don't know the buttons," Jana said, still fuming. "And slow workers at body shops who take forever to fix your car."

"And rainstorms," Ethan said.

Jana resisted smiling back at him. "And big spiders."

"And silent snakes." Ethan wrapped his arms around her. "And meerkats."

Jana leaned against his chest. "That's right."

"Tell you what," Ethan said. "Let's order Chinese tonight, and just make it Jana's Day Off."

Jana curled into the curve of his arm. "That sounds heavenly."

By the time school was out she was feeling much better, and even enjoyed telling the kids why they had to be picked up in their dad's car, instead of her soaking wet one.

That night after mutual, she asked Savannah to help her in the kitchen. "It was as if God were the choreographer," Jana found herself saying, as she told her about the missionary discussion juxtaposed with

Merry's visit in the opposite room. "Everything they asked, the missionaries answered. It was so cool."

Savannah's fury of two days ago seemed to have subsided, and she listened as the two of them unloaded the dishwasher.

"I just hope Merry overheard some of it," Jana continued, thinking aloud.

"Well," Savannah said, "She knows the truth in her heart." She put a stack of plates in the last cabinet and closed the door.

Jana felt so grateful, suddenly, for Savannah's turnaround. This looked like the perfect time to have a mother-daughter chat. "Hey, come with me," she said, leading Savannah to her bedroom.

"Can I pray with you?" Jana asked.

Savannah shrugged. "Okay."

They knelt down. Jana wondered if her daughter expected a missionary-oriented prayer about Merry. But instead she offered a prayer for the Spirit to simply be there as they talked. Rising, they sat on Savannah's bed, just like in the old days, before the specter of mistrust had cast a shadow on their relationship.

"Let's read your blessing together," Jana said.

Hesitantly, Savannah reached into a desk drawer and pulled it out. Jana fluffed pillows so they could both recline against the headboard and read it together. Slowly they took turns reading paragraphs, and then talking about what each one warned or promised.

"I like this one," Jana said, pointing to a line that described Savannah's blessing of discernment. "It's such a comfort, isn't it?"

At the part that described Savannah's future husband, Jana said, "That's the choice that's going to make all the difference in your happiness in life."

Savannah nodded.

Jana took a chance and turned to her. "Tell me what kind of man you see yourself marrying."

Savannah sighed. "I know you're doing this because of Dylan."

Jana smiled. "Yes, I am. I want you to think about your eternal goals, Savannah. I want you to be careful in your life. Careful about your choices."

"He does want to learn about the church."

Jana struggled not to say, "But then why sneak around? What kind of boy would join the church of a girl who's comfortable deceiving her parents?" Instead she just listened.

"I mean, it's not impossible," Savannah said. "People do get baptized, you know. I mean, there are some really great nonmembers out there, and some members who give the church a bad name."

Jana nodded.

"And Dylan is really smart, and has a lot of the personality traits I like. He's really considerate and helpful."

"He came to the yard cleanup," Jana said, looking for some way to agree with her.

Savannah was silent for a moment, and Jana let her think.

"If you guys would just get to know him," Savannah said, her eyes pooling with tears.

Well, you made that hard by lying about him. Even now, it's obvious he's far more than a friend. Jana took a breath, then pointed to specific direction in her daughter's blessing. "If you think he's the kind of guy who could take you to temple, and be a wonderful Priesthood holder and father to your children, then I'll give him a chance."

"Could he come to dinner on Saturday when the missionaries are here?"

Jana's heart seemed to flip over, but she found herself saying, "Okay. I think we could do that."

Savannah blinked back her tears and smiled. Then Jana gave her a hug and left. She knew Savannah was probably on the phone inviting him before she even reached her own bedroom door.

And there was Ethan, coming out. "Oh, there you are," he said.

She nodded him back into the bedroom. "I told Savannah she could invite Dylan to dinner on Saturday."

"What!"

Jana reached up to her husband's shoulders. "Hear me out."

Ethan took a huge gulp of air. *This family makes me hyperventilate.*

"We read her blessing together and had a talk. She wants us to get to know him, and as long as she understands the parameters, I think we can give the kid a chance."

Ethan's eyes were closed now, his mouth hanging open. "Why do I get the feeling that nothing good will come of this?"

"The good might be that Savannah realizes we're on her team," Jana said.

Ethan slumped down onto their bed. "But is she on ours?"

Jana sat beside him. "Well, she won't be if she sees us as totally unreasonable."

"I love it how kids can be completely unreasonable, but parents have to step it up."

JANA PICKED UP HER MINI-VAN THE NEXT DAY, LOOKING GOOD as new. Thankfully the rental car had dried without mildewing. But the rest of the week felt like an animated movie to Jana. Savannah was twirling about like a Disney princess whose dress had just been tied by perky woodland animals, while happy birds sang in the trees. She was patient with Josh and Maddie, and more helpful with chores than she had been in months.

I can't decide if this pleases me or terrifies me. On the one hand, it was a relief to have her cooperative daughter back. On the other hand, she was behaving like a swooning storybook maiden in love.

ON THURSDAY EVENING JOSH WAS HELPING ANOTHER BOY IN THE ward with an Eagle project, and Maddie was on the phone planning a science project with a classmate, so Jana started upstairs with a stack of Maddie's laundry as Savannah breezed by. "Oh—I'll take those up for you," she said. Jana shrugged and handed over the T-shirts.

Savannah bounded up the stairs and Jana felt old. When was the last time she bounded anywhere? She headed to the little room off the garage where they kept their food storage, to grab a new package of paper towels, and as she was coming back through the laundry room, she bumped into Savannah.

"Whoa—I didn't see you." Jana caught the serious look on Savannah's face, and put the towels on the dryer. "What's the matter?"

Savannah pulled Maddie's black-and-white sweater from under her shirt. "I found this stuffed in the back of Maddie's drawer."

"Oh—so it was there all the time!"

Now Savannah gave her mom a look. "Mom, she was lying. She hid it so she wouldn't have to wear it."

"Now, Savannah. You don't know that. Maybe she didn't realize it had gotten pushed to the back."

Savannah shook her head. "It was in plain view, Mom. I was looking for the drawer where she keeps her T-shirts, and there it was, behind them all."

Jana sighed. "She said she left it at school."

Savannah shrugged. "And checked Lost and Found."

Jana's face filled with disappointment, and she could almost swear her heart fell an inch. She took the sweater and marched into the kitchen where she waved it in front of Maddie.

Her daughter's face blanched and she said, "I'll have to call you back," and hung up.

"Your sister found this," Jana said.

Now Maddie spun around to face Savannah. "You were snooping? What were you doing in my dresser?"

"So you knew it was in your dresser," Savannah said.

Now Maddie burst into tears. "She was snooping, Mom!"

"Why didn't you just tell me the truth?" Jana said. "Why did you tell us you checked Lost and Found? And then said someone stole it?"

Maddie's face burned crimson, her voice chattering. "I—I hate that sweater! I never wanted to wear it."

"So why lie about that?" Savannah said. "How will Mom trust you, now?"

Maddie fired back, "Oh, like you've never told a lie?"

And there it was, an entire herd of elephants in the room. Jana didn't have to look at Savannah to see the wind leave her sails. Her daughter fell silent, and stared at the floor.

"I'll take it from here," Jana whispered, as Savannah shrunk from the room and went upstairs.

"I'm sorry," Maddie sobbed.

"Come here," Jana said, and Maddie threw herself into her mother's arms. "I just—I just didn't know what to do."

Jana held her, stroking her hair. "Maddie, you know a lie is never the right choice."

"I know. I'm so sorry." Maddie's shoulders were still heaving.

Jana led her to the sofa in the family room. "You know, Savannah's right—it's very hard to rebuild trust once you deceive someone."

Maddie nodded. "Like that story in the *Friend*."

Jana nodded. They had just read an old magazine issue about a lie that grew out of control. "First of all, Maddie, we all make mistakes." *And mine is probably making my kids feel they can't be open and honest with me. Why was Maddie too afraid to just tell me the truth?*

"Did you think I'd make you wear the sweater, even though you don't like it?"

Maddie nodded, sniffling.

"Well, I'm sorry if I made you feel I wouldn't listen. You don't have to wear the sweater, Maddie."

Maddie inhaled little staccato breaths, trying to compose herself.

"But you have to be honest, even when you're scared," Jana said. "I need to know you're telling the truth. Always. Do you understand?"

Maddie nodded. "I'm sorry, Mom."

Jana asked if they could pray together, and asked Maddie to offer the prayer. Maddie cried as she told her Father in Heaven what she had done, and asked for forgiveness. They hugged, then Jana led her over to the computer.

"Let me read you something," she said. She brought up the file of a talk by Jeffrey R. Holland, in which he shared the tale of "The Empty Pot," about a Chinese emperor who called all the young people in his kingdom together one day. He announced that he needed to choose a new emperor, and gave each of them a seed, with the counsel to come back in a year and show what they had grown with their seed.

Eagerly the children all planted their seeds in pots, including a young boy named Ping. But unlike the other children's seeds, Ping's seed would not grow. He kept watering it, but nothing happened. Finally the year passed, and one by one, the other children brought thriving plants, and even trees, to show the emperor.

Ping felt sick about his failure, but his mother encouraged him to be honest, and he took his empty pot to the emperor anyway. He placed it on the floor amidst all the beautiful plants and flowers. The emperor was watching, and had his guards bring Ping forward. Then he told the group that one year earlier he had given them all boiled seeds which could not grow. And only one boy had the integrity to bring back an empty pot. The others had cheated, substituting healthy seeds. Only Ping could be trusted to lead the kingdom, and Ping became the new emperor.

Maddie's eyes grew round, tears tumbling down her cheeks. "I want to be like Ping," she whispered.

"And you can be," Jana said. "You just have to decide that's who you are—an honest girl, even when it's hard to be honest."

Maddie nodded and hugged her mother. Jana held her, stroking her back, then turned and realized Savannah was there in the room, standing quietly behind them.

Jana kissed Maddie on the cheek, then sent her off to call her friend and get back to work on her science project.

Savannah came and sat down by her mother. She opened her mouth to speak, but her voice caught and she simply sat there, crying silently. She tucked wisps of brown hair behind one ear. Jana put her arms around her and finally whispered, "I know."

"I know you know," Savannah whispered back.

Jana looked at her daughter's tear-streaked face and smiled. "I know you know I know."

Now Savannah laughed, and wiped her eyes. "You knew I was talking with Dylan when I told you it was homework."

"Yeah. Pretty much."

"And that I've been hiding our relationship."

Jana nodded.

"Forgive me? Please?" Savannah hugged her. "When I showed you Maddie's sweater—" now she stopped again, her eyes filling to the brim. "You should have seen your face. I've never seen you look so hurt."

Jana just listened, and Savannah continued. "And I realized that's how I made you feel when I lied about Dylan."

Jana held her for a moment, the back she had rubbed so many times, the smell of her neck. Then Savannah pulled away. "And then I was so sharp with Maddie. But I had done even worse. Oh, Mom."

Jana caressed her daughter's shoulders and whispered, "We all make mistakes, Honey."

"I was scared that you and Dad would tell me I couldn't see him."

Jana looked into Savannah's eyes. "We kind of did."

"I know. I just—if he could take the missionary lessons and get baptized, then—"

"Well, that's what we'll find out on Saturday," Jana said. "If he's really interested."

"I'm going to apologize to Dad, too," Savannah said. "And to Maddie, as soon as she's off the phone."

"I have faith in you," Jana said. And she meant it. Savannah was headstrong and smart, used to getting her way. But she also had a testimony, a kind heart, and a basic understanding of why obedience and trust are so interwoven.

"I'll earn back your trust," Savannah said, wiping her cheeks and taking deep breaths.

"I have no doubt." Jana smiled, as Savannah went to find Maddie in the kitchen.

THAT NIGHT, AFTER PRAYERS, AS JANA WAS TUCKING MADDIE into bed, Maddie said, "Savannah told me she was sorry."

"I'm glad she did that."

"Me, too." Maddie turned on her side, bunching the pillow up under her head. "And I told her I forgive her."

Jana kissed Maddie's forehead. "You have a gift, Maddie. You're always quick to forgive. That's a wonderful quality."

Maddie smiled. "I have so many gifts."

Jana laughed. "Yes, you do, Sweetheart."

Ethan came home later than usual, having spent hours counseling troubled members. Jana was in bed, but she could hear the microwave beeping as he warmed up some leftover fettucine, so she slipped on her robe and joined him in the kitchen.

"You're still up?" He looked exhausted, his tie hanging crooked, his sleeves rolled up and wrinkled.

"I was waiting for you." Jana told him about Maddie and Savannah, and he squeezed her arm. "Thank you for handling that the way you did. I'm sorry I wasn't here."

"It's alright."

Ethan twirled the pasta on his fork. "No, I'm glad I wasn't here. I think I might have ruined it." He smiled. "They're so lucky to have you for a mom."

Jana laughed. "If you say so."

Ethan swallowed. "I do say so. And you're doing a great job with the folks at the El Dorado House, too."

"Oh, goodness. I'm not doing much—"

Ethan shook his head. "Not true. You, Jana Waterson, are an awesome missionary."

Now she half gasped, half coughed a laugh. "Hardly! And I think we've had enough fibbing in this house for one day."

Ethan leaned over and kissed her. "It's true. I knew you'd be the best thing that ever happened to them."

Jana shook her head and smiled. "You're biased."

"But it's still true." He finished his pasta, rinsed his dish, and the two of them headed upstairs.

In the morning, the phone rang with an entirely different opinion.

Chapter 21

JANA HAD JUST GOTTEN THE KIDS OFF TO SCHOOL WHEN HELen's son called. "Hello, Mrs. Waterson," he said, his polished voice a little louder than necessary. "This is Pastor Sturvis. We met earlier this week."

"Yes—you're Helen's son," Jana said. She had been wiping strawberry jam off the counters, but now she sat down.

"That's right. I'm calling because I want to officially terminate the discussions you're having with my mother. I hope you'll honor my request and discontinue any religious teaching at her workplace."

Jana stammered. "Wait- how- wait—Is this what Helen wants?"

"Absolutely," he said. "I want to thank you for taking an interest, but the interest is not returned. I hope we won't have to speak about this again, and there will be no Mormon literature dispensed there, either."

"Whoa, whoa," Jana managed to say. "This comes as quite a surprise, Pastor. I was under the impression that your mother wanted to be baptized—"

He managed a condescending chuckle. "She has already been baptized," he said. "And the matter is now closed."

Jana surprised herself by jumping in before he could hang up. "Wait—Is Helen there with you? May I please speak with her?"

"There's no need," he said. "It's all settled. She already has a faith, and doesn't need a new one."

"May I hear that from Helen?"

"You may not," he snapped. "You're hearing it from me and I'm hoping I won't have to take this to the authorities and file harassment charges or get a restraining order, Mrs. Waterson."

Jana fought the urge to argue with him, imagining Ernie, her hairdresser, saying that his phone call itself constituted harassment, but a small part of her wondered if Helen really had changed her mind, and had given her son permission to call. Then, just as she was going to ask how Derrick got her number, he hung up.

She called Ethan and relayed the entire conversation. "I'm going over there to hear it from Helen herself," Jana said.

"I think I'd better do that," Ethan said, "in case her son is there. I don't want you in danger, and we don't know the first thing about this guy."

Ethan asked his secretary to hold his calls and drove to the El Dorado House, where Helen looked up and smiled broadly from the reception desk. "Bishop Waterson!" she beamed.

Okay, this woman has no clue what her son just told my wife. "Good to see you, Helen," Ethan said. "Can we chat for a moment?"

"Of course!" Stanley and Marvin were in the parlor reading the newspaper, so she led Ethan into the sitting room where they sat in two wingback chairs.

He told her about Jana's phone call.

Helen burst into tears. "Oh, I am so sorry! I had no idea." Helen looked as if she might faint. "Oh, please forgive me. My son is outraged that I'm becoming a Mormon, and he must have gotten your number off the notes on my desk. I can't believe he would do this!"

Ethan held up a hand to calm her. "You don't need to apologize," he said. "I'm just relieved that you still want to get baptized."

"Oh, yes, of course I do," Helen said. "I've got to call Jana."

"Well, she'll be happy to hear that he wasn't speaking in your behalf," Ethan said. "But please don't worry. Everything is fine."

Then, just as Helen started to rise, Derrick Sturvis swept into the lobby. He was wearing a tan jacket with a maroon scarf, and brown dress pants. He glowered when he saw Ethan in the sitting room. "Mr. Waterson," he called out. "I just spoke with your wife and explained that your services will no longer be necessary here."

Stanley and Marvin looked up, lowering their newspapers.

Helen was trembling, but she stepped toward her son, trying to keep her voice down. "Derrick, this is my decision—"

"Mother, you simply don't know what you're getting into," Derrick said. "These people have hoodwinked you and it's coming to a stop."

Ethan rose, all six-feet-six inches of him, and he smiled at Derrick. He took a breath, reminded himself to avoid confrontation, and thought about the hostile people he'd had to calm down on his mission. "I understand your concern, Pastor, but—"

"Well *I* don't understand it," Stanley barked, wheeling in almost as fast as Rose could zip around in her speed-cart. "Sir, you are out of line!"

Now Derrick whirled around to face Stanley, who was seated in a wheelchair, but loomed larger than Ethan at the moment. "Excuse me?" Derrick sneered. "And you are?"

"I am a resident of this home," Stanley said. "And I will not tolerate a bully coming in here telling Helen what she can and cannot do."

"A bully?!" Derrick shouted. "I'll have you know this is my mother we're talking about, here—"

"All the more reason to respect her wishes," Stanley said. "This is the second time you've come in here trying to throw your weight around, and I won't tolerate it."

Ethan glanced over at Helen, whose eyes had been filled with fear, but now appeared filled with gratitude for Stanley's stern rebuke.

Veins were bulging in Derrick's neck as he whipped back and forth to address Stanley and then Ethan. "I'll tell you what won't be tolerated—this pushing of that religion down my mother's throat."

Helen tried to interrupt. "Derrick, nobody's pushing—"

"I told your wife and I'll tell you," Derrick said to Ethan, "I'm prepared to file harassment charges and a restraining order if you don't back off."

"You said that to Mrs. Waterson?" Stanley was building his volume, now. "How dare you threaten that dear woman! And what a preposterous idea—as if you could do either one. You have no chance of such charges sticking and you know it. These people are welcome in this establishment. It is you, Sir, who. Are. Not." Stanley punctuated those last three words like bullets, his years of elocution never more eloquent.

Derrick's nostrils flared and he spun around to leave. At the door he turned back and hissed, "This isn't the last you've heard from me." Then he stormed out.

Ethan followed him down the steps, reaching Derrick's car just as he had started the motor. Derrick rolled his window down.

"This isn't over," Derrick said.

"Pastor Sturvis," Ethan said. "I know your mother loves you and I hope this won't come between the two of you. I would always respect your parishioners' choices, and hope you'd respect mine, as well."

Derrick's eyes narrowed, but Ethan continued. "I know you have this impression of us, but it's based on misunderstanding. People have been wrong all through history, until they find out the truth."

"Oh, you're lecturing me on history, now?"

Ethan sighed. "I don't want us to be enemies, Pastor. When you've calmed down, if you have some curiosity about this, I invite you to pray about it. Pray to know if this could be true."

"Curiosity!" Derrick scoffed. "What if this were your mother?"

Ethan thought for a moment. "I'd be disappointed. But I wouldn't make threats. I would pray for her, and with her, and hope that the Holy Ghost would confirm to her what's right. And then I'd have to accept her choice."

"That's ridiculous."

Now Ethan leaned down, just inches from Derrick's face. "You may think that's ridiculous, but you asked what I would do if it were my mother. And that's what I'd do. And, Derrick, one last thing. Don't you ever speak to my wife that way again."

Derrick rolled his eyes, slammed the gear shift into drive, and took off, the gravel spraying behind his rental car as he sped away.

Ethan sighed. *God bless Stanley, for saying everything I was thinking.* Then he climbed back up the steps, quietly praying for Derrick's heart to be softened.

Several other residents had heard the commotion and were now gathered in the lobby as Helen, flushed with relief, retold the story. She quoted Stanley, who waved away her high praise, insisting he was just "glad the boy left before I had to do my Ju Jitsu on him."

The residents laughed, and Rose looked genuinely sorry to have missed a good fight.

"What did he say outside?" Helen asked.

Ethan relayed their conversation.

"Well, you handled it with tenderness, quite right," Stanley said. "You're the bishop, after all."

Marvin, who had been hanging back until now, finally spoke up. "I think we can see which one did that Jesus thing. You know, 'What Would Jesus Do.'"

Ethan felt his eyes stinging as they watered with gratitude that God had helped him take the high road with Derrick. Maybe his example would turn a few hearts. "Thank you, Marvin. And thank you, Stanley."

Helen was brimming with confidence, now. "Thank you all," she said.

Everyone milled back to their bedrooms and the recreation hall, as Ethan made sure Helen was okay. "If he comes back, you can call me," he said.

Helen winked. "Or I can call Stanley."

Ethan chuckled. "Yes, that might work a little better, actually." He tapped a goodbye knock twice on her desk, then headed back down the steps, deciding to stop by the house to tell Jana about everything in person before going back to work.

"Helen just called," she said, as she threw her arms around his neck. "I am so proud of how you handled that."

"You'd have been proud of Stanley, too."

"Both of you," she agreed. "Let's just hope Derrick goes home to Arizona and leaves us all alone, now."

Ethan smiled, and Jana smiled. But both of them knew that was probably not going to happen.

Chapter 22

ON SATURDAY MORNING ETHAN SAT IN HIS CAR WITH BOXES OF donuts, waiting for the painters to arrive. The Elders' Quorum had already filled three trucks with ladders, tarps, sprayers, and paint cans. Some of the men had come by the evening before, to tape off the windows and do some last minute sanding. At 8:05 the trucks and cars came rolling onto the property, and thirteen energetic men jumped out to get started.

Ethan shook their hands, then opened the boxes and smiled as they devoured his early morning treat in the welcome sunshine. His first counselor, Tad Lawrence, had taken on supervision of the quorum's plans, and had relayed the wishes of the owners, for a pale yellow shade of paint, trimmed with cream and gold.

"This is the white primer that's going to cover the black walls," Chad Henry was saying, as he hefted a large drum of paint from the back of his pick-up. A dozen other drums appeared to be loaded and ready as well. Chad was holding a clipboard and assigning various men to operate the sprayers, rollers, and brushes. "If we can get this thing covered by noon, we can do the top coat after lunch, and then get the trim done by evening."

Ethan slapped him on the back. "Looks like you have this all organized," he said. "I have to meet with some clients, but call me if you hit any snags. And I'll see you guys around five." Finally—that ominous black siding would be covered.

"You sure you don't want to leave it black for Halloween?" one man called, carrying the pumpkins and wreath down the stairs.

Ethan popped in to check on Herb, the man he had given a blessing, and found him sitting in a wheelchair at a table with Marvin, Howard, and Stanley. Jana would have said he looked fit as a fiddle and Savannah would have rolled her eyes.

Rose, Harriet, and Pearl were at a nearby table, playing dominoes. "So we're getting a face lift," Marvin said.

Ethan nodded. "Yep. Hopefully you won't know the place."

"Saw them sanding and prepping last night," Howard said. "I can't decide whether to go out there and supervise, or wait to be surprised. You know I've done my share of painting."

"I think you've done everything," Ethan smiled. "And they'd be happy to hear any advice you'd like to share."

"I'd like to see you on a ladder," Rose chided Howard, having over-heard their conversation.

"You think I can't climb ladders anymore? I could win a race to the roof," he shot back.

"Howard's quite the macho man," Ethan said, trying to side with Howard.

"More like nacho man," Rose said. "Nachos and a ballgame."

Howard got up and hobbled over to Rose. "I believe you were the one rooting for the 49ers last time," he said.

Rose smiled. "Yes, and I'll admit it. That's my favorite team. But you were the one eating all the nachos."

Howard slapped his flat stomach. "I can afford it. I still look like Indiana Jones."

"Indiana Jones!" Rose cackled. "You wish!"

"He does look a bit like Indiana Jones," Marvin contributed. "Same hair, similar features."

Rose studied Howard for a minute, smiled, then turned away. "Not one bit."

Satisfied with Rose's brief smile, Howard turned and hobbled back to his table. "I think she likes me," he whispered to Ethan before sitting down.

Ethan patted his shoulder. "No doubt, Howard."

"And in one more week the plants arrive," Stanley said, already antic-ipating the next step in the renovation.

"That's going to make a big difference," Ethan agreed. "I'm eager to see it." He turned to Herb. "You look like you're feeling better, Herb."

He shrugged, then slowly wheezed before coughing. "I am. Thanks."

"Well, we'll see you gentlemen later," Ethan said. He was never much for small talk, and still wondered how Jana managed to keep the conversation going for an hour or more. He headed to work imagining the final result, and the elated community members who could finally stop calling it the Witch House.

Jana, meanwhile, was picking up the soda and chips to go along with the sandwiches some of the other women were making for the workers' lunch. Her cart was piled high with 7-Ups and Doritos when she ran into Kristi Hargrove at the supermarket.

"Wow, aren't you the picture of healthy living?" Kristi teased her, glancing at the chips and sodas in Jana's cart. Kristi's short blonde hair fell to one side, and she was wearing an animal print T-shirt with a brown sweater, skinny jeans and brown ankle boots.

Jana smiled. "I've been waiting to be offended so I could go inactive, so thank you for that," she said.

"Seriously—why not just bags of sugar and bottles of oil?"

Jana laughed. "It's for the guys who are painting the El Dorado House. Mimi and some of the others are bringing sandwiches."

"The ones who refused to be seen with a cart that looks like this."

"Probably. And what have we here?" Jana looked into Kristi's cart. "Oh—Lucky Charms. Excellent choice. I believe that one's mentioned in the Word of Wisdom."

"I believe it is. In the small print."

"Yes. *Very* small print."

"The footnotes," Kristi laughed.

"Right. So why are you all dressed up?"

"I'm not all dressed up—I'm wearing jeans."

"Oh, please. You always look ready for a fashion layout," Jana said. "Look around. Who else is wearing anything remotely like this?"

Kristi glanced around and saw a chubby woman in an orange tank top and red stretch pants, facing the other way, examining onions in the produce department. Not far from her was a man in baggy pants and a wrinkled Raiders' T-shirt.

"Well, they were here a minute ago," Kristi said. She turned back to Jana. "Hey, how come you get to live in the fun ward?"

Jana raised her eyebrows.

"I mean, you guys have that cool project at the El Dorado House. Is it true it used to be a bordello?"

"Yep. It's the perfect metaphor for repentance. All refurbished, new and improved."

"And you know what a metaphor is."

Jana laughed. "Come and see it. You won't believe the difference. They're painting the exterior this afternoon."

"Cool—what color?"

"Pastel yellow, with cream and gold trim."

"I can't wait to see it," Kristi said. "Maybe I'll swing by later."

Jana took her arm. "But it's even better. The receptionist and one of the residents are investigating the church."

"Shut up!"

"Seriously. It's so exciting to see them finally finding the truth."

"At their age?"

"Hey, the gospel is true at any age."

"I want to do missionary work," Kristi whined. "I want to redo a big ol' house."

Jana laughed. "Come by and meet the folks."

Kristi laughed, and promised to check it out.

AT THE CHECKOUT COUNTER JANA WAS GREETED BY A PERKY young woman with long sandy hair and a spray of freckles across her cheeks. "How's your weekend going?" she asked. Jana noticed her tag. It said "Mandy."

"Oh, just fine, thank you." Jana placed the sodas on the conveyor belt.

"Got any big plans?" Mandy asked.

"Um . . . not really."

"Stocking up, then?" Mandy was already noticing the bags and bags of Doritos going by.

"It's, uh," Jana stumbled, trying to think. "It's for some painters. We're painting a big house."

"Oh, sounds like a lot of work," Mandy said. "And then what are you going to do tonight?"

Jana blinked. "I have no idea." *Why do I feel I owe this teenager a list of my plans for the day?*

Finally she paid, then saw Kristi again in the parking lot.

"Hey, what gives with supermarket checkers?" Jana asked. "Everywhere I go I feel like I'm being interrogated. 'What did you do last weekend? What are you doing this weekend? How about tonight?'"

Kristi laughed. "It's this new Voice of the Customer thing. Companies are telling the clerks to be more chatty, take an interest in the customers."

"Take an interest?" Jana said, unloaded sodas into her trunk. "Suddenly I have to account for every minute of my day. Like it's a courtroom cross examination."

"I know," Kristi said. "You feel like they're judging you by how you spend your time or something."

"Completely," Jana said. She piled the Dorito bags into the back seat. "And we both know she doesn't give a flying rip what I'm actually going to do, but if I point that out I look, I don't know—petulant—like I'm refusing the play the game. Why should I have to cram for an exam, just to go shopping?"

Kristi came over and put a sympathetic arm around Jana. "I think you feel guilty about buying all that junk food."

Jana laughed. "Well, I do! I never shop like this. But then to come under such scrutiny . . ."

"It's like those stress dreams," Kristi agreed. "Where you get to class and there's an exam on material you didn't even know about."

"Exactly," Jana agreed. "Welcome to my supermarket, bank, dry cleaners', and department store."

"So you need a ready response," Kristi said.

And then it hit her. Jana's eyes zinged open. "I've got it! I'm a Ward Missionary now, right? So I'll just tell her all the stuff I'm doing—and it's the truth, too. I can say I've been Visiting Teaching, or reading my scriptures, attending a baptism. And it's not being pushy because *they asked.*"

Kristi laughed. "There you go. Tell them you're a member of the Church of Jesus Christ of Latter-day Saints, and you're visiting a shut-in today. Then ask if they'd like to know more."

Jana slammed her trunk closed. "They'll either stop pummeling me with questions or they'll actually be curious—either way it's a win-win. Hey, I should have told her about our ward project at the El Dorado House!"

"You go, Girl."

"I am going," Jana said, and she turned on her heels to go back into the market. Mandy was ringing up a bald man buying boxes of wine bottles, but Jana plowed ahead. "Oh, I meant to tell you the Mormon church is painting the El Dorado House," she said.

Mandy and the bald customer both looked over at her with blank expressions.

"To answer your question," Jana stammered.

Mandy nodded, clearly confused, and Jana left. *Well, at least I have a new policy.*

On the way home she swung by David-the-burglar's house, but no one was home. Then at noon, Jana and four other women came by with lunch for the workers, and gasped as they saw the El Dorado House enveloped in white primer, a complete contrast to the formerly dark, forbidding walls.

"I can't believe how fast you did this," Jana said.

One of the brothers picked up a paint sprayer to show her the secret. "This is the only way to fly."

Jana had brought Maddie along for her art lesson with Vera, and Maddie couldn't stop whistling, a perfect imitation of her father. "It really looks like a fairy house, now," she said. "Or a temple."

Jana smiled; what a complete transformation.

After lunch, she and Maddie went inside to see Vera, Rose, and Helen. Helen was standing at the window nearest her desk, watching the painters.

"It's just amazing what everyone has done," Helen said. "This place looks completely different, now."

"And more to come," Jana said. "They're putting the final coat on right now."

"Did you come to see Vera?" Helen asked Maddie. "She's expecting you."

Maddie beamed, tickled that Vera had mentioned their plans. She and Jana headed down the hallway, but Vera wasn't in the middle room she shared with Harriet, so they stopped in the next one, where Rose was busy reading the Book of Mormon.

"Second Nephi was a bit hard," she said. "But I'm in Mosiah now. I wish I could have heard King Benjamin in person. Can you imagine what that would have been like?" Even though she was alone, she leaned in to whisper. "To tell you the truth, I wanted to finish before Helen, but I keep finding parts I like so much that I want to re-read them."

Jana felt a wave of relief sweep over her. This was what she had hoped, that Rose would read for her own edification, not to compete with Helen. "Wasn't he an incredible leader?" Jana said.

Rose nodded. "Bunch of them in here."

"Yes," Jana laughed. "A bunch. Definitely."

"My favorite is Moroni," Maddie said, then nodded and raised her eyebrows to heighten the suspense. "You'll see why."

"The boys have arranged for someone to pick us all up tomorrow for church," Rose said. By "the boys," she meant the missionaries.

"All?"

"Vera, Helen, and me," Rose said. "I asked Frances to come, since she's my roommate and we're kind of close. But she wants no part of religion. Says it goes against science."

"Hmm." *I wonder what President Eyring's dad, Henry Eyring, would have said about that.* "Maybe we can work on that," Jana said. "So have you had any more lessons?"

"Oh, yes," Rose said, holding up her arthritic fingers, laden with sparkly rings. "The boys taught me how to count it off on my hand." She started with her thumb, then went down each finger. "Faith in Jesus, Repentance, Baptism—" She stopped. "Oh, I can't remember the other two."

"The Gift of the Holy Ghost," Maddie blurted.

"That's right, and then Endure to the End," Rose crowed. "And we've talked about the commandments, tithing, and prophets, just yesterday."

Jana wanted to ask if Rose had agreed to be baptized, but decided to let Rose mention it when she was ready. "Well, we'll let you get back to your reading. Maddie has an art lesson with Vera in a few minutes."

Rose clapped her hands together. "Oh, won't that be wonderful!"

Maddie nodded and they headed to the rec room. Vera was already positioned by a window for maximum light, at a table she had covered in newsprint. Maddie put down her backpack and pulled out the supplies Vera had told her to bring—brushes, paper, markers and acrylic paints. Vera had already positioned paper plates for mixing, and paper towels and cups of water for rinsing the brushes.

Theresa, Shanika, and other nurses were cleaning up after lunch and wheeling various residents back to their rooms. But Pearl and Harriet wanted to see what Vera was teaching.

"Do you mind if we watch?" Harriet asked Maddie.

"Nope, not at all," Maddie said. If there was one thing you could count on, it was Maddie's love of an audience.

Jana pulled up a chair as well, and watched as Vera guided Maddie through basic shapes—balls, cylinders, cones, then showed her how to put them together to make objects. Right before her eyes, Maddie took a pencil, drew the components, and a unicorn took shape.

Even Maddie gasped. "It's like magic," she said. "Vera you *are* a magic fairy!"

Vera laughed, then encouraged Maddie to choose whatever colors she wanted, to paint her unicorn. Soon the creature was ablaze with a pink body, blue legs, and a turquoise mane. "The horn must be white," Maddie said.

"Beautiful!" Harriet and Pearl were clapping.

Maddie all but took a bow. "Oh, thank you so much, Vera!"

"And next time, maybe we can paint Harriet's cat, Misty," Vera said.

"Yes! I would love that," Maddie said, scooping up her supplies.

"But on paper," Harriet teased. "Not paint on my actual cat."

Maddie laughed. Jana helped roll up the newsprint and the two of them headed out again. Or tried to. Everyone seemed to want to see Maddie's artwork and stopped her to rave about her unicorn.

"I can't believe my unicorn looks so pretty," Maddie said as she and Jana finally made it to the foyer.

"Oh, let's see," Helen called, motioning them over. Maddie held up her painting. "How old are you, again?" Helen asked.

"Eight," Maddie said.

"This looks like a high school student made it," Helen said. "Maddie, you are so talented!"

"Well, Vera showed me what to do," Maddie said.

"But you're the one who did it," Jana added. "You can be proud of yourself."

"I think I'll hang it in my room," Maddie said. "Then I'll always remember this day. I'm going to call it the Painting Surprise."

Then she and Jana walked out the front door, completely unaware of the real painting surprise that awaited them.

Chapter 23

THEY DIDN'T SEE IT AT FIRST, AS THEY STEPPED ONTO THE PORCH and headed down the stairs. But then, as they turned toward the parking area and glanced back at the house, Jana nearly fainted.

"Oh, I love it!" Maddie shrieked.

Jana gulped enough air to fill a hot air balloon. She had absolutely no words.

"It's gold!" Maddie continued. "Sparkly gold!"

Ty Marks was jogging over, now, and steadied Jana who was staggering and stumbling across the dirt. "Uh, it's not what any of us expected," Ty said.

Jana could feel her head bouncing like a bobble head doll's. She was still speechless. The entire building seemed coated with gold glitter, and various men were on ladders, dabbing cream and yellow paint on the gingerbread trim and mouldings.

"I know what you're thinking," Ty said. "It was supposed to be pale yellow with gold trim, but someone messed up the order, and we ended up with a ton of gold paint and then yellow and cream for the trim."

"It's . . . it's . . . blinding," Jana finally managed to croak. You couldn't look at the place without squinting from the sunlight glinting off the metallic flecks in the paint. It was as if someone had pressed gold leaf onto the entire building.

"Do you need to sit down?" Ty asked.

Good idea, because I think my knees are buckling. Jana leaned against one of the trucks.

Ty followed her. "I know it's . . . it's—"

Jana couldn't help him find a word. She could only shake her head. And to think they were shocked by the pink and purple interior—that was nothing compared to the absolute glitziness and grandiosity before her. How could this possibly be worse?

And then, as if the cosmos chose to answer her question, a van pulled in from a local TV station. Sammy Fenton and a cameraman hopped out. Sammy was a short fellow with a red crew cut, black horn-rimmed glasses, and was the reporter who always did "you'll never believe this" stories about local people and events. Jana wanted to shrink to the size of a pixie and ride off on Maddie's unicorn.

"Uh oh," Ty said. "Don't worry. I've got this." Ty was a lobbyist at the capitol, after all, and was used to putting a good spin on things. Thanks goodness he was there. He dashed right over to Sammy and started the damage control.

"Hey, glad you heard about our exciting project," Ty began.

Sammy explained that he'd gotten permission from Helen to do a report, and asked Ty if he could interview him. Ty knew they'd film the building with or without his comments, so he consented.

"So tell us what's going on here," Sammy said, shoving a mike into Ty's face.

"Well, it's the biggest, most exciting transformation in town," Ty said. "This structure used to be painted black and was covered with thick vines—"

"Don't folks call this The Witch House?" Sammy interrupted.

"Well, they won't anymore," Ty said. "It's actually the El Dorado House, and it's been given a glamorous new look, inside and out. Now it's—" Jana could see him thinking a mile a minute. "The showpiece of the community."

"What made you decide to re-do this building?" Sammy asked.

"It needed it," Ty said. "This is a retirement facility. These people deserve to live in a beautiful home. We're members of the Church of Jesus Christ of Latter-day Saints and—well, Sammy, this is how we roll."

"How much did it cost taxpayers?"

Ty lit up. "Not a penny. Everything was donated. In fact, no one in our church is even paid—"

Sammy nodded, told the cameraman to cut, and then went looking for someone else to interview.

And there was Maddie. Jana gasped. Not Maddie! She rose to run over to her daughter, but Sammy got there first, and was already filming

Maddie twirling around as if basking in the reflected light of a thousand gold nuggets. And then, before she even realized what was happening, Sammy had turned towards Jana and had thrust a microphone into her face.

"And you're part of this?" he asked.

"Uh, yes," Jana stammered. *Oh, why couldn't Ethan be here to take over?*

"And how do you like the result?"

"Well, uh, of course it's not finished yet," she said, her mind whirling a mile a minute. "But it's—"

"It's dazzling," came a voice from the side. It was Kristi! The cameraman jerked the camera over to Jana's friend, and now Sammy had the mike in her face. "I'm not part of the project," she said. "But I live close by and I think it's the best thing to happen to our neighborhood. It's ingenious."

"And what do you think?" Sammy had turned his attention back to Maddie, who had twirled herself over to Jana's side, now.

"It's beautiful," Maddie said. "And those aren't witches who live in there, they're magical fairies!"

Sammy faced his cameraman. "Well, there you have it, Ashley and Steve—what else would you paint a house like that, except gold?"

He turned to Ty, Kristi, and Jana. "And we're out. Thanks a lot, folks. You'll be able to watch this on the six and the ten."

Jana stood with her mouth hanging open as Sammy's van screeched down the drive and off to the TV station.

Kristi came up and looped her arm through Jana's. "I forgot to tell him it's a metaphor for repentance," she said.

Jana smirked "I can't believe that just happened."

"Ty, you were spectacular," Kristi said.

"Oh, man, I was sweating bullets," Ty said.

Chad Henry and a few other men came over, all splattered with glittery gold.

"You look like Christmas trees!" Maddie exclaimed, as if this were good news.

Jana kept squinting at the house. "What are the owners going to say?"

"They're going to love it," Kristi said. "Let's face it, this place was a blight, Jana."

"Well, not really a blight," Jana said.

"Yes it was."

"Okay, a bit of a blight."

Kristi grinned. "And now it's like the Taj Mahal! I mean, this could become a tourist attraction!"

"You don't think we'll get sued?"

"No way," Ty said. "This is definitely a community improvement. And when the landscaping goes in next week—trust me, you'll love it."

Jana gulped.

"Keep an open mind," Ty said. "I know you were expecting a soft pastel, and you got—"

"A pirate's treasure chest," Jana said.

"Okay, but it's five hundred percent better than it was."

Jana smiled at him. "This is how you persuade lawmakers at the Capitol, isn't it?"

Ty laughed. "Now and again."

"I know what you're thinking," Chad said to her. "But after we painted for a while, we all kind of like it."

Yes, well, paint fumes will do that to you. "So how did it happen?"

"Who knows?" Ty said, brushing off the error. "Someone wrote down the wrong order, or filled the wrong order. The point is that it's done, and it actually looks pretty fantastic."

Maddie was running around like a new puppy, looking at the house from all different angles. "You don't love it, Mom?"

"She loves it," Kristi said. "She just doesn't know it, yet."

"But will the residents love it?" Jana asked.

Just then Helen, Frances, and Lorraine came out onto the porch, the latter two making their way down the stairs with their canes. Howard, Chester, and Marvin followed behind. As soon as they reached the ground, they all turned and looked back at the front of the house. And a film director couldn't have arranged a more unified reaction. Even though she was watching them from the back, Jana could see each startled one of them raising their hands in disbelief.

JANA AND THE OTHERS HURRIED OVER, AND BY THE TIME THEY got there, every one of the residents was clapping and cheering.

"Oh, I love it!" Helen was saying.

Can six people go blind all at the same time? "You do?" Jana asked.

"I'd jump up and down if I could," Lorraine said, staring in awe.

And the men were whooping and cheering as if this were the World Series and they had personally hit home runs.

"Thank goodness you changed it from pale yellow," Chester said. "That's such a wimpy color."

"But your jockey uniform was yellow," Frances said.

"My jockey *silks* were canary," Chester corrected. "A dark, bold yellow."

"Now this is class," Howard said.

Jana gulped.

The others were making their way down the wheelchair ramp by the back kitchen entrance, now, and craning their necks to look up at the glittering building.

Rose, of course, was first to be heard. "Have you ever! Have you ever!" she was shouting.

Ever seen anything so ghastly?

"Have you ever seen anything so magnificent?" Rose was shouting.

"Oh, someone take a picture of this," Harriet called out. "Rose, use your cell phone and let's all pose in front of it."

Every one of them loved it. *Okay, how can thirteen people agree on a hideous mistake, yet not agree on the perfection and glory of the gospel?*

"Don't you want to wait until the landscaping is in?" Chad asked.

"We can do it then, too," Vera said. "I can't wait for my kids to see this."

Ty came over to Jana and Kristi. "We still have the back side to do, and a lot of the trim," he said, wiping his hands on a rag. "But we'll be done by tonight, easy."

Chad and Ty walked off to get back to work painting, and Maddie ran over to exult with Vera. Kristi turned to Jana. "Honestly, it's going to be striking once it's landscaped. You'll see."

"Do you seriously like this?" Jana whispered. "I'm pretty sure you can see it from outer space."

Kristi laughed. "You always say I'm the fashionista, so you're going to have to trust me on this. Gold is in."

"Yeah, for earrings or a handbag or something."

"It's bold, like modern art. I've seen far worse in Architectural Digest. This is like, something Versace would do."

"Oh, help me. We have a designer rest home."

"And they love it! Isn't that the most important thing? Have you ever seen those people so happy?"

Jana looked over at the residents, their elation, their smiles, their picture-snapping. It looked as if they had never been outside before, and were suddenly marveling at sunlight, sky, and trees. "Okay," she said. "If they're happy, I'm happy."

Kristi began chatting with Maddie about her art lesson, so Jana decided to dial Ethan. "Are you sitting down?"

"I hate calls that begin this way."

"Well . . ."

"Is Helen's son leading a picket line around the El Dorado House?" Ethan asked. "I can just see a news reporter pulling up there."

"Funny you should mention the media," Jana said. "It's not a picket line—thank goodness Helen's son isn't here right now. But it's . . . well, you sound like you're in the car—are you heading over here?"

"Yes. Am I walking into some kind of disaster?" Ethan asked.

"Mmm, not a disaster *per se*," Jana said.

"Just tell me."

"The paint order got mixed up. Instead of pale yellow with gold trim, it's shiny gold with creamy yellow trim. And that Sammy Fenton guy from the news was here." She could hear Ethan sighing, and then saying he'd be there in five minutes.

Five minutes is not enough time to brace oneself. Jana watched the elated residents, still oohing and aahing over the paint as Ethan's car swung into the driveway and he slammed on the brakes.

Ethan jumped out and hurried over to her. "What on earth—" he was sputtering.

"Now, hold on," Jana said, feeling exactly like Ty Marks, spin doctoring the story for television. "The residents absolutely love it, and it's a great improvement in the community, and, and"—she was groping for another good thing to say—"and Kristi says it looks like Versace."

"What?"

"Nevermind. Just look how happy they are."

Ethan stared at the residents, then back at the dazzling gold finish. Maddie was hanging on one of his arms now, saying, "Don't you love it? Don't you love it?" until he agreed, just to get her to stop pulling him off balance. Maddie dashed off to join Vera and he turned to Jana. "So . . . this is the way it's going to look?"

"Well, unless you want to buy more paint and hire some workers."

"For thousands and thousands of dollars."

"Then, yes. This is the final coat."

Ethan whistled. Ty came over and shook his hand. "We're going with this," he said. "And it grows on you. The residents love it."

Ethan nodded. "Well, there's that."

Ty laughed. "Seriously. It's a landmark, now."

Ethan turned to the charming lobbyist and slapped his back. "You are really good at this." He took a deep breath and managed to stay upbeat about the result as he milled about, chatting with the workers and the overjoyed seniors.

Jana had to leave to pick Josh up from soccer, and they both arrived home at the same moment. Savannah had been baking a cake and had some chicken marinating in the fridge when they arrived.

"Wow—you making dinner?" Josh asked her.

"Well, Dylan's joining us for an early dinner with the elders," she said. "But Mom, can you fix that rice you make?"

Jana remembered that she and Ethan had consented to a family meal with this boy, and the elders would be joining them. "I'd be happy to."

"And then a green salad—that's enough, right? I mean, the rice has vegetables in it." Savannah was clearly trying to make the evening just right.

"Perfect," Jana said. "But first, we have some news." And then, knowing Maddie wanted to be the one to tell it, turned to her daughter. "Maddie?"

"The house is gold!" Maddie shouted. "Bright gold!"

Savannah and Josh wore matching expressions of disbelief, then wanted to go over and see it for themselves, so Ethan volunteered to drive them by. Maddie told the whole story about the paint mix-up as they headed over.

"Are you kidding?" Josh gasped as the car rounded the corner and the El Dorado House came into view.

"No way," Savannah whispered.

"Now, hold your horses," Jana said.

"Nobody has horses to hold anymore, Mom," Savannah sighed.

Jana laughed. "Okay, but just keep an open mind."

"It can't be *that* open," Josh mumbled.

"The residents love it," Jana said, and then turning to Savannah, "and Kristi says it looks like Versace."

"What is a ver-sotchy?" Ethan asked.

Savannah smiled at her dad. "It's a who," she said. "A designer."

"Okay, whatever." Ethan tried to pull over to the curb so the kids could study the house for a moment, but realized there was already a parade of cars there ahead of him, inching along as if this were an over-the-top Christmas light display.

"Looky-loos!" Josh shouted. "The whole town is here to check this out."

Maddie clapped her hands, thrilled.

"Uh-oh," Ethan said.

"No, look at them. They love it," Jana said. Sure enough, as they looked at the other drivers and passengers, they saw smiles of delight. People weren't pointing and laughing, or grimacing and shaking their heads—they honestly seemed to like the transformation.

Ethan turned the car around and headed home. "Maybe it's . . . a good thing."

"And I'm going to be on the news tonight," Maddie said.

"That's definitely a good thing," Savannah said, patting Maddie's hand.

Once home, Savannah forgot about the El Dorado House and began setting the table, arranging candlesticks and folding napkins. Josh and Maddie were in their bedrooms.

Jana chopped some peppers and mushrooms, and began stirring them with some coconut oil in a sauce pan. While Savannah was in the dining room, Ethan scooted a breakfast bar chair over by Jana.

"So it looks like gold is going to be the color," Jana said.

Ethan nodded. "That is exactly right."

"But everyone seems to like it."

"That is exactly right."

"And you're going to be nice to Dylan tonight . . ."

"That is exactly right."

Jana turned to him and laughed. "I love you."

"That is exactly right." Now he got up and hugged her. "If I can bite my tongue about that gold paint, I can be polite to Savannah's friend."

"This means so much to her," she whispered. "I mean, not just Dylan, but that you're being supportive of this."

Ethan shrugged. "I guess old dogs can learn new tricks now and then."

Jana laughed, and poured some chicken stock into the pot. "He'll be here in less than an hour."

Savannah came in just then, placed the chicken in a baking dish, covered it with salsa and cheese, then popped it into the oven. "Thanks, Mom and Dad. For letting Dylan come over."

Jana opened her mouth to say it was their pleasure just as Savannah's cell phone began playing steel drum music.

"Amy, hi," Savannah said, cradling the phone against her ear with her shoulder. "What? Are you kidding me? I'll call you back." Savannah dashed into the family room, suddenly clicking away on the computer keyboard.

Jana stared at her daughter. The color was completely drained from Savannah's face as she stared at the monitor in absolute shock and horror.

Chapter 24

"WHAT IS IT? WHAT'S WRONG?" JANA ASKED, COMING OVER.

Savannah tried to block the screen with her hands, hands that were now shaking. "No! No!" she wailed, then fumbled to exit the screen, too distraught to press the right keys. Ethan rushed over as well, and when Savannah realized her parents could see the screen, she burst into tears and collapsed over the keyboard, sobbing.

Jana stared at the monitor. There was a Facebook posting of Savannah and Dylan caught in a passionate kiss at the movie theatre where she had claimed she had gone with girlfriends only. Dylan had posted, "What movie? Teaching my babe how to kiss . . . and she's a fast learner! I guess dinner with her missionaries is a small price to pay."

Jana reached down and stroked Savannah's back. "Oh, Honey." She could hear Ethan's sharp intake of air and knew he was about to say something that would only exacerbate Savannah's anguish at the moment, so she took her arm from Savannah's back and squeezed Ethan's arm. He looked at her and she shook her head.

Savannah rose from the desk and fled upstairs, slamming her bedroom door. Ethan looked again at the screen, then turned to Jana. "I'm calling that kid."

"No you are not," Jana said. "You and I both need to calm down, and let Savannah handle this."

Ethan was sputtering now, and gesturing toward the screen. "Look at this! Look at this! That stuff goes on the internet and it stays forever!"

Jana's mouth felt dry, but she swallowed anyway. "I know. And Savannah knows. Trust me, Ethan. This thing with Dylan is over."

Ethan reached forward and turned off the computer. "What a disgusting jerk."

"Yep."

"Shall we go talk with her?"

Moments later they could hear Savannah's sobs through her bedroom door. Ethan knocked.

"I already know," she called.

Jana opened the door and saw Savannah on her bed, sobbing into her pillow. "You already know what?"

"That he's not coming to dinner. That I'm grounded. That you guys hate him and you hate me."

"Oh, Sweetheart," Ethan said, rushing to his daughter. "We don't hate you."

"But you were right about him." Savannah said.

Ethan sat on her bed and stroked her hair. "I didn't want to be right," he said. "I was really hoping he'd be a great guy."

"I'm sorry I didn't tell the truth about the movie. This whole stupid thing has been a big lie. Including Dylan saying he wanted to learn about the church."

Jana sat on the foot of the bed. "We're so sorry, Savannah."

"And now I'm totally humiliated. Everyone at school will see that picture and probably repost it. The good little Mormon girl caught making out."

Ethan handed Savannah some Keenex from her night stand, and she sat up, blowing her nose. Her cell phone was beeping with messages. "I just texted him that we're finished and dinner's off."

Ethan held her and let her cry.

"So I guess you're relieved, Dad."

He squeezed her tighter. "Never. I'll never be glad when my little girl is hurting."

Now she sobbed into his chest, and Jana rubbed her back. *Stupid kid, passing up a great girl like Savannah.*

"I can't believe all the stuff he said, just to make me think he was looking into the church. And now I have to face him at school. And his stupid friends."

"He's the one who should be embarrassed," Jana said. "Nobody will respect him for posting that."

"Or me, for being in the picture," Savannah whispered.

Jana sighed. "It was a kiss. It's not the end of the world."

Ethan held Savannah's shoulders. "Can I tell you something? He didn't deserve you."

Savannah chuckled through the tears. "You'd say that about any guy."

"Okay," Ethan admitted. "But it's especially true of Dylan." *In fact, I'd like to deck the jerk.*

Josh was coming down the hallway just then, and saw the gathering on Savannah's bed.

"Hey, what's up?"

Savannah took a deep breath. "Dylan's not coming for dinner," she said.

"You dumped him? Good—he seemed like a big phony, anyway." Josh leaned against the doorway.

Savannah smiled. "Guess I should have gotten your opinion earlier."

Josh puffed out his chest. "Well, I don't wanna brag . . ." and headed downstairs.

Savannah locked eyes with her mom and laughed through her tears. "Maybe Josh has good radar for this. I should have him screen all my future dates." Then she gasped. "Oh my gosh—Josh and Maddie are going to see that picture."

Ethan closed his eyes. *Once it's online, it's out there for the world to see.*

"I think you should show them, first," Jana said, "Before they see it at school. Tell them the truth."

"That I kissed an idiot."

"That you kissed an idiot," Jana repeated. "You're not the first girl to misjudge a situation, Honey."

Savannah laughed. "Boy, did I get conned by that jerk."

"There you go. Share the lesson you've learned."

Savannah took a giant breath, then released it. "I'm going to do that."

"Right now?" Jana asked, surprised.

"Right now. I want to get it over with," Savannah said. "Plus we have the missionaries coming."

"It's okay if you don't feel up to a dinner," Jana said. "Dad and I can even take them out for pizza—"

"No. I worked hard on that meal and I'm eating it," Savannah said, defiance in her eyes. She chuckled, and stood up. There was that trait again: Pluck.

Savannah went to her siblings' bedrooms to ask them to come downstairs, as Ethan and Jana headed the opposite way.

"That girl has an iron will," Ethan whispered as they got to the last stair.

Jana nodded. "That she does. I just hope she doesn't slam that kid into a wall at school on Monday."

Soon Savannah was pulling up the Facebook posting and showing it to her wide-eyed brother and sister. "I don't want you seeing this at school and being shocked," she said, wiping tears from her cheeks, but more angry than sad, now.

Josh visibly took a step back. "Wow."

"It's something jerks do," Savannah said. "And now we know Dylan is a jerk. And I'm embarrassed not to have realized it sooner."

Maddie kept staring from the screen to her sister, then back again. "You *kissed* him?"

"Yes, and I won't make that mistake again," Savannah said. "And when you're my age, you be careful who you kiss."

Maddie was nodding, thoroughly disgusted.

"Wow, look at all the comments pouring in," Josh said. Then, "Sorry."

Savannah scanned the list. "Some total losers piling on," she mumbled. "Oh, good—a few, at least, are calling him—well, calling him names he deserves. Good."

"This is how you find out who your friends are," Jana said.

Savannah kept reading, shaking her head. "Yep."

Soon the doorbell rang, and Elders Jamison and Torrisi stepped inside. They were momentarily disappointed that their investigator wouldn't be joining them, but Savannah assured them it was for the best. And soon they were enjoying Savannah's delicious dinner and cake as her cell phone vibrated every few seconds on the countertop.

"So it looks like we'll be baptizing Helen soon," Elder Jamison said. "She just needs her interview, and she's set to go. We've got two vans with wheelchair lifts, picking up Vera, Rose, and Helen for church tomorrow. The mission president arranged it."

"That's so incredible," Jana said. "That little Vera is some missionary."

"Well, I think this is a whole ward effort," Elder Torrisi said. "And there could be more to follow."

"What? Who?" Ethan asked.

"Well, Frances has been really against it until now," Elder Torrisi went on. "But I got some literature for her to read about LDS scientists, and she's starting to come around."

"You're kidding," Jana said. "She's been almost . . ."

"Hostile?" Elder Jamison said. "Yep. But she's smart, and that's always a good thing."

"Yes, it is," Ethan said.

"I told her this is the thinking man's religion, very logical, very sensible," Elder Torrisi said. "Now she just needs to get the spiritual witness for herself."

Jana offered the elders seconds, then said, "And that is critical. Anyone can just size it up logically. You want people to feel the spirit, and know their prayers have been answered."

"Yep. We're trying to get her to pray about it," Elder Jamison said.

"I can show her how," Maddie said.

"That might be a great idea," Elder Torrisi said. "And how about getting Sister Haines to talk with her? Isn't Merry Haines the one she saved?"

Jana sighed. "Well, that would have been perfect, but—" she glanced at Ethan.

"Sister Haines is not coming to church at present," Ethan said.

"Her family members have convinced her she joined for the wrong reasons," Jana said. "But I know she has a testimony in there. She just needs to remember it."

The elders looked stunned.

"I'm working on her," Jana smiled.

"Well, here's another surprise," Elder Jamison said. "You know the one named Pearl, the one who rooms with Lorraine?"

"She's the one with the poster of the glittery, pink cake," Maddie said.

Also the one with the exploding bra, Jana thought.

"That's right," Elder Jamison continued. "Well, Vera's home teacher has been visiting Pearl by mistake. Brother Lawrence, from the bishopric."

Ethan smiled. "What?"

"Brother Lawrence got the two of them confused, and now Pearl wants him to keep visiting."

Jana laughed. "So now he has two women to visit there."

The elders nodded. Elder Torrisi swallowed a bite of chicken. "And Pearl thinks he and his wife are fantastic, and they're going over there together, giving her gospel messages."

Ethan shook his head in amazement. "That's excellent. You just never know what can happen."

"Helen and Rose have given up coffee," Elder Torrisi went on. "They had noticed that Vera never drank it, and she basically told them all about the Word of Wisdom."

"That's hard to do," Jana said.

Elder Jamison leaned in. "But it's kind of funny—they've all had to modify their diets in their old age, so they don't think it's that big of a deal. It's just one more thing, y'know?" He turned to Jana. "We'll be asking you to sit in on some more lessons next week."

"Have you been able to meet with Stephanie again?" Jana asked.

"The librarian? Nope. She said she doesn't want any further contact." Elder Jamison took a bite of rice.

"It seems she was curious, but not sincerely seeking the truth," Elder Torrisi said. Then he shrugged. "That happens, sometimes."

Maybe so, but Jana felt the sting of personal rejection. She had felt the beginnings of a friendship. Or maybe it was just a hope of hers, something not shared by both parties. It made her think of Savannah's dreadful disappointment in Dylan, and she glanced over at her daughter. *I hope she can put this whole miserable Dylan thing behind her.*

Just then Savannah caught her mom's eye and quietly mouthed, "It's okay."

After the elders left, Maddie headed up to her room while Ethan and Josh did the dishes. Jana pulled Savannah aside. "You really okay?"

Savannah thought for a moment, then leaned back against the hallway wall. "I didn't want Dad to be right," she whispered.

Jana took Savannah's hands in hers. "He didn't want to be right, either." Then she held Savannah's shoulders. "He really is trying, you know."

"I know." Savannah glanced back to the kitchen where Ethan and Josh were talking, out of earshot. "I think Dylan is one of those charmers you're supposed to watch out for. I thought about all the things he told me . . . things he knew I wanted to hear." Her eyes watered again. "It was all just to set me up."

"I'm so sorry."

"It's okay," Savannah said, blinking back the tears. "I'm really sorry for how dishonest I was, Mom. I know I haven't earned your trust back, but I promise you nothing happened more than kissing."

Jana hugged her. "Oh, Sweetie, you don't know how hard I've been praying to hear that."

"Hey," Ethan said, coming out of the kitchen, "it's still early enough— you guys want to go to a movie? Josh was thinking of inviting Howard to that train mystery thing."

"Oh—I've been wanting to see that," Savannah said. "And that might be just what I need to get my mind off Dylan."

"But Sophie asked if I could sleep over and then come to church with her family tomorrow," Maddie said, coming down the stairs as if she had ESP.

"That could work perfectly," Ethan said. "We can drop you at Sophie's and then see you at church in the morning."

Jana smiled at Maddie. "Better pack your church clothes and tooth-brush." Maddie fled up the stairs as Josh called Howard.

"I'll set the timer to tape the news," Ethan went on, "and we can watch it when we get back."

Soon they were all standing on the El Dorado House lawn as Howard made his way down the stairs, Josh holding one arm. Howard was reminding the boy of all his experience working on trains, years ago. "I won't tell you how long it's been since I've gone out to a movie," Howard said.

"Is it longer than I've been alive?" Josh asked.

Howard winked. "Smart kid."

Josh laughed. "No—it's just that you always say everything's been longer than I've been alive."

Now Howard laughed as he climbed into the mini-van. "I do say that a lot, don't I? Well, it's true!" Howard craned his head around and saw only Savannah in the back seat. "Where's the little one?"

"Oh, Maddie's spending the night with a friend," Jana said.

Howard cleared his throat. "Stanley's heading out tonight, too. Will's in a play at his school, and his folks are picking Stanley up and taking him to see it. Nice family."

"They really are a great family," Jana said. Here was another adoptive grandpa relationship—Will and Stanley were like two peas in a pod. Even when Will gave talks in Primary, he sounded like he had the makings of a future great orator.

"So you'll have to tell us if this movie is accurate, Howard," Ethan said as they drove.

"Oh, I'll know," Howard said. "I could have been a consultant on this movie, from what I've heard."

Josh grinned. He loved Howard's bigger-than-life tales of adventure, and could hardly wait to hear more of them.

They settled into their movie seats with popcorn and drinks, Howard almost raving about the "highway robbery" prices of the refreshments. It had definitely been a long time since he'd been to the movies.

And it didn't disappoint. Grinding machinery, tracks, schedules—every time the story included the details of running a train, Howard gave an approving "Yep."

"Wow—that was really suspenseful," Jana said afterwards, as they headed down the hallway to the exit. "I'm exhausted."

"Nothing worse than a runaway train," Howard said, waving a hand for emphasis. "Nothing worse." Howard's cell phone buzzed and he looked at who was calling. "Okay, one thing worse. Rose calling on the phone."

They all laughed as Howard picked up, his booming voice seeming to fill the lobby. "You're what? Are you nuts?" and then "Of course I'm not excited. Why would I be excited about that?" Then he turned to the Watersons. "She hung up!"

"What was her big news?" Jana asked, not wanting to pry, but unable to contain her curiosity.

Howard sighed and turned to his friends. "No offense, but she says she's joining your church!"

"Wait—this is great," Ethan said. "You don't want her to get baptized?"

Howard sputtered for a few minutes as they headed across the parking lot. "It's just that . . . well . . . it's not that . . . I mean, I respect you folks and all, it's just that . . ." Howard struggled to explain and then finally blurted, "then she's gonna want some Mormon guy!"

"Oh, Howard," Jana said, realizing for the first time that he really did have feelings for Rose, and was worried that this would make a relationship impossible.

"You know," Ethan said, "You could be that Mormon guy if you wanted to."

Now Howard stopped in his tracks. "Me? Are you kidding? I'm not just rough around the edges, I'm rough right to the center!" They all started walking again. "That's not a church for a gambling, drinking guy like me who just wanders the world doing as he pleases—"

They all climbed into the car as Howard continued. "I mean, I'm a thrill seeker, you know? I take crazy chances." He raised his voice. "I'm a free spirit!"

Jana held her breath, hoping no one would point out the fact that Howard had been living in a retirement facility for years now, and hadn't done any of those things the entire time.

"But you—" Ethan started to say, and then realized it might bring Howard's world crashing down if he pointed out the difference between Howard's image of himself and the actual reality of who he was today. "But you could do the most adventurous thing ever, and look into the church," Ethan said.

"Might even impress the ladies," Savannah said, smiling from the back seat.

Howard waved it away. "Hogwash. Religion isn't for a reckless guy like me."

Jana smiled. "Howard, that's exactly who it's for."

"And I think Rose might find it charming," Ethan added. "Savannah's right."

"Well, I'm not about to join a church just to get on Rose's good side," Howard said. "That's dishonest, right there."

"But what if you really liked it?" Josh asked. "I mean, what if you looked into it and then found out you actually believed it?"

Howard was shaking his head no. "She'd always think I just did it to impress her. No thank you."

They drove a few blocks silently, then Jana said, "Well, I guess you and Rose will just have to be friends, then." She looked in the visor mirror to gauge Howard's reaction. He was scowling. "Or . . . you could just keep an open mind about it and see what happens."

By now Howard was thoroughly dismayed at his options, but tried to perk up as they arrived at the El Dorado House. Josh walked him up the steps. "I did enjoy the movie, thank you," Howard said.

"Yeah, me too," Josh said. "It was fun to go with a real train expert."

Howard shrugged and pulled open the door. "I hope I didn't offend you or your family."

"No, not at all," Josh said. "But you really would make a cool member of the church."

Howard threw his head back as if to laugh, but then just went inside.

JOSH DASHED OVER TO THE TV WHEN THEY GOT HOME, AND started fast-forwarding through the recorded news, to the report by Sammy Fenton.

"Go back, go back," Savannah said. "I want to hear how they introduced it."

Jana and Ethan joined their kids on the sofa as Josh pressed the play button. "Our own Sammy Fenton took a drive today, to the El Dorado House in Sacramento," one of the anchors said. She had short, silver-blond hair and wore a plum jacket over a white blouse and pearls. "What did you find, Sammy?"

Now Sammy was seated before a giant screen, with a freeze-frame photo of the El Dorado house on it, scaffolding and ladders dotted with workmen, and Ty Marks caught with his mouth open. "Well, it looks like folks won't be able to call this the Witch House anymore," Sammy said. "Take a look at the makeover local Mormons are giving it."

Suddenly the video came to life, Ty looking as polished as a news anchor himself, and Kristi looking like a movie star. Jana cringed as she saw herself stammer, but then Maddie finished it off with her trademark enthusiasm, and the report was over.

"Well, that was sure short," Savannah said.

Thanks heavens. Jana realized she'd been holding her breath.

"But got a nice plug in for the church," Ethan said. He turned to Jana. "You looked great."

"Well, I don't know about that, but Maddie's going to love it when she sees it," Jana said.

That night after the family prayer Savannah asked her father for a blessing. He promised her peace, comfort, and the strength to endure this embarrassing episode, which he promised her would eventually die down. He also assured Savannah that her parents loved her. When Jana went in to say goodnight one last time, Savannah was already asleep.

"I think it must be the exhaustion of such an emotional blow," Ethan said, putting toothpaste on his toothbrush.

"And the peace promised in her blessing," Jana said. "This is one of those times when natural consequences are a tough teacher. But she's not curling up and being the victim. She's taking charge of this thing."

"That's Savannah."

"Yes, it is."

THE NEXT MORNING VERA, ROSE, AND HELEN ALL ARRIVED FOR church and came into the chapel together. Rose was decked out in an orange silk evening gown, wearing every piece of jewelry she must own. Next to Vera's simple green dress and Helen's conservative brown suit, she drew immediate attention. Jana had saved them seats, and was relieved to see so many sisters rush up to greet them.

"Congratulations!" Jana said. "We heard you're going to join the church!"

Rose smiled. "Sure am," she said. Jana wanted to ask how things went with Howard after he got back from the movie, but decided to leave it alone.

Savannah was buzzing with her friends in the back of the chapel, undoubtedly about the Facebook posting. Apparently the other girls were in complete shock at Dylan's betrayal, judging from the way they clustered around Savannah, nodding at one another.

"Where's Merry?" Rose bellowed.

"Yes, we want to see Baby Aiden," Vera said.

"Oh, she's, uh . . . she's not here today," Jana said. *I am a terrible liar.*

Vera pulled on Jana's arm, then leaned in to whisper. "Has she stopped coming?"

Jana sighed.

"What happened?"

"It's her family. They were against her joining and now they've, well—"

Vera shook her head, then patted Jana's knee. "We'll see about that."

Jana smiled. If anyone could turn things around, it would be this tiny indomitable woman. "I hope you have an idea."

Vera winked. "Not yet. But I'll come up with one."

Maddie had gotten up and was now scooching between Jana and Vera, so she could sit by her magical fairy grandma. "I saw myself on the news last night," she said. "And I *love* being on TV!" This came as a surprise to exactly no one, and Jana had to smile.

Maddie's friend, Sophie, and her family were sitting right in front of them, and Sophie's mother turned around to whisper, "We taped it. Maddie stole the show!"

"What were you two whispering about?" Rose asked.

Vera leaned in and whispered about Merry to Rose, who apparently never understood the concept of lowering one's voice or keeping a secret.

"What? That's impossible!" Rose said. "Hasn't she prayed about it? Have her do that, then she'll know."

Jana started to explain, but suddenly did a double take. Stanley was coming into the chapel in his wheelchair, with Will's family leading the way. Stanley was wearing a white shirt, a tweed sports coat, and a crimson tie.

Rose and the others followed her stare and then gasped. "Stanley?" Rose called out.

He waved, then rolled his chair to the edge of a row where his new "grandson" sat happily beside him.

"Well, I'll be," Rose said. "That man told me he wasn't interested."

Jana glanced up at the stand, where Ethan and his counselors were just sitting down. Ethan's eyes were almost popping out of his head as he saw Stanley, along with the three women. He bolted from his seat and came right down to shake hands with all of them. Elders Torrisi and Jamison were scurrying around, almost unable to keep track of all the visitors—the El Dorado folks and two other visitors, as well.

"I can't believe this many of them are here," Savannah whispered, joining her mother.

"I know—it's wonderful!" Jana agreed.

"I mean, I can't believe old people want to change their religion." Savannah leaned in to Jana's ear. "I guess I just thought they wouldn't— I don't know—do something like this at their age."

Jana laughed. "I know. We always underestimate the elderly. But if you find the truth, it doesn't matter how old you are."

Josh was smiling back at them from the bench where the deacons were sitting. He held up three fingers, one for each investigator. Jana smiled.

Then she turned to Savannah. "So did all your friends see Dylan's post?"

Savannah sighed. "Yeah. I mean, it's embarrassing. But they're on my side, and they're all disgusted with him that he would post that. And say that."

Jana squeezed her shoulders.

"But," Savannah said, "I'm sure it will be a different story at school tomorrow."

"That's gonna be hard," Jana said. Her heart ached for what Savannah would have to go through until this ordeal blew over.

"But it's like you always say—it's better to be done to, than be the doer. I mean, everyone will know he's a total jerk, now." Savannah paused. "I hope."

Jana glanced up onto the stand, where Ethan was now standing off to one side, having a private chat with the chorister and Sister Friedman. Soon he sat down, and Sister Friedman began changing the posted hymn numbers. *Oh my gosh—she secretly switched the hymns to ones she likes.*

"Who's that gal up there?" Rose bellowed.

"That's Violet Friedman," Jana said.

"She looks confident and self-assured," Rose said.

"Oh, she is," Jana said. *You have no idea. Last year she tried to get the local animal shelter to give cats and dogs to all the women in Sacrament Meeting on Mother's Day, instead of flowers or chocolate.*

Rose smiled. "Maybe we could become friends."

Jana smiled and realized this was absolutely true. "I'll introduce you to her." Jana waved Sister Friedman over and the two women smiled and shook hands. Before she knew it, they were exchanging cell phone numbers so they could text one another.

Soon the meeting began, with a warm welcome from Ethan. Jana glanced at the program and said a silent prayer for the speakers—of all days, she wanted them to be outstanding.

Savannah nudged her. "I know what you're thinking," she whispered. She pointed to Brother Hausen's name on the printed program. Brother Hausen was known for his sleepy, soft delivery and Jana had to admit she had hoped for a more dynamic delivery. "But they'll feel the spirit," Savannah said.

How did we get this outstanding girl? She has ten times the testimony I had at her age. Jana found herself blinking back tears of gratitude and squeezed her daughter's hand. "Thank you. You're right."

And she was. Rose and Helen were brimming with delight after the meeting.

"This feels exactly like what I've always wanted," Helen said. "And he was completely right—so many people would embrace this if they only knew about it—what was that he said? 'But they know not where to find it.' That's me." Jana hugged her.

Maddie darted off to Primary while Savannah and Josh headed out for Sunday School.

Sister Friedman told Rose she'd meet up with her in the Gospel Essentials class, then Stanley scooted over to say hello. Rose asked him if he'd be going to the next meetings as well.

"Well, I'm not sure I can sit for three hours," Stanley said.

"Are you kidding?" Rose laughed. "What are you gonna do back home? Just sit. Right?"

A slow smile crept onto Stanley's face. "You make a good point." He turned to Will's parents. "I guess I'll try Sunday School with you."

"It does seem like a long time to be at church," Vera said. "But you're exactly right, Rose. If people go home then they usually just sit there, too."

Jana laughed. "And think about how many hours on end people are willing to sit and watch television."

"Especially us!" Rose said. "I mean, there's not a lot to do there, you know? It's like I was telling Howard last night."

Jana perked up. *Howard?*

"He says I'm going to change, now that I'm joining the church," Rose continued. "That all my life I've been so adventurous and now I'll just sit and do nothing, just watch television."

Rose rolled along down the hall as she went on. "And I said that's what we're all doing now, anyway! Who's he kidding? I'm in a wheelchair, for crying out loud. And he walks with a cane—what does he think, that suddenly he's going to climb Mount Everest?"

"How did he take that?" Jana asked.

"Well, he looked stunned for a minute," Rose said, "like I had just poured a bucket of ice water over his head. But it's the most obvious thing in the world, and it's time he faced reality. We're old! And that's fine. It's okay to close the chapter on your crazy days."

"But," Vera said, "joining the church doesn't mean slowing down—usually you speed up."

"That's true," Jana said. "You get callings, you visit teach—you stay pretty busy."

"And there are plenty of Mormons who actually do climb Mount Everest and have great adventures," Vera said. "They're in the Olympics, they travel—Howard has the wrong idea about us."

"Oh, Howard thinks of himself as a renegade. A bad boy," Rose said. "He thinks he still drinks and carries on. It's so stupid." She shook her head. "That man hasn't had a penny to gamble with in ten years. Or a drink in just as long. He just likes the image."

Jana took a breath and then went for it. "Maybe he's worried you would never be interested in a man like him, if you join the church."

Rose laughed. "Well, he's right. I like men who live in the here and now, not in the past." Then she wheeled into the Gospel Essentials classroom, and the subject of Howard was closed.

Chapter 25

THE REST OF THE MEETINGS WERE PUNCTUATED BY CRYING babies, odd class member comments, and a vent that kept blowing cold air when this was already a chilly October day. But none of it mattered to Helen or Rose, and they couldn't wait for their next missionary lesson on the laws and ordinances of the gospel. Even Stanley seemed to have enjoyed himself, and was particularly impressed with the Priesthood lesson about how the atonement of Christ actually worked.

"Well, I must admit this is the first time I've heard it explained in a way that made sense," he said, when Jana saw him in the parking lot.

Ethan was tied up with interviews for a few hours, but was brimming with excitement when he joined the family for dinner.

"I can't get over it," he said. "The work really is hastening. I'd like our family to have a fast of thanks tomorrow."

"A WHAT?" Maddie asked, fear of anticipated starvation in her eyes.

Then Ethan explained that a fast of thanks was one of the little-known reasons for fasting, and had the kids look up Alma 45:1, to show them how fasting and prayer were linked together in expressing thanks to God.

"So do we have to do this every time we're thankful for something?" Maddie asked.

"No, but when the Lord has touched our lives in a profound way and we're especially grateful for our prayers being answered, it's an appropriate thing to do," Ethan said. "And look at the amazing things happening in this ward. Especially at the El Dorado House."

Jana smiled, and thought about how grateful she was for her husband, as well. And for Savannah's heartfelt apology for seeing Dylan behind their backs. Even for Josh reaching out to Howard. In fact, the more she thought about it, the more reasons she had for stepping up her expressions of gratitude. She was even grateful for Carlita Orton, who was finally letting her guard down and allowing Cody to help with the upcoming landscaping.

She watched her kids as they stared at Ethan for a moment, then agreed to the fast. *And that. Right there. I'm grateful for that.*

"How's Savannah doing with the fallout from that Facebook thing?" Ethan asked that night, as they got undressed for bed.

Jana took off her earrings and put them in her jewelry box. "She's staying strong. Her church friends are all supportive of her. But she figures the school kids might not be as kind tomorrow."

Ethan shook his head. "Poor kid. I wish she didn't have to go through this."

"Me, too."

"Consequences."

"Unfortunately. But I honestly think she's learned her lesson. And she's braced for whatever tomorrow brings." Jana hung her jacket up. "By the way, that was a wonderful idea to fast tomorrow. And the missionaries think Frances might be interested, too. Even Pearl is being home taught. By accident, but still."

Ethan sat on the edge of the tub, pulled off his socks, then tossed them into a hamper. "You know, we're always so shocked and amazed. But we shouldn't be. I mean we're sitting on the greatest news since the resurrection. It's the restored gospel of Christ! It shouldn't surprise us one bit when people see it and get excited to join. Who wouldn't?"

Jana laughed. "Well, we can make a list . . ."

"But you know what I mean." Ethan folded his pants over a hanger.

"Yes, I do. It's so much more than just another church on the smorgasbord of choices." Jana began washing her face.

"I wonder if that's why some people fall away," Ethan said. "They never really got it. They didn't pray for a personal witness, but just grew up as cultural Mormons, following along but not actually putting in the work to get a testimony for themselves."

"You've been counseling with some less active members," Jana said.

Ethan smiled. "You can always read my mind." He tossed his white shirt into the hamper with the socks. "But if they had that witness once—if they could just remember that moment when the Holy Ghost told them it was true. If they could just remember who they are, and what this is."

"And set aside offenses, right?" Jana knew several women who believed Joseph Smith was telling the truth, who knew in their hearts that this is Christ's church again upon the earth, but who wouldn't let go of past hurts and come to church again. She imagined the same was true of many of the members Ethan was meeting with.

She looked into Ethan's face and saw his eyes well up with tears.

"I love these people so much," he said. "I had no idea I'd feel this way. I just wish I could get them to bury their weapons, lay down their grudges."

Jana dried her face and put her arms around Ethan. "If anyone can do it, you can."

Ethan scoffed. "Oh, not me. I don't even know what to say to people half the time. You and Savannah are the ones with the social skills."

"That's not what it's about," Jana said. "It isn't about making conversation or popularity. It's about what's in your heart. Ethan, you genuinely care about them, and people sense it. That's what's going to make them listen."

Ethan kissed her. "See? You always know exactly what to say."

"And I'm always right."

He cocked his head to one side and raised an eyebrow. "Most always."

Jana laughed. "Can't blame me for trying."

The next morning felt strange, not making breakfast or lunch for anyone as the kids headed off to school. But their prayer felt as if they were unified in a cause like never before, the simple cause of thanking God.

WHEN SAVANNAH CAME HOME FROM SCHOOL ON MONDAY, HER face was red from crying. Jana followed her to her bedroom.

Savannah blew her nose. "Mom, I am so glad I was fasting. If I hadn't been focusing on missionary work I think I would have punched him."

Jana smiled. "And that's the restraint that's going to serve you well all your life."

Savannah laughed and sat on her bed. "Please don't tell me I'm going to meet other jerks like him."

Jana joined her, raised her eyebrows, and said nothing.

"Oh my gosh," Savannah said, falling back on her pillow. "Maybe I'll become a nun."

Jana rubbed her daughter's feet. "You'll meet the right guy one day. For now, what's the rush, right?"

"Well, yeah, I guess."

Jana knew Savannah wasn't about to swear off dating, but at least her eyes were wider open, now, her brain a little wiser. "How were the other kids?"

"Mostly gossipy. Staring. Whispering. Some of them called me some cruel names. But I never respected them in the first place, so it wasn't much of a surprise."

"Oh, Honey," Jana said, still rubbing her feet.

"And guess who else turned out to be a total jerk? Eli Skaner. That kid from the stake. He is acting like I brought this whole thing on myself, and siding with Dylan."

"I'm so sorry."

"It's okay," Savannah said. "One of my teachers pulled me aside and said he admired how I was handling things." She turned to Jana, and sat up . "You know what I'm doing? I'm just admitting that I did a stupid thing. Never should have kissed a toad, right? And once I admit it, what can they say? I mean, I tell them it's the dumbest thing I've ever done, and how can they argue with me?"

Jana laughed. "That's true." This was the perfect way to diffuse gossip—swallow your pride and be accountable for your mistakes.

"And then I say that I've totally learned my lesson. And then you see kids nodding, like they get it. They realize I regret what I did, and that Dylan-the-Villain was the bad guy in the picture."

"So now he has a nickname."

Savannah smiled. "For the time being. Okay, it's immature, I'll admit it."

"It's far less immature than what you've been putting up with."

"What's cool is how many non-member kids are supporting me and saying Dylan was a jerk to lead me on like that."

Jana smiled. Some of her best friends through high school and college were kids who never shared her faith, but completely shared her values.

"And you know what, Mom?" Savannah continued. "I'm not the first person who regrets something that found its way onto the internet. I think a lot of kids realize the same thing could happen to them."

Jana took her hand and nodded. Everyone has to be so careful, now. "It just takes one photo, or one keystroke," she said.

"You got that right."

When Maddie and Josh got home, they didn't dash into the kitchen for snacks, and that evening they didn't pester her about when dinner would be ready. It was as if the whole family really had risen to a new spiritual plane for one amazing day.

That night Jana went by Savannah's room after the younger kids were asleep, and saw Savannah just getting up from praying at her bedside.

"You've had a quite a day," Jana said, sitting on the side of the bed.

"But this has been a—what's the word? A crystalizing experience for me," Savannah said. "I mean, the other night I was listening to the elders and I realized how much Dylan is missing. I'd never give this up for some guy."

Savannah got under her covers and Jana leaned down and hugged her.

Savannah hugged her back, then Jana sat up. "I'm proud of you."

"I mean, look at what's happening at the El Dorado House," Savannah smiled. "I want to be part of that. I want to go on a mission one day."

"Oh, Honey, you'd be the greatest missionary!" Jana's voice cracked with emotion, and she hugged her again.

"I mean, you're doing it, right? Not in some foreign country, but you're doing it."

Jana's voice caught in her throat and she felt tears welling up. *Yes. I am doing it.*

Chapter 26

CARLITA ORTON WAS SLOWLY WARMING TO THE IDEA OF HAVING a visiting teacher. At least she was returning Jana's calls, and even agreed to meet her on Tuesday morning, before heading to a late shift at work. She called, "Door's open," when Jana rang the bell.

But when Jana delivered the message and then suggested she come to Sacrament Meeting, Carlita just laughed. "No way—the building would fall down. I'm not like you other women."

"Oh, you mean us perfect ones?" Jana said.

Carlita shrugged.

"We're actresses," Jana said. "We get paid to get all dressed up and waltz in with perfect children. They're all paid actors, too—they're not really our kids."

Carlita wasn't sure where this was going, but smiled, at least.

"Carlita," Jana said, turning serious. "Every one of us is there because we're sinners, not because we're perfect."

"But I'm a single mother—"

"So are half our women. Okay, some are widows, but we have more single sisters than married ones, Carlita."

Her eyebrows lifted like wings. "Really?"

"Of course. And once you get to know us, you realize we all have problems. That's what makes it so great, though—any problem you have, someone else has had. And they can help you with it. Addictions, relatives in jail, unwed pregnancies, financial setbacks, marriage trouble, poor health—Carlita, we could spend the whole day listing ward problems."

"In the church?"

"Of course! The church is perfect and Christ runs it, but the people aren't. We're all just striving, all making mistakes and then picking ourselves up and trying again."

"But everyone looks so—so—"

"We're all just wearing Sunday best. Dresses, makeup. So what? It doesn't mean there aren't problems underneath."

Carlita inhaled, as if this were welcome perfume. She nodded. "But you all pay tithing, and you store food. I can't even afford a week's worth, much less a bunch of bins like you guys have."

Jana smiled. "Carlita, do you have a bottle of Tabasco Sauce in the kitchen?"

Confused, Carlita nodded.

"Okay. You have a year's supply of Tabasco," Jana said.

Now Carlita threw her head back and laughed.

"Hey, you have to start somewhere," Jana said. "Do you have a bunch of makeup in your bathroom?"

"Don't tell me. I have a year's supply of makeup, too."

"There you go."

Carlita shook her head, then laughed again.

"See? You're already living the gospel." Jana smiled, then headed out so Carlita could get to work.

"You don't know how much Tabasco I use," Carlita called to her from the doorway.

Jana hollered back as she opened the door to her van. "I use, like, three drops a month."

"You need to learn to cook Mexican style."

"You can teach me," Jana called. And at least Carlita didn't say no.

AFTER LEAVING CARLITA'S, JANA DROVE BY DAVID'S HOUSE again, the neighbor who had made off with the cookies. This time he was in the driveway shooting hoops with two teenage boys. Jana gulped. Okay, he does live here. And maybe he simply liked cookies. She hurried past, before he saw her stalking him, and made a note to tell the kids how she had misjudged the situation.

Next she stopped at the drugstore for some poster boards Josh needed for school. But as she came out of the store she noticed a huge dent in the front left fender.

"No way!" she gasped. How could someone else have hit her car just after it came back from repair? Jana dashed over to to survey the damage, running her hand along the concave depression in the door. She tried to scrape off the red paint that now clung to the silver finish.

"Oh, you poor thing!" A woman's voice called out behind her. Jana turned and saw a bubbly, middle-aged woman coming up behind her, with curly blonde hair and Ray-Ban sunglasses. "Did that just happen to you?"

Jana nodded, heartsick. *Ethan will flip.* And with a hit-and-run, how would insurance cover it? Their premiums would skyrocket.

"Oh, that's so awful," the woman commiserated. "Come look at it from here. You can see they dented the door, too."

Oh, not the door as well. Jana stepped back up onto the sidewalk and stared. It definitely looked worse from this angle.

"Somebody must have backed into you and then taken off," the woman said. "That's going to cost a fortune."

Jana was disgusted and shook her head, only imagining the price of this much body work.

"And a brand new Odyssey, too!" the woman said, sympathetic at the damage to so expensive a car.

Jana froze, still staring at the dent. She swallowed. *I don't own an Odyssey.* Keeping her head down, she stole a sideways glance at the license plate. She was looking at the wrong car! All silver mini-vans looked alike to her, and she was forever trying to open the wrong one until she checked the license plates. This was definitely not her van.

Her heart flooded with a mixture of elated relief, and embarrassment at accepting this woman's sympathy. She bit her lip. No way was she going to admit to this woman that she was an imbecile—what, and let her think she had wasted all this compassion on a moron?

The woman was in a chatty mood and began telling Jana that she'd thought about getting a minivan herself, but that her husband preferred sedans.

I've got to get out of here before the real owner shows up, gets in, and drives off while I'm standing here pretending to own it. "Oh, I just remembered something else I have to get," Jana said. Totally untrue, unless you count a working brain that can remember which car is which.

Jana dashed back into the drugstore and had no choice but to purchase a chocolate Dove bar on the candy aisle. Even now her heart was still pounding. What if the real owner got into the van before the woman went on her way? Her new friend would undoubtedly run into the store and tell Jana that now someone is STEALING her car!

Jana peeked out the windows to see if the woman had left. Slowly she slinked over to her real car, parked just three spots away, and got inside. But what if she drove off and pulled up to a stop light next to the Ray-Ban lady? The woman would glance over and say, "Wait a minute— what are you doing in *that* car?"

Deception whirling around her, Jana tore into the chocolate bar and ate it while she waited the length of a couple of stoplights, giving the woman plenty of time to disappear. *What if I bump into her somewhere else and she asks how much the damage estimate was? Then she'll want to see the newly repaired car. And then I'll have no choice but to tell her I decided to downsize. And then I'll have to buy chocolate Dove minis.*

Slowly Jana headed home, feeling almost bouncy with relief. Either that, or it was the chocolate. Then, just as she walked into the house, her cell phone rang.

It was Ethan, calling from work. "Well, looks like we have a lawsuit."

"No way—I just had a great visit with Carlita—" Jana put her purse down and sat on a barstool at the breakfast bar.

"Not Carlita. A Leonard Rittle."

"Who's Leonard Rittle?"

"He owns Scary Sacramento, some haunted house tour thing. And he's over at the El Dorado House claiming damages because it doesn't look haunted anymore. He's especially mad that Halloween is in three days and he can't include the house in his ghost tour anymore."

"Nobody's stopping him," Jana said.

"Yeah, but it doesn't look creepy anymore," Ethan said. "I'm going over to see what I can do."

"That is ridiculous! You can't sue someone for fixing up their property. Especially when you've been running around telling lies about it in the first place. Talk about a frivolous lawsuit—they ought to sue *him!* For, for, I don't know—defamation or something all these years." Jana could feel her blood pumping.

"I know. But apparently every city has these haunted mansion stories that someone tells tourists. It's totally bogus, of course, but if he hires an attorney we'll still have to respond. We have to hire an attorney and spend money to fight the lawsuit. Or settle out of court."

"Absolutely not," Jana said. "He just wants money. I won't hear of it. Paying someone because now they have to stop lying about you? What nonsense."

Ethan was chuckling "You should be an attorney."

"Well, you can't be everything you have talent for," Jana said. "Apparently I make a pretty convincing mime, too." She poured herself a glass of water. "Don't you dare pay that guy. Not a penny. And just use some court-appointed lawyer or something."

Ethan sighed. "We'll see. I'll call you after I talk to him."

Jana had thought she'd pop over to Merry's house, this time to deliver a pile of presents that had been delivered to Mimi's house when Merry had cancelled her baby shower. An adorable, enthusiastic member, Hannah Vasquez, had been planning the shower for months. But when Merry withdrew from church, she sent Hannah a note saying she just couldn't be a hypocrite and accept shower gifts when she had no intention of coming back to church.

Hannah, also a young mom, was not about to give up so easily, however, and asked every guest to still bring over a gift to Mimi's house. Then Mimi brought them to Jana.

"You're the only one she'll speak with," Mimi said. "I hope you can get her to take these."

Jana smiled, loading them into her van. "I'll do my best." And now she was driving over, praying that Merry would be home and would accept the offerings of so many sisters who loved her.

Merry swung the door open as soon as Jana rang the bell. Of course, Jana had been going back and forth to the porch with gifts, and Merry had probably heard her and watched from a window as the pile of gifts grew.

"What is this?" Merry was the picture of annoyed skepticism.

"I know, I know," Jana said. "You didn't want a baby shower. Everyone understands." She placed the last gifts on top of the stack. "But please don't make me haul them back to my car. The sisters still wanted you to have this stuff."

"I am not coming back, whether people give us presents or not," Merry said.

"Totally get that," Jana said. "And this isn't to change your mind. It's just what you see—a bunch of stuff they want you to have. Just because they love you. Nothing more than that."

Merry folded her arms, scowling.

"Please just open them and see if you can use some of this stuff. No strings attached."

Now Merry sighed and Jana could sense she was slowly giving in. She darted back to her car before Merry could change her mind. "And if one of them is a restaurant gift certificate or a cute nightgown or something, I want it!" Jana called.

Merry tried not to laugh, and turned away. But when she looked back at Jana, she was smiling slightly.

Jana drove off, hoping that at least Merry saw her as a friend.

Ethan saw a powdery blue Honda in the El Dorado House parking lot. *You know you're a regular when you recognize an unfamiliar car.* And the minute he walked into the lobby, he could hear Leonard Rittle's voice, the same pitch as the whining hedge trimmer Ethan had used here a couple of weeks ago.

Harriet was parked in her wheelchair by the front door with Misty on her lap, watching the hysterics along with Chester, observing from the parlor. She whispered up to Ethan, "That voice alone could scare you to death." Ethan stifled a laugh.

Leonard turned around to see who had arrived. He had slicked-back light brown hair and long sideburns, as if cast in a melodrama on his days off. His eyebrows coalesced over his nose like a solid caterpillar.

"I'm Bishop Waterson," Ethan said, striding forward with his long legs, and reaching out to shake Leonard's hand.

Leonard grabbed it. Hard. "Are you responsible for this?" Leonard waved, as if gesturing towards a murder scene.

"For what?"

"For painting the main attraction on the Scary Sacramento Tour?"

"Well," Ethan said slowly, "we didn't know you were using it to frighten people. We actually think this place is pretty wonderf—"

"Tradition in this city has established otherwise," Leonard snapped.

Ethan smiled. "Has it now?"

Rose and Howard were hovering near Helen's desk, and Ethan found himself looking around for Stanley, but didn't see him. Stanley would have had this man on the run by now, definitely.

"It certainly has," Leonard said. "I've tabulated the lost revenue I will experience this weekend and in the future, based on the three years I've been running Scary Sacramento Tours."

"Don't you have other places you can claim are haunted?" Ethan said.

"The Witch House was, and has always been, the main attraction," Leonard said.

"Which house?" Howard said.

"This house."

"Which house?" Howard pretended to be confused.

"This is the Witch House!" Leonard shouted, aggravated at Howard's attempt at a Who's-on-First joke.

"Well, the truth is that this has never been a witch house," Ethan said, as gently as possible.

"Hold on here," Rose interrupted, pulling on her blue reading glasses and staring at Leonard as if sizing him up at a butcher shop. "If you've been making money off this place without our permission, then *I'm* tabulating the cut we should get from those profits—you owe us compensation."

Gotta love that Rose. Ethan shrugged.

"If I hire an attorney—" Leonard began.

"Oh, hogwash," Howard drawled. "You'd never find a lawyer to take on such a crazy case. Matter of fact, the local news would cover it and you'll look like you're persecuting seniors."

"And boy, won't that put a dent in business," Rose added.

All the while, Helen was watching with great amusement, her eyes twinkling nearly as much as the new sparkly exterior. "Wait," she finally said. "I have an idea. Mr. Rittle, I think we could persuade some of our residents to dress up as ghosts and wander around the grounds here. We certainly have no shortage of sheets. And then you can pay them an acting fee."

Now Howard, Rose, Harriet, and Chester all raised a cheer.

Rose pivoted her chair and bellowed down the hallway, "Hey, who wants a great job opportunity?"

Vera had been wheeling her way to the lobby with a tray of cookies on her lap, and held it up just as Rose finished her question.

"Snickerdoodle?" she asked Leonard.

He snorted like an old-time steam engine, yanked his head around, sputtered, and then stormed out in a huff.

Little Vera asked, "Was it something I said?" and everyone else burst into laughter.

Ethan grinned. "You guys didn't need me here—you can take care of yourselves. But I will take a cookie for the road. And one for Jana." Then he winked and headed home.

Jana had arrived only moments before him and couldn't wait to hear what had happened with the haunted house tour operator.

"Yeah, I don't think we'll be hearing from that guy again anytime soon." Ethan helped her make sandwiches and then sat down for a rare lunch at home with her. "Wish you could have seen it," he said.

"So do I," she laughed. Then she told him about the mistaken identity van at the drugstore.

"How can you not tell the difference in van models?" Ethan laughed.

"They honestly look alike," Jana said. "And they always park right by me!"

Ethan shook his head. "So how did your visits with Carlita and Merry go?"

Jana sighed. "I'd say I made about one inch of progress with each of them," she said.

Ethan shrugged. "Well, an inch in the right direction is still an inch." He took one last bite of a snickerdoodle and a swallow of milk. "I've gotta get back to work. See you tonight."

Chapter 27

AFTER THE KIDS GOT HOME JANA TOOK SOME CHICKEN BREASTS from the fridge where they'd been marinating in Italian salad dressing, and dumped them into a baking pan. Then, just to see what would happen, she sprinkled on some Tabasco Sauce. "How did things go today?" Jana asked Savannah as she popped the chicken into the oven.

"Oh, pretty much the same," Savannah said, unloading her backpack. "Dylan is trying to defend his stupidity. I'd say I made about one inch of progress."

Jana caught her own eyebrows lifting at that phrase, then decided not to have a jinx moment with her daughter. "But you're okay?"

"I'm okay." And she seemed it—the confident teenager was back. "I'm doing that well thing, where you're in the bottom of a well and people throw rocks at you, and then you use them to climb out."

Jana smiled. "You know, you've actually turned this into a teaching moment. I'll bet the other kids are watching and learning from your example."

Now Savannah mimicked her mother. "Oh, yes, they all want to be like Super Savannah."

That had been the childhood nickname Jana and Ethan had given her. Jana laughed.

Savannah rolled her eyes. "Of course you think everyone's admiring me—you're my mom and you're biased."

"Could still be true," Jana shrugged.

That evening Ethan had to extend a calling to someone after work, so the family started dinner without him.

"Where did you get this recipe?" Savannah asked as they kids dug into their dinner.

Jana smiled. "It was inspired by Carlita Orton." She watched her daughter cut another piece. "You like it?"

"It has a kick to it," Savannah said, nodding.

"Yeah, it's good," Josh said. "Spicy."

"*Too* spicy," Maddie corrected.

Well, once again an example of the fact that you can't please everyone. Jana offered Maddie some milk to calm the heat.

Just then Ethan came home, threw his jacket over the sofa and joined them.

"Watch out," Maddie said as Ethan placed a piece of chicken on his plate. "It's prickly."

Ethan glanced at Jana, who shrugged. "Well, it's a little fiery," she admitted.

"Speaking of fires, did you tell the kids how our senior citizens put out the fire with that Rittle guy?"

"Saved it for you to tell," Jana said.

Ethan filled the kids in on the situation as they ate dinner. They all loved the way the residents had turned the tables on Rittle.

"And I have an announcement," Jana said. "David was not casing the joint, but actually lives in that house."

"The burglar?" Savannah asked.

Ethan shook his head. "'Casing the joint'? Honestly, Jana, you watch too many detective movies."

Josh finished his apple juice. "How did you figure it out?"

Jana leaned in. "Well, it took a lot of research and deduction." The kids were the picture of rapt attention. Jana laughed. "Actually, I just drove by his house and saw him playing basketball."

Maddie shook her head, disappointed. "Oh, great."

"What—you wanted a burglar as a neighbor?" Ethan asked.

She looked at him, exasperated. "I've been telling all my friends! Of course I wanted a burglar as a neighbor."

Jana shook her head. "Sorry to spoil your excitement. Maybe a pirate or a secret spy will move in."

"But it still doesn't explain him taking the cookies like that," Savannah said. "That was weird."

"Oh, I don't know," Ethan teased. "I could see your mother doing that."

Jana kicked his foot under the table.

As they cleared the dishes, Maddie looked disheartened.

"What's the matter, Sweetie?" Jana asked. "Was the chicken too hot?"

Maddie shook her head. "It wasn't the chicken."

"Then what's wrong?" Savannah asked.

"I just wish I had thought of it."

"Thought of what?" Ethan asked.

Maddie stuck her lip out. "Haunted house tours. I'd be so good at taking people around and scaring them."

Jana laughed. "Yes, you would." She could just picture Maddie's flair for the dramatic, telling ghost stories and making up wild tales. "Well, you'll just have to come up with another idea. One that's even better. Maybe fairy tours."

Maddie's eyes twinkled. "Hmm. I'll have to think about that."

ON WEDNESDAY, SINCE THE HIGH SCHOOL KIDS WERE ALL released just before noon for a district-wide teacher training meeting, the bishopric met them at the El Dorado House to clean windows. There was no sense cleaning them before the painters splattered paint on them, yet they had to climb ladders and do it before the new shrubs went in on Saturday. So a mid-week Mutual activity, between the painting and the landscaping, was the perfect solution.

Ethan and his counselors took charge of chipping the dry paint off with razor blades, while the kids sprayed and washed. Five squeegees and countless rags later, the windows sparkled. Maybe not as much as the golden house itself, but they definitely shone. The kids were drenched, a by-product of mixing teenagers with running hoses, but the final outcome was beautiful, and everyone was home in time for dinner.

Ethan popped in to say hi to "the folks," as so many were calling the residents, now. "Is it my imagination, or is it honestly brighter in here?" he asked Helen.

She looked up from her computer screen and beamed. "We might have to get sunglasses for everyone."

"How long since those windows were last cleaned?" Ethan continued as he strode through the lobby.

Helen shrugged. "I've never seen them washed before," she said. "And I've been here for six years."

The residents were all clamoring to tell Ethan how much better all the rooms looked, their spirits as cheery as the light pouring through the windows. The only one he didn't get to speak with was Herb, who was napping.

"Poor Herb," Chester said, who felt a particular friendship with the sick resident. "He's been sleeping so much it worries me."

Tall, lanky Raymond, Herb's roommate, agreed. "I try to keep him awake, but he's just plain worn out. Dr. Rashid was here earlier, and he said there's not much medical science can do for him, either."

"But the kids are coming on Friday for Halloween," Chester said. "Some of them, anyway. They want to trick-or-treat and a few of us have some candy ready. Maybe that'll lift Herb's spirits."

Ethan knew about the Halloween plan. Several of the Primary kids would be coming before the ward's Trunk-or-Treat party. Terrell Moses was already calling it "Room-or-Treat," to describe how the kids were going to go door to door to each of the six rooms there.

What Ethan didn't know was that the 10- and 11-year-olds had decided to come dressed as the residents, themselves. Since there were a total of twelve of them, and an even number of boys and girls, it worked out perfectly. And Eva Henry, the new Primary President, had kept the entire thing under wraps, hoping to surprise and delight Jana and Ethan as much as the seniors.

On Friday Maddie was throwing a fit in the bathroom as Savannah tried to help her into her Sleeping Beauty Costume, a thick blonde wig continuing to fall into Maddie's eyes, despite enough bobby pins to set off a metal detector.

"You help her," Savannah shouted to Jana, over Maddie's wails. "She's being impossible!"

"I am not!" Maddie yelled back. "I have to be Sleeping Beauty since Vera is Flora!"

"Whatever," Savannah muttered, brushing past Jana in the hallway.

Okay, so my daughter is not ready to be translated as a perfect being. And Maddie can be a brat.

Maddie's meltdown was escalating and Jana knew this was no time to be humming, *When there's love at home.* "Calm down," Jana said, taking hold of Maddie's shoulders and getting right in her face.

"I can't," Maddie whined. "Nothing is working right."

"I have an idea," Jana said. "Let me know when you're ready to hear it."

Maddie sniffled and turned off the waterworks. "What is it?"

"Instead of being Sleeping Beauty, why not be a fairy, like Vera? You could be Merryweather—with a blue dress and a wand! Then you and Vera would be just alike."

She could see Maddie's wheels turning. "A wand?"

"A sparkly wand and a blue scarf around your pointy hat," Jana said, mentally scouring her scarves in the closet, for a way to work this out. "Then you and Vera could both be magical!"

"So I'd be a fairy *with* her," Maddie said.

"Imagine!"

Maddie wiped her cheek with the back of her hand and brightened. "Let's get this wig off me."

Jana started pulling out the bobby pins, and soon they were gluing glitter onto a wooden chopstick to create a fairy wand, and cutting a blue poster board to make a cone-shaped hat.

"She should have been Maleficent," Savannah whispered as Jana poured candy into a plastic pumpkin for Josh to use, handing out candy at home. Josh had decided he was too old to trick-or-treat this year, but still wrapped up as a mummy to hand out candy.

"Honestly, Mom—Maddie is spoiled," Savannah went on.

"She's just young and dramatic," Jana said.

After the consequences Savannah had suffered for the Dylan fiasco, Jana and Ethan decided no grounding was necessary. And tonight the Young Women needed Savannah's help to run the carnival at the Ward Trunk-or Treat. Savannah had put a red rinse on her hair, and dressed up as Daphne in a purple dress and green scarf, to go as a Scooby Doo character with her friends. "Aren't you going to be anything?" she asked.

Well, I was a mime a few days ago, and we all know how that turned out. "Oh, I haven't even had time to think about it this year."

"Well you have to be *something*." Savannah was announcing this like a customs agent demanding a passport.

"There isn't time," Jana said. "It's okay to go as a mom, I hear."

"Let's look upstairs." Savannah went charging up to Jana's closet, and Jana headed after her, if only to nix what would be ideas perfect for a teenager, but ridiculous for a mother.

Savannah tapped her chin with one finger as she surveyed Jana's wardrobe. "Everything is too . . . too . . ." her frown said it all.

"Don't finish that sentence," Jana said. "I don't need a single adjective."

"Let's see what makeup you have." Savannah breezed into the bathroom. "Maybe we could give you a scar or something." The makeup rattled as Savannah rummaged through the plastic cases in Jana's drawer. "Hey—where did you get this bronzer?"

"Oh—it's the wrong color. I bought it at the drugstore last summer, but it's at least three shades too dark." Jana was hoping she'd see the uselessness of this endeavor and give up.

"That's it! You can go as a suntan!" Savannah grinned and opened the bronzer. "Come on, Mom. It will be funny, since you never lay out."

"Well some of us actually believe the reports about skin cancer," Jana said.

But Savannah was happily dusting her mother's face and neck with brown powder, blowing away the bits that fell onto her pink sweater.

"There!" Savannah stepped back to survey her work, then dashed downstairs to answer the doorbell ring of her friends, picking her up to head to the ward building.

"What are you supposed to be?" Josh asked, coming out of his room in his mummy wrappings.

"A suntan," Jana sighed.

"That's a thing?"

"Apparently."

By now Maddie was yelling up the stairs to her mother that it was time to go. Jana turned to Josh. "I wish you could go to this and I could stay home and hand out candy."

"Dad told me the same thing."

Jana laughed. "I'll bet he did. And I'll bet Savannah didn't wrangle him into a costume, either."

"He said he's going as a bishop."

"I don't think he's ever worn a costume in his life," Jana said as they walked downstairs. "I'll bet he never even trick-or-treated as a kid."

Maddie was waiting at the bottom of the steps. "Yes he did," she said. "I asked him."

"Well, what did he go as?" Josh asked.

"An accountant." Maddie flew out the door.

Jana followed behind, then turned to Josh just before leaving. "Warm up some stew for yourself. Dad's going right to the church from work, so you're on your own."

Josh saluted and Jana closed the door.

Maddie's pointy blue hat was too tall to fit inside the van without scraping the ceiling, so reluctantly she untied it and placed it on the seat beside her. This was just as well, Jana thought, since she was so bouncy it would have crushed the tip regardless.

As they pulled into the back parking lot, Maddie leapt from the back seat and shoved her hat onto her head. "Tie my scarf, tie my scarf," she said to Jana.

"Calm down," Jana said. "Good grief—you're a whirling dervish." She tied the scarf under Maddie's chin.

"What's that?"

"Oh, just another old expression," Jana said. "Maybe you should have gone as a sparkler."

"What's a sparkler?" Maddie asked.

Jana sighed. "A firework thing they had when I was your age. But they're illegal in California now."

Maddie stared at her the same way Savannah did, whenever she concluded her mother was ancient and outdated. Jana was feeling old enough to move in here.

Maddie ran off ahead, her trick-or-treat bag flapping, and Jana headed up the stairs with other parents and kids just arriving. The building still gleamed golden in the late sunlight.

Eva Henry was standing at the top of the stairs, greeting the Primary kids. "Oh, wow, look at you," she said to Jana. "You look fantastic!"

Jana chuckled and thanked her, a bit confused, and went into the lobby. Ty and Lachelle Marks were already there, and Lachelle rushed over. "Have you been on vacation?"

"Me? No," Jana said.

"Well, you look terrific."

"Uh, thanks," Jana said, stopping by the front desk to say hello to Helen. Helen was smiling and waving, wearing a headband with bouncy little jack o'lanterns on the antennae. It was a complete transformation from the first time she'd met her.

"Helen, you look awesome," Jana said.

"Thanks. You do, too."

Jana meandered past the crowd, trying to follow Maddie to the bedrooms.

The first was Pearl and Lorraine's room, and Lorraine was standing in the doorway handing out full-sized Snicker bars. Lorraine was bent over giving candy to a tiny little Sunbeam dressed as an action hero, then looked up as Jana approached. "Oh, Jana, wow—you look so healthy!"

Pearl, sitting nearby in her wheelchair, leaned around to have a look. "Oh, you do," she concurred. "Have you been getting some sun, Dear?"

Jana opened her mouth to explain that this was her *costume*, when Rose shouted from two doors down, "Look at Jana—wow—you're the picture of health, Sweetie!"

Now every parent and child in the hallway seemed to whip around to stare at her, and every one of them smiled and nodded. *Marvelous. So I've been this sickly, pale ghost until tonight, when my Halloween costume actually improves my appearance.*

She forced a smile and turned around just as Ethan arrived. "Hey, what's on your face?" he asked.

"An improvement, so I'm told."

He frowned. Sure enough, he had come from work and was dressed as an accountant.

"Thank you for liking the pasty, chalky me better," Jana said. "It was Savannah's idea to go as a suntan. But, apparently, it makes me look healthy."

She could see Ethan was trying not to laugh, so she narrowed her eyes. "Don't you dare laugh."

"I'm not," he said, clearly struggling.

"Mom and Dad, come on!" Maddie had dashed up, her bag already loaded with candy, urging her parents along. "You have to take a picture of me with Vera."

They pressed through the crowd to where Vera was decked out in a green fairy hat, and snapped a photo of the two of them. Then Simone, the activities director, appeared and offered to take a photo of all four of them.

"This is such a great idea," she said to Jana.

"Oh—it was Eva Henry's," Jana said.

"They love their duplicates," Simone said.

Duplicates? Jana looked back at her, puzzled.

"Oh—you don't know?" Simone laughed. "Come and see. You look great, by the way."

Jana sighed.

Simone led them to the men's hallway, where the older kids were posing with their counterparts, before heading to the women's side. Jana gasped. There were six boys in vests and bow ties, overalls, even a jockey suit. The one dressed as Marvin had his dark hair slicked back and was carrying a baseball. Stanley was roaring with laughter at the boy wearing a bald skull cap, who was supposed to be him. And even Herb's impersonator was carrying fake dumbbells, pretending to be a weight lifter.

Then she realized all the women were represented, too. The girls couldn't wait to rush over to the women's rooms and surprise their new friends. Though they weren't in wheel chairs, they had the costumes and props down pat. One girl depicted Rose, with a blonde French twist, blue glasses and flamboyant clothing. Another was tiny Vera in a little white wig and a shawl. One dressed as a nurse to copy Frances, Pearl was an actual cake, Lorraine was a ballerina, and Harriet's counterpart carried a stuffed cat.

And the women couldn't have been more elated. Nearly every one of them clapped, then cried, and shook their heads in amazement. Then they all headed to the rec room for a group photo. Herb looked pale and weak, but managed to smile for the photo.

That must be how I look all the time.

Howard was depicted as a swashbuckling explorer with a hat and whip, like Indiana Jones. And Howard actually blushed when everyone said it captured him perfectly.

"Best idea ever," Jana whispered to Eva.

"Thanks!" Eva squeezed her arm. "And you really do look great."

If I grit my teeth any harder they might break. Whatever.

Eva hustled the kids off to the ward Trunk-or-Treat event, and Ethan came up and whispered in Jana's ear. "I'd like to whisk you away for a piece of pie," he said.

She turned and fell into his arms. "That is exactly what I need right now."

"Can we sneak away?"

"I have to drive Maddie to the church. And you have to judge the chili cook-off."

"Oh, yeah."

"Rain check?"

"How about tomorrow night, after the landscaping?"

Jana kissed him. "Do you think life will settle down enough?"

"It has to. And no dark tans allowed."

Chapter 28

"HEY, THANKS FOR MANNING THE FORT," ETHAN SAID AS THEY came home to find Josh watching television.

Josh smiled. "It turned out fun. Cabes and Shuman came over with their candy and we made some popcorn. So I actually came out ahead." These were two neighbor boys he had known since fourth grade. And both were in the kitchen, but came out with soda pops and greeted the Watersons as they rejoined Josh on the sofa.

"*Wait* until you hear about the El Dorado House," Maddie said, flouncing in front of the TV screen. Then she gave the boys a full report of each child who dressed up as a resident, capping off the tale with a detailed description of her fairy grandmother. "Which is better than a fairy godmother," she concluded.

The boys laughed, then Jana pulled Maddie away so the guys could get back to their movie.

"I think you'll have glitter on your face for a few days," she said to Maddie as she tried to scrub it off upstairs.

Maddie shrugged. "Fairy dust."

"Very well, then. You want to come with Dad and me tomorrow morning to watch the landscaping go in?"

"Sure."

"Okay. Hop in the tub, and then off to bed."

Savannah came into their bedroom at eleven, after a pizza party at Portia Ferguson's house. "Do I have to help tomorrow?"

Jana had been lightly dozing, waiting for Savannah to get home. "No, Honey. You've done enough. Sleep in."

"Thanks."

She listened as Savannah went down the hall and closed her door. Then she rolled over.

Ethan took her hand. "Glad she's home. Were there boys there?"

"Goodnight, Ethan."

He sighed. "Goodnight."

THE ALARM WOKE ETHAN FROM A DREAM ABOUT ALL THE PLANTS going in, covered with snow, and he sat up.

"Oh, wow," he mumbled.

Jana opened her eyes. "What's the matter?" She felt groggy and wished the landscapers weren't arriving quite so early.

"I dreamed the plants were all wrong, and all frozen, covered with snow," Ethan said. He groaned, trying to make sense of his crazy dream. "I'm sure it's because of how the paint turned out. I'm worried this will be all wrong, too."

Jana reached over and rubbed his back. "It will be fine." Jack Bergman was the landscape architect from the other ward, who had volunteered to supervise the work today. "I've heard nothing but raves about Jack's work."

"I know," Ethan said, getting up and putting on his slippers. "I'm just a worrier. The sprinkler guys were supposed to meet him there yesterday, to make sure everything's okay. I'm sure he would have called if there was a problem."

Jana smiled and got up. "Oh—and I called Carlita yesterday, to remind her to bring Cody. Remember? He seemed interested in helping with it."

"Yeah, he did. I hope he comes."

"Josh wants to go, too," Jana said, heading for the hallway. "I'll make sure he's up." She figured Josh could arrive early with Ethan, then she'd show up with Maddie at around noon.

Ethan got in the shower and held his head under the running water, the warmth feeling good on a cool morning. He was glad Josh wanted to go along, but what if it turned into another disaster? The kid had injured himself two weeks ago in the big weeding project. *Maybe we should make him enroll in more sports. Build coordination. Probably help with social skills, too. And get his eyes checked; this whole thing could be a vision problem. Maybe have Gary Bloom, that neurologist guy, do a workup on him.* Ethan had several clients in medicine, why not get their opinions?

Jana opened Josh's door and stepped quietly to his bed. "Josh, Honey, time to get up."

His breathing became more deliberate and he turned to face her in the dim morning light, glancing at the clock on his nightstand.

"I hate to wake you," Jana said.

Josh yawned. "No, I want to go over there." He pulled the covers aside. "I told Howard I'd come by, too."

"Scrambled eggs sound okay?"

Josh swung his legs down, his feet resting on the brown-and-cream braided rug beside his bed. "Yeah. Thanks."

Breakfast was quiet, with Maddie still asleep. It was amazing the vacuum it created when her lively spirit wasn't in the room. "I asked Cabes and Shuman to come, but they passed," he said.

"That's nice that you asked, though," Jana said. The boys all called each other by their last names, and she imagined them telling their parents, "Waterson asked us to do a bunch of gardening this morning."

As she kissed Ethan goodbye, he whispered, "Hey, I want to talk with you about Josh tonight."

"Is something wrong?"

"No, no—I just have a couple of ideas I want to run by you."

"Okay. See you around lunch time. Some people are bringing you sub sandwiches, and Maddie and I'll be there with cookies."

"Oatmeal-Chocolate Chip?"

Jana smiled. "We'll see." She had actually planned to buy some bakery cookies, but the light caught Ethan's face for an instant and he looked exactly as he did on their wedding day, twenty years ago. The same smile, the same delight in his eyes. Okay, this time it was for cookies, but she felt herself caving in. She could make cookies for this guy any day. And had it really been two decades?

She and Maddie ran some errands, then came back and made the cookies, Maddie packing a separate one for Vera.

"I'm going to have another art lesson," Maddie said, as she dried a cookie sheet. "I think I'm going to draw Harriet's cat this time."

Jana smiled. She had noticed Maddie had been doodling cats all week.

As Ethan and Josh pulled up to the El Dorado House, two big white delivery trucks from the local nursery were already there. And Jack Bergman, thank goodness, was holding a clipboard and checking off plants as they were unloaded. Jack waved to Ethan, then went back to his task. He was short and wiry, with tousled salt-and-pepper hair. Jack's skin was a dark tan from years working outside.

Ethan and Josh unloaded their own shovels and tools, placing them behind a huge mound of soil that another truck had just dumped on the walkway. Josh saw his dad pulling on work gloves, and did the same.

"What can we do?" Ethan asked Jack.

"Nothing yet," Jack said. "Give me about fifteen minutes."

"No problem, we'll pop in and visit the folks," Ethan said. Then, as he and Josh headed through the lobby, he noticed Cody Orton in the parlor, with Stanley. They were sitting at a table, doing a jigsaw puzzle.

"Hey, good morning," Ethan said, pulling off his gloves and shaking hands with them. "I see you got sent inside, too."

Cody chuckled. "Yeah, my mom had to get to work, so she dropped me off a little early. But Stanley asked me to help him with this puzzle, so . . ."

Ethan looked at the busy street scene coming together on the table. The puzzle was about half finished. "How long you been working on it?" He figured it had been up for days, with various residents taking a turn at finding the pieces that fit.

Stanley looked up at Ethan with his trademark dry seriousness. "About half an hour."

"What?" Josh said, incredulous. "You're joking, right?"

Stanley's mouth was its usual straight line. "I do not joke."

Now Ethan gasped. "How'd you get it put together so fast?"

Stanley gestured at Cody. "I think we have a spatial reasoning prodigy, here."

Cody turned as pink as the curtains, scoffing and shaking his head. "Naw, if you knew me, Stanley—"

"I know what I see," Stanley said. "I'm guessing you're going into engineering, architecture, or technology?"

Cody's eyes bulged. He sputtered. "I . . . I'm just a . . . I'm not much of a student."

Stanley's eyes drilled into Cody's like lasers. "Well, we're going to have to fix that. No boy with talent like this should let it go to waste. Can you come over here once a week?"

Cody's head was jerking about as he seemed to be looking for an escape route. Ethan put a calming hand on his shoulder.

"First of all, you need to accept that you're a genius," Stanley continued.

A burst of disbelief escaped Cody's lips, like a laugh caught in a hand.

"No one's told you that, have they?" Stanley went on. "If you come here once a week, twice if you can, I'll help you express yourself with confidence and build the kind of vocabulary you'll need for college."

"College!?" Cody exclaimed.

Stanley just stared at him. "Certainly. You'll need a degree for those fields. And you'd be a fool not to get one. Cody—that's your name, right?"

Cody nodded, gulping.

"Cody, I've been a school instructor for forty years. I've never seen a boy like you."

Now Cody stared back. Then he looked up at Ethan, embarrassed.

"You can actually do this," Ethan said. "I'd listen to Stanley. He knows what he's talking about."

Josh was grinning, and Cody smiled back at him. "I just . . . I never . . ."

"Do it," Josh said. "That would be so cool, Man."

"I—I'll ask my mom, I guess."

"You do that," Stanley said.

Just then the front door opened and Jack called, "We're ready for you guys."

Cody stood up to head off, and Stanley tugged on his jacket. "And now we shake hands."

Embarrassed by his lack of manners, Cody pumped Stanley's hand and thanked him, then headed outside.

"You have a project," Ethan said.

Stanley interlocked his fingers together and actually smiled. "I see a world of potential in that boy."

Ethan waited as Josh darted down the hall to find Howard and say a quick hello. He felt a twinge of shame that he was Cody's bishop, yet had judged Cody so harshly, when Stanley had done just the opposite, and given the boy a chance. He hoped Cody would take advantage of Stanley's tutelage; it could be a life changer.

Soon Josh was jogging back, and they headed down the stairs to join Jack and the others. About two dozen people were scurrying about like ants now, all taking instructions from Jack, who turned out to be a ball of fire when it came to landscaping.

"This whole area will be mounding roses," Jack said, his arms sweeping wide. "Plant them about 14 inches apart. Start back here and work your way forward. It will form a blanket of color this spring. Then over here," he said, marching around to the shady, north side of the building, "we'll plant the azaleas. These are twice-blooming, spring and fall, all different shades of pink." He pointed to Cody and some of the other men. "You guys will be my camellia men. They'll start flowering this February, so we'll have something blooming in the winter. And they go against the house, but about four feet out. All the soil in this area needs to be acidic, so here's how we'll make the planting mix." He grabbed a wheelbarrow and began pouring the contents of various bags into it, reaching in and mixing it with both hands, like a pirate happily pawing through gold coins. "This is going to be great!"

Ethan had to laugh. If only everyone could find their perfect career, the one that made them want to leap from bed every morning and get to work.

"Bishop, you and your son follow me," Jack said. He led them to a sunny spot beside the wall, where the grass wasn't growing well. "Here's where we'll put a hedge of photinia. It's just now turning red and it will give them some color to see, when they look out the windows."

"You have something blooming in every season," Ethan said.

Jack grinned. "It's fast growing, so it will fill in this rough patch in no time. And the wall isn't much to look at, so this will cover it within a year or two."

"It's wonderful that you're doing this," Ethan said.

Jack waved it away. "This is fun," he said. "I get to do whatever I want. And this place has some wonderful trees already established, and great shrubs along the back side. We'll pop in some bulbs for a spring surprise, and then tidy up by evening."

Ethan was glad he could work alongside Josh, to make sure he didn't hurt himself. He watched as Josh struggled to shovel the dirt and then dump it in the wheelbarrow without missing. They planted six bushes before lunch time, tamping down the extra soil around each plant, then moving on to the next one. "Let's take a break and grab a cold drink," Ethan said, having noticed a cooler of water bottles earlier.

They threw down their gloves and shovels, and headed for the front steps, where a couple of other guys were taking a short break as well.

"Wow, look at the entry," Josh said. While their backs were turned, someone had planted gorgeous, fluffy ferns flanking the porch. On either side were dogwoods whose crimson leaves were brilliant against the greenery and the gold house.

"These are going to produce delicate white blossoms next year," Jack was saying to the nearby workers. "They'll look like little doilies of lace, floating in the air."

Cody was rolling an empty wheelbarrow by. "All gone," he said to Jack.

"Perfect." Jack turned to the workers. "This is the ideal time for pre-emergent herbicide so we won't get weeds. That, and the landscape cloth I had you put down under the new soil, should make it easier to maintain." Jack was in his glory, not only doing what he loved, but teaching his crew as well.

Ethan looked up and noticed several residents watching from the windows. Howard and Chester waved.

Josh walked over to Cody. "Hey, you like mechanics, right?"

"Yeah."

Josh nodded up at the windows where Howard was watching. "You ought to talk to Howard sometime. He can fix anything."

Cody nodded, pursing his lips in consideration of the idea. "Thanks."

Just then the sandwiches arrived, along with Jana, Maddie, and two huge trays of oversized cookies. Ethan's eyes lit up. "Oh, yeah," he mumbled.

Soon everyone had found a spot to eat on the stairs, the lawn, or in the backs of trucks. Ethan visited with Jana as Maddie scurried into the building for her art lesson.

"I can't believe the transformation," Jana said. "This is absolutely breathtaking."

Ethan nodded as he bit into his sandwich.

"Which part did you do?"

Ethan, still chewing, pointed at the bushes he and Josh had planted. "We're halfway done," he said, swallowing. "They look like they're pretty far apart, but Jack says they're going to get twelve to fifteen feet high, and about eight feet wide."

"That will be gorgeous," Jana said. Now she stood up. "I think I'll go check on Maddie and Vera."

Ethan nodded as Jana headed up the steps, then he looked around for Josh. The kid was nowhere to be seen. Ethan took his last bite, then balled up his napkin, gathered some trash from the other workers, and headed around the side of the house to the trash cans. Just before stepping onto the gravel, he caught a glimpse of Josh through the hedge. Was he sitting there with another ice pack, having hurt himself again? He almost charged through the bushes, then stopped.

There, in a secluded break in the shrubs, he saw Josh kneeling. Ethan paused, staring.

"And Heavenly Father," he heard Josh say, "Please bless Howard. He's such a good man. Bless him to accept us as his family. Bless him to listen to the missionaries and, and to join the church. Help him learn how much Christ loves him, and what he did for him."

Quietly Ethan backed out of view just as Josh ended his prayer. He listened, holding his breath, as Josh got up and walked the other way. When he was sure his son was out of sight, Ethan continued around to the trash cans and dropped the papers in. He stopped, staring at the gravel beneath his feet. Then tears tumbled from his eyes as he filled with shame, for doubting his son's abilities. Here he was, finding fault with Josh for being socially and physically awkward—and instead he should have been noticing far more important character traits. His son was a spiritual giant, a boy of faith, a boy of great compassion. Instantly Ethan prayed for forgiveness.

He wanted to rush up to Josh, sweep him into his arms, and tell him how proud of him he was. But he had intruded upon a private moment and didn't want to embarrass Josh, a kid who did, after all, have tender feelings. One thing he knew for certain: He was not going to worry about that boy. He was going to show him the respect he should have been giving him all along. Today, in Ethan's eyes, Josh had become a man.

Chapter 29

THAT NIGHT ETHAN TOOK JANA TO A LOCAL DINER WHERE THEY had that promised piece of pie—Key Lime for Jana, and Chocolate-Pecan for Ethan.

"I guess we should eat healthier than this," Jana mumbled, after swooning over the first bite.

"Come on," Ethan said. "I'll bet we haven't been here in a year. You can live it up once in a while."

Jana smiled. "I guess nobody goes on a date for celery sticks."

"Besides, we probably burned a thousand calories today, landscaping."

Just then a client of Ethan's and a family from the ward walked in at the same time, so it became a meet-and-greet, telling about the transformation at the El Dorado House. Jana watched her husband describing the residents and the hard-working youth. *Ethan is the real transformation. Look what a bold missionary he's become. This project has turned him into the kind of leader he never thought he could be.*

That night Jana said the prayer before she and Ethan climbed into bed, and when they stood up, he took her face in his hands. "Now I know where Josh gets it."

"Where Josh gets what? Oh—you said you wanted to talk to me about him tonight."

Ethan shook his head. "I was wrong." They got into bed. "I was going to talk to you about all these medical experts that I thought should check Josh out. You know how I'm always worrying that he's not . . . oh, it's so stupid. Not social enough, not athletic enough."

Jana nodded.

"But I've been completely wrong. Today I was going around to the trash area by the kitchen, and Josh doesn't know it, but I saw him kneeling there, praying."

"Really?"

"I was so close, so worried he'd see me, but there was a hedge between us. Jana, he was praying for Howard."

"For Howard? What did he say?"

Ethan teared up then, and couldn't speak for a moment. "He really loves Howard. He wants him to get a testimony."

"Oh!" Jana clasped her husband's hands. "That's so fantastic."

"That kid is a gift from God," Ethan said. "No joke. He has this absolute faith, this strong testimony. *He's* teaching *me,* Jana."

She kissed him. "What a beautiful moment. I think maybe you were meant to witness that."

"I'll tell you this," Ethan said. "I am never going to give that boy another whiff that I'm worried about him or that he has disappointed me in some way."

"You've never done that."

"Oh, kids can tell. He's seen me sigh when he's dropped a ball . . ." Ethan wiped his eyes. "I am so proud of that kid."

"Me, too."

"Talk about learning the things that matter most."

Jana nodded. "He's a great young man."

"Great *man,*" Ethan said.

THE NEXT MORNING WAS FAST SUNDAY, AND HELEN AND ROSE joined Vera again at church. Stanley was there with Will, then suddenly Raymond walked in with the Applegate family, and Frances walked in with the Holden kids.

"What on earth?" Jana could see Ethan's lips forming the same words, up on the stand. He dashed down the stairs and went over to greet them.

"Well, my new little granddaughter asked me to come," Frances said as Jana went over to greet her as well. "But I also like what I'm hearing, so far." Jana knew the elders had begun talking with her about LDS scientists; obviously it had progressed from there.

Raymond had clearly formed a friendship with Zack Applegate and looked as if he'd won the lottery to have not just Zack but four other siblings to claim as "grandkids" now.

"He likes the idea of being sealed to his wife," Elder Torrisi whispered to Jana, following her stare to the tall man in a pale blue tie.

"This is incredible," she whispered back. She glanced at Josh, on the Deacon's row, and he was holding up five fingers and grinning.

"You gonna bear your testimony?" Savannah asked her mother.

Jana smiled. "I might. I'm feeling pretty blessed right now."

And then she caught her breath. In walked Sean and Merry with their baby. Merry was frowning, but Sean looked buoyant. He must have insisted that they have their baby blessed today, and Merry had obviously acquiesced.

Ethan swept past Jana on his way to the Haines', noticing her surprise. "Sean called this morning in Bishopric Meeting."

"That's wonderful," Jana said. She hung back until Ethan had greeted them, then went over and hugged Merry.

"I'm glad you're here," she said.

Merry bristled. "It's for Sean."

Jana smiled. "It's still good to see you. And Aiden looks beautiful."

Merry scooted into a short bench against the wall, to avoid having to meet and greet, but Jana could see her eyes growing round as she spotted so many residents of the El Dorado House there.

The meeting began, and Sean gave his son a beautiful blessing. Then he bore a strong testimony, and Jana prayed that Merry would feel the Spirit.

Soon she found herself walking up to the mike and testifying of the restoration, of Christ's redeeming love, and of living prophets today. "My testimony has grown tremendously since our ward started the El Dorado House project," she said. "But it's not because of what we've been doing. It's because of the people who live there. Some of them are here today, and I want Helen to know how much it built my faith to see her standing strong for what she believes in, even standing up to a family member. And Rose, your love of the scriptures has increased my own. Vera, your missionary work has inspired me to be much better at sharing the gospel with my friends. Frances, I am grateful for your love of others and for keeping an open mind as you study. Stanley and Raymond, you are exemplary men we are honored to know.

"This church has a strong pioneer ancestry, and we often talk about covered wagons crossing the plains. We wonder what we'd be like, if we were pioneers all those many years ago. And I don't know how I would have handled it. But I know I'd want to be in Helen's, and Rose's, and Vera's, and Stanley's, and Raymond's wagon." She paused. "I guess it would have to be a really big wagon." The congregation chuckled, then Jana closed her testimony and sat down. Maddie squeezed her arm and whispered, "Me, too."

After the meeting, everyone filed slowly out into the halls, as usual. Rose zipped her wheelchair over to Merry in the hallway, catching her before she left. Jana watched from a few yards away, as Primary kids bustled by with their parents.

"I've missed seeing you and little Aiden," Rose bellowed.

Merry turned, then forced a smile and tried to be polite. "Thank you, Rose."

"And looky here," Rose went on. "Look what you missed!" Rose held out her cell phone, and let Merry watch the video she had taken of the Primary children singing "Families Can Be Together Forever" in the lobby.

Jana watched as Merry listened, too polite to hand the phone back before the song finished. Finally Merry gave it back to Rose and said, "That was lovely. Thank you."

"Did Jana tell you I'm getting baptized?" Rose asked, deliberately ignoring Merry's body language of angling towards the exit.

"No, I didn't know that," Merry said. "Congratulations."

"I'd like you to come," Rose said.

"Well, I'll see if I can."

"My only sister won't be there," Rose said.

Sean had joined his wife, now, and jumped into the conversation. "Oh—does she live too far away?"

"No, just an hour away. But she's against my joining this church. Thinks I'm just doing it to go along with the crowd. As if I've ever done that, right?" Rose cackled. "But I can't wait for her permission before I get on board with this. I could die any minute, right?" She laughed again. "So I told her I'm a grownup and I can think for myself." Rose waited for that message to sink in. Then she said, "The boys—the elders—tell me we fought a war in heaven over the freedom to choose, and I'm not about to give it up, not even for a stubborn sister I love very much."

"So is she mad at you?" Merry said.

Rose shrugged. "I can't worry about that. Mad or not, this is true and I can't deny what the Spirit has told me. Maybe when she sees how happy I am, she'll check it out, herself. But if not, I still have to follow my own heart. I can't live for some else's approval." And then she said something that thundered through Jana's heart. "My testimony is not for sale."

Aiden began fussing, and Merry dashed outside with him. Sean glanced back at Rose as he followed his wife, and winked at her. "Thank you, Rose."

Rose smiled, then turned her wheelchair toward Jana. "Oh, hi—didn't see you. Enjoyed what you had to say up there."

"Thanks. I enjoyed what I heard you say to Merry just now."

"Well, she needs to be her own woman," Rose said. "You can't let someone else keep you from the truth, even if it's a family member. Might have to cut the apron strings."

"I'm sorry about your sister. I didn't know."

"Me, too. But life is filled with people who try to hold you back. You just have to run your own course and hope they'll eventually trust your judgment. Look at Helen, standing up to her son."

Jana nodded, and thought about Howard. She truly hoped he would support Rose and open his heart to the gospel, as well. Otherwise Rose would be leaving him behind.

THAT EVENING THE WATERSONS PILED INTO THE VAN TO MEET up with the missionaries at the El Dorado House.

"Hey, guess what Sister Friedman did this morning," Josh said as they drove.

Both Jana and Ethan thought *What Now?* But didn't say anything.

"She came into Young Men's and asked if any of us were computer wizards."

Savannah shrugged. "That's not so unusual."

Josh grinned. "Yeah, but it's because she wants someone to create a Virtual Visiting Teaching App for her."

Ethan wanted to close his eyes and make all this go away, but he was driving. Still, he groaned. Jana laughed.

"She wants to be able to send the message and a picture of herself," Josh said.

Now Savannah laughed. "Yeah, like that's the same thing as a personal visit."

Jana shook her head. "I can just picture the whole church serving one another electronically. I'm surprised she didn't want to take it to Facebook or Instagram, so she could teach everyone simultaneously. Hey, instead of bringing someone a meal, I can just send them a picture of some salad and lasagna."

"Well, you've got to give her credit for creativity," Ethan said.

"Like me," Maddie piped up.

Ethan looked at Maddie in the rear view mirror. *Nothing like you. I hope.*

When they arrived, the missionaries were already in full swing teaching a lesson to Rose, Helen, Frances, Pearl, Raymond, and Stanley.

"Whoa—six!" Josh whispered to his dad, his eyes dancing.

The Watersons had come by to tell each of the investigators how nice it had been to see them at church, and had no idea half of them would be looking into the actual gospel.

Then suddenly Chester, Marvin, Lorraine and Harriet came in, Harriet rolling in with her cat on her lap. With Vera already there, the only residents missing were Herb and Howard.

"It's like a missionary party!" Maddie shouted, unable to contain her excitement. The residents all chuckled, and Jana whispered, "Let's not interrupt," even though it was too late.

Ethan was stunned, and quickly lowered himself onto the piano bench to keep from fainting. How on earth had this happened?

And then Elder Torrisi answered his question. "We asked if they'd all like to sit in on the discussion," he said to Ethan. "And they all accepted. Well, except for Herb, who isn't feeling well."

"And Howard, who's just stubborn," Rose piped up.

Jana stared, realized her mouth was hanging open, and closed it. Every one of them was holding a copy of the Book of Mormon. She felt warm tears streaking down her face.

Pearl was crocheting a salmon-colored shawl as she listened. "Pretty swell, so far," she said.

Jana could feel Savannah's eyes glancing at her. Only yesterday she had used that dated word herself, and had gotten ribbed by Savannah for it.

"Actually, a couple of the nurses were interested, too," Elder Torrisi said. "Shanika and Theresa. But they're on duty tonight."

"Come sit down by me," Vera called out to Maddie, who gladly zoomed over, curled up in a velvet chair beside Vera, and leaned her head on her shoulder.

"We're sorry to interrupt," Jana stammered.

"Oh, you're more than welcome," Elder Jamison said, gesturing to the empty sofa seats.

"Well, you kids can sit and listen," Ethan said, rising. "Maybe Mom and I will go and check on Herb."

As they left the parlor, Jana squeezed Ethan's hand. "This is incredible."

Ethan paused, leaning against the wall, his shoulders shaking as he cried. "I'm sorry. I had to leave. I'm just—" He couldn't finish.

"I know," Jana said. "It's beyond our wildest dreams."

"To be part of this, to witness this." Ethan took a huge breath and released it again, trying to calm his voice. "It's such an honor." He hugged Jana, then they stood and cried tears of joy for a few minutes.

Finally they headed down the men's hallway toward the last room, where Herb was a roommate with Raymond. Jana couldn't remember the last time she felt this happy, this light. It was as if her heart were literally dancing.

Suddenly Shanika and Theresa were walking right in their direction. Jana smiled. *Oh good, they can sit in on the discussions, after all.*

"Mr. Waterson," Theresa said as they neared them, "Were you planning to visit Herb?"

"Yes—he's been asleep all the other times that I've tried to vis—"

Now Theresa's face fell, and she glanced at Shanika, whose eyes were welling up. "I'm so sorry. I'm afraid Herb passed just a few minutes ago."

Jana gasped and Ethan drew his hands to his heart. "No!" they both said. It was as if a screen of ice had fallen.

Shanika put a comforting arm on Ethan's. "It was so peaceful, though. He was ready. He wanted to go."

"Did he—were there family members?" Jana asked.

"No; he had no one," Theresa said. "But he had everyone who lives here, and he knew they all loved him." She turned to Ethan. "And he appreciated that prayer you said for him."

Ethan swallowed. *The blessing. The blessing when I didn't feel prompted to promise him he would recover.*

Jana knew Ethan was remembering, and draped her arm across his back. "It was his time to go," she whispered. Ethan nodded and put his arms around her.

"We need to call his doctor and the coroner," Shanika said. "But if you'd like to step in to see him, you can."

"Maybe say our goodbyes," Ethan said. He and Jana let the nurses alone to make their phone calls, and stepped into Herb's room. He looked as if he were resting, completely at peace.

"Oh, I wish we'd been able to get to know him better," Jana said. "And I wish he could have looked into the gospel."

"Well, now he can," Ethan said. They stepped to his bedside, and Ethan rested a hand on Herb's shoulder. "Goodbye, Herb. You fought hard. We'll meet up again one day."

Jana cried silently, then wished him a happy reunion with loved ones. She turned to Ethan. "We'd better get back to the children. If the nurses announce this, I'd like to be there."

"Absolutely."

And they made it back to the parlor at the exact moment when Shanika apologized for interrupting the lesson, and announced Herb's passing.

Maddie, Josh, and Savannah came right to their parents.

"Just now?" Savannah whispered.

"Oh, wow," Josh said. "But he had been really sick for a long time."

Maddie's lower lip trembled and she hugged Jana's waist.

"We can come back another time," Elder Jamison was saying as the lesson broke up and the residents all tried to console one another. Raymond and Chester, Herb's closest friends, went straight to his room, both of them shaken. The rest milled about in the shock and pandemonium that so often follows a death.

As the elders stood to leave, Ethan stopped them. "Wait." Then he turned to the crowd. "If anyone feels they need a Priesthood blessing at this time—just a blessing for comfort—the elders and I would be happy to give you one."

Suddenly Howard, who had been in his room, came hobbling in on his cane, ashen and pale. He bent down and swept Rose into his arms, and they both cried.

"Oh, Howard," Rose said. "It's so sad. So awful. Poor Herb."

Howard stroked her back, then pulled up a chair beside her, and began patting her arm. Jana watched the tenderness between them and wished Howard would soften his heart and take the spiritual journey Rose was taking. The love between them was undeniable.

Helen and Pearl both wanted blessings, so Ethan and the missionaries followed them to Pearl's room for privacy. But then everyone else followed as well, and they finally came back to the parlor to accommodate everyone who wanted to see what a blessing was.

One by one, Ethan and the missionaries gave blessings to the same group that had been studying.

A beautiful, sacred quiet filled the room. "Maybe this is the best lesson of all," Jana whispered to Josh. Then she glanced at Howard, who seemed to be taking it all in, despite insisting earlier that he wanted no part of it. He seemed particularly interested in Rose's blessing.

Soon Dr. Rashid and the coroner arrived, and Jana and Ethan felt it was time to take their kids home. Ethan asked Helen to keep him apprised of the plans, and Jana promised to check in with her the next day.

On the ride home, the kids were uncharacteristically quiet. Finally Maddie said, "Well, that was a shockeroo."

Somehow it was the release everyone needed and the kids all laughed. Jana remembered how odd it was that there were always humorous moments that seemed to creep into somber occasions, if only to provide an escape for the overwhelming sadness.

"I guess we shouldn't be sad, really," Ethan said. "Herb was elderly and had lived a full life. He really was ready to go."

"It's just sad for those left behind," Jana agreed.

"And sad that he didn't get to join the church," Savannah added. "But he can do it on the other side."

"Yep." Ethan turned into the driveway.

"Maybe Chester or Raymond can do his temple work," Josh said. "That would be cool."

"That would be very cool," Jana agreed. *Swell, in fact.*

THE NEXT AFTERNOON HELEN CALLED TO SAY THAT HERB'S wishes were all in a file, and that a local mortuary was handling the details, including a burial at a cemetery nearby. There would be a viewing at the El Dorado House on Tuesday evening, and a funeral there the following Wednesday morning. "Vera was going to teach swing dancing to the teenagers that evening," she said, "but I think we'll postpone it under the circumstances."

"Oh—of course," Jana said.

"Raymond says Herb really appreciated Mr—I mean Bishop Waterson's blessing," Helen continued, "and he wanted him to conduct the funeral."

"No problem," Jana said. "We're here to help in any way we can." She called the mortuary to see how much they had already arranged, but except for taking care of the casket, they had no plans in place. So she called Mimi.

"We'll do the whole thing," Mimi said. "I'm on it. If Bishop will speak, I'll get opening and closing prayers, a couple of musical numbers, don't you worry about a thing. And I'll send out an email telling everyone in the ward, in case they'd like to attend. They may not have known Herb, but they can come to support the friends they do know. Do they need a meal afterwards?"

"No," Jana said. "Helen said they'll all just eat as usual. Lots of them are on special diets, anyway." She sighed. What did people do, who didn't have this incredible organization to plug into? She called Ethan and explained the plans.

"My first funeral," he said.

"You'll be magnificent," Jana told him.

"But I wish I had known him better," Ethan said. "All I have is the interviews the kids did. I'll go and talk with Chester and Raymond."

FOR FAMILY HOME EVENING THE NEXT NIGHT, MADDIE PREPARED a lesson about death, and pulled off a white glove to show how we leave our body behind, but our spirit still lives.

"Crazy at it sounds," Ethan said later to Jana, "I may use that in my funeral talk. This is a chance to teach about the Plan of Salvation."

"Hey," Josh said, popping into their room, "Do we have to go to the viewing?" Savannah was on his heels.

"No, I'm not much for viewings, myself," Jana said. "But it would be nice to pay your respects at the funeral."

Josh pumped his fist. "Yes! That's during History."

"Well, at least you'll be getting out of school for the right reasons," Savannah deadpanned.

"What about me?" Maddie was suddenly there as well. "I don't want to go to either one."

"I don't think you should have to go," Ethan said. "Funerals often upset little children."

"I'm not a 'little children,'" Maddie retorted. "I'm completely old enough to go."

Ethan shrugged. "Then you can go."

"But I don't want to go."

"Then you don't have to go," Jana said.

Maddie wasn't sure she had won this one. "But if I *wanted* to, then I *can.*"

Savannah was exasperated. "Oh my gosh, Mom. You are letting her think she can run the show."

"I can run *my* show," Maddie said.

Josh rolled his eyes and Jana scooted the children out. Then she called the junior high and high schools to leave dismissal messages for Wednesday. And, even though Merry hadn't known Herb either, she called and left a message on the Haines' home phone, just in case.

Chapter 30

TUESDAY WAS WINDY AND COLD, AND JANA FOUND HERSELF BUN-
dled up, clipping the last of the season's flowers from her cutting bed.
Pink roses, Peruvian lilies, even some late blooming blue hydrangeas
were still offering up their last blossoms in this northern California cli-
mate. And with ferns and greenery, she was able to make a couple of
large arrangements to take to the El Dorado House for the viewing.

She put them on tables at either end of the casket, and was relieved
to see some other sprays as well, that Simone had arranged in the
kitchen, using beautiful autumn leaves and pine cones. The Primary
Poster of Herb was on an easel as well, and Jana realized the kids would
need to make a new one for whatever new man moved in next.

All the residents had made the effort to dress up, respectfully filing
by Herb's coffin in the sitting room.

"It looks lovely," Vera whispered to Jana. "And your sweet husband
will do a fine job speaking tomorrow."

Jana smiled. "Thank you, Vera." Ethan was across the room, visiting
in hushed tones with Raymond and Stanley.

Rose was wearing a shimmering black-and-gold evening gown,
with black feathers in her trademark French twist. Howard was walking beside her as Rose wheeled past, then Francis came by with Harriet,
followed by Marvin and Chester.

Suddenly Rose's loud voice punctured the silence. "Who proposes at
a viewing?" she hollered. "I'm donating your brain to science."

Howard jutted out his chin. "I already tried to donate yours and they
didn't want it."

Now everyone's attention had turned to them, completely ignoring
the deceased Herb, the only one in the room who didn't snap around to
see what was going on.

Jana caught Ethan's eye; he was as stunned as she was.

"What on earth were you thinking?" Rose shouted.

"I was thinking that one of us could be next," Howard argued. "We're not getting any younger, Rose. I say we tie the knot."

"I say you're crazy," Rose said.

"Oh, come off it," Howard sneered. "You're in love with me and I'm in love with you. We've both known it for years."

Rose flushed crimson. "I will not be proposed to beside a corpse."

Jana winced. *Oh, well. It's not like Herb's listening. At least I hope not.*

"Then I'll wheel you outside."

Rose pushed Howard away. "You'll do nothing of the kind. It's still a funeral. And besides, you need to look into the Mormon church."

Now Howard threw his hands in the air. "Aaugh! Forget it!" Then he stormed off.

"Suit yourself," Rose called after him, always getting the last word.

Ethan was beside Jana now, and whispered, "Well, that's something new for a viewing."

Jana could feel prickly hives on her neck, and tried to avoid Rose's steely gaze. But Rose came over anyway.

"Can you believe that man asked me to marry him?" she asked, still as loud as ever. The other residents tried to filter by discreetly.

"Well, he loves you," Jana said.

"Hmph!" Rose turned her wheelchair to leave. "Then he can do what it takes to get me to say yes." And she zipped out of the room.

THE NEXT DAY HOWARD AND ROSE SAT ON OPPOSITE SIDES OF the parlor, where Ethan conducted the brief service. Savannah and Josh sat with Jana in the back. Mimi had arranged for the best singers in the ward, and everything went without a hitch.

Until the end. Howard had been asked to stand and announce where Herb would be interred, and to thank everyone who helped with the service. Holding a page of notes, he read, "Herb will be interned at Rolling Hills Cemet—"

"It's interred, not interned," Rose suddenly called out. "He's not becoming an intern. You need to wear your reading glasses."

"This from a woman with failing eyesight," Howard shot back.

"I can see better than you can," Rose argued.

"You don't shout across the room at a funeral," Howard said.

"And you don't propose at a viewing," Rose fired back.

Savannah and Josh both had bug eyes, and Jana found herself being grateful that Herb had no family in attendance.

Quickly Ethan interjected that Brother Lawrence would offer the closing prayer, and the funeral was over.

"Those two need to get married before they kill each other," Ethan whispered to Jana.

She pressed her lips between her teeth to keep from laughing.

"Howard and Rose *are* in love," Savannah whispered to her mother. "Yep."

Josh was squirming, shaking his head and trying not to laugh, and finally stood behind his father to conceal his twisting mouth. Ethan saw exactly what he was doing and smiled.

After several minutes of greeting and shaking hands, Ethan finally found himself alone with his family. "Well, I've got to get back to work," he said to Jana, but mostly for Josh, still behind him, to hear.

"I'll get the kids back to school," Jana said. By now the residents were filtering into the rec room for lunch, and Josh finally came out from behind his father, taking a deep breath and releasing it, to calm the laugh that was still trying to escape his lips. Jana put a hand on his shoulder and turned to leave.

"Hey, Savannah," Rose called. She wheeled over.

Oh, dear. What is she going to say, now?

"I'm glad to see you wore black," Rose said. "Too many kids today have no idea that you wear black to a funeral."

Little does she know that Savannah wears black more than any other color.

"Thank you," Savannah said.

"I've been wanting to talk to you about boys," Rose said, never one to approach a subject daintily.

"Oh?" Savannah smiled. Josh perked up to listen as well.

"When you were working in the yard, I noticed there was a boy who seemed pretty interested in you."

Savannah's eyebrows shot up.

"I was watching from the windows," Rose explained.

"Well, he and I are no longer seeing each other," Savannah said.

"I'm glad to hear it," Rose said. "A pretty girl like you needs to be careful. I speak from experience."

Jana was grateful that neither of her children reacted with surprise at that news.

Rose went on. "There'll be a lot of fellas who'll want to be your steady, but you hold out for the boy who loves you for who you are inside. He needs to respect you and value what you believe."

Savannah gave her a hug. "I will, Rose. Thank you."

As Jana led her kids to the door, she glanced back and caught a glimpse of Howard in the hallway, hobbling away on his cane. They stepped out onto the porch, then as they headed down the steps outside, Jana said, "Josh, do you think Howard was listening?"

Josh shrugged. "I hope so."

ON THURSDAY JANA WENT TO THE TEMPLE WITH HER BEST friends, Kristi Hargrove and Michelle Dayley. Afterwards, at lunch, Jana mentioned that she had put Merry's name on the prayer list.

"Me, too," Kristi said.

"So did I!" Michelle laughed. "I'm telling you, that girl has got to come back."

Jana told them about Rose catching Merry by the sleeve at church, and getting her to watch the Primary kids singing on her cell phone. "At least she watched it," Jana said.

"We won't give up on her," Kristi said. "Every few weeks I call to see how Aiden's doing. I really miss her."

"You guys are the best." And Jana meant it. What a blessing it was to have friends who shared her commitment and faith. It made her so much stronger on discouraging days.

"So what's the deal at the El Dorado House?" Kristi asked. "I hear you have a bunch of them coming to church, now."

"Oh, it's phenomenal," Jana said. "But we had one fellow pass away this week. And we have another man who wants to marry one of the women there, but she won't consider it unless he looks into the church."

Kristi and Michelle high-fived Jana. "Tell her to stand strong."

"Oh, I think you could look up 'stand strong' and see Rose's picture there," Jana laughed. "She is nothing if not fearless."

JANA'S PHONE RANG ON FRIDAY AFTERNOON, JUST AS SHE WAS getting into the pickup line at Maddie's school.

"I hate to bother you," Helen said, "but I'm worried about Howard."

"Why? What's going on?"

"He keeps leaving. He calls a cab to pick him up, and then he takes off for a couple of hours. I'm worried that he's looking at other care facilities."

"You think he's actually wanting to move?" Jana couldn't believe her ears.

Helen sighed. "Well, I have no evidence of it, but it's awfully suspicious that he's suddenly coming and going like this. It makes me nervous."

"Surely he wouldn't leave Rose," Jana said. *Or our family! Didn't we just make him our grandpa?*

"Well, that's what's so odd," Helen said. "I can't imagine he would leave over her decision to get baptized."

"That would be awful," Jana said.

"Maybe I'm wrong," Helen said. "I hope so. I probably shouldn't have even called. I don't want to alarm you when it's just my suspicions."

"Well, let me know if he says anything that would indicate he'll be leaving," Jana said. Then, gratefully, the conversation ended just as Maddie hopped into the car.

ON SATURDAY MORNING JANA ANNOUNCED SHE NEEDED TO GO to WalMart for some groceries for the weekend, and Ethan said he'd like to come along and get his sunglasses adjusted.

"I need to go, too," Savannah called from the family room. "I want to look at their tights and leggings."

"Let's all go," Jana suggested. "And we can get ice cream cones." She turned to Ethan. "It can be a date!"

"Okay," Ethan said, "but let the record show that you were the one who suggested a date like that."

Jana laughed. "Fine. It was my idea."

The kids ate their cones as Jana pushed the cart through the store, and soon they were heading back outside. Suddenly Jana shouted, "Stop!" holding her hands out to block her family members.

"What is it? What's wrong?" Maddie asked.

"It's a walking stick!" Jana shouted, stepping forward and bending down to look at the insect.

"A what?" Josh asked.

Jana dug through her purse for a card, and scooped the creature up onto it. "See? These are called walking sticks—they disguise themselves by looking like twigs."

"It kind of looks like a praying mantis," Josh said.

Ethan nodded, staring at the 6-inch straw-colored insect. "But what was it doing in a WalMart?"

"I don't know, but someone could've rolled their cart right over him," Jana said.

"So you're saving him," Savannah said, unimpressed.

"Of course I am," Jana said, and gingerly carried him out, across the driveway, and to the bushes by the parking lot. The family followed. Carefully Jana touched the card to the bush so the little guy could climb off and onto a branch.

But instead, he sprang into the air and went flapping and flying back across the roadway they had just crossed. And bam! Five starlings from the WalMart trees were on him like ninja warriors.

"No!" Jana shrieked. She turned to Ethan.

But Ethan and her children were all giggling, now.

"That's terrible!" Jana shouted. "And *you* are all terrible! How can you laugh about that?"

Now Ethan's shoulders were shaking. "That walking stick was probably fighting off birds all morning and finally made it to the safety of the store, when some woman scooped him up and threw him back into the jaws of death!"

The kids were all dissolved in hysterics now, Josh almost wheezing as they loaded the groceries.

"You people are sick," Jana muttered as she got into the van. "I can't believe I live with such barbarians." *Especially when I am so obviously meant to save the world.*

Finally the kids stopped howling with merriment and went about their day. Jana swung by the El Dorado House with Maddie for another art lesson, then left her with Vera for some shading instruction, and went to visit with Helen at the front desk. Rose was there, too, both of them talking about their upcoming baptisms.

Howard and Chester were in the parlor, playing cards, and Stanley was visiting with Cody Orton in the sitting room. *Good—Cody's following up on Stanley's offer.*

"I'm hoping to be baptized before Thanksgiving," Helen beamed. "Rose and I, maybe others, who knows?"

"It's just fantastic," Jana said. "The whole ward is so excited."

"Maybe Marvin, too," Rose said. "But he's taking it slow, doesn't want to rush. He's off to a ballgame with Will and his family today. Now that the World Series is over, I guess they're going to a basketball game."

"I love how so many kids have found grandparents here."

"I was hoping to get some of the cooks and other staff members interested in the church," Helen said, "but we have such a high turnover rate. I just had to replace our whole kitchen staff. Well, it's only three people, but still."

Jana marveled at how quickly the missionary spirit sprang to life in a person once they got a witness of truth from the Holy Ghost. They instantly want to share it with others. "But Shanika and Theresa are investigating it, right?"

Helen's eyes sparkled. "Yes! Two of our nurses. Isn't that great?"

"I wish a couple of the doctors had taken an interest," Jana said.

Helen shrugged. "They're here so briefly and they're so busy with their work; they don't really get to chat about other things."

"And did you know we have a new man moving in today?" Rose said.

"What? Already?"

"Oh, we have quite a waiting list, now that the place has been given a face lift," Helen smiled.

"So who's replacing Herb?" Jana felt immediately sorry for putting it that way.

Helen smiled. "His name is Gus Howell. He's coming over from the Borden-Dunn retirement facility. His kids brought him over for a tour, now that he's using a walker. And he loved the place!"

"Wow—I'll look forward to meeting him," Jana said.

"I guess I shouldn't be surprised when people love it," Helen said. "But after so many years of black paint and dim lighting, it's hard to believe people are fighting over the vacancy spots."

"It's a different place, now," Jana agreed, both of them glancing about the entirely new interior. And it wasn't just the paint and draperies that had changed—even Helen was completely different. She seemed to glow now, as if lit from within, as much as the building itself.

"Have you heard anything from your son?" Jana asked.

Helen shook her head. "I feel sad for him. But it's his loss."

Jana nodded. "It is, isn't it?" She thought for a moment. "But maybe he'll come around after some time goes by."

"I hope so. I pray for him."

"Like my sister," Rose said.

"That has to be hard for both of you," Jana said.

Helen nodded, then pointed to a little scrap of paper she had Scotch-taped to the backside of the counter, where she could see it as she worked. It said, "And every one that hath forsaken houses, or brethren, or sisters, or father, or mother, or wife, or children, or lands, for my name's sake, shall receive an hundredfold, and shall inherit everlasting life. Matthew 19:29."

Jana bent down and hugged her, then hugged Rose. And she thought of Merry. Sometimes membership in Christ's church required tremendous sacrifices.

Just then Zack Applegate came barreling through the front door with Raymond and the rest of the Applegates following behind. "Guess what?" Zack shouted. "Grandpa Raymond's getting baptized!"

Jana, Helen, and Rose exchanged glances and Helen began to cry. They rushed over to congratulate Raymond, who laughed, waving his cane in triumph. "Let's tell the gang," he said.

Soon the entire recreation room—minus Howard—was cheering.

"What helped you decide?" Helen asked.

"My wife," Raymond said. "I decided I want to be sealed to my sweetheart."

Rose glanced at Howard, who was staring at the floor, and sighed.

As they headed to the rec room, they could hear conversations in some of the bedrooms—everyone talking about their research and the discussions they were having with the missionaries. Jana had never seen anything like it, where so many people were genuinely converting to the gospel. It was as if the spirit had permeated the building, and caught everyone—well, almost everyone—in its wake.

"I'd better get back to the front desk," Helen said. "Mr. Howell could be arriving any minute." She hurried back down the hallway.

"Mom, come see what I drew," Maddie called.

Jana went over and saw Maddie's beautiful likeness of Harriet's cat, Misty. "No way—you drew that just now?" There was a portrait of Misty, licking one paw, her tail curled around herself, her delicate whiskers barely visible. Last time she had drawn Misty as well, but only the face and whiskers.

"And I learned shading, too."

Jana leaned in to see it up close. "How did you get the fur to look so real?"

Maddie smiled at Vera. "That's our little secret."

Jana grinned at Maddie's fairy grandma. "You're wonderful to do this."

"Well, Maddie happens to be very talented, or it wouldn't look this grand," Vera said.

Harriet had been watching, since the artist's model was on her lap as usual, and seemed genuinely delighted. "You could hang that in a museum," she said.

Maddie fairly floated off the ground at such praise.

"Well, time to pack it up, Sweetie," Jana said. And the two of them began cleaning up and putting the art supplies in Maddie's backpack.

Then, just as they had finished and were heading out of the rec room, in came Helen with the new resident. Handsome, with silvery hair and crystal blue eyes, he was wearing a dark blue zippered jacket and a white Polo shirt. A 50-ish couple was with him—apparently his kids who were helping him move in. Gus made his way along with his walker, then stopped as Helen began to speak.

"Everyone," Helen said, waiting for the chatter to die down. "I'd like you to meet our new resident, Gus Howell."

Gus waved, almost shyly.

Raymond went right over and shook his hand. "I'll be your room-mate," he said. "I'm happy to know you."

Gus nodded, then turned to Helen. She put a gentle hand on his back. "Let's get you all situated," she said, and Gus and his family left.

"Seems like a nice man," Jana said, turning to the others.

Pearl and Lorraine were whispering and laughing. "And pretty nice looking," Lorraine said, drawing laughter from the entire room.

"WE MET THE NEW GUY," MADDIE SHOUTED THE MINUTE THEY got home.

"What? Already?" Ethan asked. He was on a ladder, taking down the air filters for cleaning, now that brisk November weather was upon them.

"I guess they have a waiting list, now," Jana said. She started chopping vegetables for a stir fry they'd be having that night.

"So what's he like?" Josh asked, looking up from a laptop at the breakfast counter, where he was working on a report for his English class.

"Well, he's pretty old," Maddie said. "But Pearl and Lorraine thought he was handsome."

Ethan shook his head. *That's just what we need over there—another romance.*

"And Raymond is getting baptized," Jana said.

Ethan nearly fell off the ladder. "What?" He hurried down and hugged her. "Are you kidding?"

"He wants to be sealed to Mrs. Raymond," Maddie said.

"Awesome," Josh said. "Wow."

Savannah was at a school football game, but heard the full report from Maddie when she came home late that afternoon. "You should be a news reporter," she told her little sister.

"And give fairy tours, and be a famous artist," Maddie said. Then she brought out her cat picture, for the usual oohs and aahs.

"So are these people really converted?" Savannah asked. "I mean, do they know the gospel well enough to be getting baptized, or are they all just jumping on the band wagon?"

Ethan smiled and got himself a glass of water. "That's what I used to think," he said. "I always worried when people agreed kind of quickly. But my mission president told me that when someone feels the witness from the Holy Ghost to get baptized, we should do it. They have a testimony. They can fill in the blanks later."

Josh was nodding. "Makes sense. I mean, we don't make 8-year-olds wait until they're scripture scholars."

Maddie shot her brother a glance.

"Except you, Maddie," he said. "We know you know the scriptures."

Maddie seemed satisfied with that quick spin, and went into the family room to watch television. She started channel surfing for a cat show she liked on the nature channel.

"Once they know it's true, they should get baptized and get the Gift of the Holy Ghost," Jana said. "They need it. Then they can be guided to add to their knowledge line upon line."

Savannah smiled and nodded. "I guess the main thing is getting that witness. You just don't want them to fall away."

"Well, that's where we come in," Jana said. "We need to embrace them and make sure they have a nurturing ward, good friends, responsibilities—"

"And they've actually learned quite a bit," Ethan said. "The elders have taken many of them through all the lessons, and some of the Home Teachers have done an amazing job as well. You'd be surprised what they know. Nearly everyone over there has given up coffee and tea, too. It's incredible."

"They're always reading and talking together about it when I'm over there," Jana added. "It's so exciting to watch these people open their hearts."

"Maybe being old helps," Josh said.

Ethan chuckled. "I actually think it does. It's like being poor helps. You're humble, you're not preoccupied with building a fortune or social climbing."

"And it's like they're smarter or something," Josh said.

"It is," Jana agreed. "Seriously. By their age they've found out which choices in life don't lead to happiness, and their priorities are more in focus. They really do seem to recognize the truth more easily."

Just then Ethan glanced over at the TV screen where Maddie was still flipping from station to station. "Whoa, whoa. Go back one. I think I saw the El Dorado House."

Jana turned off the stove and the whole family gathered as Maddie flipped back to the same news channel where Sammy Fenton had done his report on the gold paint.

Connor Stone was at the anchor desk, with a video of the El Dorado House behind him, and a young woman standing at the ready, just outside the El Dorado House gate, the setting sun making it glimmer behind her.

". . . and now some local leaders think they know why the El Dorado House got that facelift we covered a couple of weeks ago. Angie?"

"Well, Connor, some local ministers believe the Mormon church painted this building and redecorated the interior just to get people to join their religion. I'm here with Pastor Dalton of the Sacramento Community Fellowship of Christ. Pastor Dalton?"

Now the camera shot widened to include a tall, handsome preacher with thick, wavy hair and gleaming teeth. "This isn't the first time this has happened," he said. "And we hate to see seniors taken advantage of like this. This isn't how anyone should gain converts."

"So you're saying all this landscaping and paint—"

"Well, it's pretty coincidental, isn't it?" Pastor Dalton grinned into the camera. "There are several people here—I mean, they're really trapped, aren't they? And now suddenly they're all joining that church?" He raised a skeptical brow.

Angie turned to her other side, where suddenly Raymond was standing, nervous in a plaid shirt and slacks. "And you're one of the people who are joining the Mormon church?" Angie asked.

"Yes," Raymond said.

"And you like the way this building has been re-done?" Angie asked.

"Yes," Raymond said. He swallowed, unsure what to do next.

Angie turned back to Pastor Dalton who was only too eager to begin a sermon, not even waiting for Angie to ask him a question. "The local Christian Watchdog Alliance is asking the Mormons to leave these people alone. This is not the way to increase your membership, Angie. It's just not right."

Angie turned back to the camera. "Well, there you have it. Connor?"

Connor thanked her for her report and moved on to the next story as the entire Waterson house, and eleven others in the ward, erupted into commotion.

Chapter 33

"WHAT!? WHAT?!" JANA WONDERED IF HER HEAD WOULD EXPLODE from all the capital letters filling her brain. "Poor Raymond—they didn't let him explain!"

"That guy is lying!" Savannah shouted.

"The absolute worst reporting I have ever seen," Ethan echoed.

"How can they do that?" Josh asked.

And all of it at the same time, along with Maddie screaming, "Why is he saying this?"

"They didn't even give us a chance to respond to that ridiculous accusation," Ethan said.

Suddenly their cell phones all started ringing, and for the next half hour friends and ward members—all equally outraged—wanted to know what to do.

And then the news station itself called, asking to send another reporter to the Waterson home, for a comment.

Ethan agreed to meet the reporter at the El Dorado House itself, then hung up and turned to his family. "Well, apparently their phones rang off the hook with complaints, and now they realize they should have gotten both sides of the story."

"No kidding," Savannah sneered.

"I'm going to ask Ty Marks to meet me there," Ethan said. "He's good with the press. And I need to let President Morrow know about it, too."

But President Morrow was ahead of him, and called at that same moment on the land line. "I'm just leaving the temple and heard all about it. I'll meet you there," he said.

"Shouldn't we get Helen or somebody to set them straight from a resident's point of view?" Jana said. "Maybe I should call her."

"Good idea," Ethan said, swinging on a jacket and grabbing his keys.

"I guess they'll interview us, and then run it on the late news at ten."

"Can we come?" Josh asked.

"I get to come, I get to come," Maddie began.

"No," Ethan said. "Let's not make this more of a circus than it already is. I don't want them ambushing you kids and taking your comments out of context."

"Dad, Ty, and President Morrow will be good spokesmen," Jana said, herding her kids back.

"And we've had training from Public Affairs," Ethan said. "Not that I'm some expert, but I think I can manage."

"We'll pray as you drive," Jana called as he backed out of the garage.

They all went back into the kitchen and Josh offered a prayer that the truth would come out and the nasty rumor would be proven false.

Then the phone rang. It was Helen. "I guess you've heard about the news story," she said.

"Yes—I was just going to call. Ethan—I mean Bishop Waterson—is headed there, now."

"Well, of course everyone here saw it," Helen said. "And they're all furious. Even Howard is mad because he knows what a lie it is."

"Do you want to talk to the reporter?" Jana asked.

"No, I'm not very good at that sort of thing. But the reason I'm call-ing—" Helen stopped. A moment passed.

"Helen? Are you there?"

Finally she spoke again, a catch in her throat. "Jana, I'm so sorry."

"What? What is it?"

"It's my son. He's the one behind this. He called from Arizona and got all the ministers in that alliance thing worked up, and told them to call the media."

Jana gasped. "Oh, Helen. Oh, I'm so sorry."

"No, I'm the one who's sorry. I just can't believe he would launch a vicious attack like this."

"Do you need me to come over there?"

"No. No, honestly. I'll be fine. I'm just heartbroken that he would do something like this."

"Well, it's not your fault, Helen."

"Thank you, Jana. Oh—looks like your husband just arrived. I'll talk to you later."

ETHAN DASHED ACROSS THE LOBBY TO HELEN'S DESK. "DON'T worry," he said. "We'll get this all straightened out. I have our Stake President coming, and a ward member who's a lobbyist."

Helen burst into tears and told him about her son, stirring up the accusations. Ethan listened, then clasped her hands in his. They were cold as ice. "Don't blame yourself," he said. "Everything's going to be alright."

Several residents were coming down the hallway and filling the entryway, now. Each one was echoing the same sentiments the Watersons had felt after the story had aired.

And poor Raymond was almost in tears. "I just didn't know what to say," he kept repeating. The others tried to console him, but he was devastated.

Talk about senior abuse. Ethan was angry at the novice reporter who had entrapped Raymond and then kept him from explaining.

"It's going to be fine," Ethan said, pushing the air with his hands until everyone quieted down. "Raymond, that wasn't fair how she cut you off, and we're going to set the record straight. I just ask that you all let President Morrow and Brother Marks do the talking. They're trained, they're professional, and they won't let a reporter box them in like that."

There seemed to be a mumbling consensus.

Just then Ty Marks came through the door, filling them with the same assurances that everything would be fine, and the group relaxed even more. Minutes later President Morrow arrived, and the three men stepped into the parlor to plan their response. They decided President Morrow would be the official spokesman, with Tyrell standing by to add whatever he felt inspired to say. Ethan was relieved to be there as back-up, since backing up was what he most wanted to do right now.

President Morrow nodded, then returned to the group of residents. "Let's have a prayer," he said. "Bishop Waterson?"

Ethan was eager to pray for help, really just continuing the prayer already in his heart. He also expressed gratitude that the TV station was willing to get both sides of the story. It calmed his heart, and made him able to greet Tim Jarvis with genuine affection, when the crusty reporter arrived. He'd seen Tim on air many times, and knew this report would be airing later that night. Tim had bushy gray hair he'd managed to fill with enough product to slick it down, and the deep lines of a man who'd spent many years maintaining a dark tan. Both hard-hitting and smart, Tim was a popular on-air presence.

Bright light from the camera itself bathed the lobby as the cameraman flicked on the power and Tim began his interview with President Morrow and Ty Marks. Ethan stood off to one side, Helen on the other. As usual, Ethan was aware that he was the tallest guy in the room, and hoped he wouldn't get singled out for a comment.

Tim stood in front of the cluster of residents, and Ethan found himself glad that they formed a crowd large enough to block some of the hot pink draperies. Even the new guy, Gus, was in the background, curious to see what was going on.

"We're here with Clifton Morrow, President of a Mormon organization, talking about the recent renovations here at the El Dorado House," Tim said.

Tim's a seasoned reporter. He should know to call us by our proper name.

But President Morrow was on it. "Actually, Tim, the name of our church is the Church of Jesus Christ of Latter-day Saints. Mormon is a nickname."

Tim just plowed ahead. "And the Christian Watchdog Alliance claims the improvements here have been made so that residents will join that church."

"Nothing could be further from the truth," President Morrow said. "We took this on as a community project, all done by volunteers, all paid for privately. The fact that some of the residents wish to be baptized was a very happy surprise to all of us. But no pressure whatsoever was put on any of the wonderful people who live here."

"Pastor Dalton made a claim earlier today, that you're taking advantage of the seniors living here—"

"Pastor Dalton knows better than that," Ty interrupted. "I have many friends in his congregation. They're all good people. And they all know we don't do that. This is just a Christian service project, doing what we think Christ would do if he were here."

Good, Ty—getting in the point that we're Christians. Ethan breathed a sigh of relief. And then he stiffened, as he saw Helen suddenly stepping forward.

She stood there, trembling. "Excuse me. Mr. Jarvis. I know the source of this gossip."

Now the light was drenching Helen's face as both the cameraman and reporter turned to her. Tim held a microphone to her lips. "My son is a pastor and he's angry that I'm joining the LDS faith," Helen said. "He's the one who got other ministers to spread these lies. I'm very sorry. But every one of us has chosen this faith of our own free will. We asked to learn more. This was not the condition for improvements to this facility."

A spontaneous cheer went up from the crowd and Tim turned back to President Morrow. "So you're saying you've been slandered today."

Boy and how, Ethan thought. But President Morrow held up a hand. "I'm not saying anything about that fine pastor. I'm just saying this fix-up was not contingent upon anything." *Good for him, refusing to get baited into a fight.*

Tim whirled back to Helen. "So why are you joining, then?"

And now Helen looked calmly back at Tim and said, "I have been searching for the truth my entire life, Mr. Jarvis. When I found it, I knew I had to join."

"Against your son's wishes."

Helen took a deep breath, then nodded, her eyes downcast. And that was all it took to cue Rose. Suddenly she came roaring up in her hotrod wheelchair, blue eyeglasses swinging around her neck.

"Listen here," Rose began. She was wearing a sequined blouse with a splashy coral scarf. Ethan cringed. President Morrow gulped, and he didn't even know Rose. "Mr. Jarvis," Rose started in, then interrupted herself. "I watch you on the news all the time, by the way. You seem like a nice boy."

Now Tim laughed. "Call me Tim," he said, clearly enjoying the implication that he was young.

"Very well. Tim." Rose smiled for the cameraman.

Good heavens, she's got him in the palm of her hand.

"You can't live your life trying to please family members. You'll see that's true when you get a little older, Tim."

Now Tim laughed, eager to let Rose run out her rope. And she did. "When you pray to know if something is true, you and God both know it," Rose said. "You have to act. Sometimes people get their hackles up—I have a sister who's mad at me over this—but there's a thing called integrity, and I'm sticking with it. I have to follow my conscience, Tim. And this is a free country, I believe."

Ethan wanted to give her a high five. But he just stared along with Ty and President Morrow as Tim said, "Yes, Ma'am, it is," yielding control of the interview for the first time in years.

"We're old, but we're not stupid," Rose continued, waving at the crowd of residents just five feet away. "Stanley, you talk to Tim, here."

Now, suddenly, Stanley was wheeling over, and cleared his throat. Rose picked the perfect, eloquent spokesman and she knew it.

"Perhaps you've noticed we're a fiercely independent bunch," Stanley said.

"That seems to be the case," Tim laughed, glancing at Rose.

"No one waltzes in and tells us how to live, how to vote, or what church to belong to. We decide for ourselves. All the Mormons did was make our home presentable."

"So are you joining their church?" Tim pressed.

Stanley took a deep breath, then smiled broadly. "Well, I haven't said so thus far, but yes. I've looked into it and I believe it is Christ's true church. In fact, you're welcome to attend the baptism. It would be good for you. You might learn something."

Tim's eyes were dancing with delight at having so many great sound bites to take back to the station for editing. "Well, thank you, Mr.—"

"Dr. Westminster. Stanley Westminster."

Ethan caught his breath. This was the first time he'd heard of Stanley's decision, but also the first time he'd heard Stanley's last name, or that he held a degree Ethan would later learn was a doctorate in Speech & Elocution.

Tim turned back to the camera, wrapped up the interview beaming, then shook hands with everyone there and got signed releases from those who had been on video.

"This couldn't have gone better," President Morrow whispered to Ethan and Ty.

Ty was glowing. "If they just use all the comments, what a great missionary tool, right?"

Ethan grinned. "Like a testimony meeting on the nightly news." He rushed over to congratulate Stanley on his choice to be baptized, and joined in the back-slapping.

"I spoke to my son who lives in Land Park," Stanley said, "And he's going to look into it, as well." Stanley seemed as pleased about that as he was about his own conversion.

Tim turned to Rose, who gave him a confident wink. "Rose, you are my kind of woman."

"Well, get in line," Howard sneered, stepping through the crowd. The entire cluster of residents burst out laughing and Tim blushed crimson.

Just then the front door flew open and two men in dark suits with clerical collars rushed in. One had bushy white hair, and the other looked like a fresh-faced graduate from Divinity School, both of them panting.

"Are we too late?" the older one asked. "I called the station and they said you were here doing a followup—"

Tim motioned his cameraman to turn it on again and Ethan gulped. Just when things had been going so well.

"I'm Reverend LaVon Hawkes, and this is our assistant pastor, Corbin Thorndike," the older one began, still trying to catch his breath, but speaking with command. "We'd like to offer our support of what the Mormons are doing here." His rich voice echoed through the foyer.

Ethan felt his jaw drop, then closed his mouth.

"We've had nothing but a good relationship with these folks," Reverend Hawkes continued. "They helped us when our building flooded, they've supported our food drive, and there is no reason to suspect them of doing anything but kind, charitable work here."

President Morrow looked as if he could hug the man.

"And we want folks to know that the Christian Watchdog Alliance does *not* speak for all the Christian churches in this area," Pastor Thorndike added. "We do not affiliate with them."

"So you're saying these are false charges—" Tim said, again trying to get a counter accusation on tape.

Reverend Hawkes took a deep breath. "I'm saying we work on the Interfaith Council with Mormons who have been exemplary citizens. They've built houses for the poor, right alongside us. They've supported Freedom of Religion with us. They even help us set up our Nativity Collection at Christmastime."

"And the Christian Watchdog Alliance?"

"Well," Reverend Hawkes paused for effect. "Let's just say we don't see a whole lot of them."

Now Tim's eyebrows raised and he turned to the camera himself. "Well, it looks like there are definitely two sides to this story, Jess." Then the camera shut down and Tim got the two ministers to sign more forms.

President Morrow, Ethan, and Ty rushed up to thank them, pumping their hands and almost tripping over one another in an effort to express their gratitude.

"I can't begin to tell you what this means to us," President Morrow said.

"Well, it's our pleasure. We have a good relationship and I'd hate to see it tarnished by a fringe group of hysterics," Reverend Hawkes said.

"I look forward to working with you in the future," Pastor Thorndike said. "You know, our attorney is a Latter-day Saint, and does all our work pro bono."

"I'm happy to hear that," Ethan said. "Good for him."

"Good for us," Reverend Hawkes said. Then he and his assistant shook a few more hands and headed out.

Ethan looked about for Helen, and found her already at her desk. "Helen, that took great courage," he said, shaking her hand.

She sighed. "Right is right. I just hope my son comes to accept it."

"You were amazing," Ty added, joining Ethan. "It's not easy to collect your thoughts with a camera in your face. You said the perfect things."

"Well, I couldn't just let you all try to explain things when the truth was that my son had caused all this trouble in the first place."

"I'd say you saved the whole situation," Ty said.

"Wouldn't it be something if they covered an LDS baptism?" Helen said, brightening.

"It would be a miracle," Ty laughed. "And who knows—we might get Mr. Jarvis to attend, if only to see Rose again."

So we actually came out ahead. Ethan couldn't wait to tell Jana and the kids how a seemingly horrible event had been turned on its head. It was 7:45 now, and as Tim Jarvis and his cameraman drove out onto El Dorado Street, they had a prayer of thanks before leaving for their separate homes.

NO ONE HAD FELT LIKE EATING AFTER THE NEWS REPORT THEY'D seen, so Jana warmed up the stir-fry when Ethan got home. He told them how Helen, Rose, and Stanley had become the heroes of the day, and how two protestant ministers had defended them as well. Then, with the announcement of another baptism, suddenly the whole house took on a party atmosphere and the family was famished.

At ten o'clock they gathered around the television, and at 10:20 Tim's report came on. Jana had set it to record, which was a good thing because everyone began shouting "There's Helen!" and "There's Rose!" and you couldn't hear anything they were saying. Finally they ran it back and quieted down. Incredibly, Tim had kept nearly all the comments, and then joked with the anchors about Rose calling him a boy.

"He's making this all about his age," Savannah said.

"That's okay," Ethan explained. "The public still got the facts."

"That's right," Jana said. "The anchors may care about themselves, but the viewers were set straight tonight. This ought to put those ridiculous claims to rest."

Ethan pulled out Tim's business card and called to leave his thanks on Tim's voice mail. Then he made a note to call the news director in the morning to thank him as well, for caring enough to get the story straight, and to fix the earlier one-sided report.

"And it wasn't just one-sided; it was wrong-sided," Josh pointed out.

"We always need to thank the media for fair coverage," Ethan said. "It's hard to come by."

Jana thought about Helen and the strained relationship with her son. *Good family relationships are hard to come by, too.* She said a silent prayer that they could mend theirs.

THE NEXT MORNING IN SACRAMENT MEETING JANA EXPECTED TO see Helen, Rose, Raymond, and Stanley, since they each had committed to baptism, but her jaw dropped when six more showed up as well. Chester must have borrowed one of Stanley's ties, because it hung down 5 inches past his belt. And Marvin looked as if he were a movie poster come to life—a thick, white ascot tied around his neck, and a crisp gray jacket buttoned neatly beneath.

Frances came with the Holden family, and looked every bit the grandmother in their group, beaming at the children and helping herd them into a pew. Lorraine stepped briskly with her cane, followed by Harriet and Pearl in their wheelchairs.

They must have rented hydraulic lift vans.

Vera was almost giggly, and couldn't wait to see Jana's reaction. "I know a ward about two hours north of here that had the same thing happen," she whispered. "One man went around and got *seventeen* less actives to come back."

"How did he do it?" Jana asked, astonished.

"He just made friends with them. He talked to them about their interests, really showed them respect." She shrugged. "Same thing."

Jana bit her lip. Was that what they had done, without even realizing it?

Helen and Rose were already chatting with some of the other members, making friends and getting acquainted. She glanced at Josh, seated with the deacons. This time he was holding up both hands, his fingers splayed, to show the number ten.

And then she glanced over to the bench where the Watersons usually sat. Only now it was taken.

There was Carlita, with Cody right beside her.

Chapter 32

JANA TRIED NOT TO OVERREACT AND EMBARRASS CODY OR CAR-
lita, so she just caught their eye and gave them a thumbs up. But Carlita
waved her over. "Sit on our row," she said. "So we don't look like sore
thumbs." Carlita was wearing a denim skirt and a white blouse.

Jana happily slid in beside her. "So glad you're here," she whispered
back.

"Well, it's Dr. Westminster who told Cody he had to come. That guy's
been working with Cody two days a week and it's been a godsend! Can
I say godsend?"

Jana laughed. "Of course you can. That's wonderful that he's taken
Cody under his wing."

Carlita sighed. "You're telling me."

Cody leaned forward and reached across his mother to shake Jana's
hand. He seemed like an entirely different kid. And where did that wide
smile come from?

Stanley wheeled by just then, to shake Cody's hand. "So we'll see you
at the baptism," he said, as the meeting began.

Jana's eyebrows shot up and she grinned at Carlita. "Cody's coming
to his baptism?"

Carlita smiled. "He asked Cody to *baptize* him."

Whaaat? Jana tried not to inhale all the air in the room, and just
smiled back. Soon the Young Men's President was guiding Cody to
where the Priests were sitting.

Later she found Ethan with a free moment in the bishop's office.
"Can Cody baptize Stanley?"

"Well, Stanley's a pretty heavy guy and Cody isn't that large, but we'll
tell Stanley to bend his knees—"

"No—I mean, doesn't he have to be, you know—"

"Worthy?" Ethan smiled. "Trust me. Cody is a good kid who made
a stupid mistake. He's committed to coming back to church and I think

this will be the very opportunity to get him to use his priesthood and set his course straight. I felt really good when I prayed about it."

"I wasn't second guessing you."

"Yes you were." Ethan smiled.

"Okay, a little." Jana hugged him. "But you've got to admit, it's—"

"A shockeroo?" They laughed at Ethan using Maddie's word. "I'm learning there are lots of surprises when you step back and let the Lord run things."

Jana nodded. "That's so true. It's like we actually get in the way, sometimes."

Ethan kissed her forehead. "Faith over Force."

Faith over force.

THAT AFTERNOON THE WATERSONS WENT BY TO JOIN IN MISSION-ary discussions and baptism plans. Jana had never seen such excitement. Carlita brought Cody, of course, and both of them walked in with boxes of cinnamon rolls from Carlita's bakery. Cody mingled comfortably with everyone there, shaking hands and chatting as if he'd always been confident and outgoing. Jana saw Stanley standing nearby, smiling.

The two nurses who were investigating were still interested, though not yet ready for interviews with the mission president. And although Chester, Lorraine, Harriet, and Marvin were also not ready to commit, they definitely wanted to continue the discussions. Elders Torrisi and Jamison were scrambling to organize the paperwork of the six who did want to be baptized, and visibly relaxed when their mission president came through the door.

President Yoshida reminded Jana of Chester—small in stature, but brimming with energy. Like a heat-seeking torpedo, he had made a beeline for the rec room and was quickly poring over the paperwork and setting up interviews. He was shaking hands and squeezing arms, a happy, contagious smile on his face.

Howard watched from the end of the long table where everyone was gathered, and Josh broke away from the group to sit by him. Ethan glanced over and smiled. *That kid. I love that kid.*

Jana watched as Gus hobbled in with his walker, grabbed a cinnamon roll, then sat down by Howard and Josh. She nudged Ethan.

"That's the new guy," she whispered. "He's probably wondering what all this hubbub is about."

Savannah glanced at her mother. "Hubbub?"

Jana laughed. "I should introduce all of you to him."

Soon the Watersons were gathered around Gus, and Ethan was saying, "So I'll bet you wonder what's going on, here."

Gus leaned back in his chair. "Actually, no." He smiled. "I'm already a Mormon."

"Wonderful," Ethan said, shaking his hand.

Howard's face fell, suddenly drained of all color. Quickly he glanced over at Rose, then back at Gus. Jana had never seen him look so panicky.

Oh, no. This must be his worst fear, that Rose will fall in love with a Mormon man. Make that a rather handsome Mormon man.

Rose's head whipped around. "Did you say you were already a Mormon?"

Gus nodded, chewing a bite of Carlita's delicious rolls.

Now all the other residents began buzzing, eager to ask Gus about his faith, happy to tell him they had just discovered it, themselves.

But Howard was glaring. He cleared his throat. "Well, I guess you've had a pretty simple life, Gus. Straight and narrow kind of thing. Got married. Had a bunch of kids. Right?"

Gus shrugged. "Not really."

"What does that mean?" Howard was almost sneering. "You said the other day you were in banking."

"International banking," Gus said.

"Oh, *international* banking," Howard said, dripping with sarcasm. "Is that anything like the *International* House of Pancakes?"

Rose gave him a glance, but Howard ignored it and went right on. "Must have been *really* exciting."

Gus looked over at Howard to see why he was trying to get a rise out of him, then decided to let it pass. "We had four children and lived overseas a bit. But then Dorothy passed, and—" he looked into the smiling faces of the residents who weren't glaring at him—"and now, here I am."

Howard scoffed and Rose kicked him under the table. "What is wrong with you?" she mouthed, when Gus was looking away.

Howard decided he'd had enough and scooted out, his chair screeching loudly on the floor. "Excuse me," he said.

President Yoshida continued the baptism arrangements, and Jana noticed a couple of them happily reporting that their kids were in complete support of their decision. She hoped it wasn't rubbing salt into the wound for Helen, Rose, or some of the others, but they seemed unfazed, even glad to hear it.

Helen saw Jana and Savannah standing away from the crowd for a moment, and stepped over to whisper. "I have some good news," she said. "My other son, Adam, is in complete support of my decision."

"Oh, how marvelous," Jana said. "You must be so happy."

"I am," Helen said. "He's not interested, himself, but he feels I should choose for myself and not let Derrick control my life."

"Good for him," Jana said.

"Come to think of it, Derrick probably bullied Adam as they grew up, so maybe he's particularly happy to finally see his brother isn't getting his way." Helen chuckled and went back to the crowd surrounding President Yoshida.

"Well," Savannah said, "Thank goodness she has one family member in favor of it."

Jana nodded. "Wish Rose had one."

Savannah glanced over to the table where Rose was loudly organizing the transportation to the baptism. "Rose doesn't need one. She runs her own course."

It was true. Rose was strong enough to stand up to her sister or any number of nay-sayers. "We can learn a lot from Rose," Jana smiled.

SOON PRESIDENT YOSHIDA AND THE ELDERS HAD MADE ALL THE arrangements for the baptism, and scheduled it for the Saturday before Thanksgiving.

"We're going to have so much to be thankful for," Vera said, and the residents all murmured their agreement. They turned to the Watersons.

"You have to join us for Thanksgiving dinner," Rose said.

Ethan sputtered. "Oh, I don't think they're planning on—"

"Yes, you must," Helen said. "We always budget for guests for Thanksgiving."

"Of course, they rarely come," Rose said, eliciting laughter.

Jana looked at the kids' hopeful faces, then at Ethan, and nodded.

"Okay," Ethan shrugged. "We'll come."

"And you, too, Cody and Carlita," Stanley said.

"If I can bring rolls or something," Carlita said.

"You'd *better* bring those rolls," Rose said.

Maddie dashed over and hugged Vera again, thrilled to be spending her Thanksgiving with her new fairy grandma.

Soon it was dinnertime for the seniors, and with all the arrangements made, the Watersons headed home.

"I can't b*elieve* they're renting a *bus!*" Maddie exulted, from the back seat.

"Plus two hydraulic vans," Ethan said, shaking his head in amazement.

"That's going to be so cool to have Thanksgiving with a whole room of new converts," Savannah said. "And who knows—maybe the other four will join soon."

"It really will," Jana agreed. "But Howard didn't seem too happy about Gus being a member." She turned to Josh. "Did you pick up on that?"

Josh nodded. "Poor Howard."

"Yep. Poor Howard." And according to Helen, he'd been gone all that morning, too, while the others had been at church.

That week the Young Men followed up on Ethan's request for a night of car mechanics, and Josh came home glowing. "You totally should have seen it, Mom. I got Howard to come and he knows *everything* about cars."

Jana and Maddie looked up from their reading, both of them engrossed in novels. "That's wonderful," Jana said. "What fun for Howard to be able to share his talents like that."

"And you know what? I think Stanley is right—Cody *is* a genius. When it comes to mechanical stuff, anyway."

"So Cody had a good time?"

"I'd say so. He had everything figured out even before Howard. But I could tell he was kind of hanging back and letting Howard teach it. Which was cool."

"That was very cool," Jana said. "Very considerate. How did the other boys . . . how did they . . . was everything okay with Cody?"

Ethan and Savannah came in from the garage just then, interrupting her question with leftover brownies for Jana and Maddie. "Courtesy of the Beehives," he said.

"Yay!" Maddie jumped up to devour a chocolate treat, as Jana glanced at Josh, hoping he'd answer her question. But he was right there with Maddie, tearing into the bag of brownies.

Jana turned to Ethan. "Everything go okay with Cody and the other boys?"

Now Josh swallowed and answered her, after all. "Yeah, they're all cool. Trying to help him, y'know."

Ethan smiled. "Cody's a bit of a rock star, I'd say. If you're the winning quarterback, or you sing in a rock band, or you know all about cars . . ." He shrugged.

"Or you're a math wiz," Jana said, rising to hug her husband.

Savannah released a huge sigh. "Here we go, again."

Jana laughed. "I'll have you know your dad stood out from the others the minute I met him."

"Because he's six-foot-six," Savannah teased.

"Because I'm awesome," Ethan teased back. "But seriously, Cody is doing great. And we can thank Stanley for helping him believe in himself." Then he turned to his son. "And Josh for helping Howard feel important tonight. That was great that you invited him. Gave him a chance to shine."

Josh shrugged. "Howard is cool."

Jana grabbed the last brownie just as Josh was reaching for it, then spun around and handed it to him. "But you're even cooler," she said.

THERE WAS ONE MORE SUNDAY BEFORE THE BAPTISM, WITH A late Thanksgiving falling on November 27th that year. It gave the residents plenty of teaching time with the missionaries, and gave Cody time to prepare as well.

Jana called Merry to tell her the great news, but kept getting a machine, so she just left a message. "I'll bet you dollars to donuts she's there, but just won't pick up," she said to Savannah.

"Mom," Josh said, overhearing from the family room, "Donuts do cost a dollar now, so that phrase doesn't make any sense."

"Thank you," Savannah said, pleased to have a comrade in pointing out her mother's antiquated expressions. "And we don't bet."

Jana smiled and shook her head. *When did the price of donuts go up?*

THE LAST TWO TIMES SHE HAD POPPED IN TO THE EL DORADO House, Howard had been uncharacteristically quiet, often in his room— or not there at all. Gus, meanwhile, seemed to be charming all the ladies, regaling them with stories about Europe and sitting next to Rose, noticeably, during lunch.

"Do you think Howard is pouting, or planning to move away?" she asked Ethan one night. "Do you think he's mad that Gus is LDS?"

Ethan shrugged. "Do you think the Giants will win this year?"

"Oh, stop that," Jana said. "This is not just a guessing game."

"Well, how do I know what Howard is thinking?"

Jana was exasperated. Men—at least her man—had no patience with wondering out loud.

"But I'll tell you this," Ethan said. "It's weird that Gus hasn't come to church, yet. Has he been feeling sick?"

Jana thought for a moment. "You know, in all the excitement with everyone else, I haven't really noticed. Maybe we can check on him Monday night."

Ethan nodded.

They'd been planning a Family Home Evening there for the Monday before the baptism, with the other "adopted" families. The Watersons were in charge of the prayers, the Holdens would be leading songs, the Applegates were bringing refreshments, and little Will Duarte was teaching. *Stanley will be in his glory, with his little five-year-old protégé presenting the lesson.*

After dropping Maddie off at school that morning, Jana swung by to see Helen, and make sure the Family Home Evening was still a go, and that the entire staff knew they were invited.

"Oh, definitely," Helen said. "Simone has it on the big calendar, and we're all looking forward to it. Nearly everyone's gone right now—this was museum day, but don't worry. They won't be too tire—"

Just then Jana heard Rose's distinctive voice, bellowing in the distance. Then Howard's. Then Rose's, again.

Helen shook her head. "Oh, those two. They've been quarreling all morning. Wouldn't even get on the same bus for the museum."

Jana stepped quietly down the men's hallway toward the rec room, hanging back to listen.

"Fine, I'll tell you why," Howard was saying. "Because he lived at Borden-Dunn before he came here."

"What's that got to do with anything?" Rose asked.

"It means Gus is bored and done," Howard snapped.

"Oh, that's just a ridiculous joke people make about that complex," Rose said. "Look at what they used to call this place—the Witch House!"

"Well, I still say he's boring and he's done. And I'm not going to a museum with a guy like that."

Jana began feeling guilty for snooping, and crept back to Helen's desk. "By the way, is Gus feeling okay?" she asked.

Helen shrugged. "I think so. Why?"

Jana shrugged. "Just hadn't seen him at church. Oh, well. I'll see you tonight."

SIMONE HAD DRAPED A BIG BANNER SPELLING FAMILY HOME HEAVEN in tiny burlap triangles, across one wall of the rec room, and Jana smiled when she walked in with Ethan and the kids. Simone wasn't interested in learning about the church, but she was thrilled with the joy she had seen in the residents since they'd started investigating, and she wanted to support the evening's event. Obviously she had jotted down the wrong title. Or had she? Jana wondered if maybe this label was even better.

"That's cool," Savannah said, following her gaze to the banner.

Vera had some church music playing through the speakers, and Simone had set up chairs and a table for the refreshments. The Applegates were already there, placing trays of veggies sticks and dip on the table, and Will Duarte was reaching behind a red curtain, rigged to hang from a PVC pipe frame. You could see some rustling behind the curtain, and Jana wondered who else was back there. Soon the Holdens arrived, little Lucy Holden rushing over to hug her adopted grandma, Frances.

Slowly the residents began to assemble, dressed as if this were a church service.

"Maybe you should tell them Family Home Evening is a casual thing," Savannah whispered to her mother. Rose, in particular, looked glamorous in strands of pearls and dangly earrings.

Jana nodded, then reconsidered. "I don't know. Maybe this is kind of an event for them, an excuse to get all dolled up." She knew Savannah was wrinkling her nose at the "all dolled up" expression, but ignored it, smiling at the happy residents who were filing in.

Most surprising was Howard, wearing a crisp white shirt and a purple tie. Jana saw Rose glance over at him and raise her eyebrows. Howard sat down a few seats from Rose, and began chatting with Theresa and Shanika, the two nurses who had wanted to attend, and were sitting on his other side.

Suddenly Jana noticed that Sister Friedman was there, already complimenting Simone on her banner. "This is perfect," Sister Friedman was saying. "Your wording is much better. The whole church should adopt this as the new name." Apparently there was no limit to how many conventions Sister Friedman was ready to revise.

The women always tended to cluster together, but tonight most residents had an adopted family to sit with, and the seats filled quickly. And then Gus entered. Gus looked as if he owned the place. If it were possible to stride confidently while using a walker, Gus did it. He was wearing a cranberry pullover sweater and cream-colored pants, looking like a character from *The Great Gatsby*. Nodding cordially at the group, he sat right next to Rose.

"Nice tie," Josh whispered, slipping into the open seat between Rose and Howard.

"I clean up pretty good, don't I?" Howard chuckled. "Well, I've never been to one of these things and I saw the other guys getting all fancy shmancy, so—" He shrugged.

"I'm glad you decided to come." Josh smiled.

Emery Holden whispered to Vera, who then turned down the music so they could play their own for the opening song, "Pioneer Children

Sang as They Walked." Jennifer Holden handed out copies of the lyrics so everyone could sing along, then said, "Will Duarte requested this song, to go along with his lesson." Will smiled a broad grin, missing both front teeth. Then little Lucy Holden stood up to lead the singing, her arm flailing through the air, and Stanley beaming at the poise and confidence she already possessed.

Maddie said the opening prayer, and then little Will stepped forward.

"And now, for my lesson," he said, sounding like a circus ringmaster with a lisp. Everyone laughed.

There was whispering and bumping behind the curtain, then suddenly Will yanked the curtain away to reveal a small covered wagon. Three hula hoops had been placed in a red Radio Flyer wagon, then draped with a white tablecloth. The oldest Duarte boy, Jonathan, was wearing aluminum foil steer horns, and was harnessed to the wagon by several men's belts. With much mooing and struggling, he slowly pulled the wagon across Will's "stage." Inside were Will's three- and seven-year-old sisters, Mavey, and Mia, wearing pioneer dresses and bonnets, and each holding a baby doll.

The audience dissolved into laughter and cheers as Jonathan made his way back, and then stopped and took a bow.

Unable to read, Will had to tell the story in his own words. "The pioneers crossed the plains in the 1800s," he began. "Lots of them had been killed, so they had to leave Nauvoo. Some had covered wagons and some of them had to pull hand carts. But I didn't have a hand cart." Will stopped, trying to remember the story he had evidently practiced. Jonathan cleared his throat. "Oh, yeah. They used oxen if they could," Will said.

Jonathan stepped forward and bowed again.

"Lots of them ran out of food and were starving," Will went on. His sisters held their stomachs in pain as Jonathan held up a poster of a hamburger with a big red circle and slash drawn over it.

"And, let's see," Will said, glancing back at the wagon for some clues. "Oh, yeah. Some of them had babies along the way." Now the two sisters held their baby dolls aloft with one hand, like flags, eliciting more laughter.

"They had to leave their nice homes, and everything behind, even their families sometimes."

Now the sisters began dabbing at pretend tears. Stanley was beaming and nodding as he watched Will's presentation.

"Some of them even died," Will said.

Mia hopped from the wagon and fell dramatically to the floor. *Well, at least Maddie isn't the only drama queen in the ward.* Jana glanced at her youngest, and saw her completely enthralled with the performance.

"And they had to be buried in the snow," Will said.

Now Mavis pulled a bag of white Styrofoam peanuts from the wagon and dumped it over Mia. It was hard not to smile at this presentation, even though the subject was a serious one.

"But they went through all that because they knew the church was true," Will said. "We are thankful for our pioneer ancestors. My great-great grandparents were from Mexico and they were pioneers, too. The end."

Now Mia jumped up, scattering the peanuts, and the Duarte kids all took a bow.

Those who could, gave a standing ovation, and Jana heard Stanley's robust "Bravo!" from the second row.

"I forgot some parts!" Will whispered to Jonathan, just loud enough for everyone to hear. Again, the crowd laughed, and Jonathan ruffled his brother's hair and smiled.

Brother Duarte stood up and distributed pamphlets he had put together, of actual pioneer diary entries. He urged everyone to read through them at their leisure, then said, "Tonight we pay tribute to those in attendance who are pioneers in their own right. Many of you are the first in your families to get baptized, and we salute you for your courage and faith."

Then Lucy led another song, Josh closed with prayer, and everyone headed for the refreshments. There was such a warm spirit of friendship in the room that no one seemed in a hurry to go home. Howard started chatting about car engines with Cody, Ethan found himself laughing with Chester and Marvin off to one side, and everyone seemed busy mingling. Everyone but Jana. *Well, this is a switch. Here I am alone, while Ethan's the one chatting it up.* She smiled, seeing what a different person he was in the El Dorado House.

"You seem to love it here," Harriet said, coming up behind her.

"Do I?" Jana asked, bending down to pet Misty.

"It's as if this is where you belong." Then she laughed. "Not yet, of course. But you know what I mean."

Jana smiled. "I do. You're right, Lorraine." *I'm actually happy in a rest home. Wow.*

Suddenly she saw Rose zooming in her wheelchair across the end of the room, towards the women's hallway. She looked miffed. Jana wondered if someone had disagreed with her plans.

Harriet followed her gaze. "Looks like something's upset Rose," she said.

"It does. I'll go check on her." Jana stepped quickly across the room and found Rose in her bedroom, staring at her Primary poster.

Though the door was open, she knocked on it, anyway. "Rose? Mind if I come in?"

Rose spun around. "Oh, Jana. I'm so glad it's you. Close the door, will you?"

Jana closed the door and stepped inside, sitting on a blue straight back chair near the foot of Rose's bed. "What the matter?"

Rose's eyes welled with tears. "I finally found the truth I feel I've been searching for all my life."

Jana nodded. How was this bad news?

"And I'm going to have to live the rest of my years alone."

Jana rose and went over to her, holding her hands. "What do you mean?"

"Well, I guess you've noticed Gus."

Jana nodded.

"I mean, Gus and me," Rose said.

Jana could feel her eyebrows lifting.

Rose registered her surprise. "Gus has been, well, courting me I guess you could say. He's been right beside me since he arrived. Kind of making it obvious, you know."

Jana cleared her throat. "How does Howard feel about that?"

"Oh, he's doing a slow simmer, I suppose." Rose dug through the stack of pearls around her neck, and wiped her reading glasses on a Kleenex. "But just now Gus asked if we could make a commitment of sorts."

"Oh, my. That's a bit quick."

"Not when you're my age, Honey." Rose smiled. "By this age you know what you want and you can recognize it pretty fast. Anyway, I might have said yes a few months ago. Especially with Howard being so stubborn. But now that I have the gospel—"

Jana was confused. "Wait—isn't Gus LDS?"

"Ha!" Rose threw her head back. "He may be a Mormon, but he's not the kind I want. I want what you have."

A young husband and kids?

"I want a man who believes what I do," Rose continued. "A man who'll come to church with me. Gus doesn't pray. He won't bear his testimony. He may have been baptized as a kid, but he doesn't live it, or even seem to believe it." She leaned in to whisper, as if anyone could hear them. "I think I know the Book of Mormon better than he does. He drinks, he swears—when he knows better—" She looked into Jana's eyes. "Am I expecting too much?"

Jana saw a little girl looking up at her. The daring little girl on the poster, who threw herself into life and traveled the world looking for something she finally found in her golden years. "No, you are not asking too much, Rose." Jana felt her own eyes welling up as she spoke. "You have every right to a man who's your equal."

"I just might not find him in this life."

"Well, there are worse things."

Rose pointed at her. "Exactly what I was thinking. I don't want to hook up with some guy who's gonna make me cry into my pillow every night. I honestly would be better off alone."

"You honestly would." Jana bent down and hugged her. She couldn't bear the thought of Rose ending up with a less-active husband who wouldn't share in her newfound joy.

"I can't tell your daughter to hold out for a man who shares her faith, and then not follow my own advice," Rose said.

Jana smiled. "No, that's true."

"So I was right to tell him to shove off."

"Uh . . ."

"Hey, if I can give up Howard for my faith, then I can certainly tell Gus the same thing."

Jana nodded and they hugged again.

"Thanks for listening," Rose said. "I feel better."

"Thank you for being such a strong, wonderful woman," Jana said. "You're a great example, Rose."

Rose smiled and held up a pinky finger. "Never sell out."

Jana laughed and looped her pinky around Rose's. "Never sell out."

Chapter 33

THAT SATURDAY THE AUTUMN LEAVES SEEMED TO SOAK UP THE sun's rays, almost glowing in scarlet and orange as the Watersons arrived at the stake center. Maddie hopped out of the car and raced into the building, even though Jana had told her Vera wouldn't be there, yet.

The Watersons and President Yoshida came at noon to set up, though the baptisms weren't scheduled until 1:00. Howard had asked for a ride, and Josh helped him up the steps. "So where's your sister today—the older one?" Howard asked.

"Oh, a date is bringing her," Josh said, placing the programs on a small table in the foyer. "She's meeting him at the library, then they're coming over."

"You don't say."

"I'm really glad you came to support everyone," Josh said.

Howard nodded and found a seat towards the back.

All the full-time missionaries in the stake were in the Relief Society room rehearsing a choir number they had put together, and the kitchen was bustling with ward missionaries who were providing the refreshments. Someone had made gingerbread cake with lemon sauce, and the aroma was mouthwatering. Carlita would be bringing red velvet cupcakes from her bakery, and Jana placed a tray of pumpkin bars on the counter.

She turned to Ethan. "You seem very accepting of all this."

"Are you kidding?" he said. "Why wouldn't I be accepting of six baptisms?"

Jana laughed. "I mean Savannah having a date with that kid from the Davis Stake." She had met him at a tri-stake dance just last week.

Ethan smiled. "I'm a new man. Well, new-*ish*."

"You really have lightened up a lot."

Ethan shrugged. "Not really."

She laughed again. "Well, then you're a great actor."

"No, I just have to let her be a teenage girl. I can't smother her. You were right."

"It means so much to her."

Ethan sighed. "It better." Then he smiled at his bride. She had no idea how hard it was for him to back off and give Savannah some breathing room. But being an ogre was backfiring, and the adoring look in Savannah's eyes when he nodded his approval of this date—was priceless. Besides, this was a good way to underscore the fact that she had moved on from the travesty with Dylan.

Carlita came in with her cupcakes just then, everyone oohing and aahing over the swirly cream cheese frosting. Cody looked relieved to see Ethan. Immediately they stepped aside so Cody could get some last-minute help with Stanley's baptism.

Soon the bus arrived and the seniors piled out, all excited and talking at once. The back had a special door for the wheelchair lift, and soon everyone was heading into the building. The dressing rooms filled as members helped them change into their white clothing, voices echoing against the tile.

Vera helped greet the visiting family members, and soon Savannah and Brady, her date, were helping to usher in the crowds as well. Brady was tall and slim, almost a young, brunette version of Ethan, Jana thought. He was shaking hands and looking every bit like a missionary in the making.

It seemed half the ward wanted to be on hand for this historic event, along with the stake presidency, and the chapel began to fill. Jana was astounded at how many youth came, every one of them beaming as if this were their own grandparents' baptisms. Soon the accordion doors opened to the cultural hall, for overflow seating. Josh and Terrell Moses scrambled to help the missionaries set up extra chairs.

Helen was craning around the visitors trying to find Jana, and came right over when she spotted her. She was pulling a handsome man along, and introduced him as her son, Adam. He seemed to be everything his brother, Derrick, was not—warm, gentle, polite, and engaging. "My mother has never seemed so happy," he said. And Helen did look truly overjoyed. Jana was so grateful she had to hug him. "I think she's very happy to have a son like you, too," Jana said. "How nice that you came all the way from Arizona for this."

Adam smiled. "Wouldn't have missed it." And his mother looked more at peace than Jana had ever seen her.

Several men had been asked to baptize, in addition to Elders Jamison and Torrisi. Pearl wanted Tad Lawrence to baptize her, of course, and Frances wanted Eric Holden. A few others would be assisting with those who couldn't go down the steps unaided.

"Have you ever seen so many men in white outfits?" Maddie asked, pulling on Jana's hand.

Only at the temple. "It's amazing," Jana said. *And maybe in a year they'll all be getting endowed, as well.* It made her cry to think of it.

The nurses, Shanika and Theresa, came in, both buzzing with anticipation of their own future baptisms. And Dr. Rashid followed close behind, cordially nodding and whispering that he wouldn't have missed this important event. Simone was there to lend support as well.

Michelle Dayley and Kristi Hargrove came with their families and sat behind Jana, while Ethan dressed in white to baptize Helen and Rose.

The baptismal room couldn't accommodate a crowd this size, so the music and talks had to be presented in the chapel. President Morrow gave a beautiful talk about baptism being just the beginning, then as many as could fit, gathered in the other room where the font was waiting.

One by one, the seniors either stepped into the font for their ordinance, or were assisted by Ethan and the missionaries, if they couldn't walk on their own. Jana saw cheeks wet with tears everywhere she looked. Rose was first, with Ethan performing the baptism. When she came out of the water, she honestly looked like an angel. Quickly Jana met Rose in the locker room to help her change back into dry clothes. *I so hope Howard saw that.* But the crowd was so large she wasn't even sure where he was. Regardless, Rose was elated and threw her arms around the other women who were waiting their turn. "This is the best day of our lives!" Rose told them. And they agreed.

Rose was first to dress and return to the baptismal room, and was in time to see Helen, Frances, and Raymond get baptized. Then Cody stepped into the water, and Stanley joined him, assisted by Ethan and Terrell. Cody spoke clearly and confidently, and when Stanley rose from the water he threw his arms around Cody as if he were his own son. Cody broke down and cried, clinging to Stanley for a full minute before the two of them pulled apart and climbed out, both forever changed.

"Well, I guess that's it," Rose said, knowing Cody had asked to go last so he could watch it done several times first.

Then Ethan turned to the crowd and said, "If you'll all just wait a moment, we have one more." His eyes danced as he glanced over at Jana, and she could tell he was as surprised as anyone.

Suddenly, there was Howard, dressed in white, coming down the steps into the font. He looked up for Rose, caught her eye, and winked. If Rose hadn't been sitting down, she would have fainted. She turned at least three shades whiter, her jaw dropped, and she stared, unblinking.

Ethan stepped down into the font to meet Howard, and before a stunned audience, baptized him a member of the Church of Jesus Christ of Latter-day Saints.

He and Ethan hugged, then Howard turned and grinned at Rose. She was still speechless. He chuckled, then climbed out and went to get dressed.

Rose turned to Jana. "Did you know about this?"

Jana was as stunned as she was. "Not a whiff."

There was a palpable buzz of exhilaration in the room, and soon Howard came back to the chapel, dressed and dry, and sat with the other men.

But before anyone could ask Howard how it happened, President Yoshida stood and spoke about the Gift of the Holy Ghost that they would receive tomorrow in Sacrament Meeting. He even shared a personal story of his father's conversion, and the Holy Ghost saving his life. The spirit filled the room and nearly everyone seemed to be wiping their eyes. Ethan welcomed them all into the ward, then, as if seven baptisms and three inspiring talks weren't enough, the full-time elders and sisters sang the most heartfelt version of "Lord, Accept into Thy Kingdom" Jana had ever heard. She was not the only one there weeping openly.

Right after the closing prayer the various grown children of the senior residents gathered around to congratulate their parents, and meet one another. The entire building was humming with excitement, and Elders Jamison and Torrisi were posing for picture after picture.

Howard made his way to Rose, and Jana—along with her family and a growing crowd—couldn't resist gathering around to see how on earth Howard managed this surprise.

"I've been taking the lessons in another ward," he said. "That's why you haven't seen so much of me, lately. Only the mission president and the elders knew. I've even been going to another ward, so I could keep it a surprise."

Rose was just shaking her head in amazement. "Why didn't you tell me?"

Howard laughed. "Aw, I didn't want you to think I was just doing it because—well, for the wrong reasons. I only wanted to do it if I really knew it was right."

"How long have you been studying?" Rose was almost speechless, but not quite.

"Well, it started when I heard Josh's prayer," Howard said.

Josh did a double-take, but kept listening.

"His prayer at Family Home Evening?" Rose asked.

"No, no. Long before that." Howard looked over at Josh, whose eyes widened. "You didn't know it, but that day when you were landscaping, I was coming outside from the kitchen. I saw you praying there, on the side of the house," Howard said. "It was weeks ago."

Josh gulped. "You . . . you heard that?"

"Well, I didn't mean to," Howard explained. "But I heard you pray—" Howard stopped, tears tumbling down his cheeks and a lump in his throat. "You prayed for me to listen to the missionaries, and to learn what Christ did for me—" Howard stopped again, and wiped his eyes with both his palms. "Nobody's ever loved me like that."

Now Josh stepped forward and threw his arms around Howard's neck. No one said a word until Josh pulled away, his eyes moist.

"May I hug you, Howard?" Rose asked. Josh stepped back, and Howard leaned down and held her tight.

"Howard overheard the same prayer I did," Ethan whispered to Jana. "I had no idea."

Rose pulled back and looked into Howard's eyes. "So you really believe it."

"I do. And I decided to get baptized no matter what you decide to do. Even if you leave me for stupid ol' Gus."

Rose laughed. "I gave him the heave-ho the other night."

Now Howard was the one to be surprised. "You did?"

"I certainly did. I watched those little kids telling about the pioneers, and I knew I could never be happy with someone who wouldn't have crossed the plains for this."

Howard dropped to one knee and held Rose's hands in his. "Rose, will you be in my wagon?"

Rose pulled his hands to her lips and kissed them. "There's no one I'd rather be with," she said.

The crowd cheered, then quieted to hear what else Howard would say. "So you'll marry me? I mean, I want to be clear about this because you know how you are—you don't always understand—"

"Oh, shut up and kiss me, Howard," Rose laughed. "I understand you perfectly, you old goat."

Howard and Rose kissed, and Jana wasn't the only one who caught her breath. To be so close to a proposal was an honor no one could misunderstand, but added to this already amazing day, it felt as if the whole assemblage was floating on air.

Chapter 34

DOZENS OF WELL-WISHERS BEGAN TO CROWD AROUND ROSE AND Howard, with Sister Friedman at the forefront, saying, "I think all baptisms should be required to have a surprise like this." Jana just laughed and shook her head, then decided to check on the refreshments, especially since the ward missionaries were in charge of them. As she pushed open the door to the kitchen she saw Carlita arranging cookies and sugar-dusted lemon bars on a tray, her expert touch evident in the perfectly displayed items.

"Oh—someone brought lemon bars!" Jana exclaimed. "Oh, I so wish Merry could be here. Those are her favorites."

"I brought those."

Jana turned around and gasped—Merry was behind the door, holding Aiden. "You—are those—are those your lemon bars?"

Merry smiled and nodded. Jana threw her arms around her.

"Don't y'all get me crying, now," Merry said.

Jana whispered into her hair. "Are you back?"

Merry nodded and pulled back. "I hope you'll forgive me for being so stupid."

Jana felt relief sweep through her body. "Oh, I'm so happy, Merry. Oh, this is the answer to my prayers."

"I slipped in a little late, but I saw most of the baptisms," Merry said.

"What—what made you come back?" Jana glanced around, looking for a private place to talk, but the kitchen was bustling with workers, and Carlita seemed to be listening as well.

"So many things," Merry said, not seeming to mind the crowd. "That time we went to the El Dorado House and I could overhear the elders teaching. I felt like such a phony trying to pretend I didn't know it was true. Then Rose played me the tape of those kids singing and I tell you what—I thought about little Aiden doing that someday—" Her voice caught and her lip trembled. "I knew I had to come back, Jana. I knew it was time to put on my big girl panties and stand up to my family." She and Jana laughed. "So I did."

Jana kept looking from Aiden to Merry, and couldn't stop smiling. "I'm so proud of you. How did they take it?"

"Just like I thought they would," Merry said. "Mad as hornets." Then she smiled. "But Rose was right—my testimony can't be for sale."

Never sell out.

"And don't *even* get me started about that report on the evening news," Merry went on. "No way did I want to be part of that anti-Mormon camp, spreading lies and ganging up, saying it's in the name of Christianity."

Carlita stood a bit closer, now, and Jana could see her smiling.

"I felt the same way," she said.

"So here I am!" Merry smiled. "Want a lemon bar?"

Jana laughed and hugged her again. "Sean must be thrilled."

"Oh, that man is ready to buy me a Mercedes," Merry laughed. "Not that we can afford one."

Jana realized Carlita had never met Merry, and introduced them.

"Don't tell me you're going to count this as a visit," Carlita teased.

"More details on that, later," Jana said to Merry. Then she glanced around. The kids who always swarmed the refreshments first were heading out with their families, and the seniors were already boarding the bus to go home.

"Looks like we'll have some extra treats," Jana said. "Maybe we should take them to the El Dorado house for all the visiting family members."

"Oh, that's a perfect idea," Merry said. "I need to get Aiden home for his nap—can you two manage without me?"

Carlita glanced at Jana, then smiled. "I'd like to help do that. And Cody can visit with Stanley, too."

"I'll call you later," Merry said, giving Jana a last hug and stepping into the hall.

Jana and Carlita loaded their cars, then gathered their families. Savannah waved goodbye to Brady, and hopped into the family's van.

"How was your date? How was your date?" Maddie was bouncing on the seat, despite wearing a seatbelt. *Thank you, Maddie, for asking that, so Ethan and I don't have to.*

Savannah laughed. "It was fine. He's a nice guy."

"I can't believe Howard proposed to Rose," Josh said, beaming.

"And she said *yes!*" Maddie said. "That was a shockeroo."

"This has been a whole day of shockeroos," Jana said, and told the family about Merry coming back. She thought Ethan might start to cry, and rested her hand on his arm.

"I just don't know if I can process all this," he said, his voice cracking. "Seven people joining the church, and now—"

Savannah reached forward and patted her dad's shoulder. "You can do it. If you can watch me go on a date, you can do anything."

Ethan laughed and wiped his eyes. "I believe you're right."

The bus that had been carrying the seniors was just pulling out as they arrived, so the Watersons waited before pulling into the driveway. Jana glanced at the scene before her—family members milling about on the beautiful grounds, a sparkling gold building—and then she caught her breath.

"Oh, look," she said, "The poplars have changed color for autumn— they're all completely gold."

The family turned and saw the backdrop of foliage lining the wall behind the house. Brilliant yellow leaves fluttered in the breeze as if an impressionistic painter had rolled a giant mural in for the occasion.

"Wow," Maddie whispered.

"That is absolutely gorgeous," Ethan agreed.

"I'm going to get a picture of that," Jana said, rolling down her window. She held up her cell phone and snapped a shot.

Soon she, Carlita, and Simone were arranging the extra refreshments on a long table for the visiting relatives. Even the seniors who didn't have family attending, were happily mingling with one another, sharing their conversion stories, and congratulating Howard and Rose.

"Congratulations," Gus said, shaking Howard's hand. "I hadn't realized you two were an item."

"Glad he's being a gentleman," Jana whispered to Ethan.

She and Carlita poured cups of water and placed them at one end of the table.

"Oh, Carlita, you have to see this," Jana said, pulling her phone out to show her the photo.

"Oh, that's beautiful," Carlita said. "It looks like a painting or something."

"Everything's gold," Jana said. "Hey. Maybe we should ask the owners if we can rename it, now. I mean, I know it's on El Dorado Street, but maybe we should call it Golden House or something."

Carlita laughed. "That's already its name."

"What do you mean?"

Carlita smiled. "You need to learn Spanish, mi amiga. El Dorado means golden."

Jana gasped. *Why didn't somebody tell me this? But of course.*

"I thought that's why you painted it gold," Carlita said.

Jana smiled and remembered Elder Torrisi telling the residents they were golden investigators. It was all fitting together.

Helen and Adam came over, bubbling with excitement about her baptism, and Rose and Howard's engagement. "And Mom says you're coming for Thanksgiving."

"Oh, yes," Jana said. "Will you be here as well?"

"No; my wife and I have to visit her parents this year," Adam said. "So I'm really glad you'll be here for her. After all, I hear you're like family, now."

She felt a rush of warmth at his words, and turned to Helen. "Yes," she said. "It really is like that."

Then Jana looked around the room at the people she had come to love, and felt more gratitude welling up in her heart than she would ever have thought possible. She couldn't imagine anywhere she would rather be.

About the Author

JONI HILTON HAS WRITTEN 24 BOOKS, SEVERAL AWARD-WINNING plays, and dozens of magazine articles. She holds a Master of Fine Arts degree in Professional Writing from USC, and writes regularly for MeridianMagazine.com. She also writes for *Music and the Spoken Word.*

She is currently serving as Relief Society President in her ward in northern California and has previously served as a Regional Media Specialist for Public Affairs, First Counselor in a Stake Relief Society, Relief Society President and Counselor, Seminary Teacher, Gospel Doctrine Teacher, and has worked in the Primary and Young Women organizations.

She is a former TV talk show host and radio host. Hilton is currently The YouTube Mom, and continues to tour the U.S. as a corporate spokeswoman on TV. She is also a busy motivational speaker and the founder and former CEO of an organic line of cleaning products. An avid cook, Hilton has won more than 70 cook-offs and recipe contests. She is married to Bob Hilton and is the mother of four children. Her website is jonihilton.com.

Made in the USA
Lexington, KY
28 June 2016